MIKE NELSON'S DEATH RAT!

Mike Nelson's Movie Megacheese
Mike Nelson's Mind Over Matters

MIKE NELSON'S DEATH RAT!

a novel

MICHAEL J. NELSON

HarperEntertainment
An Imprint of HarperCollinsPublishers

HarperCollins books may be purchased for educational, business, or
sales promotional use. For information please write: Special Markets
Department, HarperCollins Publishers Inc., 10 East 53rd Street,
New York, NY 10022.

FIRST EDITION

Designed by Chris Welch

Library of Congress Cataloging-in-Publication Data

Nelson, Michael J.
Mike Nelson's death rat! : a novel / Michael J. Nelson.—1st ed.
p.   cm.
ISBN 0-06-093472-7
1. Minneapolis (Minn.)—Fiction.   2. Periodicals—Publishing—
Fiction.   I. Title: Death rat!   II. Title.

PS3614.E447 D43   2003
813'.6—dc21   2002027323

03   04   05   06   07   WBC/RRD   10   9   8   7   6   5   4   3   2   1

MIKE NELSON'S DEATH RAT!

CHAPTER 1

iven his advancing age and his current stature in the business community, Pontius Feeb knew that it was unseemly for him to be driving giddily through town at mid-day, whistling and thinking fondly of spit-roasted chicken and buttered fingerling potatoes. Ponty sensed that a vehemently antilunch prejudice had infected many in the Minneapolis trade-magazine community. "You can eat on your own time" was the unspoken rule.

Would it change matters if they knew that he was to lunch at Beret, the hot new downtown bistro that had been visited by none other than former *Good Morning America* host David Hartman shortly after its grand opening? No, sadly, it probably wouldn't. The people in his industry were notoriously inflexible in their attitudes. But Ponty would not let them dampen his spirits.

He weaved his way through Minneapolis's light noon-time traffic and pulled onto fourth Street, fully expecting to have to make the long ascent up the ConFac Building's massive parking ramp. But this lunch bestowed an unforeseen blessing in the form of a metered parking space directly in front of Beret's entrance.

As he fed the meter, he scanned the faces sitting at the half dozen tables that Beret had set out on the sidewalk and called their patio, seeing if perhaps he couldn't gloat a little over his parking spot. If anyone was impressed, they did not give him the satisfaction.

Ponty had entered, secured a table by the window, and was already nibbling a sourdough roll when his lunch partner arrived several minutes later, trying his best to look harried and important. To Ponty he simply looked thin and fey.

Here was the only downside to a repast at Beret: his lunch companion, Craig Thurston. In Ponty's opinion, the midday meal was too good for Craig, who he felt strongly was a wee-nie. But he was also Ponty's boss. And he did occasionally buy lunch, a rare positive trait. Ponty tried not to stare at Craig's hair, which challenged conventional notions of male dignity. It was a limp, gray-blond, windblown mess, dully supported here and there by light spritzings of some cheap fixative, and his shiny scalp showed through at various locations across his skull. Craig was a man who wore a collar pin, a sign of deep moral failing. That his collar was often a different color from his shirt only cemented Ponty's opinion regarding his character.

"Whew," said Craig, apparently winded by the effort of driving to Beret. "Did you order?"

"No, no. Waited for you."

"Good, good," said Craig, sighing again, smoothing the hair on the sides of his head and looking about the dining room as though he suspected he might be missing other lunch meetings at some of the other Beret tables. A waitress appeared.

"Hey, there you are," said Craig, and without letting her

reply, he continued, "Why don't you give me the smoked trout hot dish and an Egret Springs water, can you? Oh, and bring the Egret Springs in the bottle."

"Actually, we don't have the smoked trout hot dish on the menu anymore. I'm sorry about—"

"I know, but they'll make it for me. They've done it before."

The young woman scribbled on her pad. "You know what? We're out of the Egret Springs. Will Anoka Creek Flowage do?"

"Hmm. No. No. I've been to Anoka, no thanks. What kind of iced tea do you have?"

The waitress answered flatly, "It's in small whitish bags." She gestured with her thumb and forefinger. "We brew it and then chill it by pouring it over ice."

"No, no, no—what *kind* of tea?" Craig pushed.

"As far as I know, it comes in bulk from a food service. It's called Allied Grocer Groups brand," she said wearily.

"Oh, no. That won't do," said Craig, as though she had just offered him a glass of room-temperature egg whites. "Bring me some apricot-blackberry Assam blend, a pot of hot water, and a huge glass of ice."

Ponty ordered his meal as efficiently as possible, trying not cause the waitress further distress. Time dragged on as he waited for Craig to get to the point of their meeting, but Craig seemed content to nurture the pained silence between them. So Ponty had to search for a topic of conversation among Craig's non-work-based interests. So far as he knew, they included his car, a BMW 7-something, and ordering effete iced teas at upscale lunch places. Since Ponty's knowledge of cars was limited to the cockpit of his own Tempo, he tried for a more general topic.

"The Twins are in town today," Ponty offered.

"Really?" said Craig, regarding him suspiciously.

Ponty, who was not in the habit of inventing major sporting events and certainly could not see how anything could be gained by it, nevertheless grew doubtful under Craig's skeptical stare.

"They're not in Detroit?"

"They just finished a three-game series there," Ponty said, feeling his confidence flagging.

"I think they have one more in Detroit," said Craig, craning his neck to look at a table across the dining room.

Could you just let me have this one thing? thought Ponty as he looked at the side of Craig's tanned head. It was never like this with Craig's father, Ponty's former boss at Jack Pine Publications. Tom Thurston was a man of principle, a man who used hair fixatives sparingly, if at all. He and Ponty had virtually grown up in the publishing business together, and in twenty-four years Tom Thurston had never ordered water by a brand name. But Tom had died suddenly, tragically, when a trailer loaded with sod had jumped its ball hitch, sped down the hill near his home, and hit Tom full on as he stood in black socks and sandals, smoking a cigar and watering his wife's hostas. Craig had then "taken over," if that term could properly be applied to his thin-legged managerial style.

When the food finally came, Craig got down to business. "Ponty," he said, "Jack Pine Publications is in for some changes."

Ponty cleared his throat and dabbed his mouth with a napkin. "Well, good. High time. I'd start with those cheap green partitions of ours, but I'm sure everyone has his two cents to—"

"Adapt or die, that's the new business model."

"It is?" asked Ponty. "How is the hot dish? Enough smoked trout in there?"

"There's a vibrant young market out there, and we're missing it."

"But," Ponty struggled, "vibrant young markets require mature, experienced people to—"

"You and I, we're not getting any younger."

Ponty nearly dropped his buttered roll. "Well, I would like to point out that that's true of most people."

"This is a strange—I don't know—almost mysterious business," Craig said. He was gazing off into the middle distance as though recalling fantastical things.

"It is?" said Ponty, turning to look at the same spot as Craig was.

"Ponty, I'm getting ready to sell the company."

Ponty froze momentarily, then looked with scorn at his chicken. All that morning just the thought of it had filled him with bright promise. But now, because he knew with certainty that he was to be fired and that his entree had played even a tangential role in the dirty business, he hated it bitterly.

"Well," said Ponty shakily, "that's a lot of work. I'll need new stationery, of course. But let's roll up our sleeves and—"

"You're an anachronism, Ponty. You're sixty years old. You're not integral to the magazines, and, let's face it, your books don't sell worth beans. The last one sold seventy-eight copies, you'll recall."

"And I for one was encouraged by those numbers."

"I can't have you there as a wrench in the works."

Ponty grasped for rebuttals. "Now, Craig, remember when you were shaping that deal with—what's it?—*Extrusion Die Journal*? I was no wrench there, Craig. I was deal lubricant."

"You got Bill Muncie some nondairy creamer from the supply room. I don't think that's what sealed the deal."

"It certainly didn't hurt. A fresh jar of creamer delivered politely and in a timely manner can—"

"Look, I don't want to argue, Ponty. I'm letting you go."

"But I don't want to go, Craig, so you don't have to *let* me."

"Ponty? You're fired."

"Fired? I'm fired?" said Ponty, as though trying to grasp the meaning of the word.

"Yes. Let's not make a big deal of it, shall we? Hey, look, take a second with this. I got to go tap a kidney," said Craig, and he left the table.

Though he fought them viciously, tears pooled in Ponty's eyes until Beret's dining room became a haze of indistinct designer colors. Finally the tears spilled over, and Ponty reached numbly for his napkin, grabbing the tablecloth by mistake, causing a loud jangle of flatware, and upsetting the remainder of Craig's apricot-blackberry Assam iced tea. A busboy quickly materialized and began soaking up the spill. By the time Craig returned, a new tea had been delivered and Ponty was nearly composed again.

"Whew," said Craig, again seeming winded from the journey, "there's some lookers in here." After a moment he pulled his gaze away from a "looker" and directed it at Ponty. "So anyway," he continued, "as I said, you're fired. Now, if you don't mind, I'm shaping up this deal quickly, so if you could clear out your stuff in the next couple of days and haul away those dirty old bookcases in your office, that'd be great."

"Haul away my bookcases?" Ponty asked incredulously.

"Fine," said Craig, slapping the table. "If you're gonna make trouble about this, I'll hire someone to take them out. I'd have thought, given your history at Jack Pine, that you could do me that little favor, but hey!" he said and took a sip of tea. "What is this crap?" he exclaimed, spitting it back into his glass.

"Allied Grocer Groups brand. I spilled your Assam," Ponty confessed miserably.

"I suppose I had that coming." Craig sighed. "Well, I got to get going. I'll pay on my way out." He left quickly, tossing "Take it easy, Ponty" over his shoulder as he did.

Leaving his half chicken nearly intact, Ponty made his way zombielike to his car and sat for a moment staring straight ahead before absently starting it and putting it in first. He let his eyes go out of focus and a moment later realized that something other than the loss of his job was troubling him. He blamed this new discomfiture on the position of his driver's seat and with sudden, violent anger, reached for its adjustment lever, pushing with his legs and slamming his back against the seat at the same time. With a horrible gear-grinding noise, the internal mechanics of the seat completely gave out, causing it to fly down and backward with tremendous speed and force to its maximally reclined position.

"Ow," Ponty moaned, trying to keep his voice down so that passersby would not become alarmed.

When the initial shock of the seat's collapse had passed, Ponty noticed that his left hand was quite stuck between the seat base and the doorpost. What a mistake it had been to start his car and put it in gear before breaking his seat. For now it was impossible to keep the clutch depressed and still reach the shift knob to get the car out of first gear.

An athletic man might have been able to pull off some move that simultaneously extracted his hand and raised him to a driving position without even stalling the Tempo. Ponty was not

such a man. Yes, he'd been a wrestler at Coulberry High, but
not the kind of wrestler who wins his matches. He ended his
career with a dismal 2–34 record (one of those wins a forfeit).
Knowing what he did about his own abilities, he decided to lie
there thinking it over for a minute while listening to the Twins
game that he just now realized was playing on his radio.

As the starter for Baltimore attempted to pitch out of a jam in
the sixth (he'd been right about the blasted Twins—they *were* at
home!), Ponty thought bitterly about how pleased he'd been to
find parking directly in front of Beret. Now it looked as though
his "rock star" position would contribute greatly to a nadir of
his personal dignity, as there was no way to extricate himself
without a humiliating display in front of Beret's clientele. He
wondered how it must have looked to the patrons at the sidewalk tables to see an obviously agitated man of sixty climb into
his white Tempo, start it, and then shake violently for several
seconds before disappearing under the level of the windows.

He tugged on his left hand, testing it for resistance. It was
stuck, and it hurt. In a moment of clarity Ponty decided he must
try to thrust his torso up, attempt to reach the forward/back-
ward seat-adjustment bar beneath his legs, pull it up, and move
the seat to free his hand. The Tempo would probably stall without lurching into the car in front of him, he reasoned, because it
was a Tempo and it stalled often.

"Okay. Here, we go Ponty," he said to himself out loud, and
then he was shocked by a dark object at his passenger-seat window. Ponty shrieked in a manner a good deal less manly than he
would have liked.

The dark object that had frightened him was an older man
wearing a colorful, wispy, sleeveless running shirt. He'd encir-
cled his face with his hands and had the whole business pushed

directly against the Tempo's window. His brow was severely furrowed, his top lip drawn up, presumably to aid his vision.

"Y'all right?" he asked, scanning the backseat with a look of aggressive confusion. With some embarrassment, Ponty thought of the unopened hot-dog steamer that he'd received as a gift and thrown in his backseat with the intention of exchanging it at Target. It had been there now for over a year.

"Yes, I'm al—"

"You hurt?"

"No, I'm not hurt. Could you—"

" 'S that a hot-dog steamer?"

"Yes," said Ponty impatiently. "Yes it is."

"What are you doing with it?"

"Nothing. I got my hand stuck. Could you—"

"Shall I get someone?"

"Could you do me a favor? Just come around and open my door."

"What are you up to?"

"I'm not up to anything. Look, just come around—"

"I'll go get someone," he said pausing briefly to stare at Ponty with vague distaste as though his predicament were a personal insult.

"No! Wait, please!" Ponty was just about to add "You *are* someone!" but he was gone. Ponty felt reasonably sure that his "someone" meant someone official in some capacity—possibly the police—and this notion hastened his sense of urgency. Police officers made him nervous, and when he got nervous, he would involuntarily smirk. In his experience no officer while dutifully enforcing the community's laws liked to be smirked at by a short, chubby man. Inevitably they would say something like "Am I making you laugh, funny man?" or "Glad I could give you a chuckle there, Gallagher." He wanted to avoid this, especially in his vulnerable, freshly fired state.

Ponty made his move. He thrust his right shoulder upward, his abdominals working harder than they had in some time, and attempted to reach his seat-adjustment bar. While that maneuver was an utter failure, it was spectacularly successful at pulling his left foot off the clutch and allowing his right foot to depress the accelerator. The Tempo shot forward more smoothly than *it* had in some time. Ponty screamed, clutched the right side of the steering wheel, and pulled himself up, at the same time steering himself over the curb. His left hand was still quite pinned.

The Tempo shot toward Beret's outdoor bus stand, missing it by inches. Ponty did not have time to celebrate. His potential death car was heading for the patio tables, and the few lingering diners screamed as Ponty raced toward them. Using his free right hand, he jerked the wheel hard and steered it successfully away from them. Emboldened by this, he made a quick decision to try to steer back onto the road. But his control was only marginal, and for twenty yards or so he cruised straight down the mostly empty sidewalk.

Of the two people between himself and the sweet freedom of Fourth Street, one was a bike cop. Until the Tempo began its odd journey around Beret's patio and bore down upon him, the officer had been perched on his leaning bike talking with the old man in the running outfit. The old man was using huge, grandiloquent hand gestures, apparently in an attempt to describe to the cop how Ponty was lying down in his car. Now both of them stopped and stared. Ponty's eyes and the cop's locked.

In that moment Ponty's confidence in his plan, such as it was, evaporated, as memories of past humiliations rushed in and invaded his senses: the look on the face of a date's father after he'd backed his car over the family dog. The shattered sense of betrayal in the eyes of Mr. Blanding, his favorite high school teacher when on a dare, Ponty had attempted to trap the old man in the boys' bathroom by tipping a bank of lockers against the door—but the door was hinged the wrong way, and poor Mr. Blanding had stepped out and caught him easily. The bottomless disappointment in his father's voice upon taking the splitting maul from Ponty's young hands after Ponty had cleanly missed a sizable chunk of elm eight times in a row. "Just . . . son, just—give me that thing," he'd said sadly.

Now the old man threw up his arms like a music-hall actor and ran. The cop made a confused attempt to mount his bike but couldn't find the right pedal position, so he held up a hand toward Ponty in a "stop" gesture. The Tempo's radio projected the tinny cheers of the hometown Twins crowd, seeming almost to be nightmarishly urging him on.

Ponty knew that if he stopped, he would most assuredly see that look in the eyes of the cop, the old guy, the representative members of the attractive Beret lunch crowd, that look that said, "You, more than any other person I've yet known, more than any other person could be, are a failure." He could not bear that.

So he stuck with his plan and kept going, immediately running over the cop.

CHAPTER 2

Gus Bromstad was the first non–team member to be featured as a bobble-head doll and given away to ten thousand fans at a Minnesota Twins game. He wasn't so sure he liked it. Ross Barnier, his agent, had talked him into allowing it, not knowing that Bromstad nurtured a secret fear that his real head was conspicuously outsize when compared with the heads of most other people. The bobble-head dolls would highlight this feature, make it inescapably noticeable on the real version of himself. Within weeks of the dolls' release, he'd be known predominantly for having a big head, as was always the case with Lee Marvin. However, Gus was reluctant to confess in public just how much he'd thought about his head size. So he simply pouted to Ross:

"I'll look silly."

"Bobble-head dolls are supposed to look silly, Gus. Do you think Bert Blylevyn or . . . or Christian Guzman or Doug *Mientkiewicz* worried about that?"

". . . I don't know." He recognized only one name out of Ross's three examples, Bert Blyleven, and that only vaguely. He had never really been able to come to grips with sports, and they tended to confound and irritate him as a whole.

"No, they didn't. It's an honor, Gus. You're an icon."

Bromstad couldn't argue with that. At fifty-two, he had silver-haired, squinchy-eyed, trim, Roger Whittaker–like good looks that were as recognizable as any author's; even more so, Gus was proud to note, than those of prolific military thriller writer Bunt Casey. The elements were an omnipresent fisherman's sweater and Greek fisherman's cap, a look he'd decided on for the dust-jacket photo of his second book, *Dogwood Downs*. His first book, *Letters from Jenny*, had featured a drab jacket photo, which he always thought made him look like an uninspired junior high school principal. It did not sell well at all, and though a Dwee Award winner, it still had received largely tepid reviews. Gus blamed the photo and planned on someday releasing a special edition of *Letters*, each copy personally autographed (by machine).

But *Dogwood Downs*, featuring his new look, was an absolute sensation, remaining on the bestseller list for 148 weeks, far longer than Bunt Casey's *Go Skyward, Missile*. Since that time, some fifteen years ago, a supremely superstitious Bromstad had doggedly kept his "look" intact, donning the sweater and cap at all events, even throughout the humid Minnesota summers. Once he even wore them to a pool party where the mercury hit 103 and the humidity 90 percent. The navy blue of his cap had made his head an extremely effective solar collector, and despite the alleged "breathability" of wool, he'd become woozy from heat exhaustion and pitched clumsily over a chaise longue before passing out. Ross had carted him home, explaining to the other guests that he'd "probably eaten some bad shrimp," in order to dodge questions about why he didn't just off take his sweater and cap. Despite the heat-related danger and his staggeringly high dry-cleaning bills, he remained unswervingly loyal to his look.

Though Bromstad had verbally agreed to the bobble-head doll, he had not come to terms with it in his own heart. He'd bullied everyone involved, and late one night he'd even called the subcontractor in charge of manufacturing the thing, after browbeating a young man from the answering service into giving him the number.

"This . . . doll? I understand it will have a big head?" he'd asked accusingly, after introducing himself.

The man laughed.

"Is this funny to you?" Bromstad thundered into the phone.

"What? Oh, you're not kidding. Well, yes, yes, it will have a big head."

"How big will it be, exactly?"

"Um, I don't keep my doll specs here at home, but it'll be about six inches."

"The head? The head will be six inches? The head?" Bromstad asked in a nearly hysterical voice.

"No, um, sorry, the doll will be about six. Sorry, it's late; I'm a little confused. The head—I-I don't have the specs with me—but it should be about two-and-a-half inches."

"And the body?" Bromstad pressed.

"Well, that should be about three inches, with a small base, um, about half an inch. Making six inches, total."

"That's an unacceptably huge head. I'm sorry."

"Now remember, the doll is six inches. The head, as I said, is gonna run just two-and-a-half inches."

"Who has a head that big? Who? Why is it so important that the head be disproportionate? Why?"

"It's just been that way for as long as I've been in the bobble-head game. I'm telling you, Mr. Bromstad, you make the thing realistic and to scale and all that—it's gonna look mighty disturbing. It's a funny thing about dolls."

"So the answer is to make the head long and . . . and . . . and swollen? No, I won't have it. That head will have to be smaller. It just has to be."

The man whistled through his teeth. "If you want to shrink

that head down, you're talking about new plans, new molds and retooling. The molds are all . . ."

"And why the palsy? What is that supposed to be?"

"Palsy? Oh, you mean the bobbling? Well, I don't know. I guess, whimsy, if I had to take a guess. Maybe it's supposed to be amusing."

"I don't find that funny! And the head's just too big! It'll have to be smaller," Bromstad nearly shrieked. "As it is, it's nearly fifty-percent head. Is that what you people think I look like? A brobdingnagian head floating above a tiny, shrimp body?"

"Brob—?"

"You're going to have to scale it back, or my skull will be—" And then his voice abruptly cut out and was replaced by some dull thuds and then some minor crashing sounds.

"Mr. Bromstad?" But that was the end of the call.

Alarmed, the man had thought about calling the police and had just resolved to do so when he fell asleep. Ross had called him early the next morning, the second time a representative of the Bromstad camp had awoken him in seven hours, to apologize. He left out the detail that Bromstad often prowled his Victorian mansion in St. Paul late into the night, making abusive phone calls to those he considered underlings.

After much wheedling on Ross's part and a great deal of expert whining on Bromstad's—including a tense week before the actual giveaway when Bromstad had become convinced that recipients of the doll would assume they were being handed a small likeness of Pete Seeger—it was finally game day: officially the Gus Bromstad PederCo Bobblehead Doll Giveaway Day.

Bromstad, the honored guest of PederCo—a local hospitality conglomerate with substantial travel agency, hotel, and restaurant holdings—and its owner, Darlene Pedersen, stood in her moderately luxurious skybox picking through a pile of steaming chicken wings.

"Are there any drummies?" he said to no one in particular.

Of the fifteen or so other people in the room, sitting in the row seats watching the game or hanging about the beverage table, not one seemed to have any idea to whom or about what he was talking. Ms. Pedersen's assistant, a pleasantly bland woman of twenty-eight whose ID badge read JENNIFER, moved efficiently over to Bromstad, placed a hand lightly on his shoulder and said, "Mister Bromstad, can I get you something?"

"Drummies? There are usually a couple of 'em floating around in here. Somebody already pick 'em out and got 'em rat-holed somewhere?" he asked accusingly.

"I. . . . I'm afraid—" Jennifer stammered.

"Is this hard?" he asked, his hat trembling ever so slightly.

"Oh . . . um," said Jennifer, not wanting to respond honestly.

Ms. Pedersen, with her extensive knowledge of appetizers, tried to clarify matters, voicing gently but firmly from across the suite, "Chicken legs are also known as drumsticks, Jennifer. Mr. Bromstad would like some of those."

"Oh. I'll go talk to catering." Jennifer bustled out of the room on the hunt for the desired chicken parts.

Human interaction often went this way for Gus Bromstad: unpleasant, coming in fits and starts, leading to blunt tension and, often, tears. It used to concern him, his inability to communicate with people in any meaningful way, other than to make them cry. But then success had come, and he hadn't worried about it since. It was perhaps most troubling in the area of romance. He'd had four dates in the last fifteen years (coincidentally, all of them had been with local television news anchors), and none of them had gone very well. For an hour or so during one of them, he held hope for a relationship with Rebecca Sparks, the coanchor of the ABC affiliate. She was attractive, meticulously groomed, bright, flirty. Bromstad had felt himself becoming interested, but then, when he'd tried to act flirty in return, not his specialty, he'd bungled it and come off as menacing. She cooled on him; he blamed her and became sullen. They parted on chilly terms. For several months afterward he'd watch her broadcasts, eat pizza rolls, and wonder if she was thinking of him.

Years ago there had been his common-law wife, Marion, but that had been a match of convenience; they'd remained a couple mainly because after college, on a whim, they'd purchased a duplex together. They'd met in the St. Odo the Good marching band, and the first time he'd kissed her, they were both wearing three-foot-tall white, fur-covered hats. Later he wondered if that wasn't perhaps the first of many, bright, legible signs that theirs wasn't exactly a romance for the ages.

Still, after she moved out, he was morose. He had a night job at a low-wattage radio station at the time, and when he wasn't working, he padded around the duplex wearing flannel pajamas and mixing himself strawberry daiquiris, sometimes as early as nine-thirty in the morning. When the renters on the other side of the duplex moved away, he didn't bother renting it out again; he simply moved over to that side, leaving the newly vacant portion nearly condemnable.

But he did find love again, a far deeper love than Marion could ever have given him. With Marion, even had it lasted, there would always have been her stinky herbal teas, her cut-off military pants, her belief that *Watership Down* was one of the greatest novels of the century. His true love had none of these rather serious blemishes. No, his love was perfect and pure, unchanging.

His public. That was his true love. They understood him, they did not judge or condemn; they simply adored him. And in return he loved them—or rather loved their love of him. Not as individuals and not in person, however. To him that was horrible. It was too close. Like trying to see your lover by examining her scalp with a microscope or by looking under her toenails. No, his lover was best loved from afar, and as a whole. Not as each separate, lumpy, often unattractive subunit.

His love was here today, ringing a field of green beneath him. When they'd introduced him before the game, the roar from the crowd was their declaration of love, and it satisfied him deeply. They cheered loudly when he threw out the first pitch, despite the fact that it was a good thirty-five feet short and halfagain as many wide of the plate. Love was like that, always forgiving and supportive. It was a glorious display of their love and a glorious day, despite the strong smell of beer, which he detested. In fact, he avoided alcohol altogether, mainly because the first time he'd tried it, he felt out of control the whole time, and when he woke up, he discovered that he had wet the bed.

"Mr. Bromstad, I think today's event can be classified as a great success, don't you?" asked Darlene Pedersen, eager to get past the unpleasantness with the chicken legs.

"Well, I have very little experience with bobble-head doll

promotions," he said without a hint of humor. Most of the people in the suite laughed, but he was able to shrug off the jocularity and continue to be prickly. "But, yes, I suppose it's going as well as one would hope."

Bromstad, snackless but with drink in hand, sat down again next to his hostess in what he imagined was supposed to be the seat of honor. Since the suite had three rows of identical purple plastic stadium seats, the only clue that he was being feted was that he was positioned roughly in the middle of the row next to the stately Ms. Pedersen. As he fumbled to his chair, struggling to keep his Mr. Pibb upright, she smiled understandingly, dispensing a benevolence that made him resent her without even having to register it consciously. Roughly his same age, pinched but pretty, with graying blond hair, she possessed an easy grace, a dignified mien that made Bromstad feel quite large and clumsy in comparison, which indeed he was.

Flanking Ms. Pedersen were PederCo's high-ranking officers. Bromstad had been introduced to them all but was unable to recall anyone's name—or rather he recalled one name, Carlos, but had applied it to the wrong person twice already.

"Isn't it wonderful how Minnesota embraces her own?" Ms. Pedersen asked, her tone low and pleasant.

"Yes. Yes it is," Bromstad answered, assuming she meant him.

"Yes, you are a true Minnesota original, Mr. Bromstad. We're lucky to have you." Bromstad nodded, ostensibly in thorough agreement, during the lengthy pause that followed. "As you might know, we, too—PederCo, that is—originated right here in Minnesota, back in 1921, when my Grandfather, August—"

"Who's that guy?" Bromstad asked with sudden, jarring

energy. Darlene stopped short, obviously annoyed that she was unable to complete what she thought was a better-than-average corporate history.

"I'm sorry. Who?" she asked reasonably, for Bromstad was not pointing at anyone. "Ron? Our business-affairs manager?" she attempted, smiling wanly at a slender fellow in khakis and a light blue shirt leaning against the side wall eating a piece of deep-fried ravioli.

"No, down there." Now Bromstad gestured down toward the field. "The guy in the mask."

"Well," Ms. Pedersen explained patiently, "that's the catcher."

This seemed to satisfy Bromstad's inexplicably sudden, childish interest. "Okay," he said. There was a long silence. The PederCo employees subtly abandoned their company's owner by starting their own low conversations.

"Mr. Bromstad," Ms. Pedersen began, a little unsteadily, "I can't imagine your chicken drummies will take much longer."

"Let's keep our fingers crossed," he said grimly. Their discourse vaporized. Ms. Pedersen glanced around for help and, finding none, gently and silently cursed her traitorous employees.

"You enjoy drummies, hm, Mr. Bromstad?"

"Every right-thinking person does," he responded grumpily.

"Ha, ha. Yes." More punishing silence followed, and there was a lull in the game, so Ms. Pedersen could not reasonably turn her focus to that. She tried to meet Bromstad on his own level. "If you could have only one snack, Mr. Bromstad, which would it be?" she asked sweetly.

"Hm? Snack?" He formed his face into an expression suggesting that he was being bothered by unseen biting flies. "I don't know," he said, shrugging dismissively, "something fried or . . ."

There was more intense nothingness. Her last push had failed. Ms. Pedersen glanced at the side of his irritable head, looking for a way in. She was about to make an uncontroversial statement about the pleasant weather when Bromstad again burst forth with unexpected vigor.

"How about a reading?" he asked.

Ms. Pedersen's employees looked to her for guidance.

"I think that would be splendid," she said, clasping her hands near her chest.

"Yes, great!" "Oh, that'd be super!" "Please, please!" came the chorus of voices from PederCo staff. Cheatham Imprint Books, Bromstad's publisher, had sent over a case of his latest, *Dogwood, Anyone?* as thanks to the PederCo staff. Ron fetched a copy of it from a stack on the counter near the tortilla chips.

Ms. Pedersen and the staff gathered around, ignoring the baseball game (which was going south for the Twins, as Baltimore's shortstop had just hit a three-run shot), and Bromstad began reading from Chapter 6.

"Bip Stuyvesant called his brother Ewell at 10:00 A.M. every day of the week. 'Ewell has his head in the clouds,' Bip would say when people asked why. 'He's a dreamer, and someday he's gonna dream hisself into a big load of trouble.' "

Gus's voice was in good form and as he affected Bip's tone, and the people in the skybox noticeably relaxed, if only slightly.

"It was the Tuesday after the big Sugar Beet Daze parade when Bip called Ewell at the usual time and Ewell didn't answer. Bip let the phone ring twenty-three times (he counted), figuring that Ewell might be down in his root cellar sorting tubers, but even those twenty-three rings weren't enough to raise Ewell."

Bromstad was lost in his reading now, really warming to his own material. PederCo's staff, witnessing Bromstad's transformation from the odd, belligerent man who had oppressed the skybox into the warm, engaging, public Bromstad, began to loosen noticeably.

"Oh, Ewell,' said Bip, crawling onto his Massey-Ferguson, turning it over and speeding down county Y the two miles to Ewell's place. Pulling it up in front, he hopped from his seat and burst through the front door. There in the front room he found poor Ewell, passed out, buried under a large pile of frozen fish fillets, in the early stages of hypothermia."

Sensing that at last they were in good hands, the PederCo staff began to fall into the story, and Bromstad, who throughout his years had honed a keen sense of his audience, pushed his characterizations even more.

" 'Ewell! Oh, Ewell, what kind of a loony scheme are you up to?' Bip cried as he pushed and clawed the fish fillets off his unconscious brother and scooped him up into his powerful arms. He mounted his Massey-Ferguson, pulled Ewell up onto his lap, and floored it speeding toward the Dogwood Downs Community Hospital. Bip paced the floor for two hours before he was allowed to see him.

" 'Ewell, you dreamer! What in the name of mercy were you up to?' Bip asked.

" 'Oh, Bip,' said Ewell weakly, 'It ain't what you think.'

" 'Well, it can't be,' said Bip. ' 'Cause I ain't the foggiest what you were doin' under those fillets.'

" 'Well, I was watching the *Top of the Day* program out of Duluth, when Tina starts a-talking about how if you got the dry skin, there's a remedy you can do right at home, with ingredients you already got. Now, Bip, you know I got the dry skin.'

" 'I know,' Bip said, tears in his eyes.

" 'Well, they says where if you make a paste of salmon, it was, and lemon juice and some other things I don't remember and put it on your dry skin, it'd work wonders.'

" 'Oh, Ewell,' said Bip, guessing what had happened.

" 'But I didn't have no salmon, just those fifty pounds of perch fillets that Mr. Clousin give me after his trip to Lake of the Woods. So——' "

At that moment Jennifer fairly burst through the door and announced triumphantly, "I have your drummies, Mr. Bromstad!"

This interruption clearly upset Gus Bromstad considerably. His face darkened as he stared, eyes wide, at the poisonous intrusion. Jennifer immediately sensed that it was the wrong time to be cheerily presenting steaming trays of drummies.

"Whoops," she said quietly.

Bromstad began by hurling the book at her, which missed by more than a dozen feet. Then he rose from his seat and, cursing most foully, made his way to the snack area, where he began to upend trays, never stopping the steady stream of obscenities.

So violent and unexpected was this outburst that it was impossible for the PederCo employees to laugh even when Bromstad ran out of snack trays to upset and in his rage tried to uproot one of the heavily anchored stadium seats, presumably to throw that as well, sputtering and cursing at it as he did. He even comically anthropomorphized it, referring to it several times as "you"—and then a rapid-fire set of vulgarities—"stadium chair," but no one had the slightest inclination to smile or titter.

It was his thorough condemnation of young Jennifer that was perhaps most upsetting. She was obviously not "a stupid breeder cow" as Bromstad had called her. Nor was she a "witch" or a "filthy spy." There was a great deal of wincing when Bromstad called her a "stupid, sobbing chickenmonger." She was indeed pitiful, standing in the doorway, crying openly, wearing large oven mitts, barely holding on to a sizable pan of steaming fowl.

Once Bromstad had finished his tirade and stood spent and panting in the middle of the suite, it was nearly a minute before Ms. Pedersen's skill and instinct in the hospitality arts finally reengaged. "Well. Thank you for the reading, Mr. Bromstad. I think we all enjoyed it. Jennifer, set that down, get some buckets, and start sponging some of that sauce off the carpet, will you?"

Several minutes later, from a camera platform on the upper deck, Bromstad, smiling warmly and accompanying himself on the banjo, sang "Take Me Out to the Ballgame" to the rowdy and appreciative crowd of 44,873 people at the Hubert H. Humphrey Metrodome. They roared their approval when he finished and roared louder as he continued in his reedy tenor, doing a second verse with lyrics of his own composition:

"Bus me out to the big dome, / Bus me out to the hump. / Maybe I'll catch me a foul ball, and get me a big-headed Gus Bromstad doll." The crowd cheered and clapped wildly. Bromstad handed off his banjo, mounted a railing, and fell back into the waiting arms of the fans, where he was passed around for nearly a full revolution of the stadium seats.

ndignities are not nearly so unbearable if no one is there to notice them. Or so thought Pontius Feeb upon suffering yet another indignity in a remarkable and consistent string of them. Starting, of course, with his being fired, followed closely by his running over a police officer and being jailed for nearly twenty-four hours. (He was told that if the police officer had died, he—Pontius—would have been charged with vehicular manslaughter instead of reckless driving. Luckily, Pontius had only run over the officer's ankle, and the men had fully recovered after two weeks in an inflatable cast.)

The story had made the Metro section of the *Minneapolis Star-Tribune*, with a headline reading DRIVER JUMPS CURB, HITS POLICE OFFICER. Pontius, rightly or wrongly, perceived a bit of editorializing in that comma. It might as well have read DRIVER JUMPS CURB *TO* hit police officer. Or DRIVER JUMPS CURB *AND CRUELLY* hits police officer. Plus, there was the word "jumps." It was entirely too forceful a word to describe the leisurely pace at which he *drove over* the curb. "Jumps" connotes high speed— seventies-cop-show-type speed—the driver hunched over the wheel, grinning fiendishly, bearing down on his prey with murder in his eyes. A Tempo in first gear was wholly incapable of jumping anything, he thought.

The story itself was pretty dry and brief, but there was the inflammatory quote by the officer he'd hit: " 'I don't know what he was thinking,' said Pierce, an eight-year veteran. 'Maybe he went a little nuts, or maybe he hates cops. I don't know.' " *Why in the world didn't they ask me?* Ponty thought. The cop had said it himself: "I don't know what he was thinking." If they had asked, they would have found out that there was no murderous intent, no going nuts, not cop hating, just a simple case of a human hand's getting caught in the broken seat of a Ford Tempo. *I'm sure it happens every day*, thought Ponty.

If he felt ill used by the headline and the officer's wild speculation, he was more stung by the fact that they'd published his mug shot next to the story. Even under the most favorable of conditions, Pontius did not photograph well. He was, as his father had often told him, "not much to look at" or "like a bum at a ballpark" to begin with, and, since he was five foot eight, too often the camera was literally looking down on him. This made for an unfortunate angle at which to capture his slightly heavy brow, as his eyes ended up peering out of the shadows of his own forehead, which was prodigious. Photos often made a bad show of his smile, too, which in person could be quite warm. As seen by the camera, it looked like a pained grimace, frozen in time by a flash, only top teeth apparent. There was no opportunity, as there was when he spoke, to see the bottom teeth, the friendlier of the two rows by far. His hair, what was left of it, was an undistinguished gray and very badly behaved, sitting well back on his head, parts of it always poking straight up and out, as though he'd "combed it with an eggbeater" (his father again).

His ability to select and purchase unflattering clothes was seemingly unerring. He'd given up on even trying to reverse the trend and settled on the idea that if there was a style that made him look sharp and dapper, it had yet to be invented or had fallen out of fashion hundreds of years ago and would not be seen again in his lifetime. In fact, he had hard evidence that this was true. The two times in his life that he felt he'd looked good in his clothes, and had in fact received more than one compliment, he'd been wearing a costume. Once for a Halloween party he'd dressed as the Roman Praetorian prefect Sejanus and felt quite at home in the toga. Many years later, for a very strange murder-mystery evening at a fellow employee's house, he'd been instructed to show up in character as someone named Sir Reginald Twyhammer. He'd rented a Sherlock Holmes outfit, jettisoned the deerstalker and the meerschaum, added a monocle and a snuffbox, and, in the opinion of more than one female guest, looked very dapper. But aside from these rare and minor victories, his had been a life of steady sartorial defeats. For the past twenty-five years or so, he'd stuck with plain brown shoes, a solid-colored wool/poly blend slack and a cotton/poly blend short-sleeved, button-collar business shirt. In the winter he often added an Orlon crewneck, also solid-colored.

Given all this, the odds were that his mug shot would be utilitarian at best and, at worst, severely unflattering. And in fact it was worse than that. He had been slightly dazed by the stress of being arrested, handcuffed, and processed. But he'd been unprepared for just how shockingly criminal he could look, even in a setting conducive to it. His hair was thoroughly out of order, twisting this way and that, a few strands pasted down on his greasy-looking forehead (and he had never before had a problem with oily skin). One eyebrow was slightly raised, something he didn't even know he was capable of, his head tilted forward with apparent threat. His lip was curled as though he had just finished uttering a curse at the police photographer, perhaps even taken a desperate swing at him. He had to admit he looked the type of character who would jump a curb and try to run down a cop. He could not even pretend that it wouldn't be noticed, as it had been placed above the fold on the same page as the local celebrity gossip column.

The newspaper story it had lead directly to his next humiliation. A week after the incident, a letter arrived at his rented house in South Minneapolis:

Dear Mr. Feeb,
Given your recent public behavior, regrettably, my client has chosen to invoke the moral-turpitude clause in your lease. You have thirty (30) days to vacate the premises. As you know, Mrs. Parsons is a frail woman and has been weakened by the shock of this scandal. The sooner the strain of it can be relieved, the better for her health, which as you know is not optimal at this time. Should you choose to vacate even earlier than thirty (30) days from today, she would be most grateful, as it is her desire to have a garage sale, and she does not wish to have your presence there driving prices down. Please notify me if this is your intention. Otherwise, mail your keys to my address within thirty (30) days.
Sincerely,
J. Michael Winslow
Howard-Stritch Attorneys

Pontius was unaware of a moral-turpitude clause in his lease, because he had signed it more than fourteen years ago. Plus he had yet to be convicted, and he doubted that his arrest, as shameful as it might have been, would qualify as an act of moral turpitude. It seemed to lack the depravity and baseness that he'd always associated with turpitude. Still, he did not want to upset Mrs. Parsons or J. Michael Winslow. He moved out three weeks later after a frantic search for a new place.

And now, his freshest humiliation, perhaps his deepest, made endurable only because there was no one around to point and laugh. At sixty, Pontius Feeb, former trade-magazine editor, former writer of little-read history books, was alone in the tiny kitchen he shared with four roommates, leaning over the sink eating Our Pride brand macaroni and cheese out of the pan using the spoon with which he had prepared it. When, mid-bite, the bitter sting of this indignity overtook him, he set the pan down, perched on the edge of a vinyl-covered kitchen chair, and wept quietly for a minute before returning to finish his lunch.

PONTY SAT DOWN with his roommates, Sags, Beater, Scotty, and Phil—all summer students at the University of Minnesota, for a meal of packaged ramen noodles that had been dressed up with browned hamburger. When Ponty had resigned himself to living with fraternity buddies, he'd imagined that the only time they got together as a group was to put Volkswagens on roofs or construct and drink lustily from beer bongs. That they ate all their meals together and were a reasonably sober bunch was a surprise to him, and he told them as much.

"Yeah," said Sags, fork poised at mouth, "we've been in school together since kindergarten, so we're used to it." Ponty had been at his new home for just a week, and of his room-mates, Sags stood out as the cleanest. His hair reminded Ponty of John Denver's or perhaps John Davidson's, and his array of clean and pressed button-collar oxfords was seemingly endless.

"And you decided to go to college together?" Ponty asked.

"Yeah, it just seemed easier. You don't have to make new friends if you don't want to," Sags replied, pushing up his delicate horn-rimmed glasses.

"So you're a writer?" Scotty asked. He hadn't been at any meals yet because he'd been working evenings at Blimpie's. Scotty had only one eyebrow. It covered both eyes, luckily, but its deviation from a straight line was only slight, dipping minutely above his nose. Ponty had already noticed, in his brief time there, that Scotty was not meticulous where fingernail cleanliness was concerned, and there was always some dark matter beneath them. He made a mental note not to eat at Blimpie's U of M location.

"Yes. Yes, I am," said Ponty tentatively, knowing that his current situation threatened to prejudice them regarding how good a writer he might be.

"Would I know any of the books you've written?" asked Beater. Beater, or William Beatty, was enormously tall, to the point that Ponty felt slightly irritated by it. The last three or four inches of his height seemed to be pure self-indulgence. Beater had a clear and resonant voice and very mature comportment. The whole package made Ponty feel small and somewhat elfish.

"Well," Ponty said, swallowing some noodles, "I write books about history, so they're a little off the beaten path." They all looked at him expectantly. "Let's see, I wrote, um,

Push Me, Pull You: The Importance of Railroad Handcars to an Emerging Industry, um, and . . ." he said, trailing off with some barely audible noises in his throat. Silence followed. Ponty felt compelled to fill it. "That was interesting. Um, I also wrote *Where Did Amerigo?: Vespucci and the New World,*" he said, chuckling self-consciously at his own title. When he conceived it, he'd been quite proud, thinking it both spicy and commercial. Now, after speaking it here, he tasted ashes in his mouth.

"Uh-huh," said Phil, in the same tone he might have used had Ponty just revealed his favorite brand of linoleum. Phil had the traditional look of a skinny stoner, with long, unkempt hair, jeans so ragged they threatened to disintegrate at any moment, and dingy, almost yellow T-shirts bearing logos and icons that Ponty could only guess represented a taste for irreverent, disenfranchised music groups who recorded on independent labels. Still, so far as he could tell, Phil was not a stoner. There was no smell about him other than what you would expect from any college student, he did not use patchouli oil, and once Ponty thought he'd heard him say to Sags, "back when I was still doin' rope," strongly implying that his THC days were behind him.

"Let's see," said Ponty. "I wrote one that sold quite a number of copies out of the Gooseberry Falls State Park's gift shop. It was called *Old von Steuben Had a Farm: The German-American Settlement of the Midwest.* Maybe you . . . you might have seen that."

Far away a dog barked.

"Did you have a publisher, or did you just do these yourself?" asked Beater, with a scrutiny in his deep voice that made Ponty uncomfortable.

"No, no. No. No. All of them were published through Jack Pine Publications, right here in Minneapolis. They made their name back in the fifties with the Rick Darling mysteries. . . ." he said, making a question out of it on the last three words. None of his roommates showed any sign of recognition, so he continued, "And also, they did Gus Bromstad's first book. . . ."

All of them now made exclamations of familiarity. "Oh, no kidding?" said Phil. "I just assumed those were published out of New York."

"Well, they are now," said Ponty, "But Jack Pine did *Letters from Jenny*," he said, again making a question of it.

"That's a Gus Bromstad book?"

Ponty, disoriented by the attention he was receiving, allowed his pride to lead him into a conversational trap.

"Oh, yeah, that's Bromstad. I know him, you know."

"Really?" said his roommates in unison.

Ponty now realized he had to reveal the shameful truth of his association with his fellow author. "I, um . . . well, I know him in the sense that he and I once had a bit of a contretemps at the Russell L. Dwee Book Awards ceremony."

"Russell Dwee? What's that?" asked Phil with a slightly accusatory tone, as though it were Ponty's fault that there was something called the Russell L. Dwee Awards.

"Russell L. Dwee? Grain magnate. Founded Pulstrom Mills. He was a great lover of literature, so he started the Dwee Awards."

"And that's where you met Bromstad?" asked Beater, leaning toward Ponty.

"Well, had a bit of a contretemps, yes."

"Right," Beater confirmed. "And what is that?"

"An embarrassing moment. A little tiff, actually." They

stared at him. "Things went badly. I was forced to give him a wedgie."

There followed a stunned silence.

"My reasons were sound. He threw a dinner roll at my friend and refused to apologize."

"Gus Bromstad did that?" said Sags. "The Dogwood guy? I can't believe it. He's all—what do you call it?—homespun and stuff."

"You sure it didn't slip out of his hand?" asked Beater.

"He was four tables away," said Ponty. "I went over and demanded an apology, he got lippy and then pushed me, so I wrestled him to the ground and, you know . . ."

"Gave him a wedgie," said Sags helpfully.

"Exactly."

"Why a wedgie? That seems a little . . . well, unconventional, don't you think?" asked Beater.

"I guess it's a primal response. Growing up, I was always the smallest one in my class, I had to defend myself, and I found the best way to do that was to take away the perceived power of my attackers. A wedgie does that—and safely, I might add. I don't know, it seemed the right thing at the time. Almost seems kind of silly now. Didn't really help my career all that much either. Word gets around, you know." Ponty faded into a reverie.

"What book of yours was up for the award?" asked Beater.

Ponty was glad the topic had shifted slightly from his assault on Bromstad. "Oh, I was nominated for *Old von Steuben*."

"Did you win?"

"Nnno. Bromstad's *Letters from Jenny* took the prize, so they put some advertising dollars behind it, but it still didn't really take off. But Bromstad left, and Jack Pine kind of shifted most of their business to trade magazines, so I ended up being their only author, really—in addition to spearheading a few of the trades," Ponty said.

"Wow, so Bromstad beat you like a drum and then jumped ship, huh? You pretty bitter?" asked Beater, not even looking at Ponty.

"No, actually. I always loved what I did. Bromstad didn't have anything to do with me. I may not like him personally, but—"

"What's that you were talking about, the trades?" asked Phil, who was currently sporting a particularly undignified milk mustache.

"Oh, right. Well, like *Variety* for the entertainment industry, the trades just keep everyone in a specific business up-to-date with the latest news, technology, business trends, that kind of thing," said Ponty, warming to his topic.

"What did you work on?" asked Scotty politely.

"Well, I worked on the *Journal of Plasma Beam Annealing*, which was pretty cool. And there was the journal of the bar-code-scanning industry, *Bar Code Solutions*. I did a lot with that particular mag," said Ponty, and then he waited for more questions.

"But they fired you, huh?" asked Beater.

Ponty shifted his weight in his chair. "Well, they . . . it's more that they eliminated their entire book-publishing division, which was, as I said, really just me."

"Is that why you went berserker on that cop?" asked Scotty.

"That was an accident, man," said Phil. "His hand got pinned in his car, okay?"

"No, it's all right," Ponty said, looking down.

Ponty carried his shame with him into the evening like a knapsack. As he sat in the cramped room he shared with Sags, he thought about calling his younger brother in Tucson, but he knew he couldn't face any questions about the accident, his job, his new living situation. Scotty, Phil and Sags, were playing hockey in the hallway, too, and it would be difficult for him to hear anyway. In adulthood their relationship had not been one of big brother/little brother. It was Thaddeus, the successful one, who had been watching over Ponty, and since Ponty had hit his mid-fifties, Thad had been, consciously or not, trying to prematurely age him, blaming any problem he might have on his advancing years. These latest events would only further Ponty's growing belief that he was eighty-five and feeble of mind and body, so he decided to send his brother a change-of-address card tomorrow and deal with the questions later.

Weaving his way through the hockey game in the hall, Ponty made his way to the street, wandered about the neighborhood in distracted thought for a time, and presently found himself at Prospero's Bookstore. He pushed open the door, heard the tinkling of the bell, and was greeted with the traditional smells of a college bookstore: the dusty, dry-moldy scent of the books themselves, an undertone of coffee, a dirty whiff of patchouli oil, and a hint of body odor. His attention was arrested almost immediately by a large cardboard cutout of a man with books in his chest. It was a corrugated likeness of Bunt Casey, dressed in a flight suit, arms akimbo, dispensing copies of his latest military thriller, *Shall Not Perish*, from his midsection. Ponty, almost to make himself feel worse, fished a copy from an area near Bunt's heart and turned it over to read the jacket copy. "Trent Corby has discovered a shocking secret: The president of the United States of America is a spy." Ponty snorted derisively, then realized he was compelled to keep reading. "If he follows his training and eliminates the president, the secret—

and Trent himself—could die; if he doesn't, the most powerful country in the world could fall victim to an insidious plot involving corrupt coffee-plantation owners, the Russian mafia, and a secret organization known only as the Silent Arm."

Ponty opened the book to read the bio on the dust jacket. "Bunt Casey is the bestselling author of *Red Debt; Go Skyward, Missile;* and the book that Colin Powell called 'a quick read': *He Lived to Die.* He lives in Virginia with his Jack Russell terrier, Sun-tzu, his collection of antique muzzle-loaders, and one fully restored Patton tank. He owns a controlling share of the Washington Redskins."

"Oh, for the . . ." Ponty said out loud. He knew, as anyone who bothered to check could, that Bunt Casey was a former finance manager for a medium-size GMC dealership in Topeka, Kansas, who just happened to have an interest in military hardware. In 1984 his first novel, *The Hammer of Nippon*, featured his picture on the dust jacket wearing his signature flight suit and baseball cap with the scrambled eggs on the brim. Though he had never served, people just assumed he was in the military, and he did nothing to dispel that belief. He made the news in 1990 when he blew off his left index finger while reloading his German-made Göerck 470, the model he used to shoot steel targets at the range behind his home in Virginia.

Critics were none too fond of his work, coming down especially hard on his propensity to write extended and agonizingly detailed descriptions of antitank missiles. Still, Ponty noted with some self-pity, even Casey's least successful book, *O'er the Ramparts*, sold close to 5 million copies, some twenty-three thousand times more than his own *Better than Great: A Maritime History of Lake Superior*.

He pushed the book back into its grim-faced author's

abdomen and headed off to find the history section, pausing at a display table situated on the end of an aisle. LIVE THE ADVENTURE, read a hand-lettered sign. Ponty, though in no mood to live any adventures, examined a few books and discovered that three of the ones featured—*Man One, Mountain Zero; White Pyramid of Doom*; and *On Belay*—were about the same ill-fated expedition up Nanga Parbat. Two more were about shipwrecks in which men ate each other, and another was about a man who got lost in the Canadian wilderness, killed a moose, and lived inside its body until he was found several weeks later. Grim, thought Ponty, though he admired the cover art, which featured a helicopter shot of a man on a frozen lake surrounded by thick woods. Knowing that he ended up in a moose somehow made it very effective.

He searched the history section. If he could see only one of his books sitting on a shelf in its natural habitat, he thought, he might mute the failure of the day and place himself, however insignificantly, in the world. But after about five minutes of unsuccessful hunting, he gave up and timidly approached the young woman at the information counter. Despite his inherently charitable nature, he had to suppress the thought that she was the filthiest-looking creature he had ever seen. She had on an array of tank tops, all of slightly varying shapes and sizes, most of them—and he guessed there might be six in total—bleached and frayed; a pair of shockingly dirty jeans cut off at the knees, replete with penned words of an indeterminate, though probably Germanic, language; and studs gracing numerous piercings, most noticeably in her tongue, each nostril, and her bottom lip. Most of her head was shaved to Curly Howard length, though from the right lower half a shock of chartreuse hair hung greasily down.

"Hi! Can I help you?" she said in a bright, enthusiastic manner that for some reason made Ponty feel ashamed.

"Um. Yes. Do you have *Without an Ore: The Decline of Minnesota's Mining Industry?*" he asked. "I didn't see it on the shelves," he added in a tone that let her know that it was probably his fault.

"Do you know the author?" she asked kindly.

"No, never met him," he said guiltily before realizing he had misinterpreted her meaning. "Oh, wait. Um, yeah. Pontius Feeb."

"Feeb, F-E-E-B?" she asked, already tapping it into the computer.

"Yes."

She entered a surprising amount of additional keystrokes, staring at the screen with concern.

She hit a few sharp backspaces and then an emphatic enter. "Hm. Okay, I'm not showing anything. And you didn't see it on the shelves?"

"No, that's okay. Could you maybe look for *Better than Great: A Maritime History of Lake Superior?*"

She looked at him blankly for a moment, then began entering keystrokes. "Okay. I'm not seeing it."

"How about *Old von Steuben Had a Farm*? Same author," he said, leaning over the counter slightly to look at the computer's monitor, as if doing that might somehow help.

"*Had a Farm?*" she asked.

"*Had a Farm*, correct."

"*The Old Man and the Sea,*" she offered weakly while still staring at the screen. "But . . . no. Don't have *Old von Steuben Had a Farm.*"

He had thrown his best at her. These were easily his most

popular books, and if *Old von Steuben* was not in stock, *And Tyler, Too: In the Shadow of Harrison* most certainly would not be. And forget about *Czech and Sea: Dvo˘rák's Voyages to America.* There was no more chance of that's being in stock than there was the dismal failure *You Can Bank On It: Senator Carter Glass and the Federal Deposit Insurance Corporation.* He bought the latest Bunt Casey and went home, defeated.

That evening Ponty sat at the small desk in the untidy second-story room he shared with Sags distractedly doodling small, neat cartoons of men with large noses and blank expressions.

"Look Skyward, Missile," Ponty whispered to himself with deep bitterness, while inking an obscenely large mustache onto one of his creations. He sniffed derisively through his nose and circled his pen over his yellow legal pad, waiting sarcastically for inspiration.

Ten Thousand Leagues, Ponty wrote mockingly, then sat staring at it for half a minute before adding, *of Intrigue.* He crossed it out. *I Kill for a Fee,* he wrote and did not cross it out. After twenty minutes of thinking and scribbling, he had a small, messy column of titles that included *Three Men, Two Guns, . . . Or Give Me Death, To Sleep with Weapons, The Magna Cartel, My War Never Ended,* and *Over a (Gun) Barrel.* He reread them, laughing mirthlessly, before scratching them out, tearing the page from the tablet, ripping it into pieces, and depositing it in Sags's Chicago Bulls trash can.

Later, as he sat on a beanbag chair in Beater's room watching a Twins game, his thoughts strayed back to the book about the man and the moose. There was something compelling about it, something elemental—a man facing death, facing nature without technology to rescue him. And also life *from* death, the inescapable theme of birth, and, holding it all together, the notion that God's universe, even in the modern age, still had the ability to surprise. His blessings weren't always neat and tidy. Now and again it came down to a lone, dying man crawling into the chest cavity of a deceased ruminant.

Ponty abandoned the game (the Twins were down 16–3 to the Indians anyway) and returned to his desk. He began to ink more titles on the page now, and with more purpose. *Killer Caribou,* he wrote, just to get his mind working. *Combat,* he wrote, and quickly added *Wombat. Antlers of Horror* was followed by *White Bison of Death.* He was unsatisfied with the direction in which the large mammals were taking him, so he tried a new tack. *Lizard! They Chew Your Flesh, Day of the Kangaroo Mice,* and *Wrath of the Rodents"* soon joined the list. He then wrote down *Rat Patrol,* before quickly realizing that it had already been a TV series with Christopher George. Ponty flipped the page, wet the point of his pencil with his tongue, and wrote the two words that would change his life and shape his future.

Death Rat, wrote Ponty.

He was on to the next, *Death Pig,* before he stopped and lightly circled *Death Rat.*

"Death Rat," he said quietly before circling it again.

"Death Rat," he said, with a little more force.

All through the night Ponty lay still in his bunk, quite awake, staring at the ceiling.

THE NEXT AFTERNOON Phil padded downstairs after an especially long night of sleep—somewhere close to thirteen hours spent in bed—to find Ponty stretched out on their living room couch reading a book with color pictures.

"Didn't know you were into picture books," he said good-naturedly.

Ponty started. "Daaa! Don't do that!" he said sharply.

"Sorry, man. So what is that? You looked pretty engrossed," asked Phil while readjusting his sweatpants.

"It's just a book on . . . this . . . stuff, that I have to do," Ponty said nervously.

"Uh-huh," said Phil. Ponty read some suspicion into his answer.

"A book on capybaras," said Ponty quietly. Phil said nothing. "They're a—"

"Yeah, I know. They're kind of like a hutia."

"A hutia?"

"Yeah. Hutia."

The word "hutia" hung in the air, and there was palpable tension between the two roommates. Ponty did not want to discuss capybaras any further, but he did not want to rouse Phil's suspicions by cutting short their conversation. And he was tantalized by this "hutia," whatever it might be.

"What . . . what is a hutia?" he asked finally.

"Cuban rat. Pretty good-sized. Not as big as a capybara."

"No? No. No, I guess it wouldn't be."

"Why you readin' about capybaras?" Phil asked casually, while yawning and running a hand through his wispy tangle of hair.

"Because," said Ponty defensively, his ears reddening, "I heard it was a good book."

"What else you got there?" Phil asked, gesturing halfheartedly at the small stack of books on the end table next to Ponty.

"Just some books. A thing on the—what do you call it . . . ?" he said, and pretended to think. "Well, anyway," he finished, waving at the air. Phil, he knew, wouldn't understand *Death Rat,* wouldn't know the costs. He glanced at Phil's yellowing T-shirt with its cryptic slogan, BREAK IT IF YOU GOT IT, and decided *Death Rat* was too good for Phil.

He did not want to answer his roommate's questions, so, to preserve secrecy, Ponty shifted his base of research to a public library in Pelican Falls, a suburb of Minneapolis just fifteen minutes away by bus. The Pelican Falls public library remained largely unvisited at most times, and Ponty was free to use its resources without having to answer to anyone. Ponty enjoyed research, and for this project he was committed and excited by the material even more than he had been for *Everett M. Dirksen: The* Other *McKinley*, a topic that had energized him greatly.

For three weeks his days consisted of waking, showering, eating Fam-a-lee Brand bagged cereal with his roommates, and catching the 8:42 bus to Pelican Falls, where he would spend the morning researching. Here Ponty was fully in his element, impressing the librarian, a fastidious man in his early thirties, with his extensive knowledge of the Dewey decimal system.

When he had completed his research, he returned his base of operations to his room, because for his actual writing, Ponty needed even more solitude than could be provided by the oft-empty Pelican Falls branch. On a warm, windy day in early July, Ponty sat down with nearly one hundred pages of hand-written notes by his side and began work on the manuscript.

Though he was on fire to complete it, progress went more slowly than he thought it might. Sags, who Ponty knew was within his right to do so, would come in and out of the room dozens of times a day. That was not so much a distraction as was his absurdly exaggerated "sneaking" demeanor. He produced the same amount of noise no matter what he did, but his tiptoeing with hands at his side like an actor at a children's theater disturbed Ponty more than anything. He would have preferred the earsplitting levels of old Ted Nugent albums to Sags's histrionics.

"Try the attic," Scotty had suggested when Ponty had laid out his problem before him.

"There's an attic?" Ponty asked. He'd never been good with houses. He didn't get them. The reason he'd never bought a house was that a drain trap in the extra bathroom of a place he was renting had once corroded through when his landlord was away. This alone had put him off houses forever.

When Scotty suggested the attic, Ponty had imagined a quaint, dusty, and spacious room littered charmingly with old oak-based dressmaking forms, steamer trunks and yellowing silk lampshades. The attic in which he set up his writing space was more like a medium-size closet with a peaked ceiling. It smelled like discarded sneaker inserts, and it was hellaciously hot. Ponty brought a thermometer up with him, and one day when the temperature outside reached 95 degrees, it was 126 in the attic. The next morning, for the first time in his life, he made a trip to the Tom Thumb convenience store and invested in a "sports drink," figuring that if he ever needed to replace his electrolytes, now was the time. It tasted like Kool-Aid made with melted plastic instead of water.

He devoted himself to his book throughout the days and into the evenings, often shirtless, a fact that was as upsetting to himself as it was to anyone who happened to see him in such a state. Access to his space was available only through a ladder that went up into the ceiling of Beater's room, so he would have to peek through the trapdoor to see if the coast was clear and then maneuver his sweaty body down the ladder, refill his thermos with water, perhaps grab a box of one of the many varieties of snack crackers from their cupboard, and return to his labor. He wrote in longhand on yellow legal pads, stopping occasionally to fan himself with his own prose.

Ponty had always had confidence that he was a good, if not great, writer—even before his nomination for the Dwee Award. And as he toiled, he found himself recalling an incident that began to grow in significance: When he was a sophomore in high school, he'd penned a rather purple short story in the style of Poe for his creative-writing class, and Mr. Blanding had called him aside to offer special, pointed praise.

"Marvelous, Pontius. Just marvelous," he'd said.

"Thank you, sir."

" 'From The Murderer's Gibbet,' " Mr. Blanding said with admiration.

"Yes," said Ponty.

" 'And the final desperate thrum of some distant, dying night, the weak but incessant beat of its faint, clashing overtones sounding in the hollows of my heart, signaled the end, not of the darkness, but of my hope' " he quoted in his reedy tenor. "Quite evocative."

"Thanks."

"And the bit about the thrush trapped in the quadrangle, screaming—very good."

"Oh, thank you, sir."

"The narrator's vision of fighting with his mother's 'rag-covered, rattling skeleton.' Quite good."

"Uh-huh. Thanks."

"Everything all right at home?"

Mr. Blanding need not have worried. Ponty knew then how to tailor his writing to Mr. Blanding's tastes, yet somehow, as he'd grown and found his interests in history and honed the discipline his chosen field required, he'd forgotten that he once knew very well how to give the public what they wanted. He was now rediscovering the skill.

Spurred on by some encouraging early chapters, his dwindling supply of cash, and the life-threatening heat, Ponty began to make accelerated progress on the book. His lack of money was of special concern, for he felt certain that when fall came, his roommates would be looking for someone else who shared more of their interests. Someone nicknamed "Moose" or "Hud." Someone who knew the rules to drinking games and had never written a book on Senator Carter Glass.

After three weeks of labor, he took dinner with his roommates, and they grilled him on his progress.

"That book of yours?" asked Scotty. "How's it coming?"

"Well, I think it's coming along quite well," Ponty said mysteriously.

"What's it about?" asked Sags.

"I'm afraid I'll have to keep that a secret," Ponty said, pointing at Sags with a fish stick.

"Is it about hutias?" Phil asked. He had on yet another T-shirt with a puzzling slogan: AIN'T NO CRIME IN THAT, it said above a silhouette of what appeared to be a conventional Old West cowboy. He was committing no crime that Ponty could see, which in his mind made the slogan unnecessary.

"No. No, it's a short history of . . . of the covered wagon," he offered weakly.

"What's a hutia?" Beater asked.

"It's a Cuban rat," said Phil. "Ponty there seemed pretty engrossed by 'em one day when I saw him."

"Why you readin' about Cuban rats?" asked Scotty.

"I *wasn't* reading about Cuban rats," Ponty said defensively. "I was reading about capybaras."

"Oh, that's right," said Phil, through a mouthful of potatoes.

"What's a capybara?" asked Sags.

"It's a . . . well, it's a large South American rat," Ponty conceded.

"Your book's about rats?" accused Beater.

"Well, no," said Ponty, "it's about intolerance and man's arrogant disbelief of . . ." Ponty was about to add "anything that intrudes on his natural reality," but he could not. In his nervousness he had been careless with the mastication of his fish stick and had allowed an oversize bit of crunchy coating to slide into his windpipe. He coughed violently for nearly a minute while Phil and Beater took turns pounding on his back. Finally, when his eyes had stopped watering enough that he could see, he continued. "It's about adventure and mysticism, a monumental clash between two men of strong will. . . . Let's see, it's got strong elements of history, and ultimately, I suppose, it's about faith and deliverance."

"And there's a large South American rat in it?" asked Beater.

"No, no, no, no," Ponty said firmly. "He's not South American, my rat. He's just a rat." Ponty took a sip of milk. "Just a regular old six-foot-long rat."

n a newly clear-cut swath of woods eighty-five feet above St. Paul's locks on the Mississippi River, Ross Barnier stood staring in stunned amazement as a monstrous structure was being made even more monstrous by a legion of workers and a fleet of heavy machinery.

"It's starting to look like a high-rise log cabin," he shouted over the din of a backhoe.

"It sure is!" Gus Bromstad shouted with obvious pride. He was standing in a construction area and was required by law to wear a hard hat, but because he refused to take off his Greek fisherman's cap, he was using both hands to hold the hard hat several inches above his head.

"How big is it going to get?" Ross shouted.

"Bigger than any log cabin you've ever seen, or these guys are all fired," Gus shouted back. "Those big logs there?" he said, gesturing with a tilt of his head.

"Gus, they're all big logs."

"Those along that wall there?" Gus held his hard hat with one hand so he could point. "Those are flaming red birch, three hundred years old."

"Where do you get three hundred year old birch logs?"

"They're not cheap, I won't kid you. They come off the bottom of Lake Superior. They either fell off of chain-boomed rafts or just got waterlogged during floats and sank to the bottom. There's a salvage company that hauls them up and sells them."

"Can they do that?"

"Who's gonna stop 'em? The beams along the third story

there are walnut, not nearly as old, only about two hundred years, but I had to make some compromises. The hardest thing is going to be prewiring it for my stereo system. Apparently there are some major fire concerns, and I had to spread the money around pretty—"

"Gus," Ross interrupted, motioning for Gus to step farther away from the cranes. "Gus, let me ask you something: do you have any *budgetary* concerns?"

Bromstad frowned. He stopped holding the hard hat above him and with his right hand let it drop to his side. He tugged on his lip with his left hand.

"No," he said finally, shaking his head.

"But, Gus, this . . . this thing is massive. It's a fortune. You don't want to be house-poor, do you? Sitting in your grand home, not able to afford a nice night out because of a big, clunky mortgage—ow!" he concluded, as Gus had just given him a sharp rap upside the head with his hard hat.

"Hey. Hey! This is practically a wash. This location, everybody can see it. Right on the Mississippi—who doesn't love the Mississippi? The Mississippi is my river. It's like an advertisement for my books."

"Ow. You hit me," Ross whined, daubing the side of his head to check for blood.

"You're not bleeding, Ross. Hard hats aren't very sharp. Now, listen. I've got another Dogwood book in the can. A single Dogwood book is like a money press, Ross, you know that. Now, stop raining on my . . . my, house."

"Okay. Okay. You're right. You've worked hard. You deserve a high-rise log cabin, Gus."

"That's right. If I don't, who does?"

"No one, Gus."

They stood for a moment in silence watching a thirty-five foot preserved cherry log being set into the gable of Gus's new home.

"Bow down before me, St. Paul," said Gus quietly.

"Ow," said Ross.

"DEATH RAT WORKS on a number of levels: On the one hand it is high adventure, man against nature, the elements gone wild. Yet on another level it slowly lays bare the emptiness and futility of man's—and in this case, *a* man's—hubris," Ponty said while swabbing his face with a 3 percent hydrogen peroxide solution. He squinted into the bathroom mirror. "This is not to say that there isn't something very cinematic about its story arc, if that's what you're asking." The weather had remained unbearably hot for three weeks now, parching the lawns and heating Ponty's attic writing space to a temperature beyond belief. This was not a worry, for Ponty and *Death Rat* were ready to go to market.

"Mister Feeb, I need the check for your part of the cable, or Beater says you can't come in his room to watch it anymore, okay?" Scotty shouted from outside the door.

"Oh, right. Scotty, I hate to be a bother, but do you think you could cover me just for a week or two?"

He heard a huge sigh outside the door.

"Fine."

Ponty donned his best dun-colored wool/poly-blend slacks and a pale yellow cotton/poly-blend short-sleeved, button-collar business shirt. Because Ponty's license was still suspended, Sags drove. Soon both he and Ponty were sitting in the spacious lobby of Todd Fetters, Literary Agent, in the magnificently restored Pork Exchange Building in downtown Minneapolis, being offered water by Mr. Fetters's model-thin assistant, Petra.

"And, sir, would you like a water?" she asked Sags timidly, unsure exactly who or what Sags was supposed to be.

"No thanks."

Ponty looked past her at the walls, clutching *Death Rat* to his chest.

"Um, I'm sorry," Petra said looking at Sags, "but are there going to be two of you for the meeting?"

"No," Ponty broke in. "He's my ride."

"He hit a cop and lost his license," Sags informed Petra.

"Oh, dear."

"Not in the face, or anything like that. With his car. It was—"

"Thank you, Sags," Ponty said.

"Is it okay if I sit out here?" Sags asked.

"Oh, of course," she said, though clearly it was not. She sat back down behind her desk and emanated disapproval.

"Nervous?" asked Sags.

"No, not really," answered Ponty.

"Aw, why should you be? He's gonna love *Death Rat.*"

"Thank you, Sags," said Ponty, patting Sage's knee.

After a very long time they heard a burst of laughter from behind Fetters's closed door, and a moment after it settled down, legendary local newscaster Daniel Turnbow emerged, followed by a sharply dressed young man that Ponty presumed was Todd Fetters.

"Dan," Fetters said, laughing, "you have to tell that story to McDonald when we go to New York."

Dan promised he would, and just the promise of it made Fetters laugh again. The fact that the pair was planning to go to New York at some future date and repeat jokes to someone named McDonald somehow made Ponty feel ashamed and unsure of himself.

"Now, get out of here," Fetters said. When the door had closed behind Turnbow and Fetters's delight had faded almost entirely, he turned to Sags.

"Sorry to keep you waiting, Mister Fleeb," he said.

Sags, lost in a magazine article about a rare endangered parrot, said nothing. Ponty made vague gestures with his body to try to get Fetters's attention. Fetters only stared at Sags, a smile frozen on his face.

"Mister Fleeb?"

"Um, Feeb," said Ponty weakly, holding his hand up halfway like a schoolboy uncertain of his answer.

"I beg your pardon?" said Fetters.

Petra arose from her desk and interceded. "This is Mr. Pontius Feeb, sir," she said, gesturing to Ponty.

"Ah, nice to meet you, Mr. Feeb," he said offering his hand.

"Ponty, please."

"And you are?" Fetters asked Sags emphatically.

"Hm? Oh! Jim Sagawski, sir," he said politely, rising.

"Nice to meet you," said Fetters, making it obvious that it had so far, on the whole, not been all that nice to meet him. "Come on in, Ponty."

They moved into Fetters's office, which Ponty complimented profusely even though he found it cold and uninviting.

"Well," said Todd Fetters after settling into his chromed steel and black leather chair and somehow managing to make it look comfortable, "I'm glad we were able to get you in today, Ponty. Normally we wouldn't. Now, what can I do for you?"

"Well, as I think I explained to Petra on the phone, I'm an author."

"Yes."

"I've published eighteen books, all of them with Jack Pine Publications."

"Hm. I'm not familiar with that outfit."

This confession threw Ponty for a loop, as he felt it was the strongest point in his plus column. Because of that, he did not want to give up on it. "Their operation is right down the street—right there, in fact," he said, nodding toward the window.

"Hm. I don't get down that way very often."

"Well, it's not important *where* they were published, I suppose. The point is, I've got a track record."

"Hm."

"And now I have a new book. A book just packed with thrills, adventure, and taut mystery." Fetters stared at him. "It's a survival/adventure kind of thing. And I don't have to tell you, they're all the rage right now."

"Hm."

There was a pause, and then they both started to speak at the same time.

"Would you like to—" Ponty began.

"Why isn't Jack Pine—"

"I'm sorry," Ponty said.

"Why isn't Jack Pine publishing this one?"

"Well, they just sold their operation to some outfit out of Denver—you didn't hear about this?"

"I do most of my stuff with New York houses. The Denver publishing scene is off my radar."

"Well, anyway they sold, so that avenue is gone for me."

"Can I speak frankly, Ponty?"

"I guess so."

"I like you. You're a smart guy. You know the business. I have no doubt that your book is as taut and adventurous as you say. But—how can I say this?—you look about sixty, maybe sixty-three. Am I close?"

"Maybe."

"Well, I should have said that you're pushing sixty."

"I know. I can't help it."

"It's not your fault, really. But in this business, sixty is old. And you'll forgive me, but it's always a plus if the author looks the part. Now, I don't know you from a hole in the ground, but you don't look like the adventurous type. Am I wrong? Are you the adventurous type?"

"I have a yearly pass to the Larssen Mountain Ski Resort."

"Exactly. I knew you'd see my point. Besides, I'm not taking any new clients right now."

"Well, why did you take this meeting with me?"

"I like these little meet-and-greets. They help me stay in touch. I want to know everyone and everything that's going on in the publishing world. Good luck. Now, if you do sell your epic adventure, you give me a call, and we can talk about representing you on a trial basis—for that book only, of course."

"Of course."

"Would you like a water for the road?"

Ponty accepted and was hustled out of the office.

"Did you get a deal?" Sags asked expectantly as they walked to his car.

"I'm afraid not."

"Well, I got a date with Petra," Sags said.

"She seemed nice," Ponty said, his voice sounding dazed and defeated.

 PONTY LAY IN bed that night thinking over what Fetters had said. *Am I really that old?* he wondered? Sixty? Buckminster Fuller, he remembered hearing, had accomplished some of his greatest achievements when he was well into his sixties. And Grandma Moses, she was seventy before she even got out of the gate. Still, as he thought about it, he realized there were many more examples of those who had done their best work while young, and on the whole they were more convincing than either the guy who invented those weird-looking dome houses or some old lady who was famous for not painting very well. He also realized that the only time either of their names came up, it was in desperate defense of being old and worthless. And it was also true that there were plenty examples of people who were dead by sixty. And still more who were alive but really just spent, burned out husks, barely recognizable as human beings.

How ridiculous, he thought, *to hang your hopes on a ridiculous, rat-based book. You are what you are—a dull, paunchy bachelor and the unattractive author of staggeringly unsuccessful books on crashingly boring subjects. You can no more change that than you can the fact that you have large pores.*

Also, you are broke. This, he thought, *should be your most immediate concern. If you could just get some money, you could perhaps claw your way back to some semblance of self-respect and from there form a realistic plan for the reconstruction of your life and, most important, some decorum in your impending old age.*

After one stinging meeting, a deflated Pontius Feeb decided

that night to abandon *Death Rat* and seek the reclamation of his dignity. The very next morning, with the help of a recommendation from Phil, he secured a position at the U of M branch of Medieval Burger.

CHAPTER 5

"Here's your time card. Do you know how to work these?" asked Ponty's trainer, Suzanne.

"You push it into the slot, right?"

"Right. This end first. You take and push it into the slot like this." She pushed a dummy card into the slot. "Just like that. Why don't you take and grab this card and go ahead and try it?"

Pontius took the dummy card from her, pushed it into the slot, and at that moment in his life achieved an unsurpassable, almost transcendent new low.

"Let's go get you a uniform."

The official Medieval Burger hat troubled Ponty a great deal. Six inches tall, constructed of some sort of synthetic mesh, puffy foam, and high-impact plastic, it was the first hat he'd ever worn to feature a battlement—or any kind of defensive structure, for that matter. Besides feeling that they were wholly incompatible with one's inalienable right to dignity, Ponty simply could not believe that colorful hats were an effective tool for selling lunch items. More than that, he had strong reservations about the whole medieval theme. One didn't have to be an expert in European history—and Ponty wasn't—to know that medieval sanitary conditions were nothing to be admired or emulated. Sewage was disposed of openly, ditches flowed with filth, people relieved themselves out of windows, and there were few clean water sources. Plus, there were no such things as hamburgers, let alone Knave Burger Meal Combos. Still, his position there kept the wolves from the door, so he put his head down and did his job.

He worked efficiently and stayed to himself, taking extra shifts when they were offered and squirreling away as much money as he could. He stitched a terry headband into the inside of his hat to prevent itching and chafing. If it was slowly eroding his soul to have to fill the drawbridge-shaped ketchup dispensers or wipe down the trompe l'oeil house depicting ancient masonry, he ignored it as best he was able.

If not for his singular purpose of making a living, Ponty knew he would be lost. Where was he going with his life? Had *Death Rat* been some strange cul-de-sac along the road to his inevitable ruin? Would he spin out his golden years like Macbeth, his way of life fallen into the sere, the yellow leaf? Honor, love, obedience, troops of friends—should he expect to have none of these? Would he die alone in his shabby little room (assuming Sags was out when he passed), a tall foam novelty hat on his head, an unpublished rat novel tucked pathetically in his desk drawer? He had now fulfilled what he believed were his brother's expectations by failing.

A month into his ignominious tenure at Medieval Burger, he was frying taco salad baskets and, to his further disgrace, doing an excellent job of it, when Sheila, one of the very few front-of-house workers who would talk to him, passed behind and said in a conspiratorial sotto voce, "Check out the new stiff."

Suzanne was at a register, and though Ponty could not make out her words over the din of the exhaust fans and the spattering grease, he presumed she was brusquely and condescendingly issuing instructions. This was not unusual at all. What *was* strange was that she was dispensing her tutelage to a very large, virile man, the type who, at least in Ponty's prejudicial view, steered clear not only of preparing Medieval Burger's fare but of eating it or even setting foot in one of their restaurants. What with his cotton poly mock-peasant tunic and ridiculous headgear, he looked even more out of place than Ponty did. At six foot five, he was the tallest person in the place by a fair amount, and the battlements on his hat were raised to an impressive height. He appeared to be in his early thirties and had a long, thin face, a muscular build, and very serious eyes that seemed to slightly intimidate even Suzanne. His hair was jet-black, and though it was obvious he had recently shaved, his slight growth of beard was as dark and apparent as if he had rubbed it on using charred cork.

Throughout his shift Ponty stole glances at the new guy as he learned about portioning, grease traps, and filling out time cards. For a moment Ponty felt guiltily pleased that someone besides himself had run his life aground to the point that he would end up here. But the feeling was short-lived and unsatisfying and made him feel ashamed.

It was several days later till Ponty saw the man again. They were working a closing shift, but he was front of house and Ponty was back, so they had no occasion to speak. Ponty was doing his closing duties and had inventoried prepackaged sauces, completed a line cleaning, filtered and replaced the frying medium, and was just stripping off his apron when he heard a resonant voice directly over his left shoulder.

"I know you," it said.

Ponty turned to see the man, smiling down on him from underneath his hat. "You're Pontius Feeb," he said.

"I know, yes," said Ponty, trying to be agreeable.

" 'We must consider John Tyler one of our most important presidents, one who should be lauded as much for his administration of The Webster-Ashburton Treaty as he should be upbraided for his annexation of Texas.' "

"Okay. Thanks," said Ponty, nodding, completely mystified as to why the man was offering him such an odd phrase.

"No, no. That's yours, from *And Tyler, Too: In the Shadow of Harrison.* I used it as the opening line of a paper I wrote on Tyler when I was in college."

The panic disappeared from Ponty's face. "Ooooh. I'm sorry, I didn't recognize it. It's been so long."

"Yeah, sorry. My fault. It's still fresh with me because it's the only thing I did in college that I got a B on."

"Oh. I hope it wasn't because of me."

"Oh, no, it was—but that's a good thing. The rest of my grades were all Cs and Ds. Jack Ryback," he said, putting out his hand.

Ponty shook it and was acutely aware that as cold and fishy was his hand was, Jack's was strong, solid, and free of any hint of clamminess. "Ponty Feeb."

"Can I buy you a beer?"

"Yes, thank you. But I'm afraid I won't be able to reciprocate till Friday, when I get my check," said Ponty.

Ensconced in a booth at the Point After Bar, a microbrewery and sports bar a few doors down from the Medieval Burger, Belgian ale in hand, Jack Ryback elaborated.

"Yup, that's why I recognized you. I lived with your book

for a couple of weeks at least, so your face was always staring back at me from my desk."

"All I can do is apologize."

Jack laughed. "No, really, you saved me. I hope you don't mind, but I took bits of it for my paper that I left unattributed."

"Ah, what author doesn't cadge a bit here and there?"

"Really, quite large passages, to tell you the truth."

"Hm. Well, doesn't matter." Ponty took a sip. "How many words, about?"

"Oh, man, I don't remember word counts anymore. A lot."

"Hundreds? Thousands?"

"How many words on a page usually?"

"Normal formatting, say, three hundred."

"Okay." Jack thought for a moment. "Fifteen thousand, or so," he said, casting his eyes down.

Ponty aspirated a small amount of Hefeweizen and expelled it quickly, forcing it into his sinuses. He wiped his nose with a beverage napkin. "Well, I suppose it doesn't matter. But weren't you worried your professor might have recognized my writing?"

"No. When I found it in the library, it had never been checked out." He noticed Ponty's hurt look. "Sorry."

"No, no. It's all right. That was never one of my bigger hits. You probably doubled its audience." They sat without speaking for a moment. "So how do you like Medieval Burger?" Ponty asked, realizing at once that it was wholly inconceivable that a human being would harbor pleasant thoughts about Medieval Burger.

"It's great. I think it's going to be a lot of fun," Jack lied, in the event that his new acquaintance had some unknown head injury that caused him to enjoy his hours behind the counter.

"Have you always wanted to do something like that?" Ponty asked, hoping his voice sounded light and inquisitive.

"You know, I never did see myself working in the food-service industry," said Jack, while at the same time searching Ponty's face yet again to see if he was being made fun of. It didn't look that way, so he continued, "But heck, it could be good for me, and if I can get a decent schedule, I can keep plugging away with my acting career."

Ponty was hugely relieved that a new topic had been introduced, and he leaped it on it a bit too enthusiastically.

"Wow. You're an actor, huh? Would I have seen you in anything?"

"Well, that's hard to know. I just finished a run of *Strindberg's Wallet* at the Bleeding Vein Theater."

"I didn't get to that one. I think I was working. . . ." Ponty trailed off a bit on the last few words and conveniently took a sip of beer.

"Before that I did *Oh, for a Dram of Hemlock*, also with Bleeding Vein." Jack started peeling strips of soggy blue label off his bottle of ale.

"I think I heard of that one," Ponty said weakly, before quickly asking, "Say, where is the Bleeding Vein Theater again?"

"Oh, it's not an actual place. It's a cooperative of artists run by two women who are really committed to doing works by newer, weirder playwrights. The hemlock play was put up at My Foot Theater, down by the old grain-storage mill." Ponty nodded as if he drove by it every morning, even though he hadn't the foggiest notion of where it might be. "And *Strindberg's Wallet* we did in the subbasement of the H. Biddle Building in the warehouse district. I do that stuff because I love it, but I was making my living doing commercial work, until that dried up on me."

"Why is that, if you don't mind me asking?"

"Well, the whole business kind of shifted, so that now you really need to be kind of scrawny and, well, I call it 'heroin-y,' if you know what I mean?"

"Oh, right. I see a lot of those pale guys with the dead eyes and the undernourished little beards. They're the thing now, aren't they?"

"Yup. In the current climate, if you're emaciated from substance abuse, you can write your own ticket. Me, I'd be lucky to get catalog work posing in canvas coveralls or thermal underwear holding a cup of coffee."

"Well, you've got the stage acting," said Ponty to bolster him.

"There were three people at the opening performance of *Stringberg's Wallet*. The rest of the run saw considerably lighter houses." He seemed to rouse himself from his self-pity. "What about you? How long have you been with Medieval Burger?"

"It seems like I started in about the year 1050, but actually it's just been a few weeks. You see, I got fired, then ran over a cop and got kicked out of my house."

Jack considered this for a moment. "Hey, it happens," he said.

The pair finished their beers and parted, Jack to his car and Ponty to catch the 17B bus over by the Tom Thumb convenience store.

As Ponty walked into his house, Scotty handed him the phone.

"It's your brother," he said.

"What?" Ponty whispered, pushing the phone back at him. "Tell him I'm not here."

"I already told him you were. You should talk to him, 'cause I forgot to tell you he called about a week ago. And a couple times after that. But I forgot to tell you, sorry."

Ponty handled the phone as though it were a small asp. Ponty was fond of that. He was a rock of a human being, confident where Ponty was unsure, successful where Ponty was not, and he had a wonderful family that he loved, while Ponty had college roommates.

"Hey, little Feeb," he said.

"Hey, big Feeb. What's going on with you?"

"How do you mean?"

"I got a change-of-address card from you, no explanation. I called your work number, but it was disconnected. I had to do a search for your phone number, and then you don't call a brother back when I leave messages for you. Who are those people who answer when I call?"

"That was Scotty."

Scotty called over his shoulder from where he was now sitting in the living room watching television. "Phil took some of those messages, I think."

"And Phil, too."

"Who are these guys?"

"They're my roommates."

"Roommates? What happened to you? You didn't fall, did you? Are you hurt? You need me to wire you some money?"

"No," he said with some effort, trying simultaneously to wad up a piece of message paper to throw at Scotty. "No, I'm—I'm fine. Mrs. Parsons got a little confused and kicked me out. I think that place had some weird mold spores anyway. And as far as work . . . well, my number isn't, um, active anymore," he said and launched a piece of paper at the back of Scotty's head.

"Why don't I come there this week? You can come back to Tucson with me, we'll get you a job down at the store? Nothing too taxing. I know you got health problems."

"I don't have health problems. I'm as sound as a horse. Thad, no, no." Scotty brushed at the back of his head, so Ponty wadded and launched another piece of paper.

"Sure you're okay?"

"Yes. Yes. How are you? How's Melissa and the kids?"

"They're fine. They miss you. Say, I'm worried with you on your own. Are you eating?"

"Why in the world would I stop eating, Thad? I like eating. It comes easily to me."

Ponty now had Scotty's attention. He quickly scribbled on a sheet of paper and flashed it at him.

"What are you doing?" his brother asked.

"What? Oh, working. Writing, you know."

"What are you doing right now? Your breathing sounds constricted."

"I'm just . . . I'm trying to get a centipede."

"Your place has bugs?"

Scotty came close and read the message, then nodded in understanding.

"Hey, Ponty, that guy is here for you," he said unconvincingly.

"What's that?"

"That guy," Scotty said again.

"Oh, say, Thad, I've got to go. Craig is here to go over that thing. I'll call you real soon."

"Well, all right. You sure you don't want me to come?"

"Positive. I'll call you later."

Scotty smiled smugly at Ponty and gave him the thumbs-up before sitting back down to watch a documentary on sand crabs.

The next afternoon Ponty sat in the 17B commuter bus trying to ignore the rattling of the windows and the jarring to his kidneys. A portly man wearing a short-sleeved shirt bearing a pattern often seen on tablecloths in low-rent Italian eateries sat down heavily next to him.

"Haven't seen you on this route before," the man said, and then he exhaled heavily.

"I'm a little late today," Ponty admitted.

"Hey, I *hear* you," said the man with unwarranted enthusiasm. He produced a book from the filthy green backpack he had deposited on the floor of the bus and turned it over in his hands. It seemed to Ponty that the man was doing it for his benefit. "Man, you read this?" the guy said loudly.

"What's that?" asked Ponty dutifully.

"*White Pyramid of Doom?*"

"No, no. Haven't read it yet."

"It's *awesome*." The man hefted the book slightly, to show how awesome it was.

"Well, good. Have you read *In the Belly of the Moose?*"

"No, is it good?" the man fairly shouted.

"I don't know. I bought it, but I haven't read it yet," said Ponty.

"If I see you on this route again, you can tell me about it," the man suggested.

"Sure, sure."

The man turned his attention back to his book. He smiled admiringly and turned it over to gaze at the author's picture on the dust jacket. Ponty saw again the unsmiling, somewhat grim and rugged face he had seen in the bookstore.

"It's amazing. This guy retraced the steps of that expedition up Nanga Parbat. Got into a bit of a scrape himself. But he looks like he can handle himself all right."

"He sure does," agreed Ponty.

THE NEXT DAY Jack slid his long body into a booth at the Gopher Café, where bad coffee and Ponty sat waiting for him.

"You do any mountain climbing, Jack?"

"Me? No, no. Had a friend who injured himself on the rocks in the St. Croix Valley, and that kind of put me off it. Course, he was drunk, so I suppose it isn't all the rocks' fault. Why, you want to go sometime?"

"No, no. It's just . . . I couldn't help but notice that you're a pretty rugged guy, Jack."

Jack stared at him.

"Look at you. You're a heck of guy," he said, holding his hands apart to approximate the span of Jack's shoulders. "Are you married, Jack?"

"Where are you going with this?" Jack asked flatly.

"Did you ever read *In the Belly of the Moose?*" Ponty asked, leaning toward Jack intently. Jack in turn leaned back to preserve the amount of space between them. "It's the one about the guy who survives by living in the body cavity of a moose."

"While it's still alive?" Jack asked with a look of distaste.

"I really don't think you could live inside of a moose that's still alive. I mean, he's bound to object."

"Okay, I see that now," Jack said, holding up a conciliatory hand and then sipping some coffee.

"Anyway, what about *Sailors Take Warning*, the book about that shipwreck where the survivors killed each other fighting over a sea tortoise?"

"I heard about that. Didn't read it. Sounds kind of grim."

"I guess. I didn't read it either. But—but you must have read *Hell, Oh, Copter* about that crash in Uruguay?"

"Saw the movie. Never read the book."

"Well, there's one thing all these books have in common, Jack. Do you know what that is?"

"Ponty, I didn't read them."

"They were all extremely popular, and each one of the authors looked remarkably like you."

"Really?"

"Big, tall guys with big handsome heads. Fisherman sweaters. Rugged jaws. Broad shoulders."

"Ponty, please stop that."

"Now, take me, Jack. I am not a handsome man. I do not inspire a sense of strength and ruggedness. At best I inspire vague, disinterested pity. I look like a sloppy caricature of Gorbachev without the wine stain."

"No . . ."

"Yes. My point is, I think you should write a book. Or rather be an author."

Jack poured himself more coffee from the brown plastic pot. "Well, now I really don't follow you, Ponty."

"I guess I'm taking about kind of an odd acting job. This is gonna sound pretty strange, but you see, I've written a sort of rugged adventure story that I can't possibly sell. You *look* like you've written a rugged adventure story, so you take my book and sell it as your own, and we split the profits."

Jack distractedly poured some half-and-half into his coffee and, without stirring it, took a sip. "Wait, your acting job is you want me to go around pretending I wrote your book?"

"Well, you don't just walk up to people and pretend you wrote it—you try to sell it," Ponty said with strained mirth in his voice.

"Because you can't sell?"

"Right."

Jack held his cup several inches from his face and stared into it. "Is it a good book?" he asked.

"Well, that's hardly the point, but, yes, I think it is, in a kind of overwrought fashion."

"What's this book called, Ponty?"

Ponty cleared his throat and lowered his voice. *"Death Rat,"* he said.

"Deaf Rat?" Jack said, putting the emphasis on "rat."

"There are no deaf rats anywhere near this book. The hearing of my rat is impeccable."

"Okay. Whatever you say. *Death Rat,"* Jack said, testing it out. *"Death Rat,"* he repeated just as the waiter approached.

"Deaf rat?" said the waiter. "You guys must be having fun over here."

Ponty gave him a pained smile and nodded slightly.

"I'll get you some more coffee," he said, taking the pot and withdrawing.

"So what do you think?" asked Ponty.

"Now, wait a minute. You see, Ponty, the thing is I'm not an author, and . . . well, I don't know—it doesn't seem right."

"Doesn't—doesn't seem right? But you've already done it. With your paper."

"Oh, come on. That's low. That was a long time ago. I used to tip over vending machines and steal Twix bars, but that doesn't mean I still do. So—if you couldn't sell this *Death Rat* thing, then maybe it just isn't very good."

Ponty's face reddened slightly. "It *is* good," he said firmly. "It *is*. But I'm just old, and . . . well, to sell a book nowadays, you need the whole package. You, you're the whole package. Well, besides the book, but I've got that covered for you."

Jack shook his head and stabbed a few strawberries with his fork. "Boy, I don't know."

Ponty seemed slightly deflated, but he rallied. "Look, Jack, half the books out there are ghost-written. Think of this as a ghost-written book, nothing more."

"Ha!" said Jack, making his voice go high. "That's possibly the weakest argument I have ever heard in defense of anything in my entire life."

"Oh, come on. *Profiles in Courage*. Extremely ghost-written."

Jack considered this for a moment. "Well, it sounds like you need a U.S. president to be your front man. Thanks anyway, but I'm gonna say no."

"Maybe you want to think it over? You're still suffering the effects of a full shift at Medieval Burger."

Jack repeated it, with finality: "No. Thanks anyway, Ponty."

"Oh, please, Jack! I need the money. You need the money. And it will work, you know."

"No."

Ponty pouted briefly and then dug into his pocket. "Well,"

he said, laying down some change for his coffee, "I can't get too full of caffeine or they won't buy my plasma. I'll see you tomorrow, Jack."

AMID THE DROWSY bustle of the evening crowd, Ponty morosely wandered the sidewalks near his home, lost in thought. As he strolled the tree-lined boulevards, he noticed with umbrage the spectacular beauty of the flame-orange leaves fringing the smaller maples, for all he could see in them was the long, unendurable death march of winter ahead. He saw shovels and mukluks, mittens and gigantic bags of ice-melt, oil-saturated slush thrown from passing trucks hitting him in the ear. And he saw himself, in the packaged-food aisle of Betsy's Quik Mart trying to decide if he should buy the Our Family brand of macaroni and cheese and walk home, or leave it on the shelf and take the bus.

Was it really wrong, what he was suggesting to Jack? When a film is projected, it is not explicitly stated that the skin tone Bruce Willis is presenting to the world is actually makeup master Ben Nye's, and is that wrong? Is it wrong that a toaster is marketed and sold under one name when it was in fact the product of a great number of people, and not someone named General Electric? When a team of dolphins makes a synchronized leap into the air to ring bells simultaneously, does it matter that the maneuver was invented by trainers and not the dolphins themselves? (Ponty made a mental note not to lead with this particular argument.)

No, it was not wrong, he concluded—not when compared to the many horrible things he could potentially be doing, like carjacking or arson. Though it was true that these would not be easily accessible occupations, given the circles he usually ran in, he had no doubt he could find that kind of work within a couple of weeks. But he chose not to do these things, even though they were perfectly viable options, given the two-to three-week period of searching. No, it was, if not exactly right, then not wrong. Especially when one considered that the alternative was a retirement spent dispensing sauces from a caulking gun.

And his little brother: What would he think if Ponty bottomed out? If he were to be forced to fall back into Thad's safety net, he could not bear the shame.

The next day, his day off, he phoned Suzanne and told her that he needed Jack's home address so that he could return the work hat that he'd borrowed. Suzanne seemed especially pinched even over the phone, but after clicking her tongue and offering a terse lecture on keeping track of his property, she finally acquiesced.

Jack answered the door at his duplex in the bohemian Lyn-Lake area of Minneapolis wearing a faded green Henley shirt, tan cotton painter's pants, and worn brown work boots.

Ponty smiled at him. "Would you look at yourself? You look like you're ready to go live in a moose or go conquer a mountain."

"Knock it off, will you?"

"What are you doing, can I ask? Are you building something?"

"I was just having some cereal. What do you want, Ponty?"

"Jack," he began, "about yesterday. I feel like I should explain."

"Yes?"

Ponty sighed. "I'll give you sixty percent of all profits from *Death Rat*."

Jack shook his head and sighed. There was a pause. He fixed his eyes on Ponty "How much does that amount to?"

"I don't know. We haven't sold it yet."

"What do you usually get for your books?"

"I got four thousand for my last one. But if you adjust for inflation—"

"Fine. I'll do it. I'm not crazy about it, but . . .'"

"Okay! Okay, great. Fine."

"Well, I suppose I ought to know what it's about?"

"Yeah, good idea. I didn't bring the manuscript with me, but . . . can I come in?"

"Yeah, get in here." Jack ushered him into an unspectacular and very actorly living room, packed with bookcases, both darkly stained built-ins and several more made of medium-density fiberboard and laminated in white plastic. There was no art on the walls, only one cheap torchier lamp and one exercise bike sitting behind the heavy glass-and-wood door. Ponty noted approvingly that, in contrast to his own place, there were no dirty clothes or crumpled beer cans lying about.

"Why don't you take the chair," Jack offered, referring to the only piece of furniture in the room, a worn, green-velour-covered recliner. Though it was in the middle of the room, it did not face a television but simply sat alone, as though it had become unmoored from purpose.

"Thank you," said Ponty as he sank into it, stressing its already tired springs.

"If we sell your book, I'll be able to get a couch," said Jack, sitting on the floor and leaning his back against his buffet.

"Oh, we'll sell it," said Ponty, rubbing his palms together and looking around Jack's living room. "Nice place. Yes, indeed. But it'll be nicer after—"

"Ponty? Could you tell me what the book's about?"

"Yes. Yes I can," said Ponty, leaning toward Jack, causing the recliner to tip dangerously on its base. He settled back a bit and continued. "The year is 1865. The place is a town up in northern Minnesota called Holey. Do you know it?"

"I've heard of it," said Jack.

"In connection with the Lake Vermilion gold rush of 1865," said Ponty, raising his eyebrows like a villain in a nickel melodrama.

"There was no gold rush in Minn—"

"Ah, but there was!" said Ponty, springing the trap. "Like so many things in Minnesota, it turned out to be not nearly as big a deal as the one in California. The gold was embedded in rock that was so hard it was shattering the equipment used to extract it. But there *was* a gold rush." He waited for questions from Jack, but none came, so he continued. "During that year a lot of unsavory people had made their way up there. People from strange places like Illinois and Indiana, even New York. The town had become a hotbed of gambling and prostitution, not like San Francisco or anything, but for Minnesota it was pretty wild. So when a charismatic preacher named Isaiah Fuller rolled into town and kind of took control, the people really rallied around him. Though he didn't have much to do with it—it was the lack of gold that did it—the town returned to its quiet ways in just about a year, and Fuller became a powerful man. But there was one local, a man named Edward Lynch—sort of a wild character, a professed atheist, a guy who had never married, made strange inventions, built his own weapons, ate mostly pemmican and kept bees, lived in a one-room shack just outside of town—he butted heads with the parson, so Fuller whipped up the town against this fellow, tried to drive him out. Well, Lynch would have none of it. He stayed put. Now and then he'd confront the Reverend Fuller in public, or it'd be the other way around, and they'd have words, but this went on for a couple of years. Then, in about 1868, some weird things started to happen around Holey." He leaned forward with more care this time.

"Weird things?" said Jack, taking the bait again.

"Right. Cattle mutilations. Disappearances. Strange noises after dark. Well, one night a farmer's horses broke from their stalls, and when he tried to lead them back into the barn, they went crazy with fear and tried to eat each other. The townspeople got spooked, and they looked to the Reverend Fuller for the explanation. Well, Fuller was spooked, too. About the only thing he could think to do was to blame it on Lynch. He got the folks believing that Lynch was up to some sort of witchcraft that was bringing the evil to their town. Lynch, of course, was furious at their accusations and superstitions. Being a real woodsman and a crack hunter, he went out to solve the 'mystery' of the strange doings all by himself. One day he followed some very bizarre and unfamiliar tracks into the woods. Deeper he went, until he noticed a change in the air, a strange silence that seemed to weigh on his mind. His heart began to beat faster, and he felt strongly as though he were being watched. Something pressed in on him. His steps became measured, and he could hear his own blood beating in his temples. He took a cautious step—and suddenly darkness, crashing, pain." Ponty leaned back in his chair with a look of self-satisfaction.

"Yes?" said Jack coolly.

"He had crashed through a closed-off area of the deserted

gold mine. And now he lay at the bottom, injured, terrified, almost—but not quite—alone. For with him in the cold, cramped space was—"

Just then the front door of Jack's duplex flew open, and into the room burst a thin, bewhiskered man with a backpack slung over one shoulder.

"Hey," he said, a look of cheerful bemusement on his scraggly face.

Jack rose and made an apologetic gesture toward Ponty. "Hey, Denny. This is a friend from work. Ponty, this is my roommate, Denny."

Ponty rose and greeted Denny, then made an excuse to leave as Denny shuffled off to his room.

"All right, so long, Jack!" Ponty said cartoonishly as Jack showed him to the door. Then he whispered, "I'll get you the manuscript tomorrow at Medieval Burger, okay? Bring a backpack or something, so I can slip it to you without having anyone see it."

"Okay, yeah. 'Cause I have to know what happens," Jack said.

ONE WEEK LATER Ponty approached Jack near Medieval Burger's garbage area, and they huddled in a corner like teens discussing the purchase of a dime bag.

"Did you finish it?" Ponty asked, his head pivoting nervously around. Suzanne was condescending to another employee near the meat well.

"Yeah," Jack said.

"And? What'd you think?"

"Really, really good," said Jack.

Ponty stared at him for a moment without blinking. "Anything else?" he asked.

"No. No, I don't think so."

"Jack? I'm going to have to insist that when you speak to people about this book, you are a little more articulate about it, okay?"

"I will. Be," he added.

That same evening a jumpy Ponty rang Jack at home.

"Is it okay to speak?"

"Yes. I'm sorry, though. I had just taken a bite of carrot when you called."

"That's okay. Listen, I think that as we get nearer to selling this thing, I should quit the Medieval Burger so it doesn't look too strange—you, a first-time author, working side by side with a well-known history author."

"Whatever you think," Jack said, swallowing.

"But I'm going to need your financial support just until this thing sells. You might have to work a lot of double shifts."

Ponty heard the crack of a carrot chunk being severed from its source, then some muted crunching, a pause, then more crunching.

"Don't you think I ought to quit so that I can concentrate on getting an agent for this thing?"

"No, no, no, no, no, no, no, no. No," Ponty said. "It's part of the Jack Ryback lore: 'He toiled at a burger joint, often working double shifts to support himself, in the meantime working on his true passion in the small hours of the morning in the kitchen of his modest apartment.'"

Ponty listened to nearly half a minute of contemplative mastication.

"Ponty? Why does that part of it have to be true, when it's not even true that I wrote the book?" Now Jack heard silence, so he chewed as he waited for Ponty to respond.

"You're getting the lion's share of the take from this thing. You sling the burgers, okay?" came the reply.

"Fine. But I've got a meeting with Todd Fetters tomorrow. Think you can cover my shift?"

That night Ponty dreamed. His dreams were often flatly prosaic, revealing nothing. When he was younger, he often flew in his dreams, arms outstretched, fingertips touching treetops, wind whipping hair against forehead. These days his dreams were about bringing his shirts in to be laundered or shopping for a new mattress.

Now he dreamed he was at work, putting bun tops on a row of hamburgers.

Many miles away and across the wide Mississippi, Gus Bromstad dreamed he was a rat.

CHAPTER 6

The instructions on a package of Mrs. Condresi's Crab Enchiladas are unequivocal: DO NOT THAW BEFORE COOKING! KEEP FROZEN! These words are printed on the front and the back of the sturdy paper microwave- and oven-safe package. The test kitchens of Mrs. Condresi's parent company, Telron Foods, had found a very slight risk that if the product were thawed in such a manner, naturally occurring bacteria present in the extruded pollock used to manufacture the imitation crab could grow to toxic levels and cause illness.

Gus Bromstad was in a hurry to use his new FlameMaster convection oven and did not read the label. He glanced at it only briefly before cooking his enchiladas, ignoring everything but the suggested oven temperature. He did not even wait long enough for the oven to preheat, and this gave the naturally occurring bacteria an even more conducive environment in which to grow. It was, in fact, not he who had thawed the Mrs. Condresi's Crab Enchiladas in the refrigerator; it was his buying service. But that was of no help to Gus Bromstad on this particular night.

As Telron might have predicted, it was a fairly small amount of bacteria that affected him, and his most marked symptom was a low-grade fever that did not even come over him until the very early morning when Gus was dead asleep. He did not awake, but he dreamed fiercely.

Time, emotions, color, texture all smeared together, separated into meaningless parts, swirled, converged again, and finally came into focus. Bill Yaster, a guy in his poly sci class at St. Odo, was offering to paint Gus's old Mustang. Gus felt nothing so much as pure terror at the thought, and he was filled with a wild sense of betrayal. He shook his head furiously and tried to scream, but he couldn't. Bill Yaster made a mocking face back to him and then started laughing, his laugh a choked, deathly harsh noise with no antecedent in the natural world.

Suddenly Bill Yaster became Gus's aunt Pearl, and they were sharing poppy-seed cake. Aunt Pearl kept eating it, but the cake kept growing, and as it did, Aunt Pearl ate more and more, making obscene yummy noises and swallowing loudly. Gus tried to chat amiably and pretend it wasn't happening, but it was too ghastly a display. He got up and ran.

Now he was at a rally, standing before a massive, cheering crowd at the Capitol Mall. He was vaguely aware that there were other celebrities onstage with him, but he had only the sense of them, as they were to his side or behind him. Ron Wood maybe. Tom Wolfe. Yevgeny Kafelnikov, the tennis player. He couldn't be sure. He distrusted the crowd for some reason, but they seemed pleased with him. He clasped his hands above his head in a victory gesture, and the people cheered wildly. When he brought his hands back down, he noticed that they had become paws. Gray-brown hair covered the backs of them, but otherwise they were thin, pink, the skin soft and nearly translucent, finished with tapered, sinister-looking claws. He immediately tried to hide them behind him, but he couldn't bend his arms enough to get them there. The crowd gasped, then started hissing, their sibiliant Ss hurting Gus's now-sensitive rodent ears.

"Please, please, stop! I'll take care of it!" he yelled to the crowd. He turned to ask a handler what he ought to do about this transformation, but when he did, his horrible, hairless tail whipped from behind him and came to rest, swaying gently right before his eyes. Gus woke up and clutched his stomach. He was breathing heavily, and a nocturnal flop sweat was evenly distributed about his ample body. He'd been in his new log home only a week now, so it took a moment for Gus to place himself spatially in his universe; his sense of self, his life experiences, his metaphysical beliefs soon followed.

"I'm Gus Bromstad," he said quietly in the dark.

This dream was deeply disquieting, especially as the capper to a somewhat ominous day. He had been on KDQT's morning

show promoting the new Dogwood, and though the hosts had
been fawning, the call volume brisk and their content nothing
but loving, Gus couldn't seem to shake a sense that the very
next caller was about to attack him as a fraud, accuse him of
being, *au fond*, a mean-spirited hack. But of course it didn't
happen. The next call would play out very like the one before it:
an acknowledgment of love, some light banter, the quoting of a
favorite passage, the promise to come to his signing. The caller
would sign off, and as Gus exchanged the familiar patter with
the hosts, he would feel a slight tugging of discomfiture, and it
would unwillingly enter his consciousness that the next call
would be pure condemnation—and so on throughout the
morning.

And then there was the signing itself: long lines stretching
outside the store and down Nicollet Avenue, great weather, a
buoyant mood prevailing over the whole proceeding. And yet
there was the comment by that woman. He was processing
them through at a good clip (when it came to signings, Gus was
obsessed with volume and would often compare the numbers of
books he'd signed to those at previous signings), all was proceeding as normal, when a middle-aged woman wearing blue
sweatpants and a Minnesota Wild T-shirt, holding a plastic
shopping bag with THE DILLY LILY printed on the side, flopped
her book in front of him and said, "I really love the new Dogwood, Gus."

"Yup," he said, scribbling his signature.

"When do you think you're going to do something new, like
not Dogwood?" she asked. "I'd buy anything you write."

He'd handed her book back without answering, of course,
and her comment had caused him enough stress to throw him
pretty badly off a very good signing pace (he was nearing the

record clip he'd managed at Atlanta's H. Thomas Booksellers in '96).

Write something new? he thought now as he lay rolling slightly in his bed, kicking his legs and rubbing his stomach. *No. Make me, lady.*

Besides, each Dogwood book was nothing if not new. Each word was hand-selected from the hundreds of thousands of words available at any given time. Its placement in the Dogwood firmament was not fickle, not based on past successes, not put there by rote experience. It was selected fresh, each and every time, you hockey-loving rube! What do you want from me, stark Russian novels set in gulags? Moist southern gothic? Military techno-fiction, like that idiot Bunt Casey? Bunt Casey who when he dons one of those ridiculous—and too tight, mind you—flight suits, actually stuffs to his advantage, the poor, insecure, underendowed idiot!

No, Mrs. Sweatpants. You'll get Dogwood and like it, do you hear?

As HE CRUISED past the timidly seedy shops of East Lake Street, Jack Ryback wrestled with his conflicting emotions. In part he was ecstatic over the sale of his book, yet he was also severely apprehensive over the fact that when he'd called Ponty to tell him the news, Ponty had cut him off abruptly, then given him an unknown address and told him to show up there at two o'clock the next afternoon. He was to ask for "Earl." Jack was not used to going to mysterious addresses on East Lake Street and asking for unknown people by name. Earls in general, he felt, were not to be trusted. Those lurking about at the old buildings and shops across 35W at two in the afternoon waiting to be asked for by name were especially suspect.

He parked his Buick Somerset on a side street, found the address he needed, and entered the narrow building, a pool hall called The Rack, situated between a massage parlor disguised as the "Utopia Health Club" and a store selling military memorabilia. Inside, there were three people: a middle-aged woman behind a counter reading a book, a man in a dirty T-shirt lining up a rail shot, and, sitting on a bench along the wall with his hands on his knees, Ponty, inexplicably decked out in a pair of stiff new blue jeans, cowboy boots, an embroidered gabardine western shirt with pearl snap buttons, and, pasted on his upper lip, a large, crepe-hair, "cookie duster"–style mustache. Jack wondered briefly if there were any conceivable way that Ponty could look more uncomfortable and out of place, but his effort yielded no fruit. He strode up to him.

"Ah, good, you've gone mad," he said.

"Quiet. Sit down."

"Earl?"

"Yes."

"Ponty, why are you Earl?"

"Sit down."

Jack sat down next to him.

"Well?" Ponty asked.

"*Death Rat* . . . is officially sold," Jack said, patting the breast pocket of his jacket.

"Yes!"

They embraced briefly and clumsily, simultaneously hopping excitedly up and down on their bench, before parting just as clumsily. The man in the dirty T-shirt looked over at them.

"For the amount we discussed?" Ponty asked, his voice quite low.

"What?" Jack whispered.

"The amount? For the amount we discussed?"

Jack narrowed his eyes in thought. "I don't remember what that was the last time we talked."

"It was—" Ponty began, before stopping himself and looking around the pool hall with great suspicion. Then, with some difficulty, due to the snug fit and fresh-off-the-rack stiffness of his boot-cut jeans, he reached into his back pocket and fished out his wallet. He produced a short stack of business cards from a subpocket of the wallet and shuffled through them, peering at each side, dismissing one, then moving to the next, finally finding one that seemed to satisfy him. Jack looked on in confusion as Ponty then patted his chest, produced a ballpoint pen from his right breast pocket, and leaned over to write on the card. Ponty could get nothing from his pen, so he shook it, tried again, and, when it failed, touched the tip to his tongue and tried again. It would not write. He held up his finger in a "hang on a second" gesture and was standing up when Jack yanked him back down.

"Would you just tell me the amount, Ponty? I just don't remember the amount."

Ponty whispered in Jack's ear.

"Stop spitting. I can't hear you."

Ponty tried again.

"Yes, exactly. That was the amount, exactly. I signed the contract a few days ago," Jack said. "Fetters took his share and cut me a check yesterday. And don't forget the back end!"

"Yes!" said Ponty triumphantly.

They celebrated again in a more muted fashion, Jack more so than Ponty because he was now slightly frightened by both the elder man's behavior and his tight-fitting trucker's outfit.

When they'd settled down again, Jack gave Ponty a look of distaste mixed with pity.

"Ponty, what is this? The jeans and the 'Earl' and the mustache? What's happened to you? You're not line-dancing are
you?"

"It's nothing. I'm just trying to be careful. My picture was in
the paper after my . . . accident, so I'm known all over town.
And besides, these past few weeks I've had dreams. I never have
dreams."

"I agree—we do have to be careful, but there have got to be
better ways to go about it than dressing up like Richard
Farnsworth."

"You laugh. Go get a rack, will you, before we start to look
conspicuous."

Jack returned with a tray of balls and racked them. Ponty
broke, the cue ball glancing off the side of the rack gently, free-
ing up exactly two balls.

Looking at the floor Ponty half mumbled, "Oh, I'm going to
need a few percentages of your share to buy off my roommates.
It's in our best interest."

"What?" said Jack, standing up straight. "You told them
about this?"

"Well, they know enough about the plot that when it comes
out, they'll know I wrote it. It won't take much. They're good
guys. They understand the drill, and they're not going to get in
our way. I just need to give them a good-faith bribe."

"I can't believe you told them about it."

"I didn't know at the time that you were going to be its
author. It's just two percent."

"Man," said Jack, "I liked my percentage the way it was. It

was so symmetrical. It hadn't been pecked at by roommates."
He waved away the issue with his hand. "Fine. Have your
stinkin' little two percent back."

"You're a pal. Okay, so tell me how it went down."

"Well," said Jack, expertly sinking one of the freed balls,
taking the cue ball off the railing, and breaking up the rack,
"there's not much to tell. Fetters took it right away, and, like I
told you, there was interest within the week." He sank another
while simultaneously looking over his shoulder at Ponty, "He
told me he sold it at auction."

"Auction? Hm, sounds a little farm implement–y to me. But
whatever works."

"Yup. Can't argue with the results," Jack agreed, using the
bridge to put one in the side and one in the corner with one
shot. "He said they were all blown away by the fact that it was a
true story. He warned that with a nonfiction book like this we
have to be pretty hush-hush to the press, because another publisher can pay some other hack journalist to whip one up, and
they'll rush into print before we get ours out." He sank a long
rail shot and pointed at it in a playfully self-satisfied manner.

Ponty blacked out for an instant, and when he woke, he was
in the exact same spot watching Jack line up a shot. He shook
his head.

"Jack, what are you talking about?" he said, his voice trembling.

"Yeah, I guess it can happen. There was another book about
that moose deal—you remember that?—but it got to market a
little late and didn't do much. This is going off the rail into the
side, Ponty."

"Jack. You said 'nonfiction.' What book were you talking
about when you said nonfiction?"

"Ponty, are you getting a little too into the Earl thing? I'm talking about *Death Rat*. Our book—your book." He took his shot, finally missing. Ponty blacked out again. He awoke to see the rubber end of a cue stick several inches from his face. "Your shot there, Earl," Jack said.

"Jack. I need to ask you a very important question now: You didn't read the book, did you?" Ponty said quietly.

Jack removed the stick from in front of Ponty's face. "What? Ponty. I read it. It was really, really good." Ponty stared at him. "I leafed here and there, might have missed some of the subtler character shading. Perhaps the smaller subplots escaped me. Why?"

"Give me a rough outline of *Death Rat*, Jack."

"True-life adventure of . . . oh, what's his name . . . falls into a mine. A gold mine. Minnesota had a gold rush—1865. That's the gist of it anyway. I'm sure I missed something." Ponty stared at him. He was trembling. Jack set down his cue. "Look, Ponty," he said, "don't be hurt—I'm not much of a reader. When I'm in a play, it's everything I can do to read the thing."

"What happens when he falls into the mine, Jack?" Ponty asked, his voice quiet and scratchy.

Jack made vague gestures with left hand. "He battles the odds. He fights a cruel, indifferent nature and eventually triumphs."

"Yeah, yeah, Jack. It's something like that. Actually, he's attacked by a giant, intelligent rat."

"Really? How big?"

"Six feet." Ponty now had his head in his hands and was pressing on his skull.

"Rats can't get that big, can they?" Jack asked himself, leaning on his cue stick. "Well, now, capybaras can get to be pretty good-sized, can't they? But in Minnesota, with its short growing seasons, I wouldn't think—"

"No, they can't get that big, you idiot!" he shrieked. His mustache rustled in rhythm with his labored breathing. The man playing at a table by himself stopped and looked over at them.

"You all right?" he asked.

"Yes, thank you," said Jack, giving him a friendly wave. "Just practicing for a play, thanks."

Ponty charged on. "They can't get to be giant and intelligent and malevolent like my rat either."

"Yeah, I know. So how do you explain how one got up in there in Holey anyway?"

"It didn't! It didn't happen, okay? I made it up."

Jack put his hands on his hips. His face blanched.

"*Death Rat* is a novel, Jack," Ponty said quietly. "A silly novel about a giant rat."

Jack paced back and forth for a second as Ponty buried his head in his hands and shifted around to relieve the itchiness of his new jeans.

"We're ruined," Ponty said.

Jack stopped pacing. "You're sure it's not true?" he asked.

"Yes I'm sure it's not true, you moron! I wrote it."

"Please, I get very uncomfortable when I'm called a moron. I don't know what it is. You notice the idiot thing didn't bother me? There's something about 'moron.'"

"Why didn't you read the book? You told me you read it, you, you . . ." He trailed off.

Jack pointed at him accusingly. "You know, if anyone here

has cause to blame, it's me. You don't write novels, Ponty. You should have told me this was a novel. *I* should be yelling at *you*."

"Oh, oh, oh! We're ruined," Ponty said again, softly.

Jack lowered his pointed finger and relaxed his stance.

"Well, we can't really be ruined, 'cause we don't have much. Except all this money."

Ponty looked up at him, eyes rimmed with tears. "Why didn't you just read the book?"

"I kind of got busy with other things." Jack tried to be cheerful. "Well, not a big deal, but what happens after he battles the rat anyway?

Ponty sat up with a spasm and sighed deliberately. "He—" Involuntarily, a strangled cry interrupted his words. "Oh," he said with bottomless misery.

"You don't have to tell me," Jack offered.

"He's cornered by the rat. It's closing in. It's going to kill him. He says a prayer. He passes out. He wakes up—oh!" Tears fell from his eyes. He covered his face.

"Ponty, really. I can read it later."

Ponty rubbed his face, shook his head, and went on. "He wakes up and he's outside the mine. Someone or something saved him. He thinks it's God." He delivered every point automatically, but with great apparent strain. "He goes into town, to the local tavern, he tells his story, how God saved him. They think he's crazy. Suddenly the rat itself busts open the tavern door. Lynch battles it, kills it. Skins it in the street. He and the preacher reconcile. Lynch becomes a town legend. The rat pelt hangs there to this very day— Look, what did you tell Fetters when he asked you about the book?"

"Well, we didn't talk much about it. We kind of started talking about squash." Jack made half a motion to line up another shot but apparently thought better of it and instead sat on the edge of the table.

"Squash? What—what does squash have to do with anything?"

"The game. He plays squash, and so do I. It was fun. Anyway, he didn't ask. I just told him it was an amazing story, and when he asked if it was nonfiction I said yes, and then I handed him the manuscript. He said he'd have Petra read it and give him a summary. Then we talked a little about boast shots and nick-kills. He called me later in the week and said he'd read it—I thought he meant the book. Hm, he must have meant Petra's summary. Anyway, he said it was fantastic and that he'd sent it on to a friend of his at P. Dingman Press, and he loved it—must have meant the summary again. I guess he played it off a few of his contacts and they all loved it, and I guess P. Dingman won the auction, and here we are."

"So no one read it? They bought a book they didn't even read?" Ponty's voice was shrill.

"Well, in fairness these are busy people. I know that—"

"We've got to give the money back," Ponty said. "And then I suppose we should turn ourselves in."

"Wha—? To who? The Library of Congress? We don't know if what we've done is illegal, Ponty." He got up off the pool table and sat down next to Ponty. "Yes, I should have read 'my own' book, but I didn't. Next time I will." Jack thought for a moment while Ponty mourned. "Here's what I think we ought to do: I think we ought to just wait until someone actually reads the book—which is bound to happen—P. Dingman will be so embarrassed about the whole thing that they won't want it to get out. So we just offer them the money back. Actually, *I* offer them the money back. No harm done. They never even have to know that you were involved."

"The money. I really could have used that money."

Jack put a hand on Ponty's back. "I'm sorry."

"It's my fault. I pushed you into it."

"I know," Jack said tenderly. "But I'll fix it for you."

CHAPTER 7

From the pungent acridity of the burned coffee, Timm Leint guessed that it was about 9:45 P.M. On any normal day he could have gone home at a reasonable 8:30, but the scuttlebutt was that *she* was prowling the halls at P. Dingman, and he didn't want her to see his empty office. He wanted to appear as eager and productive as he could, so at 4:30, when he had finished his work for the day, he stayed at his desk and began the first of what would end up to be more than 226 games of Minesweeper. He had just resolved to shut down his computer and go home when something materialized in his doorway.

"Leint?" said Kay Dingman-Mulch.

"Indeed," he said, springing up from his desk with the least amount of alarm he could manage.

"I just had lunch with Bob Poston." Leint was about to look at his watch and thought better of it. "He told me that Williamson-Funk just secured a property about a safari where several people were mauled by hippopotami. Is this true?"

"Um, yes, ma'am, I do believe I heard that, too."

"Why wasn't I told about this?"

"I was waiting for the right time."

"My door is always open," she said accusingly.

Leint mentally noted that though this was technically true, Kay Dingman-Mulch hadn't been *in* the office for fourteen weeks.

"What's happening with that rat manuscript, the one by that large man from Kansas?" she asked, looking over the top of her glasses at him.

"Ummmm . . . oh, you mean the one from that fellow in Minneapolis. I . . . um—"

"I signed the check for that one, Leint. I think I know from where my rat-attack stories are coming, don't you?"

"Of course, ma'am. I think that one is in line to be fact-checked."

"What's to check? There are rats. They attack. Some guy from Kansas writes it down.

Rush it along, Leint. Get a piece on the author in one of the entertainment rags. He's handsome, right? Rugged, well spoken?"

Again Leint demurred. "Ruggedness is so subjective." Dingman-Mulch frowned at him. "But, yes, I think he is rather on the rugged side, in a kind of long-limbed, midwestern way."

"Then what in the name of Samuel Taylor Coleridge are we waiting for? I want a big first run, and I want it out before the hippopotamus story hits. Frankly, I don't believe for a minute that a bunch of goofy-looking zoo animals mauled anyone, but I'm not taking any chances. I want those hippos buried up to their ears in rats, okay?"

* * *

JACK WAS FIDDLING with the radio knob as Ponty drove, the dented grill of his Tempo pointed north, toward Holey, Minnesota, population thirty-eight.

"Yes, I'm disturbed by the radio stations in northern Minnesota," Jack declared, though he and Ponty had not been discussing it. He locked in a station playing Boz Scaggs's "Lido Shuffle." "There. Boz Scaggs. When was the last time you heard that song? Nothing at all wrong with it, it just isn't played in the real world anymore. Next there'll be a farm report, and then they'll play, oh, say, 'Bluer Than Blue' by Michael Johnson. This is not normal behavior, playing Michael Johnson songs for others to hear. People got together a long time ago and agreed to stop doing that. Ponty, I'll make you a bet that we hear 'Wildfire,' by . . . um, that guy who sang 'Wildfire,' at least three times on the way up and on the way back. Is it a bet? Ponty? 'Wildfire'? Which side of the bet do you want?"

Ponty grunted.

"Okay, I'll give you the pro-'Wildfire' side of it. You're right, it's a sure winner." He fished around for a blister pack full of beef jerky, zipped it open, and held it out toward Ponty. "Ponty, can I offer you some jerky?"

Ponty shook his head distastefully. With great difficulty, Jack snapped a piece off and began chewing laboriously.

"Man," he said with emphasis, through a mouthful of meat, "sometimes I wonder if they should have just left it as steak. That is to say, I'm sure it wasn't the greatest cut of meat ever, but it had to be more tender than this is." He chewed thoughtfully for a moment. "Course, I suppose you can't go around eating pieces of room-temperature steak from a plastic bag, can you?"

They drove on in silence, but not for long.

"It must be nice to have your license back, huh?" Jack asked.

Ponty grunted a noncommittal response.

"I would not feel like a complete man if I had my license revoked. It had to be hard on you." Jack snapped off another piece of jerky. "Ow, I'm getting hurt by my own food over here," he said, then chewed for another moment, before picking up a newspaper off the floor mat. "Did you read about this? They found some new carvings right in the area where the Kensington Rune Stone was found? It got me thinking, Ponty, and I have a proposal for you. Don't say no before you hear the whole thing. Well, you know about the Kensington Rune Stone, right? Found on a farm, years ago. The writings indicate that the Vikings got to central Minnesota in 1392? What am I saying—the man's a historian. Of course he knows about it! Anyway. You remember what it says on the stone? Here, it's right here in the paper: 'Eight Swedes and twenty-two Norwegians on an exploration journey from Vinland westward. We had our camp by two rocky islets one day's journey north of this stone. We were out fishing one day. When we came home, we found ten men red with blood and dead.' That's pretty good stuff, Ponty. Almost too good to pass up. My proposal is, if this book works out well for us, we write another about this, maybe plant another rune stone. We assert that the Vikings did battle with some strange creature. We can brainstorm about the creature later. The sky's the limit though, really. What do you think? Hey, I just realized something: If that farmer, the one who supposedly found the stone, if he forged it, we owe him a hearty tip of our caps, don't we? That's a good one. I wonder what he got out of it? He didn't write a book, I know that. Can you make good money forging stones about Viking expeditions?"

Ponty ignored the steady stream of rhetorical questions. In fact, he did not really hear them. He was busy thinking, wondering if St. Cloud State Penitentiary was really as damp and drafty as it was rumored to be. And could the prison kitchen accommodate his slight case of lactose intolerance?

LAKE VERMILION IS a large one: 40,000 acres, with 1,200 miles of coastline and 365 islands. It stretches 35 miles, tipped diagonally northwest to southeast, across Minnesota's arrowhead region. The town of Holey is not nearly so big. Its "downtown" area is anchored by ten buildings, five interconnected buildings on either side of County Road II, just one mile from the southeast edge of the lake. Various small buildings and homes scattered outward from the center of town, but those ten were really where anything of note took place.

Jack and Ponty pulled into the main drag just after lunch and went in search of the town's tavern. It was not difficult to find. A cluster of diagonally parked American sedans, all at least ten years old, led them to the Taconite Saloon. They disembarked from the Tempo, Jack brushing off crumbs and detritus from the various snacks he'd consumed, and walked cautiously toward the bar's entrance. Ponty was disposing of some spent coffee cups into a sidewalk trash can, when Jack, with subtlety at all, pressed his face against the window of the bar, squinting to shut out some of the day's bright, cold sunlight.

A small outburst of surprise escaped him, as he was greeted by a face on the other side of the glass, not two inches from his own, staring back. It was the rugged, unshaven face of man wearing a blaze orange hunting cap and a look of mild hostility. Jack pulled back quickly and offered an apologetic wave.

"Sorry," he said.

"Can we just get inside, please?" Ponty urged. "And let's try not to stick out too much."

They pushed open the door, and the sunlight stabbed into the bar's dark interior. Every head in the place swiveled to look, amounting to about twelve heads. Jack, turning to his left, understood why the man in the hunting cap had been so close to the window: There was a pinball machine positioned along the front wall. The man was just disengaging from it, so Jack offered another apology.

"Sorry," he said. "Didn't mean to alarm you with my face there." The man simply nodded at him, took a sip of his longneck, and sat down at a tall bar table to work on a half-finished plate of nachos.

Conversations had been halted. The jukebox was playing something just below the threshold of comprehension, possibly country rock. The attention was too much for Ponty, and he became quite aware of the shockingly loud hue of Jack's very new puffy yellow coat, one of his first purchases after they'd cashed the check for their book advance. It was enormous, and thoroughly overstuffed. On the ride up, Jack had presented a spirited apologia of it, claiming that with Minnesota winters' being so life-threateningly severe, there was no room for fashion. In defense of its intense hue, he offered a parade of illustrative scenarios, many including imagined head injuries, stranded cars, and animal attacks, all ending with rescue squads or search helicopters spotting his colorful jacket. Ponty had listened to his defense and, while not disagreeing, told Jack that he looked like the Michelin Man with severe jaundice. He feared he'd hurt Jack's feelings.

While their eyes adjusted to the dark, Ponty and Jack stood uncomfortably near the door, rubbing their hands and unzip-

ping their coats. Ponty scoped out the long bar to his right and
the game room/dining area to his left and decided it would be
easier to blend in if they simply bellied up to the bar. He was
just about to nudge Jack and motion in that direction when Jack
took off on his own, striding confidently toward the bartender.

"Whoa," he said to no one and everyone, ignoring Ponty's
instructions to lie low and let him do the talking, "it's so cold
the dogs are sticking to the fire hydrants out there."

Because Jack's joke had come from an outsider, it had little
chance of hitting its mark to begin with. But it was hampered
even more by the fact that it had been heard and repeated by the
twelve people in the bar hundreds of times before. Jack, hearing no laughter, provided some of his own.

"Ah, well, what are you going to do?" he said as he mounted
a stool. "Barkeep, what have you that will warm these chilly
gizzards?" Ponty, giving Jack's banter an internal grimace, took
a seat next to him.

"What do you want?" asked the bartender, a tall, pleasant-
looking blonde in her mid-fifties wearing a sweatshirt whose
front featured an embroidered loon.

"How 'bout a Woodpecker Cider? You got a bottle of that
floating around?"

"Nope."

"Whatever hard cider you have, I'll take that."

"Don't have hard cider."

"Okay. Well, I'll take a Smokehouse Nut Brown Ale," Jack
said, rubbing his hands together vigorously.

"Hm, don't have that."

"Do you have the Smokehouse Pale Ale?"

"No."

"Well, then just give me your Samuel Taddy India Pale Ale."

"We've got Grain Belt, Grain Belt Premium, Bud Light, and Leinenkugel's."

"Grain Belt. Premium Grain Belt. That sounds good."

"You?" she asked, looking at the red-faced Ponty.

"Coffee, please," he said.

Ponty was leaning over to whisper discreetly in Jack's ear when Jack leaned in the other direction to speak to a middle-aged man two barstools to his left.

"Hi there, Sonny, is it?" he said, making a gesture toward the name stitched on the breast pocket of the man's corduroy work coat. The man did not look up from his paper. "Sonny, how are you today?" he asked again, but there was no response. Jack looked around for assistance, and the man, sensing something, looked over at Jack.

"Pardon?" he said.

"Sonny, right?"

The man looked thoroughly mystified for a moment. Then he shook his head in understanding. "Oh! The coat. No, no, I'm not Sonny. Got this down at a secondhand store in the Cities last year." He did not offer his name.

"The name's Jack," Jack said.

The man, who had already looked back down at his paper, raised his head again. "You ought to get that stitched on your coat," he said. The bartender laughed as she set down their beers.

"Say, Jack," Ponty whispered when she had withdrawn, "be cool, okay?"

"Yeah, yeah. I'm just trying to be friendly."

"Well, maybe it's the coat or something, but right now I think you're scaring everyone."

"Well, your coat isn't exactly a paragon of good taste," Jack said, casting a critical eye over Ponty's blue parka. "Should I call you Nanook? How would you like that?"

"Jack, please. Why don't we take off our coats and just get comfortable. Try to blend in."

They settled in and began silently watching the television that sat in a corner over the bar. It was tuned to a medical program that was showcasing a hernia operation. A few minutes went by. A short, stocky older man with a camouflage coat and a battered baseball cap that read DEKALB on its front approached the bar to pay his check. Ponty noticed Jack eyeing him up, itching to say something to him as he stood waiting for his change, so he tapped Jack's leg as a warning.

"Yeah, yeah, yeah," Jack whispered impatiently. "I got you."

They went back to watching the muted television. After about ten minutes, just as the surgeon had begun stapling a synthetic fabric to the patient's abdominal wall, Jack asked Ponty, "Have we blended in enough yet?"

"All right, fine. Let me do the talking," he said, smoothing down his hair. "Excuse me," he said to the bartender, and she approached. "We're . . . um, we're both writers from the Twin Cities," he said, and swallowed.

"Well, good," she said, smiling.

"What I mean is, we're interested in the history of this town, and we're wondering who we might talk to about that?"

"You're interested in this town?"

"Yes, right."

"You're in Holey, you know?"

"Yes."

"Minnesota."

"Right."

"And you're still interested?"

"Yes. Yes, we are."

"Well," she said, crossing her arms, "I guess I know about as much as anyone. Ask away."

Ponty leaned into the bar. "Well, actually, we were wondering if there's a historical society or something like that."

"The Holey Historical Society? Something along those lines?"

"Yes, yes. Exactly."

"There isn't one." Seeing Ponty's look of profound disappointment, she quickly added, "But the mayor is in charge of what few historical documents there are in Holey, and I'm the mayor."

Ponty returned her smile. "Really?"

"Yes. Name is Sandi Knutson," she said, offering her hand.

"Ponty Feeb. And this is Jack Ryback. Can you imagine that, Jack? She's the mayor," Ponty said, slapping the back of his hand on Jack's shoulder.

"I'm pleased to meet you both," she said. "Why don't you hang around till four, when Ralph comes in, and I'll be able to take you to my office and answer your questions."

"Oh, terrific," Ponty said, using a word he had not used in this manner for some twenty-eight years.

"All right," Sandi said, leaning back against the bar, there being really no place she needed to go. Because of this, the conversation was left in a state of limbo, having not been fully severed by her leaving, yet practically hampered by the fact that their business was concluded for the moment. Ponty looked self-consciously up at the television, not really seeing it. Jack drummed lightly on the bar and stared at the walls.

"How are your cheeks?" he asked suddenly.

"I'm sorry?" Sandi asked.

"I noticed you had walleye cheeks on the menu there," he said, pointing to the hand-lettered menu above the bar. "I'm thinking I need a little something to munch on."

"Oh, they're fine. Ralph, my partner, he caught 'em this last summer, so they're frozen. Ralph doesn't ice-fish." Ponty surprised himself by feeling disappointed that Sandi had a partner. "Been a bad year anyway, hasn't it, Chet?" she said to the man with Sonny's jacket.

"'S that?" Chet said, looking up from his paper.

"Been a bad year for walleye, hasn't it?"

"Oh, yah. Lots of eelpout, but the walleyes are being coy."

"Eelpout, huh?" said Jack, as though he had fished for them his whole life.

"Yup."

"What are they?"

"Well, they're freshwater cod—little bearded things. Kind of slimy. Ain't you never caught an eelpout?"

"No, sir."

"Well, you usually hook 'em when you're going after walleye, but some like to fish 'em 'cause they're good fighters."

"Are they?"

"Yah. Don't listen to those guys who go after 'em with leeches, though," Chet said, shaking his head and putting on a look of extreme censure.

"I won't."

"You just take a Lindy rig and jig it off the bottom, real slow-like."

"I'll do that," Jack promised.

"Yup," he said with finality and went back to his paper.

"You got any eelpout on the menu?" Jack asked.

"Oh, gosh, no," said Sandi.

"Well, could you give me the cheeks and some of those deep-fried minitacos? Ponty, I'm buying the deep-fried minitacos?"

"No, no thanks."

When Jack's food arrived, Ponty decided that in the interest of their relationship, he would look away as Jack ate. He had been traumatized by Jack's snack consumption on the trip up and needed time to heal. He spun around on his barstool and gazed about the Taconite Saloon. On the far wall, past a pool table and just above the table of a young couple holding hands and drinking Budweisers with their free hands, he saw several dioramas featuring dead animals. In one, a large muskellunge pursued a "buck tail" lure, its mouth opened wide in preparation for chomping down. Ponty immediately thought of Jack, tearing into his plate of batter-coated walleye cheeks, and shuddered. Another diorama featured a stuffed bobcat poised on hind legs near a crystalline lake, batting at a butterfly. Next to it a largemouth bass broke the water's surface, again, mouth wide. It was very nicely done, but Ponty got stuck thinking about the poor bass, having been necessarily sawed off at an angle just behind the head, in order to make it appear to be rising out of the lake that had been painted on the bottom of the display case.

He tapped Jack. "I'm gonna look around," he said.

"Sure, sure," said Jack, mouth full.

Picking up his coffee, Ponty got out of his chair to see if there were any more dioramas on the far wall of the tavern, which was obscured from his view by a half wall. He took a few steps to see and stopped up short, nearly choking on a sip of coffee. There, hanging on the far wall, was the pelt that he had written about, the huge, gray-black pelt of the death rat it. He took several steps toward it and then stood, gape-mouthed, his heartbeat quickening.

Good gravy, he thought, *it's true! But it can't be.* His eyes went out of focus, his mind raced. *Did I make it up? Or did I read it?* He stepped beneath it now, reached up slowly, and touched the bristly hair. He gasped and took a step back. Off to his left, he heard a small giggle.

"Hey there. You all right?" He turned to see the couple who'd been holding hands looking at him with amused smiles. She was turned fully around in her chair to get a good look at him.

"Yeah," Ponty mumbled. "Yeah, I'm fine."

"Don't be afraid of it. It's dead," said the girl, and they both laughed.

Ponty hurried back across the bar and jumped onto the stool next to Jack.

"Jack," he whispered loudly, "the pelt. The pelt of the death rat. It's over there on the wall. *The* death rat! How can that be, Jack? It's not true, is it?"

Jack looked at Ponty in disbelief. "Ponty, did you take a pool cue to the noggin? No, it can't be. There's no such thing as a six-foot rat, remember? Heck, I learned that the hard way."

"But it's over there. It's right over there."

"Okay, Ponty, honey," Jack said with mock condescension. "I'll just go take a look."

Jack wiped his mouth, stood up, and crossed the bar, out of Ponty's sight for a moment, then returned. Nonplussed, he sat back down.

"Well?" Ponty said. "Isn't that bizarre? It's just like I wrote it, don't you think?"

"Did you?" said Jack with a guilty look.

Ponty studied his face for a moment. "Oh, my—I thought you said you'd read it?" he accused, his voice incredulous.

"I did. I did read it. I just didn't remember that part. Anyway, Ponty, that's a bearskin. So you can calm down and stop accusing people of not reading your book." He bent over his appetizers again.

"That's a bearskin? A bear—are there bears around here?"

"Ponty, how long have you lived in this state? Yes, there are bears around here. Black bears."

"Well, how come he looks gray?"

"He didn't use Grecian Formula—I don't know."

"Well, I think it's odd. I don't know. It just seems like it must be a sign," said Ponty, affecting a look of intense, almost rapturous depth.

Jack finished, or rather half finished, chewing. "Ponty, there's a bearskin on the wall of every tavern from here to Mankato," he said as chunks of congealed taco meat rolled down the back of his hand, leaving red-brown slug trails of grease. "It's a sign that you don't get out much, is all it is."

"Maybe," said Ponty, disappearing into his own thoughts.

WHEN RALPH ARRIVED and took over bartending duties, Sandi led Jack and Ponty back to her office, the storeroom of the bar. They pulled up two gray metal office chairs in front of her gray metal desk, and, amid #10 cans of wax beans and plastic pails of dill pickles—sliced—they got to their official business.

"I understand there was a gold mine here at one time, is that correct?" asked Ponty.

"Yes, it's still there, just outside of town," Sandi answered.

Ponty scribbled silly unintelligible lines into a notebook. "Mmm-hmm, mm-hmm, still there, I see," he said. "And, and . . . did it yield a lot of gold?"

"I don't believe so, no. I think the rock they were trying to extract it from was too hard." She shifted forward. "Say, what is this for anyway? Why are you writing about Holey?"

"Well, I think it has a fascinating history," Ponty said, and, out of nervousness, he pretended to write another note on his pad. "The discovery of gold right here in Minnesota."

"Yes, but there sure wasn't much to it. The way I understand it, they were here in 1865 and by the next year the whole thing was kaput. All they had to show for it was some broken mining equipment."

"Kaput. You used the word 'kaput.' Are you German?"

"No, my grandmother was. You?" she asked with a tilt of her head.

"My father. My mother was Irish, mostly," he said, his fingers nearly twiddling.

"Ponty is such an unusual name. Is it short for something?"

"Yes, Pontius, as in Pilate. My father was always intrigued by Pilate's ambiguity, his helplessness. I guess when I was born, he saw that in me, so he named me Pontius."

"Well, if there's any ambiguity to you, I'm sure the majority of it is on the good side," she said, smiling. "What are some of the books you've written so far?"

Ponty sat up straight to look more important. "Well, perhaps you've heard of *Worse than Her Bite: The FBI's Vilification of Ma Barker?*"

"I haven't, but that sounds fascinating. Is your wife a writer as well?"

"I'm not married, actually. What about your partner, Ralph, is he a writer?"

"Well . . . no, he's a bartender."

"Oh, right."

"We own this place together. We're not . . ."

"Oooh. I'm sorry. In the Twin Cities, 'partner' means . . . I'm sorry." Ponty began fidgeting and blushing, so Jack threw in.

"Wasn't there some weird story about a guy who fell into a mine and was attacked by a giant rat?" he asked. Ponty stopped fidgeting and sat up straight, looking at Jack with alarm.

"I'm sorry, a giant rat?" Sandi asked.

"Yeah, we were doing some research and came upon the story of some guy—don't remember his name—was attacked by a rat in the gold mine."

"Um, no, not that I ever heard," she said, raising her eyebrows, looking uncertain as to whether he was having her on.

"Ah, but you don't know that this *didn't* happen, do you?"

"I'm pretty sure it didn't," she said, laughing.

"Well, there are a lot of weird and unexplained things in this world. It would be pretty arrogant of us to rule out this giant-rat thing just because—"

"Jack," said Ponty.

"There is starting to be a lot of evidence about capybaras now that is blowing to smithereens basically everything that scientists had ever known about rodentia. Why do—"

"I think we ought to just go ahead and be straight with her," Ponty said.

Jack considered this. "I thought we agreed *not* to be straight about this?"

"When?"

"In the Tempo," Jack said in a stage whisper. "Look, can't we—you know," he said, tossing his head toward Sandi.

"No. Whatever we said in the Tempo is water under the bridge. I just can't continue to lie anymore," Ponty said, quickly adding, "to her, I mean." He turned toward Sandi, who sat staring at them with a half-frightened, half-amused look, and told her everything about his writing, his decision to do a really stupid book, his inability to sell it, making his deal with Jack, and Jack's tremendous blunder with the sale. The only thing he left out was the embarrassing incident in which he ran over the police officer, so Jack told her that.

"Thank you, Jack," Ponty said when he was done. "The upshot of all this—what we're asking is, please, if anyone should ask, publishers, reporters . . . lawyers, or what have you, could you possibly just go ahead and tell them—Well, here, I've written it down."

He leafed through his notebook, found a typewritten sheet of paper, and handed it to her tentatively, as though she might slap his hand in the process. She studied the paper like a judge looking over a piece of evidence, read through it, mouthing a few words, saying a few out loud in a low voice: ". . . was named Lynch, and he . . . tracked the creature to a . . . eventually . . . battle with the giant rat . . . ."

When she was finished, she handed it back to Ponty, braced both hands against her desk, pursed her lips, and stared as if in deep thought.

After a moment Jack shifted in his chair and asked her abruptly, "So? Will you do it?"

She broke her reverie. "Sure," she said, slapping the desk with both hands for emphasis. "For ten percent of everything the book makes." She smiled pleasantly. Ponty and Jack stared at her for a moment. Then at each other. Then back at her.

"Done," they said in unison.

"Good," said Ponty, rising and handing her the sheet of paper. "You'll probably want to keep that."

"Yes, thank you," she said pleasantly.

"We'll get you a copy of the book contract and sort out the details tomorrow. How does that sound?"

"Perfect," she said. "So where are you staying?"

"Can you recommend a place?"

"Yes. I would try the Bugling Moose Lodge. It's the only place in town."

"Then that's for us," said Ponty. "Sounds nice."

"Their breakfasts are famous."

"I look forward to them," said Ponty. They were about to leave when Ponty stopped and put a finger in the air. "Oh," he said, "one more thing. As the mayor, do you think you could do us a favor and just tell everyone else in town to cover for us, too?"

LATER THAT EVENING Jack, wearing a red union suit, leaned against the wall and stared out the sliding glass door of cabin number three at the Bugling Moose Lodge.

"Wish we would have gotten a better lake view," he said wistfully. "The one with the better lake view wasn't winterized."

"This is never going to work. We're going to jail." Ponty said from a cocoon of quilts and wool blankets lumped atop his cot.

"Are you kidding? I now have a high degree of confidence in our plan," said Jack. He turned to look back out the window. "I want to drag me an eelpout out of that ice before we go back home."

"It's not going to work," said Ponty.

"If we can get leeches, I don't see why not."

"Not the—the *plan*. The plan isn't going to work. We're going to get caught," Ponty said miserably. "And I'm going to freeze to death. Which is probably for the best," he added.

"No, no. You heard what Sandi said, right?" Jack turned to look at Ponty, but he was buried beneath his bedding and did not respond. "Ponty? Sandi, you know, your sweetheart?" He saw Ponty's eyes peek out from under his quilt. "She got us the town meeting. We pitch it to the rest of this burg and see what happens. She thinks it'll work."

"She smells the money," Ponty's muffled voice said.

"Well, so will the rest of the town," said Jack, turning away from the window and adjusting the seat of his union suit.

"They'll run us out on a rail. After they've tarred and feathered us. And I'm going to freeze to death tonight. Which is probably for the best," Ponty added.

"Just make it through till breakfast. They're famous for their breakfasts," said Jack, still looking out the window and thinking of eelpout.

PONTY AND JACK sat in straight-backed chairs on the dais of the Holey Town Hall, feeling every bit like schoolboys about to do a recitation of "The Village Blacksmith" before the faculty. Jack was trying to disguise the fact that he was a bit logy, having consumed a four-egg venison omelette and a towering stack of buckwheat pancakes with wild blueberry syrup for breakfast. Standing at the podium, Sandi addressed nearly the entire town of Holey, most of whom had walked over to their mayor's emergency meeting directly from church.

"Thank you, everyone, let's come to order. Bob," she said to a man in the front row of folding chairs, "do we have a quo-rum?"

Bob, a thin, nervous-looking man in his forties, stood up, his hat literally in hand. "Oh, yes, Mayor. There's thirty-six of us here. Betty Leustek is visiting her daughter in Coon Rapids and . . . um, Gerry Iverson, I don't think he got the message." He shuffled even more nervously at having to report the news on Gerry Iverson. The crowd exchanged knowing glances.

Jack leaned over to Ponty. "Gerry must be an alkie or some-thing," he said.

"Shh."

Sandy continued. "As you all know, I haven't called an emergency meeting for some time—in fact, when was that?" she asked, mostly to herself. An elderly woman near the back stood up.

"It was year before last. The mayfly problem."

"Right," said Sandi. "Well, the reason—"

"Got so bad we needed to use money from the next year's snowplowing budget to get 'em off the roads."

"Exactly. Thank you, Rose."

"Yup."

"The reason I called this one will become clear very shortly. I'm going to turn it over now to a writer from Minneapolis. He's written, among other things, a book called—what is it called?" she said, turning away from the microphone and look-ing at Ponty.

"Oh . . . um, *Worse than Her Bite: The FBI's Vilification of Ma Barker*," he answered.

"Worse than her bite. The—what?" she stage-whispered to him.

Ponty, who lately had had diminishing confidence in speaking his book titles out loud, now had none at all.

"It doesn't matter," he said, smiling nervously at the town of Holey.

"No, I want to get it right. *Worse than Her Bite. Ma Barker's Vilification.*"

"*The FBI's Vilification of Ma Barker,*" he whispered frantically.

"But there's the *Worse than Her Bite* part, right?" she asked. "I liked it. That's why I don't want to mess it up." The crowd was growing restless. She turned back to speak into the mike. "Anyway, he's written a book called *Worse than Her Bite: The Vilification—— The* FBI's *Vilification of Ma Barker*. Please welcome Ponty Feeb."

The applause was at best light, the mood reserved.

"Um, thank you," he said. "We, my friend Jack Ryback and I, are here to ask a favor of you, the town of Holey. We——" Ponty was thrown suddenly when the appearance of a man in the front row caught his eye: He was wearing jeans, soiled work boots, and an extraordinarily dirty and frayed baseball cap. But it was the slogan on his black T-shirt that most arrested Ponty's attention, and he took the time to read it. It read BEAUTY IS IN THE EYE OF THE BEER HOLDER and featured a cartoon drawing of a google-eyed man, gargantuan tongue hanging from a snaggletoothed mouth, looking lovingly at a stein of foamy beer. Ponty was amazed that this was the outfit he had chosen for a Sunday-morning meeting, and by the time he had finished reading the shirt and being amazed, he had completely taxed the slim reserves of patience the crowd had for him.

"Well, get on with it," called a voice.

"Yes. Thank you. You see, I . . . we wrote a book about your town, Holey, and—"

"Yeah, we know where we live," called the woman sitting next to the BEER HOLDER man.

"Of course," he said as the crowd laughed halfheartedly. "Your town, as you well know, has a very old and fascinating history. Why, in 1865 there were more than two thousand people living in Holey, many of them in search of gold. Now, years later, there are thirty-eight of you—" Realizing how this might sound, he tried to tack on a more positive addendum. "Which is not a judgment. I'm sure you all had very good reasons for staying. Your families did, that is." And again realizing he had not successfully patched it up, he tried again. "Or perhaps you or your families came long after that, and why not? It's a lovely place, and I understand the fishing's very good. Which leads me to the thrust of my speech," he said quickly, abandoning a fair amount of prepared material to get to the thrust of his speech. "We, Jack and I"—he turned and gestured to Jack, who was slumped in his chair now, his eyes at half mast—"have written a book."

"Well hoo-ray," someone said, and no one even laughed.

"Yes, thank you. The book we wrote was a story about some citizens of your town, right after the gold rush. Anyway, there's a small inaccuracy in the story, a mistake—I don't want to say whose fault it is. What good is finger-pointing when it comes to minor mistakes of detail in history books, right?"

There was no reaction to this, so he plowed forward.

"But anyway, with a rather large first printing of the book about to come out, we'd like to pay you to back us up on this one little, really rather small inaccuracy in the text. If anyone should ask. And I can't imagine they would. But if they do.

That's about all there is to it. Thank you." He gave a tiny, nearly imperceptible bow toward the crowd. "Questions?"

"What is it?"

"What is it? Yes, good question. It's a story about two men, essentially. A fellow named Edward Lynch and another named Isaiah Fuller—you know of them both, I would guess—well, it's about the elemental clash of these two strong-willed men. And the history of the gold rush, too."

"I mean, what's the inaccuracy?"

Ponty inclined his head toward the crowd and put a cupped hand aside his ear in a theatrical gesture. "I'm sorry?"

"The mistake? What's the mistake you want us to lie about?"

Ponty laughed nervously. "Well, it's not lying so much as it is, I don't know, covering up *a* mistake so that the true history of Holey can be told to the world." He turned to look upstage. "Jack, wouldn't you say that's a good way of putting it?" Jack, arms crossed, long legs thrust straight out, gave Ponty an affirmative nod. "Yes, my partner agrees with me on that point." Ponty swabbed his sweating forehead, which in the midday light looked fully and expertly greased, with the short sleeve of his pale yellow business shirt.

Now the crowd worked itself up into an irritable buzz. A man in the second row, who Ponty thought resembled Robert Shaw enough to be disturbing, leaned forward and spoke up.

"You still haven't told us what we're supposed to cover up for you," he said, and the crowd murmured its approval of his analysis.

Ponty put a hand to his chest coyly. "Didn't I? Ah, well, it would probably do best for us to determine whether or not this was of interest to you, and what kind of fee you'd need, before we discussed what you would actually have to say."

"Well, that ain't the way I see it!" the Robert Shaw simu-lacrum nearly shouted.

"I don't lie for authors unless I know what the lie is," said a woman in the third row, stating a policy that seemed to be gen-erally agreed upon by the crowd.

"Yeah!" shouted many, and someone threw a projectile with-out much force, but it clunked near Ponty and frightened him.

"Hey, now! Let's settle down," said Ponty, backing up from the podium. Sandi stood up and looked disapprovingly at the assembly.

Ponty was surprised to see that something in this plea seemed to calm the crowd and was about to press this advantage to admonish them further when he felt a hand on his shoulder. He turned to see Jack smiling benevolently at him.

"Why don't you grab a chair, there, Ponty," he said smoothly. "Maybe I can explain it to them."

Ponty moved to his seat without turning his back on the crowd, a hurt look on his face.

Jack began. "Now, you don't know me from a hole in the ground, and what you've seen of Ponty, I gather you haven't thought much of."

The crowd seemed to agree quite emphatically to this state-ment.

"You know, that's one of the problems right there," he said thoughtfully, and then he stepped down off the dais with one lanky stride and approached the man with the beer shirt in the front row, his hand extended. "How are you, friend? Jack Ryback's the name." Ponty, who was slumped in his chair, breathing heavily from the emotion of his confrontation, now rolled his eyes at Jack's ham-fisted approach.

"Howdy," the man said, and he shook Jack's hand, nodding

vague approval. Jack repeated the action with the rest of the front row before moving back to the second, shaking hands or just nodding his greeting to the people he couldn't reach, until he had worked the whole crowd. When he was done, he strode back up onstage and reclaimed the podium.

"That's a little more like it. A fella can't very well waltz into town and ask a favor of a stranger before he's even had a chance to shake his—or her—hand." A few people smiled at this. "Now, Ponty, he's a nice enough guy once you get past all that bluster, and you won't find smarter in all the world, but sometimes he can't communicate worth sour owl guano, pardon my French," Jack said, using the saltiest colloquialism he knew. "He's a history author—what can you say? Sorry, Ponty, you know I love you," he said, shaping his hand into a "gun" and pointing it at Ponty. It got a few laughs. Ponty, unable to come up with anything better on such short notice, rolled his eyes again.

Jack slumped his shoulders to show that all the kidding and the good times were over—that it was time for honesty. "Here's what happened: Ponty come to me with this book, this history book about your gold rush."

Ponty squinted with distaste, noting Jack's deliberately corn-pone grammar and thinking he heard a previously absent twang reminiscent of Andy Griffith.

"It was good, but nap-inducing. You know what I mean— again, no offense, Ponty," Jack continued. "So I suggested he let me take it and spice it up a little, you know. So I came up with this crazy story about—you're gonna laugh at me—but it was about a guy getting attacked by a giant rat." The town of Holey laughed. "Sure, sure, dumbest thing you ever heard, but you know how sometimes dumb ideas can kind of rattle around and come back to you and all of a sudden they're not so dumb anymore? Well, that's how the book turned out. And Jack agreed, so I took it to an agent, and he sold the dang thing, and you're never gonna guess what happened next."

Jack let it hang in the air for a moment, till someone finally said, "What? What happened?"

"I'll tell you what happened: It got into the hands of a New York book publisher—you ever seen one of these guys? No? Well, you take yourself the slickest Philadelphia lawyer you've ever laid eyes on and you slap a tweed coat on his back and throw some leather patches on his elbows, set him in a Manhattan restaurant in front of a fifty-dollar lunch, and I'd have to think you're about as near to a New York book publisher as you could get."

This incited laughter in most everyone but Ponty, who was convinced that Jack had breezed past Andy Griffith–level hominess and had his sights set on Will Rogers now.

"Well, this agent guy"—and here he turned to look at his partner—"Ponty, what was that poor dope's name? Todd, was that it?"

"Yes, I believe Todd was his name," said Ponty, making it sound no more convincing than a confession coerced by KGB agents.

"Yeah, Todd. He was a piece of work. Well, he sells it to his bosses as a—get this—a true story!" This got some bigger laughs. "Yeah. What can you say? He's from New York. So they buy this thing and print up a couple hundred thousand copies and paste the words 'a thrilling true story' on the cover with one of those stickers, all ready to go market before they realize—'Hey, this can't be true, can it?' So they come back to me and say"—and here he put on a weak, reedy voice as parody of his New York publisher—" 'Ah, Jack, this is a true story right? You checked it out, didn't you?' So I realized what had happened. They messed up, and now it's up to *me* to pull *their* bacon out of the fire. Well, at first I said, 'You gotta be kidding me!' Then I realized they're gonna yank this book, they're gonna blame it on us, they're gonna get themselves about a football team's worth of those fancy lawyers, and they're gonna take our money away. For something that was *their* fault." Jack shook his head with frustration.

"Then I thought, well, maybe there's a way we can keep our money, even spread some of it around to the good folks of Holey, and at the same time pull a pretty good joke over on Todd and his buddies in that glass skyscraper in Manhattan. So I said, 'Well, of course Todd. It's all true. Every word of it.' " There was a spark in Jack's dark eyes as he finished. Then it faded and he dropped his eyes and ran a hand through his wavy hair. "Ahhh. Now that I get up here and talk it through, it sounds pretty silly," he said. Then he paused, made a motion to say something more, stopped himself, and walked to his seat, giving a little wave of thanks as he did. The crowd was silent.

Sandi approached the podium. "Okay, well, thank you, Mr. Ryback," she said, sounding a little too impressed for Ponty's taste. "Why don't we have our guests withdraw, and we'll discuss and have their answer shortly—how does that sound?"

THAT EVENING, BACK at the Bugling Moose, Ponty sipped a cup of cider while Jack flossed. "Jack?" Ponty called from his chair at their knotty-pine table. "Did you mean that about my book being a real snooze? Is it, do you think?" There was a long pause as Jack withdrew his floss, rolled and disposed of it, then rinsed. He appeared at Ponty's side and crouched down to his level, which took a good amount of crouching.

"Ponty," he said cajolingly. "Hey, Ponty." He lightly punched Ponty's shoulder. "Come on, Ponty," he plead, trying to incline his face under Ponty's to get a look at his expression. "No, I don't think your book is a snooze."

"No?" Ponty said, peeking out from under his hand.

"No," Jack said with emphasis. "It's not my cup of tea, but it's good. I made up all that stuff, Ponty. I was just trying to get us out of a jam."

"Yeah. Those were some real whoppers you told."

"Yeah, I kind of poached a lot of the attitude of it from a play called *Log jam of Dreams* by Samuel Boathers."

"I've never heard of that one. It's about logging, huh?"

"No. It's about men returning home after the Spanish-American War."

"So no logs?"

"No, not that I recall."

"So why the log-based title?"

"I couldn't say. It's been a while."

Ponty sat up and sighed deeply. "Well, you had me worried at the bar the other day, but you did do a great job up there today. Perhaps we're just delaying our arrests and subsequent jail terms, but still, nicely done."

"Hey, no doom and gloom, now. The whole town is behind us. They love us, Ponty. I made a lot of friends at the doughnut table there, after they took the vote. And I saw you cozying up to Sandi. We got it made. There's a pile of our books coming out. What could possibly go wrong now?"

CHAPTER 8

The rustic back porch of Gus Bromstad's log home was best accessed by the southern elevator, the route Ross Barnier took one winter night to answer a summons by his employer. The elevator door slid open, and Ross beheld Bromstad sitting in his rocking chair, bathed in a pool of yellow light, whittling.

"How do, Ross?" Bromstad said in his familiar radio voice.

"Good, Gus. You?" Ross could not see how Bromstad was getting his chair to rock; then he noticed that it was plugged in to a wall outlet.

"Have a sit-down, Ross, and I'll tell you how I am."

Ross took off his coat, selected a hickory-stick chair with a gingham cushion, and sat down. "This sure turned out nice," he said, settling into the cushion's comfortable gel insert.

"Yes, I'm glad I decided on a retractable roof for the porch, or this weather would have chased us inside to the great room."

Ross sat quietly, being dutifully impressed by the spoils of Gus's light and charming prose. "Yup," he said. "Turned out real, real nice."

"Mm-hm," Gus agreed, a curl of oak falling lazily to the unfinished ash flooring.

"Yes, sir."

"Ayup."

Ross thought for a moment that he heard crickets chirping, but he dismissed it as impossible.

"Mmm. Nice night."

"That it is."

During this artificial lull, Ross pretended to be taking in a view of the boxcar siding over Gus's shoulder but was really spying the whittling knife with his peripheral vision, so that in the very likely event that Gus hurled it, he would have a sporting chance of getting his head out of the way.

"Did you go with forced-air heat?" Ross asked.

"Except for out here—this has baseboard heat."

"Mmm."

"Yup."

Gus suddenly exploded out of his chair and surprised Ross by stabbing the whittling knife into the table next to him and throwing the chunk of wood instead. It missed Ross by about thirteen feet and clunked weakly to the floor.

"Who is he, Ross?" Gus sputtered. "Who's Jack Ryback?"

"Jack . . . ? The guy from that game-show scandal in the fifties?"

"Don't toy with me, Ross. An adventure book outselling me? The Dogwood books are adventure-book-proof. How did this happen?" Bromstad thundered.

Ross crossed his legs and cleared his throat. "What can I say? People are fickle. Right now they like true stories of people overcoming odds—or huge rats, as the case may be. But when that dies down, they'll come back home. To you." He looked at Gus's frown. "One would think," he added.

"Ross, I'd like to do a dramatic reading now from the St. Paul Pioneer Press, if I may?" Gus reached beneath his rocker where the paper sat loaded and ready, pulled it out, folded and smoothed it. "Ahem. 'Jack Ryback just might be the perfect author for the nouveau-pop age. Hip, smart, and studly, he is both self-aware and disarmingly guileless.' And I'm gonna stop right there, Ross. How can one be both self-aware and disarmingly guileless?" asked Bromstad sarcastically while resting his head in his free hand.

Ross coughed demurely. "It's not easy, no question about it. I can't pull it off, that's for sure. But this Ryback fellow . . . I don't know. Maybe there's something to it."

"Is there any bad press for that stupid rat book, Ross? Is there? 'Cause I called our clipping service, and I—"

"You called our clipping service? You shouldn't do that, Gus. That's my job."

"*And* they couldn't find any review of *Death Rat* that was flat-out negative. Who's his press agent? How is he doing this?"

"Gus, please let me call the clipping service for whatever you might need. They're very fickle over there, and I don't want—"

"Look, shut up about the clipping service, will you? *Death Rat* sold more in its second week than *Dogwood* did in its first. We're in trouble here, Ross."

"What trouble are we in?" asked Ross. "What do you care about this guy? Your book still sells the same. His just sells more."

"What do I care about this? He's wearing a fisherman's sweater in all his press photos, Ross. The fisherman's sweater, in case anyone happens to drive up and ask you sometime, *is my deal! Mine!* I invented wearing fisherman's sweaters, not him."

"Well, now, Gus. In all fairness, he's wearing it in a kind of straightforward, 'I'm rugged' kind of way. I really don't think he's even trying to step on your modified Burl Ives, folksy, backwoods thing."

"And the scuttlebutt is—and this had better not be true—

he's been short-listed for the Russell Dwee Award. Who always wins the Russell Dwee Award, Ross? Do guys named Jack Ryback win it? Or do I?"

"You do, always, Gus."

Gus grabbed a wicker chair, placed it front of Ross, and sat down, leaning into him. Then Gus Bromstad, the beloved author of the series of Dogwood books, editor of a bestselling book of light verse, and writer of the libretto for the long-running children's musical *Harry H. Hare: Hare for Hire,* quietly ordered the death of Jack Ryback.

Ross was horrified. "Gus, I don't think I can do that," he said.

Gus rolled his eyes toward the ceiling and nodded in understanding, pointing to imagined listening devices. He nodded conspiratorially at Ross.

"Well, good. I was just kidding anyway," he said in a thick voice.

Gus then arranged his hand into the classic pantomime "phone" shape and wiggled it next to his head. *"Call . . . me . . . when . . . he's . . . dead, "* he mouthed deliberately to Ross.

"Gus, no. I think you've been working too hard."

Bromstad came at it from a different angle.

"I want him hurt—bad—or restrained indefinitely so that he can never write again," he said.

"Gus, no. I can't and I won't."

"Well, then, I'm just going to have to find someone who can. You're fired," he said, standing. "Here, let me punch in the code to let you out."

"WHAT S MARVELOUS ABOUT it is that it puts Minnesota on the map," Darlene Pederson said. "It lets the rest of the country know that things other than playoff losses and blizzards do happen here. It says, 'Hey, we're not just odd, silent people who hoard gasoline and wear puffy coats.' "

"Exactly. We're that and so much more," said Jack. Ms. Pederson was one of an army of Minnesota's brightest lights, and the whole bright lot of them, at Fetters's invitation, had stormed Beret for a nine o'clock cocktail reception in Jack's honor.

"Well, this is it," Ms. Pederson agreed, holding out her left hand while sipping her old-Fashioned with the other. "But your average New Yorker doesn't even know we have electricity here, let alone culture, theater, and the arts—and bestselling authors like yourself."

"Oh, please. This whole book basically fell into my lap," Jack said, fishing another stuffed mushroom from a plate.

"You're too modest. I think a book reception like this is a marvelous thing, and I adore Mr. Fetters. Don't you just love him?"

"He's the most well groomed man I've ever met," said Jack honestly.

"And a thing like this can only be good for our state. Anything that's not bingo, or pull tabs, or one of those horrible meat raffles, is a cultural step up."

"Well, now, there's nothing wrong with a good meat raffle. I once won over eighty dollars' worth of kielbasa for an investment of five! And the beer was insanely cheap. Less than a dollar a glass—though it was Carling, I believe. But you take the good with the bad."

Ms. Pedersen's smile, which had been broad and open, was beginning to show signs of strain.

"Well," she said, "look around. There's Thomas Kaat over there. He chairs the—"

"I'm sorry, that guy, with the . . . uh, the, um . . ." Jack was trying to describe a man standing near Beret's kitchen entrance without having to refer to his gigantic puffy hairpiece, which in Jack's opinion appeared a full forty years younger than the face beneath it. "With the marinated asparagus—there, he's trying to scissor it off with his dentures there. That guy?"

"Um, yes. He chairs the Greater Twin Cities and Southern First Tier Suburb and Council for the Arts. Lovely man. And that's Erica Sturgeon. She did so much work last year to send the Chamber Orchestra to Russia."

"They're that bad, huh?" The smile dropped fully from Darlene Pedersen's face. "Just kidding," said Jack.

"Well, anyway, it's lovely to have something come out of Minnesota that's a little more serious in tone, a little more ambitious in its scope than the usual fare," Ms. Pedersen continued. "With Gus Bromstad, frankly, all that banjo music begins to grate, and with the forced homespun thing, that hat of his . . . well, it diminishes the image of our state in the eyes of the rest of the country."

"No place associated with banjo music can ever succeed on a national level," said Jack.

"It's so true," she said, apparently mistaking his joke for a comment with some depth.

"So forgive me for putting you on the spot, but you liked *Death Rat?*" he asked, because he wanted time to try a cream cheese wonton and needed to get her talking.

"Oh, yes. Very, very, very good, it was. And I understand it's just flying off the shelves. Number one this week, right?"

He was caught by surprise at the compendiousness of her answer and had barely begun to chew his wonton when she'd answered, so he simply nodded and gave her an apologetic wink. She waited patiently, looking at the inside of her glass and smiling wistfully. Jack had a way to go before his wonton could be safely swallowed, so they both waited. Salvation came in the form of a waiter who sidled up next to them.

"Mr. Ryback," he said in the hostile but officious manner of Minnesota's service industry, "there is a phone call for you."

Jack begged his leave of Ms. Pedersen with a hand signal, and she waved him away graciously. "Oh, yes, please, you are a busy man."

He was shown to a phone in the coatroom, where, because of the length of the cord and the unergonomic placement of the door, he had little choice but to stand less than three feet away from the young woman doing the coat checking.

"Sorry," he told her. She smiled at him weakly. "Hello?" he said very quietly into the phone.

"Jack Ryback?" said a deep male voice.

"Yes, this is Jack Ryback."

"The author?"

"Who is this?"

There was a pause, then a click on the line, then a beeping sound. The voice came back on. "Do I have your permission to tape this conversation?"

"What? No. Who is this?" Jack heard the beep again.

"Hang on." There was some more clicking, then a beep cut off midway. "Okay. I'm not taping this anymore. But I am going to have to ask you to keep this conversation in the strictest of confidence."

"We haven't said anything yet. Is this Earl?"

"Who's Earl?"

"Never mind. Look, who is this?" Jack said, dodging the accusing look of the coat-check woman.

"If I tell you, will you keep it under the bulldozer?" said the voice.

"Well, okay, I suppose."

"Can I ask you that part again and tape *just* that?"

"No! Look, I'm hanging up if—"

"Okay. I think I can count on you. I work for a certain person."

Jack waited. "I trust you'll tell me who it is at some point?"

"Do I have your solemn vow that you'll not say anything to anyone, under penalty of death?"

"All right, I'm hanging up." He made a motion with the phone and heard the voice pleading, "No! Don't hang up."

Jack put the phone to his ear.

"I'll tell you. I work—for King Leo." He let it sink in.

"Well," said Jack, "I thank you for your frankness. Now I have to be getting back to—"

"You do know who he is?"

"Didn't he do that song 'LoveDeathTomorrowJelly'?"

"Yes. That is he."

"That was a very weird song."

"King Leo thanks you."

"I—"

"He has asked me to contact you because he wishes to have an audience with you."

"And who are you?"

"I am—Why don't you just call me . . ." And there was a pause that Jack assumed was supposed to be mysterious but then carried on a little too long.

It was Jack who broke the silence. "Hel—" he began, but the caller had mistimed his cryptic pause, and Jack had stepped on the payoff. The voice spoke at the same time as Jack.

"Mr. Gray."

"What?" said Jack.

"Mister—"

Jack interrupted again. "Sorry, didn't mean to step on you there."

"No, it's all right. I was going to say 'Mr. Gray,' but I guess you can just call me Don."

"Okay, Don. Don Gray?"

"No, I made that part up. The Mr. Gray part."

"Well, Don, why does King Leo want to see me?"

"It has something to do with your book. That's all I know."

Jack's scalp tingled with panic, a panic that was exacerbated by the fact that the coat-check woman was now staring straight at him with a strange expression. "What about my book?" Jack asked in a quiet voice.

"I don't know. He just wants to see you. May we come for you now?"

"No, I'm at a party."

"After the party?"

"It will be quite late."

"King Leo doesn't sleep," Don said crisply.

This caught Jack at a loss and found him defenseless. "All right. One-thirty, here at Beret. You know where it is?"

"King Leo knows where everything is."

Jack became impatient. "Okay, okay. Fine. Just be here at one-thirty, or I'll go home." Jack hung up. Despite the note of danger to the call, he was mostly annoyed with having his unwanted party abut an unwanted and late-night meeting.

"Pardon me. I couldn't help but overhearing. King Leo wants to see you?" said the coat woman, her eyes wide.

"Apparently."

"Wow. Tell him I loved 'Your Velvet Flower'!"

"I sure will," Jack said distractedly. It had been more than a month since he'd spoken to Ponty, at Ponty's request, but he thought it was time to break radio silence. He dialed Ponty's number and, asking for Earl, got him on the phone.

"Earl?" Jack asked, so upset by recent events that he forgot to be annoyed by Ponty's insistence on the ridiculous smoke screen.

"Yes, this is Earl," Ponty said in a manner sure to arouse the suspicions of anyone who might be tapping his phone.

"Say, concerning 'the thing'? I just got a call from King Leo. He wants to see me about the thing." Calling the book "the thing" had been Jack's idea, a compromise arrived at when Jack bucked mightily at Ponty's suggestion that they call it "Delta Romeo," a radio-language abbreviation of its initials.

There was silence on the other end of the line. After a moment Ponty spoke. "What's a King Leo?" he asked.

"Pont—Earl, come on! How out of touch are you? He's the funk guy, lives here in town? He did . . . um, 'PeneTrain Station'?"

"I'll take your word for it," Ponty said.

"I get very nervous when funk superstars call me out of the blue and ask to see me," Jack said. "What do I do?"

"Jack, I'm sure you can appreciate that I, too, have very little experience having audiences with funk superstars? Just go talk to him. Maybe it's nothing."

"A one-thirty A.M. meeting with King Leo? It's bound to be something. Do you think he knows? Hang on, Earl." Jack had stopped because Fetters was peeking into the coatroom making a complicated series of hand signals, mouthing inde-terminate words along with them. Jack could make no sense

of any of them, but he nodded back his understanding anyway. "Earl, I have to run. I'll give you the full report later."

"Ten-four," said Ponty. Jack thought his weak voice
sounded very much at odds with his military sign-off.

Jack made his way, not too quickly, back to the reception and
was soon engaged in dangerous small talk with the chair of the
Greater Twin Cities and Southern First Tier Suburban Council
for the Arts.

"That's a big rat you've got there, young man. Congratula-
tions," said Thomas Kaat, shaking Jack's hand.

Jack struggled to look into his eyes. "Thank you, sir."

"I'm going to be seeing Dirk and Fiona in a couple of weeks,
and you can bet your hat I'm going to mention the fine work
you've done on this rat story."

Jack hadn't the faintest shadow of an idea who Dirk and
Fiona were, but he guessed from context that he was supposed
to be pleased that they were going to be informed about his
book. "Well, good. Please give them my regards when you do
see them."

"You know Dirk and Fiona?" Kaat turned away before Jack
could protest. "Leslie! Leslie, Mr. Ryback knows Dirk and
Fiona."

Leslie, overjoyed to hear the news, disengaged from her conversation and joined them at once. "Oh, you're kidding! What a
small world. When did you last see them?"

"Dirk and Fiona are our favorite people in the world. We
just love them to death," said Thomas Kaat, his eyes moist with
emotion.

"No. No. I'm sorry. I don't know Dirk and Fiona at all.
Never met them."

Jack had let down the pleasant old couple in a very profound way. Thomas attempted to understand Jack's having misrepresented himself concerning his relationship with Dirk and Fiona. "Why . . . ? Why did you say you knew them?" he asked.

"I misunderstood," Jack was beginning to explain when Leslie took Thomas by the arm.

"Come along, Thomas. Let's be getting home."

The crowd was thinning, drifting away with the disappointed Kaats. Fetters came over and grasped Jack's right hand with his own, supporting Jack's elbow with his left. It seemed to Jack as though Fetters were about to teach him a secret lumberjack handshake.

"You did a fantastic job tonight, Jack. This town is now completely a pro-Ryback town."

"The Kaats need some convincing."

Fetters ignored him. "Everyone loves the book. Did Christine get plenty of good shots of you?" Fetters asked, referring to the photographer he'd hired.

"I think so. I see flashbulbs in my retinas when I close my eyes," Jack said, his voice sounding weary.

Fetters laughed. "Well, you look great. Just great. We're on our way, Jack. We'll be talking about the next book soon enough. I've got to go. Petra is here if you need anything," and Fetters glided insincerely away.

JACK WAS RELIEVED when King Leo did not show up, and he was getting into his car, nearly hungry for sleep, when he heard a hollow sound he thought very much like the clattering of hooves. Jack concluded that it was unlikely he was being attacked by a division of light cavalrymen, so he turned to see what the source of the sound might be. When he saw an obscenely overdecorated horse-drawn carriage making its way up Fourth Street toward him, and when it then pulled up next to his car and the coachman had dismounted, approached him, and said, "Mr. Ryback, King Leo thanks you for agreeing to see him," he knew he was one unwanted King Leo meeting away from crawling into his bed.

"Don?" Jack asked the coachman.

"Don is in the landau, sir," he said. "Watch your head, sir," he said, just as Jack cracked the top of his head violently against the carriage's frame. The first thing Jack noticed, after he had sworn, rubbed his head for a minute, and managed to scramble into the carriage without concussing himself, was that in the design and construction of landaus (as he now knew this carriage to be), obviously precious little attention had been paid to providing adequate headroom for such as Jack Ryback. The pressure of his head on the carriage's fabric roof made him worry for its continued integrity. The next thing he noticed was that Don, a small man of about forty with a fiery red mustache and even fierier hair, seemed to have more than his share of headroom. Jack immediately resented him for that, if not for Don's coming to collect him using excessively fey transportation.

"Mr. Ryback?" said Don.

"Yes. Don?" said Jack.

"For now, yes, 'Don' will do. I must apologize for our tardiness. King Leo found it necessary to dispatch the last three limos to a party in Wisconsin to retrieve some . . . items. A brilliant man, but if I had to level any criticism, it would be at his inability to stick to the published schedule as regards his fleet of personal luxury transportation."

"Well, if that's the worst you can say about the guy," said Jack, tossing his head in an "oh, well" manner and immediately feeling a buildup of static electricity in his scalp.

"I assure you, it is. But it was that misstep that caused us to have to use backup transport to retrieve you. The stable is a drive from the main house as it is, and, as you can see, the tack for this rig is elaborate, and it takes time to properly hitch up the team."

"If I'd known, I could have driven myself."

"King Leo would be ashamed if it had come to that."

"Are we going to his house?"

"I think it's safe to say now that, yes, we're going to his house."

"And where is that?"

"I'm afraid I can't tell you. That's why I've rolled down the curtains on this carriage, so you cannot see its location."

"Isn't it . . . ?" Jack thought for a moment. "Wait, I've heard where he lives before. Isn't it in Deephaven or Mound or one of those?"

Don started. "Who told you that?" he demanded.

"I think I read it in *Us* magazine."

Don retrieved a small notepad and pen from the inside pocket of his London Fog coat and, swearing under his breath, scribbled furiously for half a minute. Then he pushed the notepad back to its home.

"Security issues plague us. We can't be too careful," Don explained.

Jack nodded, somehow using only his face, as he'd resolved to try not to move the whole head unit again until it was time to extract himself from the carriage. "I don't think I've ever had an 'audience' with anyone before. What usually happens?"

"I couldn't say."

"Well, what does he want with me?"

"I'm afraid I don't know, Mr. Ryback."

There was silence, save for the sounds of traffic and the clattering of horseshoes on asphalt.

"Will anyone be with him?"

"I don't know."

"Should I have brought something?"

"Sir, really. I don't know."

There was more silence as Jack thought of more questions, but it was Don who spoke next. "Can I get you something to drink?" Don asked.

"What have you got?"

"Nothing. But we could certainly stop and get whatever you'd like us to get at a 7-Eleven or something. We didn't have time to stock beverages in this thing. I am sorry."

"No, let's not stop this at a 7-Eleven. I'm fine. Can you get any heat in this thing, though? I'm kind of cold."

"I'm afraid not. We could stop somewhere, you could warm yourself briefly, and we could continue."

"No, that's okay."

"Or we could call around to see if any of the Fleet Farm stores stay open twenty-four hours, and, if so, I could call ahead and order, then hire a delivery service to pick up a catalytic-type heater or camp stove and then meet us at spot somewhere—"

"No. That's okay, really."

"I am sorry."

"Not at all." Jack closed his eyes and let the pressure of the roof support his head.

"Music?" Don asked.

Jack's eyes flew open, and he drew in breath. "What?" he asked.

"Would you like some music? I've got a CD player and headphones in my briefcase. Ooh. Though I should check to see if there's any battery life before I offer."

"No, really. I'm fine. Good night, Don," Jack said, and he fell asleep, missing most of his first and only ride in a horse-drawn carriage.

Jack awoke when the landau bounced, creating a sudden increase in pressure on the top of his head. With no objections from Don, he lifted a curtain and saw that they were passing through an iron gate. They continued on past dense hedges, their progress broken by topiaries trimmed into the shapes of curvy women, until they arrived at the grand entrance of a large, colonial-style manor, rather conventional in appearance except for the fact that it was painted hot pink. It also had spotlights trained symmetrically on either side of its facade fitted with gobos projecting the classic "naked-lady mud flap" shapes in bright white. When they came to a stop, the coachman helped them down and Don led them quickly through the front door. They weaved expediently through some darkened hallways, and Jack was shown to a small, upholstered chair situated in a room that nearly hurt his eyes. His coat was taken, and he was told to wait while Don fetched King Leo. The room was medium-size, decorated, Jack guessed, in a kind of rococo/baroque/neoclassical/Wild West/risqué lingerie shop–style. On the walls hung naked paintings from nearly every major period save the Neolithic and before. Every style of design from every country in Europe—every royal house, even—had apparently sent a representative piece of furniture to be shown in King Leo's waiting room.

As Jack waited, he heard intermittent sounds outside his door. First some hysterical screaming that had him momentarily worried, followed quickly by laughter from the same apparent source. He mused briefly on what could have caused the extremes of emotion. Being set upon by wolves only to discover that they were quite tame, that each one wanted to lick your hand more vigorously than the last? A knife-wielding intruder waiting for you around a corner who turned out to be your husband, wearing an apron, cutting a lime, just about to ask you where the Captain Morgan's was? Jack was just working out a third possibility when he did indeed hear the cry of some beast, probably canine, possibly a large cat. Then some silence. Then he heard a shattering, as of a large terra-cotta pot falling from some height and hitting a tiled pool deck. Then low voices and soon the sound of a hutch being shoved, three feet at a time, across a wooden floor. Then more low voices, the brief sound of a radio being turned on at explosive volume and turned off very quickly. Just as Jack had made a commitment to investigate and was rising from his chair, an apparently insane man entered the room and strode up to him.

"Jack, Jack, Jack, Jack, Jack, Jack, Jack, Jack, Jack, Jack, Jack, Jack! Jack Ryback!" said the man, though the reason for his saying it so many times still was not clear to Jack.

"Hello," said Jack.

Jack recognized the insane man as King Leo, a handsome, open-faced, bright-eyed man with closely cropped hair. He was small and fairly well muscled, with a hairless chest and just a small fringe of hair around his belly button. Jack wished he did not have access to this information, but it couldn't be helped, as King Leo entered wearing a pair of very low-cut, red leather pants—and that was it. He hugged Jack, and Jack realized that King Leo was a good deal moister than he needed to be.

"Forgive me! I've been doing some things, and I'm a little sweaty because of it. Jack! Jack, Jack, Jack—"

"Yes," said Jack, trying to stop King Leo's momentum before he got onto another tear with his name. But King Leo plowed on.

"Jack, Jack, *Jack*. Jack Ryback," he said.

"King Leo," Jack responded.

"You can call me King Leo, or you can call me the Sovereign Ruler of Groove, Milord Nasty Pants, the Magistrate of Penetrate, the Pharaoh of Funk, Maharaja of the Mojo, Caesar the Pleaser, Benevolent Despot of the Lower Places, the Commander in Chief in the Overstuffed Briefs, or the Exchequer of Milk Chocolate Soul. Wooo!" He ended this obviously practiced bit of elocution by leaning back with his arms out at his sides, looking up at his cove ceiling.

"Uh-huh. May I call you King Leo?" asked Jack.

"Absolutely. I trust my barouche conveyed you here in adequate comfort?"

"We took the landau, actually," said Jack.

"Ah, I'm so pleased. That is a fine coach."

"Oh, yes, it is. Cold but pleasant."

"Didn't Don provide blankets? Did he bring the space heater?"

"No, but it's no big deal."

"Your comfort is my number-one priority. I'll have to have strong words with Don. Now—Jack! Jack, are you ready for a revival?"

"I'm not sure," said Jack honestly.

"Your book! *Death Rat*. It is a sign, Jack, very clearly a sign."

"Is it a sign?" asked Jack. He turned to look at his chair.

"Yes, yes, sit, sit, sit, sit."

Jack was already discovering King Leo's love of repetition to make points, no matter how minor. Jack sat, and King Leo pulled up a Queen Anne side chair, leaning in close.

"When I heard you on the radio a few weeks back, and I heard the story of what happened in Holey, I was so moved I nearly messed my drawers," said King Leo.

"Ah, really? So you liked *Death Rat*?"

"Oh, yes, yes, yes, yes. It is the most important work of ours or of any time."

"Well, I don't think I'd go near that far. Kind of a fun read is about all I'd—"

"Jack, before we get any further along, may I get you a drink of some kind?" King Leo asked, placing a hand on Jack's arm.

"Hm. You know, I could stand—"

"I will be partaking of a frozen Down Under Snowball, but I also have a Goom Bay Smash, or we could do a Yank Me, Crank Me as well." He looked earnestly into Jack's eyes as he said this.

"Well, are they all frozen drinks, or . . . ?"

"Actually, the Yank Me, Crank Me is not frozen, but I highly recommend it."

"I'll have one of those."

"You will not regret it. Now, let's talk about you," said King Leo, his arm still on Jack's.

Jack looked around nervously. "Oh, your drink will be here in a second, Jack. My crack staff listens in and makes whatever it is you order. Say hello to them."

"Hello, everyone," Jack said, looking around.

"I'm sure they say hello back. We do it this way so we don't have to have someone from the wait staff standing here invading our privacy. Now, tell me all about Holey, Jack. Tell me everything about it."

Jack started with what he knew, which was very little. "Well, there's good fishin' there. And I know—"

"Jack, do you remember a work of mine from some time ago called 'Wash Me Lower'?"

Jack recovered quickly from being interrupted. "Yes! Yeah, I remember that," Jack said, happy to be able to tell the truth.

"Do you remember the spoken-word part of that, after the second chorus?"

"Um . . . I . . . I don't think so. But the hour is advanced, and I'm pretty tired, so—"

"It goes like this: 'If you gotta ask what I want, baby then you ain't been listening no no no no no no. Why'n'cha throw away that loofah, sugar loaf Grab the big sponge, honey sweet.' "

Jack cleared his throat and raised his eyebrows, trying to disguise his embarrassment as a method to stay awake. King Leo did not notice.

" 'And oooooooh, wash me lower.' And then I scream a little, and the bass and drums kick in, and I say, 'Get down, make it fat, hit me with that holy rat.' " King Leo added special emphasis to the last three words. Jack stared at him with eyes wide. "Is that the freakiest thing you've ever heard?" King Leo asked. Although Jack thought that it was easily one of the five or six most disturbing things he'd ever heard, he thought better of telling King Leo that. As he was formulating a safe reply, an elderly man in white gloves and topcoat entered and presented them their drinks.

"Thanks, Pops," said King Leo.

"Mm-hmm," said the man, who then turned to Jack. "And, hello, sir," he said, then left quietly.

Jack sipped his drink, and though he did not find it unpleasant, he was unable to identify even what neighborhood of flavor it resided in. Was it fruity or somewhat hoppy? Blandly alcoholic like a vodka, or was there a mellow heat in the undertones suggesting brandy? He simply could not tell. King Leo licked off a white mustache of Down Under Snowball. "You like it, Jack?" he asked.

"I think so, yes," said Jack.

"Jack, Jack, Jack, Jack, Jack. This is big. Big, big, big, big. Something's coming. Do you feel it?"

Jack thought about it. "I don't think so, no. Not yet anyway. Perhaps if you explained what it is, I could keep a lookout for it?"

"Something. Something's coming. Got to get to Holey, Jack. Got to get there," said King Leo, narrowing his eyes. He finished off his drink and sat staring straight ahead, past Jack's right ear. "I'll have another, please," he said quietly and held out his glass.

Jack shifted in his chair. "Um, sure," he said tentatively. "What's in a Down Under Snowball again?"

King Leo shook his head. "No, I was talking to the wait staff."

"Ah," said Jack. "They're listening in."

"You said on the radio that Lynch claimed it was God who saved him. Now, you obviously researched this thing up, down, over, under, this way, out the other side—what do you think. Do you think it's true?"

Jack stalled by saying, "Well," and taking a very big gulp of his Yank Me, Crank Me. He swallowed laboriously and then lightly smacked his lips. "Mm. Very good. Very nice flavor," he said, looking with a good deal of interest into the interior of his glass for a moment before looking up. "Well," he began again, "as you know, a lot of solid research has been put into it, and we're no closer to getting a decisive answer to the whole God question, so it's not surprising that this one unexplained animal-attack rescue . . . um, doesn't yield a definitive answer either. . . ." He took another sip of his drink and virtually re-created his previous stall. "Mm, that has some very unidentifiable taste to it. What's in it, do you know?"

King Leo looked at him penetratingly. "I don't know Jack, but I'll find out." He kept his eyes on Jack and did not move.

Jack waited for something to happen. "Well, it's not important," he said after a moment.

"Now, back to—"

A phone on an intricately carved, eight-sided Moorish table rang sharply, and King Leo rose and picked up the receiver.

"Yes?" he said. "Uh-huh. Okay." He hung up and returned to his spot in front of Jack. "Vodka, Old Milwaukee beer, Country Time Lemonade and Mello Yello," he said.

"I'm sorry?" said Jack.

"My people tell me those are the ingredients of a proper Yank Me, Crank Me."

"Oh, right. Well, I'll have to make them at home some time. Have a Yank Me, Crank Me party. Very good."

"You were telling me if you believed it was God who rescued Lynch," said King Leo, fixing his eyes on Jack.

"Right. Well . . ." Jack sensed that King Leo was looking for an affirmative answer, and, hoping to end their meeting expediently, he gave one. "I think so, yes," he said, then added, "Absolutely," just to be safe.

"Forgive me, Jack, but I think you're wrong," said King Leo bluntly.

"Well. Wouldn't be the first time, that's for sure."

"I think he was saved by the one Funka-Lovely-Creative-Spirit-Being, the Rodent of Dee-vine Power. That's what I think," said King Leo importantly. Jack waited for him to smile, but it didn't happen. "It was his spirit that gave Lynch new life and a new beginning, pushed him into another level of consciousness," King Leo said, taking a sip. "That's what this whole world needs, to be pushed by the rat of dee-vine power into another level of consciousness. If we could manage that as a nation again, as a world, then I think we would truly be great. So. What do you think, Jack? Do you think it could have been the one Funka-Lovely-Creative-Spirit-Being, the Rodent of Dee-vine Power?"

"Well," Jack said, "maybe we're just splitting hairs, semantically. Probably talking about the same thing."

"Yes!" King Leo shouted, startling Jack enough that a good portion of his remaining drink sloshed onto the leg of his khaki pants. "I knew it! It's coming! Through the power of music, my music, we will connect with the rat of dee-vine power."

"How will that work, exactly?" Jack asked.

"You seek answers where there are none, Jack. That is so very lower-self of you and nothing to be ashamed of." Jack nodded his basic agreement. "It will be a musical extravaganza such as has never been seen by our time or by any time. Our concession will do well, too," he said, his eyes far away. "It's time for a revival. We're going to Holey, Jack. You and I. You'll be my guide."

"Oh, I don't know. I'm not a good guide. I get lost finding bathrooms at unfamiliar restaurants. And with all my interviews, I don't have time for much of anything, let alone a revival."

"We can do satellite video and radio uplinks from Funkabus, my touring cruiser. You won't miss a one."

"Sorry, but my agent's got me on a tight schedule, and—"

"Who's your agent? Fetters?" Jack nodded. "No problem. He's an old friend. We used to shop for Italian cotton T-shirts together. I'll take care of it."

"No, really. Thank you anyway," Jack said as he dabbed his pant leg with a wet cocktail napkin. King Leo rose, came to his side, and hugged him clumsily with what seemed like an inappropriate amount of affection.

"Please, Jack. Come with me," he said, and squeezed Jack more firmly around the shoulders.

Jack was relieved to discover that King Leo was no longer as overheated as when they'd first embraced, but the body-to-red-leather-pants contact that the hug was causing was entirely too much for Jack's continued comfort.

"Jack, Jack, Jack, Jack. Let's do it, you and I. Let's go to Holey," King Leo pleaded, pulling Jack's head closer to his bare stomach. Jack's desire to be far away overcame his extreme reluctance to agree.

"Okay," said Jack without enthusiasm.

"Good," said King Leo. "It's coming, Jack. And we're going to be there to see it."

"All right then," said Jack, disentangling himself from King Leo. "I think I'm gonna get going."

"I would helicopter you home, but they tell me I can't at this hour. Is it okay if I send you in one of the limos? The coach driver is off at two?"

"Perfect."

"And I'll be contacting you soon to arrange our triumphant arrival in Holey."

"Okay," Jack said through a panicked smile. He felt as alarmed as he imagined Ponty felt most of the time, and this thought alarmed him even more.

CHAPTER 9

Gus Bromstad did not have to wait long in the austere lobby of Den Institut Dansk before Thorkild Blixen, secretary to the institute's president, Stig Stou-Thorup, glided into position in front of him and spoke coolly.

"Come," he commanded. Without waiting to see if Bromstad was following, he accelerated back out of the lobby, barely leaving a slipstream. Bromstad hurried to keep up.

"And how are you, Thorkild?" Bromstad asked from a position some five steps behind him. "I haven't seen you in a while." Bromstad heard only the small, efficient wisps of friction as Thorkild's long, gabardine clad legs converged and diverged. After a moment Thorkild replied.

"Well," he said.

"That's good. Everything going good at the institute?" Bromstad waited for an answer, but it was clear he had explored the whole of Thorkild's conversational range. He was ushered into Stig Stou-Thorup's office and shown an austere and witty chair positioned in front of Stou-Thorup's desk with its clean lines and, behind it, the clean lines of Stou-Thorup himself. Thorkild withdrew noiselessly.

Stou-Thorup was a tall man, his blond-brown hair swept back (though a portion of it resisted, making the top of his head look like a cresting wave). His mustache was faint, blond and neatly trimmed. It appeared to Bromstad as though his face had made only a halfhearted commitment to its facial hair and was ready to recall it should anyone object. He wore a blindingly white shirt and a cool blue tie accented in a fish pattern so subtle as to be nearly undetectable. He smelled clean, like a finely sanded cedar board. Facing Bromstad, in a semicircle around Stou-Thorup's desk, were four chairs filled with men who seemed intent on looking and acting, as much as was possible, like each other. Stou-Thorup leaned forward over his desk, unsmiling, and addressed Bromstad.

"Gus Bromstad," he said, his American accent eerily perfect, in the manner of a Dane who held his dual citizenship in high regard. "You've come back to us."

"I never left you," Bromstad said, his voice uncharacteristically lacking that final bit of smoothness for which he was known.

"You remember Per," Stou-Thorup said, directing a subtle nod in the direction of a trim blond man wearing exceedingly small granny glasses, which he never seemed to put to use, for he was always looking over the tops of them or wearing them up on his forehead. "Vagns. Jørgen. And of course Ülo," he said, giving each man a similar nod.

"Vagns, how are you?" Bromstad asked. Vagn, the only dark-haired member of Stig's entourage—a fact that seemed to have made him somewhat bitter—moved his head almost imperceptibly in response. "Per. Jørgen, nice to see you again. Ülo," said Bromstad.

"Gus," Ülo responded. He was considered somewhat flighty and loquacious by his mates.

Stig continued. "Let's see, the last time I saw you, Gus, you had come here to these very offices to ask for our help, you remember? Now you're back. Did you come to say hello? To thank us for our help? To bring us a fresh-baked wienerbrød?"

Bromstad laughed, making the total number of people in the room laughing exactly one. "No. No. The truth is, I do need your help again," he said.

Stou-Thorup picked up a pencil and read the side of it before continuing. "Really? I would have thought you'd have wanted to stay far away from us . . . 'the thick-necked Danes, those inveterate church-skippers.' " Bromstad's strained smile faded into confusion before being replaced by a look of pained recognition. "Page sixty-eight, paragraph four, *Absolutely Dogwood*, A Cheatham Imprint book."

Bromstad adjusted his fisherman's cap, feeling perspiration around its brim. "Did I write that?"

Before Bromstad had finished his sentence, Stou-Thorup continued, " 'Stig Stangerup, a thick-necked Dane with a wide face and misshapen toes, was at all times boiling, or about to boil, a large piece of salmon.' Page one hundred forty-three, paragraph one, *A Dogwood Primer*, A Cheatham Imprint book."

"Look, Stig, these are jokes. I'm Danish after all. I can say these things."

"We at Den Institut Dansk, those of us charged with protecting our precious Danish heritage, are less amused, Mr.

Bromstad. You do not nourish our Danish heritage, you—what is the word?—malnourish it. Yes, I should think that is it. You write cheap and demeaning jokes while wearing a hat meant for Greek fisherman. You, Gus Bromstad, as far as I can tell, are not a Greek fisherman. Are you currently dropping your net into the blue Ionian Sea somewhere off the island of Corfu?"

"Stig—"

"Are you?"

"No, of course not."

"Then by my reckoning you are not a Greek fisherman."

"Stig—"

" 'Stig Stangerup had the red ears typical of his race, and they stood a good deal away from his head, as though they were embarrassed to be seen with it.' Page one hundred forty-three, paragraph two, *A Dogwood Primer*, A Cheatham Imprint book."

"Now, Stig—"

"I can laugh just as hard at the shape of my own ears as the next human being, Mr. Bromstad. But I like to keep the circle of people laughing at them to a reasonable minimum. For reasons I can't fathom, great hordes of people enjoy reading your disrespectful prose, meaning, of course, that whether they know it or not, these great hordes of people are having a good laugh over the placement of my ears on my head." He sat back and crossed his arms. Jørgen and Per did the same. "That distresses me."

"Stig, that's not supposed to be you," Bromstad pleaded weakly.

"Shut up, Gus. Shut up and let me guess why you're here. Your precious little Dogwood is getting gnawed by a rat—a big, fat rat. Does that square with your thinking, Ülo, Vagn?"

All four of his associates laughed mirthlessly.

"It certainly does, Stig," said Vagns.

"I think you've assessed the situation correctly, Stig," said Ülo.

"Jørgen, what do you think? Is that why Bromstad is here?"

"I think so," said Jørgen.

"*Ja,*" agreed Per.

"And what would you have us do?" Stig asked.

Bromstad sighed. "You must know. He's not who he says he is. How could he have just appeared out of thin air and uncovered such a wild story? I've never before heard of this thing, this rat thing that happened in Holey. Have you?"

"Well, now, there was no Danish settlement in this Holey, so it is of little concern to the institute, but I admit, no."

"Then I need you to help me discredit him."

"And why in the world would you imagine we would help you?" said Stou-Thorup, his voice rising in pitch.

"I don't know. Because I'm Danish?" Bromstad said brightly.

Stou-Thorup laughed deliberately. "Ha!" he said. "Ha, ha! You are not Danish, no matter how Danish you are. You are as Danish as a muffin pan," he said, and though Bromstad was aware he was being severely upbraided, he wondered what characteristic of a muffin pan made it particularly un-Danish. "If you were standing in a room full of Finns, Swedes, and Laplanders, you would be the least Danish person there! Danish! *Ha!*"

Bromstad let his scolding sink in. "I have not been a good Dane, I'll admit that. But I have nowhere else to turn. Word is they are going to give him the Dwee Award. I don't think I could take that, Stig."

"And what would that matter to me, do you suppose?" said

Stou-Thorup with surprising anger, setting his quasi pom-
padour to shaking. The room grew silent.

"I don't suppose it would matter at all," said Bromstad, his
bottom lip large.

Finally Stou-Thorup said, "Look at you. Your family comes
to the New World, and within several generations you are a
wreck of a human being. And you prosper in this country. *Blind
høne kan ogs°a finde et korn,*" he said, looking at the other
Danes. They laughed bitterly. "Ah, still, you are all that we
have. We Danes are seriously and tragically underrepresented
in these United States. You, despite your severe and obvious
flaws, are the most visible presence we have. We will help you,
though you do not deserve it. We will find out about your Mister Ryback."

"Thank you, Stig," said Bromstad.

"And when it is over," said Stou-Thorup, ignoring Bromstad, "you will write us a book. It will be filled with Danes, true
Danes—strong, noble Danes. Not the red-faced buffoons of
your past books. Is this acceptable to you?"

"Maybe. Yes. It certainly could be. I'll try."

"Though I, too, have doubts that you will be able to turn in
something of quality, I need more solid assurances that you will
try, or you cannot expect our help," said Stig.

"I can do it. Sure."

"Good. Then we will shake your Mister Ryback's tree and
see what falls out. Ülo, break out the aquavit, and let us celebrate our alliance."

CHAPTER 10

High noon on an uncharacteristically warm March day in Calhoun Park. A tall man in a cream-colored fisherman's sweater, holding a brown paper bag, approached a bench occupied by a stiff-looking little man with a bushy mustache and sat.

"Earl," he said.

"What did he say? Does he know?" whispered the smaller man.

"No. He hugged me, and his pants touched me. It was horrible."

"His pants touched you? What does that mean?"

"Nothing, unless you're the person who has been touched by his pants. Then it means a great deal."

The smaller man ignored him. "Is he bribing us? I never thought I'd be the victim of a bribing crime. I've never done anything worthy of bribing me over. Not that I can recall. I'm not saying I've lived a sinless life, but to this point I've kept it bribe-free. Now look at me. I've—"

"He doesn't know, Ponty." Jack reached into the paper bag and took out something wrapped in butcher paper. "I brought you a sandwich."

"What? You can't bring me a sandwich!"

"Why not?"

"We don't know each other. Strangers don't bring each other sandwiches."

"Where is that written? Besides, a guy doesn't sit right next to some other strange guy when there's an empty bench ten feet away either. Ponty, I knew you wouldn't have eaten, so I brought you a sandwich."

"Put it in my coat pocket," whispered Ponty. "Don't be obvious about it."

Jack shoved the sandwich into the outer pocket of Ponty's parka and began unwrapping his own sandwich. "Nope. He doesn't know."

"Well, that's good news, at least."

"Sort of," he said, slurring his words because his mouth was full of egg salad and rye bread. "He wants to visit Holey, to see the spot where it happened. Maybe have a revival there."

"A what?"

"A revival."

"A revival of *what*?"

"I don't know. That's just what he said. He kept saying that something was coming. That we needed to be there for it. And, as I said, he hugged me."

"Is he insane?"

"I think so."

Ponty took out his sandwich and began unwrapping it. "I borrowed one of his albums and listened to it. Filthy stuff. I'm still shaking."

"Yeah, it ain't pretty. But it gets the job done. He's got quite a little ranch house all set up for himself."

"Do you think he'll go to Holey?" asked Ponty.

"Well," said Jack, chewing, "I think so. He asked me to go with him, and I don't know if it was the hour or the Yank Me, Crank Me, but I said yes."

"What?"

"He's very persuasive. You'll see when you meet him."

"I'm not meeting that weirdo. Why did his pants touch you?"

"I'd rather not relive it."

"Why—*why* did you say you'd go with him?"

"Well, I figured I could keep him from finding anything out."

Ponty shook his head and swallowed. "Oh, this is bad. Very bad. Strange people up there. All the attention. They're bound to find out. Someone will spill it. We're going to get caught."

The two sat eating in silence.

"Well," said Jack finally, "no reason to worry until we have to. You want an M&M cookie or a Rice Krispie bar?"

Across Lake Calhoun a blue Volvo idled, a German-made Leica APO Televid 77 Angled Spotting Scope pressed against the tempered glass of the driver's-seat window. Pressed against the eyepiece was the compact head of Jørgen Hunk, Den Institut Dansk's finest man in the field. Vagns sat in the passenger's seat reading *Death Rat*. Ülo sat in the back, humming quietly; Bromstad sat next to him, twitching.

"What's he doing now? Jørgen, what's he doing?" pestered Bromstad.

Jørgen did not immediately answer, but when he spoke, his voice was even. "It was not necessary for you to accompany us, Mr. Bromstad."

"Oh, I wouldn't miss it for the world. I want to nail this guy," said Bromstad, rubbing his soft writer's hands together.

"Do you not have to be writing, or perhaps doing a book signing?" asked Vagns, without looking up from *Death Rat*.

Bromstad looked at his watch. "You know what? I think I *am* missing a signing, but spying on this guy is a higher priority right now."

"It is extremely unlikely that anything of interest will occur," said Jørgen, adjusting the eyepiece of the scope. "We have just begun our surveill— Oh, my."

"What? What?" said Bromstad, leaning into the front seat.

"He has taken a seat next to a smaller, mustachioed man."

"A smaller, mustachioed man?" mused Bromstad. "What's he look like?"

"He is somewhat smaller and has a mustache. For now that will suffice. We will get photographs. Ülo," Jørgen commanded briskly.

"Right," said Ülo, taking a camera bag from the floor.

"He is handing the mustachioed man a small package," said Jørgen.

"Drugs?" said Vagns, without looking up.

"With Americans it is so often the case," said Jørgen sternly.

"I knew it. Get him! Get him!" shrieked Bromstad.

"The mustachioed man is refusing the package," said Jørgen. "They are exchanging words."

Ülo began snapping pictures through the telephoto lens of his Nordisk ;tOresundsbron M6 TTL.

"He is placing it surreptitiously into the pocket of the other man," said Jørgen.

"It is probably scag," said Ülo contemptuously. "Americans and their scag."

"Hey—now, not all of us use scag," Bromstad objected.

"That is only because of economic barriers. If it were cheap enough, you would all use scag," averred Ülo.

"Quiet. The other man is eating something. It is a sandwich. I . . . cannot . . ." Jørgen adjusted the eyepiece. "I cannot make out the filling. If I had the fifty-millimeter eyepiece perhaps.

Now the mustachioed man is taking the package out of his pocket. He is unwrapping it. He is sniffing it."

"Scag," said Ülo.

Jørgen strained to see, making fine adjustments to the scope. He scowled with the passion of a Dane unable to get a good look at a drug deal that he is highly committed to seeing, and seeing well. After a tense moment he separated his head from the eyepiece. Then he turned to look at Ülo.

"I am sorry to say it is not scag. It, too, is a sandwich. He is consuming it now. Great bites is he taking," he said sadly.

Bromstad was reeling himself back in preparation for loosing curses but was stopped short by a rapping on the passenger-seat window. Their four heads swiveled to see a park police officer crouching down, peering in with a dispassionate expression. He made the "roll down the window" gesture, and Vagns obeyed, while Bromstad crouched low and pulled his hat over his eyes.

"What you fellas up to?" he asked casually, as though Volvos stuffed with Danish ex-pats wielding spotting scopes and cameras were not at all an uncommon sight.

Without pausing, Jørgen replied, "We are looking at the ducks." The officer stood up, put a hand over his eyes, and peered across the lake to see the only ducks anywhere on the horizon. They were at least half a mile away. He crouched back down.

"You'd get a better look at 'em if you drove over to the other side of the lake," he said.

"You don't say?" said Jørgen.

"Oh, yeah. Much better view. Probably wouldn't even need the spotting scope."

"Okay, thank you," said Vagns, improvising.

"Yep. Just take this road right around."

"We will do that," Jørgen promised earnestly.

"All righty," said the officer, giving a friendly salute and strolling away.

Vagns rolled up the window, and there was silence in the Volvo save for the purr of its 2.3-liter 5-cylinder intercooled engine.

"That was sloppy," Jørgen said.

"Is he gone," asked Bromstad, from underneath his hat.

PONTY'S CAREFUL PLANS to pack hurriedly, almost frantically, and drive wildly up to Holey in preparation for King Leo's arrival were thwarted just as soon as he walked in the door to his house and Scotty handed off the phone to him like a football.

"Whoa—hang on there. It's your brother," he said.

"Son of a . . ." said Ponty, taking it from Scotty. "Hey, Thad. How are you?"

"Hey, bro, "you sound like you're under a lot of stress. Are you?"

"No, not at all. Especially now that I'm not working—you know I'm not at Jack Pine anymore?"

"What? What happened? You need me to wire you some sawbucks?"

"No. No, don't. Yeah, Jack Pine did a little downsizing, and I was lucky enough to get in on their outplacement program. You know, got a pretty sweet golden parachute."

"Hey, that's great. So you're eating?"

"What? Right now?" Ponty said with irritation.

"You're eating well and all?"

"Why wouldn't I be eating well?" he asked, thinking of the dinner of Chicken in a Biskit crackers and dill dip he'd had the night before.

"Look. Melissa, and I were talking, we thought you might want to get into the Meals on Wheels program, so that you can get your basic nutrition at least."

"You mean delivering it to the seniors, right?"

"Ha, ha! No, no. You know, you just get into the program. Get some good food delivered to your house."

"What? No! I'm sixty years old. And I'm not homebound. Heck, *you're* fifty-five," Ponty objected shrilly.

"All right, all right. I'm just looking out for you, brother." Thad sighed deeply, apparently wounded that Ponty had refused to accept his offer of hospital food delivered to his door. "When you moving to Tucson?"

Ponty fended off his brother's well-meaning advances, exchanged the usual pleasantries, and hustled Thad off the phone before he could make any plans for Ponty's hospitalization. Then he packed hastily and headed north to Holey, determined not to fail, steeled for whatever lay ahead, a bag of corn chips at his side.

JACK HAD FOLDED himself onto his couch and was asleep in front of the television when he heard the *QE2* sound her horn in preparation for sailing at his front door. His limbs leaped into the air, followed by his body, and he gathered himself into a sitting position. After a moment he was able to piece together a vague semiconsciousness. The horn sounded again, and he realized now that it had the quality of a landgoing vessel, possibly an eighteen-wheeler. It sounded again in a short-long combination, and he thought he detected a beckoning tone to it, which he acknowledged by standing up and separating a portion of his front window blinds to see if it was meant for him. Idling out in front of his house was the hugest, most hot pink bus that he had ever seen, a sight made no less impressive by the fact that it was the *only* hot pink bus he'd ever seen.

He padded outside in his socks. A tinted tilt-out window popped open, and though he could not see its source, he heard a voice say, "Woooooooo! Woo! Let's go, Jack!"

"I thought you were going to call first!" Jack yelled at the side of the bus. There was a twenty-second silence. Jack called out, "Hello?"

"What?" called King Leo in a distracted voice.

"I'm not ready."

"Wooooooooo!" said King Leo. "We're going to Holey, gonna get holy! Wooooo!"

"I'm not ready. Why don't you go ahead without me. Unless you want to come inside for a minute?"

"Wooo—all right. Hang on."

The door hissed open, and a parade of people began flowing out of the bus and through Jack's front door—seven people in all, including King Leo. The only member of the group not wearing a colorful feather boa—a middle-aged man in a gray coat with a patch above the pocket that read GARY—Jack guessed to be the driver. They stood in an awkward knot in his entryway.

"Step into the living room there, why don't you, while I go throw a bag together. No, you don't have to take your shoes off," he said to a guy in a red headband and huge diamond-shaped sunglasses who had made a motion to begin unlacing his thigh-high leather boots.

"Let me do some intros," King Leo offered. "Jack, that's Sir

Shock-a-Lot there. And Kaptain Kinetik. And that's Wigs Jackson, and Tarzan Moe, Billy Moonbeam, and that's Gary."

"Well, welcome, all of you. Have a seat while I rush off and get this done. Just throw your coats over the coach there, and . . . ah, help yourself to anything in the kitchen. Sorry, I don't have much."

As they filed into his living room, Jack pulled King Leo aside. "I thought you were going to call first."

"Jack, Jack, Jack. I am sorry. I thought Don had called," King Leo said, pulling off a pair of granny glasses with yellow lenses and polishing them on his silk peasant top.

"No. No one called. I didn't hear a thing."

"Well, that doesn't surprise me in the least," said King Leo with faint disgust. "Anyway, I had to fire Don."

"What? Why?" asked Jack, though he had no stake in it.

King Leo shook his head vigorously. "I don't remember. You can ask his replacement if you're really interested. Jack, don't be mad. We can't have you going to the revival all mad."

"I'm not mad—I'm just not ready. 'Cause Don never called."

"As I said, I had to fire him. Now, get packing. We'll wait." Something caught his eye. "Billy! Get your feet off the man's couch!" Billy Moonbeam looked sheepish and quickly put his feet on the floor. King Leo turned back to Jack and threw his arms out. "Jack, Jack, Jack. I'm sorry, my man," he said and stepped forward to hug him.

"No, really," Jack objected, backing up a step. "I'm not much of a hugger. Well . . . okay." And he received King Leo's hug, relieved that he was not also receiving some of King Leo's sweat.

"There, there, there, there, Jack. Go throw a bag together,"

King Leo said, and he patted Jack's back. Jack took a step toward his room and then turned back.

"I guess I don't know what to pack," he said.

King Leo gave it some thought. "Well," he said, "I packed my Jimmy Choo calfskin slingbacks, a tulle bodysuit, some jersey-knit sweaters, a couple three chiffon peasant tops, my python pants, a Fendi cape . . . um, my Manolo Blahnik heels, a few sleeveless turtlenecks. Oh, and my mink sweatpants for just hanging around."

Sleep, for Jack, was difficult in the Funkabus. At all times Kaptain Kinetik was drumming on some surface: the large mahogany table, the cabinets above the stove, even the head of Billy Moonbeam. And Wigs Jackson was playing a video golf game against Sir Shock-a-Lot, who seemingly could play nearly flawless video golf, causing Wigs to yell and hit him on the shoulder. King Leo strummed mindlessly on a hollow-bodied Gibson and sang indeterminate words in a wavering falsetto. With the hum of the bus's tires and the other riders' conversations obfuscating his voice, to Jack it might just as well have been Tiny Tim.

He was watching the yellow lines fly by when King Leo swung into the seat next to him. "Jack, Jack, Jack," he said, a strange smile on his face that reminded Jack of his perpetually stoned freshman roommate, only a good deal less stupid-looking.

"King Leo."

"You're a writer, Jack."

"I am," Jack lied.

"I don't want to put you on the spot, but I want you to take a look at something." Jack became quickly and appropriately terrified. "I've written some poetry. . . ." said King Leo, producing a notebook.

Jack scanned surreptitiously about him for an escape route, noticing with disappointment that his seat was not positioned near one of the emergency windows. "Well, King Leo, I'm really more of a journalist, you know. Not really a good judge of poetry, per se."

"But you know words, Jack. You bend them to your will."

"Oh, not so much bending, really."

King Leo thrust the notebook at him. "I'd be honored."

Jack was about to formulate a new line of objections when he concluded that it would probably be easier to capitulate and accept an inevitable fact of life: at some point some person will force you to look at his poetry. In any calendar year half of the people on the planet collar the other half and cajole them into looking at their bad rhymed couplets, free verse, poems about horses accompanied by crude drawings, or what have you. It was simply his turn. He took the notebook gingerly from King Leo's hand.

"Okay. I'll take a look at it—though understand, I'm no judge."

"Thank you," said King Leo.

"Sure," said Jack with finality.

Jack saw fresh difficulty on the horizon when King Leo, who by all accepted rules of human interaction surrounding the exchange of poetry should now have been leaving, was doing nothing of the sort. In fact, he was looking at Jack with an eager expression, as though Jack were about to bite into his famous home-baked Dutch apple pie. Jack devised a way to test his theory that King Leo was going nowhere until some unit of poetry was read by him. "Okay, I'll take a look at it when I've got a minute," he said, and turned away. Unfortunately, he was unable to begin any activity that seemed more important than reading poetry, and King Leo pounced.

"What are you doing now?" he asked reasonably.

"Oh. Now?"

"Yeah. Read it now. Go ahead." King Leo was excited.

Jack thought briefly how nice it would be to die, but he simply smiled at King Leo and thumbed open the notebook.

"All right. I'm excited," said Jack. "First page, here?"

"Yeah, yeah. Start there."

Jack noticed his use of the phrase "*start* there" and despaired. He tried to get the first page to come into focus, but it was difficult with the low light and the distraction of being able to hear its author breathing. Finally it did, and he read the title, written in flowery script with a gel pen: "My Flute," it read. Because he couldn't think of anything else to do, Jack coughed. He pointed to the page. "Right here?" he asked.

"Yeah, yeah, yeah, yeah. Right there."

He was cornered now, with nowhere to go, so he read King Leo's poem entitled "My Flute."

Toot, man.
That what it says, says my flute.
You'd think it would be a hoot.
But it ain't a hoot to toot my flute, brute.
My life—my blood, my sweat, my tears—MY LIFE
Is in that toot.
That toot,
From my flute.

Toot.

Jack was so delighted that it wasn't filthy, he was certain he would be able to pretend that it was good, even though he felt very strongly that, like 99 percent of all the poetry ever produced, it was not good.

"Wow. That's . . . that's very good. There's a real dark edge to it."

"Yeah, I meant that," said King Leo.

"Your music?" Jack offered as his analysis.

"What's that?" asked King Leo.

"It's about your music?"

King Leo thought about it. "Well, that's one reading, I suppose." Jack closed the notebook and made half a motion to return it. "No, no, no. Read more," King Leo commanded.

"More? Well, I'm just kind of letting that one sink in." King Leo smiled at him. "Okay. I'll read more. Good." And Jack read King Leo's entire notebook, two hours' worth, as King Leo looked on, the bus speeding northward. And while he read, he thought how much better off he would be if he had stayed at Medieval Burger and worked his way up to register.

Everyone on the Funkabus was so engrossed in his task, and the video-golf music was turned up to so needlessly intense a level, that no one noticed a cool blue Volvo keeping pace with them until about an hour outside of Holey, when there came a bright white flash originating in the Volvo's interior compartment. Nor did they see the car swerve out of control, its right front tire catching the gravel on the shoulder of the road. And they did not notice as the car flipped and rolled off into the woods, where it came to stop some fifteen yards off the road, its roof propped up against a red oak.

CHAPTER 11

When Ponty returned to Holey, he was not exactly expecting to be welcomed as a long-departed hero, but neither did he expect the extreme and tangible apathy that greeted him as he entered the Taconite Saloon.

"Hey, Ralph," he said.

Ralph didn't look away from the television. "Hey," he replied.

"Hey, Chet!" Ponty said, and, noticing that Chet was no longer wearing Sonny's jacket, added, "Got a new coat, huh?"

"Hm?" Chet said, glancing up from his paper. "No. Well, I suppose it's new to you." And he looked back down at his paper.

Ponty, who, despite having paid the citizens of Holey a decent amount of money, did not consider himself their employer, nevertheless decided it was time to take a firm hand.

"Where's Sandi?" he asked sharply, and then quickly added, less sharply, "Have you seen her, or . . . ?"

"Sandi?" said Chet. "Oh, I think she's taking a delivery in back."

"Thank you, Chet," said Ponty, satisfied that he'd got some solid results. He decided to press his advantage. "Say, everything going okay around here?

"Oh, yeah. Everything's fine."

Ponty thought perhaps Chet was missing his deeper meaning, so he spelled it out. "No strangers poking around asking questions?"

"Nope. Just you— Well, you know what I mean," said Chet.

"Yes, thank you."

Chet's intelligence had been excellent: Sandi was indeed just finishing up unloading produce in the back.

"Hello, stranger," she said cheerfully.

"Hello. How's everything going?" he said, adding an extra edge of conspiracy to his voice.

"Good."

"Really?" he said doubtfully.

"Yes."

"No . . . problems?"

"No. Well, the grinder on the dishwasher went out and the whole drain line clogged, so Ralph and I were doing dishes by hand for nearly a week."

"But no one calling, no visitors asking uncomfortable questions about the book?"

"Oh, there've been a few calls, an interested person will stop by the Taconite—nothing I haven't been able to handle. I understand the book is doing real good, which is nice for all of us. We can all use a little extra walkin'-around money. Come on in and have a cup of coffee with me."

They convened at a table near the bearskin, poured coffee, and settled in. Sandi stared at him penetratingly. "You look like you've been rode hard and put away wet," she said, employing an equine saying unfamiliar to Ponty. He used context to guess at its basic meaning but still proceeded cautiously in case he'd erred horribly.

"Really? Well, I suppose I was not as dry as I could have been . . . when . . . um . . ."

"Have you been sleeping well?" she asked with what looked like genuine concern.

"Frankly, no. This whole business, the book thing, it takes it out of you. Lots of bad dreams. I'm being chased in my dreams quite a bit lately, and the people chasing me seem more and more committed. Overall, they're worse than the falling dreams, and I don't like those much either."

"Falling off of cliffs or what?"

"Sometimes. Sometimes buildings. Sometimes I just fall down and hurt myself. Shorter dreams, but no less frightening, 'cause I don't wake up before I hit the ground, like in the others. But those aren't as bad as the dreams where I'm on trial—they go on forever. The evidence against me is usually presented by my family and friends. And there's always a lot of it, cataloged and presented methodically. Why am I telling you this?"

"No. It's okay."

"Well, my uncle Barn is usually the prosecutor—he was a sweet guy. Not in my dreams, though. There he gets pretty nasty. Shouts down all my own attorney's objections—not that that guy's good for much anyway. But, as I said, it just goes on and on. I have to sit there and watch."

"You poor thing."

"Oh, it's okay. Usually if I cry too loudly in my dreams, my roommate kicks the top of my bed, and then I stop." He realized that this sudden confessional left him a bit exposed, so he took a sip of coffee to quell his embarrassment. He swallowed. "What about you? Sleeping well?" he said, and immediately regretted its inadvertently personal nature.

"Me? No problems, no. I don't dream often, but when I do, it's usually about just me lounging at a little house by the sea. I don't know where it is, but the curtains on the little yellow house always blow in the breeze, and the waves are always calm. I stand with my hands over my eyes looking out at the ocean for something." Realizing that this revelation, with its distinct lack of angst, might hurt his feelings, she added,

"Could be something bad that I'm waiting for, like . . . like Viking raiders or something. Luckily, I always wake up before it comes." She shifted gears. "So you have room*mates* or room*mate*?"

"Roommates, four. They're hardly even around during the school year."

"Are they teachers?"

"No, students," he said, as though the question were odd.

"And are you . . . involved with any of them?" she asked.

Before he could stop himself, Ponty screamed. It wasn't much of a scream, but still, the half-dozen or so people in the Taconite Saloon turned to look at him, none of them with fondness or admiration. He gathered himself enough to say, "No! No! Whatever would give you that idea? No, no, ouch!" he said as he sloshed some coffee into his lap. "No."

"I'm sorry. Are you okay?" she asked, referring to his potential groin burn.

"Yes. Yes, I'm fine. Sorry I overreacted. You'd have to know my roommates."

"I thought perhaps 'roommate' was a new term for 'girlfriend' that people were using in the Cities. We get things late here."

"No. Roommate means roommate in this case, probably more than it ever has before."

"I believe you."

Ponty, fearing he had frightened her with all his histrionics, tried to stay calm as he asked, "And you don't—that is Ralph, you mentioned—he's not your husband—or partner, I think you said—but he and you aren't—aren't—that is to say— you're not married to him—or anyone? Right now?"

"Ralph and I? No! No. He's a good man, Ralph but—no. Not ever. I was married once, a long time ago. I lost him."

"I'm so sorry."

"Back in '78, we were in the BWCA—the Boundary Waters Canoe Area—when he wandered off to get firewood. Never found him. No bones or anything. They tell me if he met with some accident or something (which is probably the case) and couldn't move, then he most likely got eaten by wolves."

"Oh, that's horrible."

"It's actually a great comfort to me to know he didn't suffer for long if those wolves got him. Course, I don't know if they got him, but I like to think that."

"Of course. I didn't mean to bring up a painful subject. Forgive me."

"No, please. Don't worry about it."

"Well, speaking of painful subjects. The reason I'm up here, King Leo took a fancy to the book, and he's planning a visit here at any time."

"King Leo! Oh, dear. I don't think there's much here in Holey for King Leo," said Sandi, taking a sip of coffee. "But we'll try to make him feel welcome."

Ponty, while not wanting to judge unkindly, felt that she was not displaying the appropriate amount of panic. "He's apparently insane and . . . and slightly obsessed with the book. . . . And he'll be bringing a lot of media attention here," he said forcefully, trying to replace her apparent sangfroid with a reasonable and proper amount of fear, such as the kind he felt nearly always.

"Well, I know most of the folks around here won't much like it, but everyone could stand to have his cage rattled every now and then."

"I don't think you understand. If he finds out the truth, so will everyone else who matters. Our little gravy train will be off the rails right quick."

"How would he find out our secret?"

"Well . . ." He looked around for an audience to do an arms-out-at-the-side, "can you believe this?" take to, but finding none, he did it to the wall. "Somebody might let it slip. Is everyone in town properly motivated? Everyone's happy with his pay? You're in charge of all this, you know? It's in our contract."

"I know that, you big dope," she said, not without affection. "The people of Holey have given you their word, and I don't know how things are in your St. Pauls and your Minneapolises, but around here that's . . . well, that's as good as gold, if you'll pardon the expression. I have only one concern, and that's with Gerry Iverson. The mine's on his land, and . . ." she said, seemingly reluctant to continue.

"Why? What's . . . ? What's his deal?"

"Well . . . he's different," she said cryptically.

"Different? Different from what?"

"Well, he doesn't have electricity . . . and he does really *interesting* chain-saw art. . . . I think he used to be on the goof-balls or something. He's different."

"Well, is he one of those guys whose brain is fried? You know, one of those guys who laughs a lot at nothing? Are we trusting someone who's not all there?" Ponty was getting worked up. Sandi tried to calm him.

"Ooohhh, noooo. He's a nice fellow. Well, you'll see. I'll take you out to meet him. It'll be fine. Hey, maybe you can give him a little extra piece of the book! Or maybe buy one of his chain-saw sculptures. That might help."

"I vowed I'd never buy chain-saw art."

"Well, take a look at it anyway. Look, Gerry's fine. Don't worry."

Ponty was not calmed by her reassurances. "Oh, we're doomed," he said.

"I doubt it. Can I get you a warm-up?" she asked softly, proffering the pot.

"Doomed," he said miserably. "Absol—that's good," he said as she filled his cup, "—lutely doomed."

PONTY WAS UNWRAPPING a complimentary bar of Lux facial soap at the Bugling Moose when he heard an unsteady thudding sound coming from the vicinity of his entryway. Aside from the fact that it sounded very much like a human fist making rapid contact with the outside of his door, it otherwise had none of the qualities of someone knocking in an attempt to get his attention. Its rhythm and intensity were too unsteady. With curiosity and slight trepidation, he opened his door partially and peered through, expecting to find something in the neighborhood of a handyman nailing up aluminum chimney flashing, or perhaps a badger trying to snare a sausage rind from a garbage can. Instead he found the apparent source of the thudding to be Ralph. He opened the door wider.

"Ralph," he said. "I'm sorry—I thought you were a badger."

"Nope. How are you, Ponty?" Ralph asked, his hands jammed into the pockets of his polyester bar jacket.

"I'm good. How are you, Ralph?"

"Good." There was a long enough pause that Ponty thought perhaps their business was concluded for the evening, but

Ralph soon followed up with "I was talking to Sandi. She said you been having kind of a rough time of it lately."

"Did she?" Ponty said, suppressing a grimace. Probably because he was framed in the doorway, he noticed for the first time how much space Ralph took up and, again, because he had the right angle of the doorframe as his guide, how his head was not completely symmetrical.

"Yeah. So I thought maybe to kind of unwind a little you might want to go out with me tomorrow."

Ponty stopped breathing. His heart continued to beat, but arrhythmically. Breathing resumed shortly, followed by severe tachyarrhythmia. His vision pixelated slightly, and he felt hot, as unconsciousness loomed. He was saved by an important clarification from Ralph.

"I'm going turkey hunting tomorrow. Thought you might want to go out with me? Help you get your mind off your troubles."

Under normal circumstances the question "Would you like to go turkey hunting?" would have been greeted with as much enthusiasm by Ponty as "Would you like to see a four-hour showcase of performance art?" But given his enormous relief over the fact that a large man had not come to his door at a late hour to ask him out on a date, it seemed extremely welcome. He accepted without hesitation.

"Okay. I'll see you at five, then," said Ralph. "You can use my old bow."

Ponty had said his good-bye to Ralph and stepped inside to resume his appointment with the Lux when he suddenly realized that Ralph's parting sentence made less than no sense to him. Five, he'd said? P.M., surely. But hunting in the late afternoon? It couldn't be. Still, it was less improbable than 5:00 A.M., a time that, when presented as the hour to meet, should raise in the presentee serious suspicions of insanity about the presenter. There was, he was fairly certain, no molecular movement of any kind before at least 6:30. And what could Ralph possibly have meant by "You can use my old bow"? Did one wear a colorful ribbon around one's head for maximum visibility when hunting turkeys? No, couldn't be. He didn't mean a bow, as in the bow that propels arrows? This was not a weapon commonly used for the hunting of any fowl, was it? No, certainly not. But perhaps. Too much about the whole scenario had already shown itself to be extraordinarily improbable to begin discounting the smaller absurdities out of hand.

For one thing, Ponty had always assumed that turkeys were raised on farms, obviating the need for hunting them. Could they possibly be going out to hunt for escaped, renegade turkeys? And if that was the case, were the turkeys desperate not to get caught and therefore reckless and dangerous? It seemed likely. Or *were* there wild turkeys? Wild as in "feral"? As in "wily"? As in likely to sense Ponty's obvious weakness and attack? He hoped not. He had compiled sixty Thanksgiving dinners' worth of evidence that turkeys were not small animals—imagine how much larger they grew in the wild.

And did they herd up when left to their own devices? Were there prides, or pods, or murders of turkeys out defending themselves against natural and human enemies? If memory served, live, unpackaged turkeys have some kind of spur on the inside of their legs used to slash and hack at their opponent's tender flesh. Ponty was not tall. He wondered if a turkey could climb him and shred him up pretty good with those spurs before he even got off a shot. Probably, if his luck continued to go the way it had been. If that was the case, he was certain his bones would be picked clean by a murder of turkeys by a quarter to six in the morning, at the very latest. At 5:28 or so, a minute before his final breath on earth, he'd see a big mess of red wattles bearing down on his tender face, pecking his very life away.

The fact that he was entertaining such thoughts provided all the testimony he needed that it was quite time for bed. He set an alarm for 4:45 in the event that madness ruled and people did indeed get up 5:00 A.M. to shoot arrows at turkeys.

His night of sleep consisted of very little actual sleep, and what there was, was riddled with anxious dreams filled with killer turkeys, rats, falling, and episodes of being chased by a crazy man with a chain saw. Throughout them all he had lost the ability to scream for help, and he was naked for fairly half of them.

RALPH CONFIRMED HIS fears by knocking tentatively on his door at 5:03 A.M. He crept in covered head to toe in camouflage.

"You ready?" he asked, sounding nearly chipper, something Ponty hadn't imagined he was capable of—that anyone was capable of at 5:03 A.M.

"Oh, heck yeah," said Ponty. "Let's get some turkey." He thought for a second. "*Turkeys?* Or turkey?"

"What's that?"

"Nothing."

They climbed into what was left of Ralph's '81 Malibu (it was very badly rusted) and drove off into the darkness. Quite a lot of driving, Ponty thought. Then they drove some more, through the darkness, and into the onset of sunrise, the pair speaking little, mostly listening to oldies on Ralph's AM radio over the roar of the Malibu's throaty engine.

Finally Ponty tried to get something going. "Civil twilight, they call that," he said, pointing to the diffuse pink light filtering through the trees on the horizon.

"Who does?" demanded Ralph.

"Astronomers."

"Twilight is at night, I think," said Ralph, looking at Ponty with barely disguised pity.

"Well, yes, it's both, in astronomical terms. I did a book on Vespucci, so I had to do some research on nautical astronomy."

"So it's twilight right now?"

"I think so, yes."

"In the morning? Twilight?"

Ponty nodded. It was clear from Ralph's reaction that he did not agree and certainly did not like people misapplying the word "twilight" to other times of day.

"So, Ralph, where are we going to get these turkeys?" said Ponty.

"Oh, just a little farther now, to a place I know near Round Lake. You got to go where the turkeys are, you know?"

"That's for sure," said Ponty confidently.

"Have you hunted them before?"

"No."

"You've handled a bow, though, haven't you?"

"Oh, yeah. A little," he said, thinking back to a suction-cup bow-and-arrow set he'd had as a child.

"It's a little tricky with turkeys. They've got keen eyesight for movement, so a lot of times you'll have to hold the draw a good while before you've got a clean shot."

"Right," said Ponty, without having a basic understanding of what was just said.

"And you'll want to go for a shot at his spine, or else they can just run off, and you'll never find 'em."

"So spine shots?" said Ponty, rubbing his hands on his knees.

"That's right. The good thing is that in the spring those toms are looking to find themselves a nice hen, so if we call 'em close enough, they'll strut their stuff with their backs to us, and it's easier to get a shot at the base of the spine."

"Call 'em? How do we call 'em?"

"You never . . . ? oh, that's right. I've got a turkey call. We do a couple of hen calls—some purrs, a yelp or two—and with any luck those big toms'll come running. Then bam."

Ponty hadn't realized how dire was the situation. He was venturing into the remotest woods with a virtual stranger about to imitate the call of a large, sexually excited fowl and then shoot its romantically charged mate through like St. Sebastian. Another upsetting thought came to mind:

"Do we have to rub on turkey-gland oil, anything from their giblets or the like? Don't they do that for deer hunting?"

"Doe urine, yeah. But, no, we don't have to do that. They got no sense of smell."

Here was a small consolation: He would not be asked to splash on turkey pee. Then another thought:

"Do I need to buy a license?"

"I got you one."

"Really? Well, thanks, Ralph." Despite his reservations, Ponty felt a measure of pride that he was now a fully licensed turkey killer.

"You just have to pretend to be my brother if we get stopped," Ralph said.

"What? How do I do that?"

"You don't have to imitate his voice or anything," Ralph said, trying to quell Ponty's obvious alarm. "If we get stopped, just say your name is Brian Wrobleski."

"But what if he asks for my driver's license?"

"Just tell him you lost it."

"What if he frisks me and gets it out of my pocket?"

"I don't think the DNR has the right to frisk you. Lawsuits, I think." He paused. "I don't know—maybe they *can* frisk you, but if he does that, I'll pay your fine for you."

"What is the fine for illegally hunting turkeys?"

"If you have to ask, you can't afford it. We just have to make sure not to get caught."

They drove another twenty minutes or so and pulled over onto the shoulder of a deserted dirt road. Ralph opened the topper of his truck and began pulling out gear, handing Ponty a camouflage jacket and hat and what looked to Ponty like an enormously complex bow. He had remembered them as being bent-wood objects with a string connecting the two ends. Ralph's old bow was strung this way and that like a cat's cradle—the string passing over cams and wheels—and had a quiver attached to its right side that was bristling with broadhead studded arrows.

"This is your *old* bow?" Ponty asked.

"Yeah, but there ain't a turkey alive that wouldn't die after being hit by it."

"Oh, no. I don't doubt it. What I meant is, it doesn't look old."

"No, it's not. But here's my new one." Ralph pulled out a more complex-looking model with even more pulleys and levers and some sort of extension and what looked like a laser sight. "Got this with the money you guys paid us," he said.

Ponty whistled. "Wow. That's a peach," he said, and then he realized how effete the word "peach" sounded when applied to hunting tackle.

"Okay, here's what we do: We're gonna drive alongside this stand of trees up here and just listen for the call of a crow, okay?"

"A crow? Not a turkey?"

"A crow. We'll blast this—"

"Now, hang on. You keep saying 'crow.' You know that, right?"

"Yeah. When we hear the crows, we blast the crow call, and then—"

"I hate to be a pest," Ponty interrupted, "but bothering the crows seems a little off mission for a turkey hunt."

"Would you let me finish? When we hear the crows, we blast the crow caller real loud, and if there are any turkeys around, they'll gobble when they hear it."

"Really?"

"That's right."

"Brilliant. Let's do it."

They drove slowly up and down the dirt roads in the area and listened, Ralph leaning forward and looking to his right, Ponty concentrating hard. They did this for some time. Ponty did not keep track of the minutes, but, had he been on his own, he would have lost patience with the search some 700 percent earlier than Ralph did. The sun was fairly high in the sky when Ralph made the official announcement that they had been skunked. "Well. I s'pose," he said.

"Yup," Ponty seconded.

"Let's make one more pass down this side," said Ralph, swinging the truck around.

"Yup," Ponty agreed, for he was now a turkey hunter.

As he had previously, Ralph sounded the call when he heard some crows in the tall oaks. It was Ponty who heard the gobble.

"Hey, hey. Turkey," he said excitedly.

"You sure?"

"They gobble, right?"

"Yes."

"Something gobbled."

"Probably a turkey," said Ralph.

"That's what I'm saying."

They jumped out and collected their gear, Ralph restraining Ponty from dashing haphazardly into the woods like an excited child. They walked slowly and as quietly as possible down into a thicket of poplar, and when they were about a hundred yards from the road, they crouched low for cover and Ralph produced two small boxes of the same size, one with what looked like a piece of chalk protruding from one of its short sides, and began drawing the chalklike protrusion over the broad side of the other box (Ponty later learned that the chalklike protrusion was chalk). Against all logic, it produced a sound that Ponty could easily believe was similar to that made by a randy turkey. At first there was no reaction. But after a few calls they heard a response from an interested suitor.

"Go ahead and draw back an arrow," Ralph whispered.

Ponty gingerly removed an arrow from the bow's onboard quiver and, with only a basic sense of physics as his guide, successfully loaded it into the arrow rest and nocked it to the bowstring. Then he began to draw it back. This was harder than he might have imagined, and he had quite forgotten about the turkey as he concentrated all his might on simply pulling as hard as he could. Ralph gave his elbow a prodding squeeze, and Ponty redoubled his efforts to get the arrow back.

"C'mon, c'mon!" Ralph frantically whispered, and then he sounded off another turkey call. Ponty had the bow halfway back, with little confidence in moving it the rest of the way. Suddenly, frustrated with his own lack of strength, he made one last attempt to bully his trembling muscles into giving it another go. Just as he was about to abandon it all and suffer the inevitable contumely from Ralph, the effort of drawing it back diminished greatly and the arrow seemed to fly back to its ready position. Ponty, without realizing it, was taking sweet advantage of the "eccentric cam" system of a compound bow, and his first experience with "let-off," or the diminished resistance at the end of the draw, would always be his favorite.

Unfortunately, the feeling of elation was short-lived. Oxygen debt in the muscles of his right arm and shoulder was currently being paid with lactic acid, and this would not do. A slight spasm in his biceps caused the whole system to break down. His elbow unlocked, his fingers lost their grip on the string, and the arrow jumped from the bow, realizing all at once its potential energy. Ponty gave a little cry of panic, which mingled with the cry of a randy tom as an arrow pierced its spine.

"Yeah!" cried Ralph. "What a shot! Come on!" He grabbed Ponty by the coat and pulled him through the underbrush to where the poor trusting turkey lay, quite dead.

Ponty stared numbly at the noble creature, strange and beautiful at once, its gorgeous iridescent feathers so at odds with its bald blue head and grotesque dangling snood and wattles, stilled forever by Ponty's cruel arrow. He watched in silence as Ralph bent down and pulled the shaft from its limp body. Ralph whistled with his tongue. "This is a beaut, Ponty. Just a beaut."

Ponty did not answer. He was thinking about Benjamin Franklin and how he'd been so impressed by wild turkeys that he wanted them to be a symbol of the new country. Ponty had just killed the runner-up to the bald eagle, a poor, helpless beast that had gone looking for *l'amour* and was betrayed to *la mort*.

"Man," said Ralph, hefting it by its legs, "I'd say sixteen pounds. That's decent. Nicely done."

Ralph's words were sinking in.

"Really?" Ponty managed to say. He only now realized that he was trembling. "That's good, huh?"

"Oh, that's a real nice tom. Nice beard, good-looking spurs," Ralph said, pawing roughly over the corpse. "Here."

Ralph handed the turkey to Ponty, who was amazed at the weight and size of the thing. "Man," he said. "That *is* a nice one, isn't it?"

"Oh, yeah. Real nice. Heck of a shot there. Heck of a shot."

"Yeah, yeah, it was, wasn't it?" The heady rush of Ralph's praise, the buildup of adrenaline, and the sheer thrill of the hunt combined to wipe away all of Ponty's reservations about his kill. "Are we gonna get another?" he asked.

"Well, we could, I s'pose," said Ralph. "We got two permits."

"Darn right. Let's do it," said Ponty.

"Okay," said Ralph, and they trudged back toward the truck.

"Am I supposed to eat his liver raw or anything like that?" asked Ponty.

"I wouldn't think so. I've got some jerky in the glove box if you're really that hungry," said Ralph, smiling.

"I just thought I'd heard something about that."

"No, that's deer. And only crazy fellas do that."

"Let's just have some jerky," said Ponty, slinging the turkey over his back. In the course of a morning, he had become a turkey hunter.

CHAPTER 12

"'ll tell you what. I don't see that Danish ham is anything to write home about," Bromstad said, baiting his three traveling companions. "Watery. No flavor. Not a spice to be seen anywhere in it, or on it, even near it." No one responded, so Bromstad was encouraged. "And those open-faced sand-wiches you Danish like—what are they called, sauerbraten or or s'mores, or what is it?"

Vagns caved in. "Smørrebrød," he said thickly.

"Smørrebrød. That's it. It seems to me the need for an open-faced sandwich was obviated by the development of the second slice of bread placed on top in the traditional sandwich, holding everything together, and—let's face it—preventing you from having to stick your hand into all that ham and dill sauce and what-have-you. Have regular sandwiches made it to Denmark yet?" There was no response. "Well, doesn't matter. And those Danish pastries: sure they're good, but I don't know that we have to keep referring to them as 'Danish.' Unless I'm wrong, it's just a buttery dough with some sort of wet filling, right? There's no reason a person of any nationality—say, a Lithuan-ian or . . . or a Pole—couldn't make it. I don't know, you guys are Danish—you tell me if I'm wrong." There was silence, so

Bromstad looked out the window. The Volvo was following the Funkabus expertly, a discreet twenty car lengths behind. Bromstad sighed. "I'm particularly mystified by herring. Raw fish soaked in sugary vinegar? Tiny balls of . . . what, exactly? Floating in that cloudy brine. Is it bits of fish dust making it cloudy? Or is there—"

"Stop it!" screamed Jørgen. "Shut your mouth right now! I will not have herring maligned! You may taunt us all you want, and your prattling does not bother me. But you leave the herring out of it." The overtones of his vociferous rant bounced around the interior of the Volvo for a second, and then all was silent. Bromstad, who, probably because of his staggering narcissism, was not easily cowable, was now nearly completely cowed.

"Herring is good," said Ülo, coming out in strong support of Jørgen.

"Ja," said Vagns, backing them up.

"Whatever you say," said Bromstad quietly.

"Ridiculous," averred Jørgen. "We shouldn't even be helping this . . . American."

"Ja," said Vagns.

"It is part of my job that now and again I am forced to suffer fools, but I don't have to do it gladly," said Jørgen. "I don't have to tolerate such personal attacks."

"And not from an author," said Ülo with disgust.

Bromstad had not had anyone refer to him as a fool—and one who needed to be suffered, at that—for some thirteen years. At least within earshot. With some effort, he forced his dander up.

"Now, hold on," he said, but couldn't for the life of him think of how to follow it up. "You . . ." he ended weakly.

How had he fallen so precipitously in such a short time? he

wondered. Not long ago, on even his least energetic days, he could make ten people cry, not even counting those in the service industry. Now he was thoroughly beholden to a small squadron of viciously passionate pickled-fish apologists.

And it was all Jack Ryback's fault, he of the big, handsome head, the well-modulated voice, and, as Bromstad had noticed during an appearance by Ryback on the local-events program *Dill Morton's Tuesday Wrap-Up,* the absurdly large feet. Though Bromstad was well aware that television added several pounds to one's perceived size, by his reckoning that couldn't amount to more than a centimeter of apparent foot lengthening, and he felt confident guessing that Ryback strode around atop silverbacklike feet in the neighborhood of a size thirteen (forty-eight, in European sizing, he noted with empty triumph, upon converting it later). He picked up Vagns's copy of *Death Rat* off the seat next to him where it lay, actively mocking him. There it was on the back cover, that outsize, rugged head perched confidently atop a well-used fisherman's sweater *(big fat thief!),* the face careworn and perfectly unshaven. *What,* he thought, *are we being asked to make of that growth?* That its owner was too busy being rugged to bother with anything so prissy as scraping whiskers off his chin? That he had been felling redwoods and wrestling b'ar all day and plumb forgotten about the photo shoot for his only book? "That's today? Why, can we make this quick, fellas? I've got an oxcart full of rails to split before I break camp."

Bromstad decided to do something he had not yet done: actually look between the covers of *Death Rat.* He opened it gingerly, with a look of distaste, as though he were a vegan and the book were constructed wholly of room-temperature raw bacon. He thumbed randomly to a page somewhere near the middle and reluctantly allowed himself to comprehend small groups of words: "toe box" was one set, followed by "not known to have," and, after letting a few more pages slip past his thumb, a phrase that without benefit of context seemed especially irritating to its reader, "cornmeal in burlap sacks." Bromstad knew that it would be unfair to condemn Ryback's prose on the basis of such a sparse reading of it, but he decided to anyway.

"Phhhhttt," he said. "What a load of manure."

"What is it you are comparing with manure, Mr. Bromstad?" Jørgen snapped.

"No, don't worry Jørgen. I wasn't talking to *you*," he said petulantly.

"If you have any complaints about our arrangement, you should speak them in the open, as a man might, not in the whispered tones of a schoolgirl."

"Is that how it works in Denmark—schoolgirls must exclusively whisper their complaints?" Bromstad asked, allowing his voice to drift toward the sarcasm it went to naturally in times of stress. He was in the process of constructing a follow-up riposte involving a critique of constitutional monarchies and how they often lead to the development of draconian rules with regard to the voicing of complaints by matriculating young ladies—but he lost his nerve.

"You are childish in the extreme," noted Jørgen. "From now on I shall not speak to you directly. If you want to address me, ask Vagns or Ülo, and they will speak for you."

Bromstad sighed deeply and readjusted his cap, partially replacing the stale, abused hat air that had been trapped beneath it for more than ten hours.

"It is now dark enough, with enough contrasting light in the passenger cabin of the bus, that I believe we can get some passable photos of Mr. Ryback and this King Leo," Jørgen said, closing the distance between the Volvo and the Funkabus. "Ülo, please tell Mr. Bromstad that because of where he is seated, he will have to make himself useful and snap the shots as we pull abreast of the bus."

"Mr. Bromstad, Jørgen wishes me to tell you that your assistance is required in getting the shots as we pull aside the funk star's bus," said Ülo dutifully.

"Ülo, will you tell Vagns to tell Jørgen that I'd be more than happy to do that?" said Bromstad.

"I will not," said Ülo, "because as you well know, Vagns heard you and can do it himself."

"*Ja,*" said Vagns. "Jørgen, Mr. Bromstad said he would be more than happy to take the pictures."

Ülo gave him a brief lesson on the proper use of his rather expensive and complicated camera. "Here," he said, "is the button," pointing to a button, "that you press to take the picture."

Bromstad asked for a clarification. "Just this?" he said, pointing to the button in question.

"*Ja,*" said Ülo.

Bromstad had a follow-up. "I don't have to focus?" he asked, but Ülo had lost patience with his student and did not instruct him in the finer details of the M6's autofocus features, but said only, "No."

"Okay," said Bromstad with extreme, almost theatrical skepticism upon taking the camera from Ülo. He then turned it over a few times in a manner intended to indicate that, due to shoddy and inadequate schooling, he couldn't be sure whether to put his eye to the viewfinder or perhaps to the plastic buckle of the camera's strap.

"Have you got it?" Ülo tested.

"I guess," said Bromstad shakily.

What Jørgen could not have known was that thirty-nine hours before, drivers on the stretch of hilly road along which he now traveled had been less than impressed with the top speed of Tom Anderson's new Massey-Ferguson 8200 tractor (36.5 mph) as it cruised along in front of them, effectively blocking their way. Even though it was easily the fastest tractor he had ever owned, Tom began to see their point, especially when the driver of the 1997 Ford F-150 directly behind him demonstrated his displeasure by flashing his lights, swerving wildly back and forth across the blacktop, and sounding his horn, the final and most effectively communicative blast lasting more than fifty-three seconds. Tom pulled off to the right and reluctantly throttled back the new Massey, the tread of its massive tires leaving deep, Volvo-grabbing ruts in the soft gravel of the shoulder, to let the speedier drivers pass. ("Get a farm!" the driver of the truck had yelled, rather unhelpfully, as he passed.)

And none of them could have guessed that while Bromstad was deliberately being a pain in the handling of the camera, he had been more effective at it than he could have imagined when he thumbed the tiny silver button and put the camera into autoflash mode. Just as Jørgen began to accelerate, gaining speed with the intent of passing the bus to give Bromstad the proper vantage to snap photos, Bromstad had become even more of a pain by accidentally pressing the one button that Ülo had instructed him, however sketchily, in the proper use of. This caused the automatic focus to adjust the cameras lens to the exact focal length necessary to pick up the finest detail of their dome light, the shutter to snap open and close again quickly, the film to advance automatically, and, most unfortunately, the flash to pop, fully blinding every occupant of the Volvo. Jørgen then found that, though there is most probably never a very convenient time for the driver of a moving automobile to be fully blind, Bromstad's choice had been particularly ill timed. It was precisely at a moment when he should have been fully sighted, which would have aided him greatly in avoiding the road shoulder and its tire-grabbing ruts. As it was, Jørgen could see neither the shoulder, the ruts, nor anything really, save the bright crimson of his own assaulted retinas, so he was unable to avoid the danger. All he could do was flip over one hundred and eighty degrees and scream in terror, which was of little use to anyone. Despite its lack of efficacy, the other occupants found this to be the most convenient course of action as well.

Fortunately for most everyone involved, there were only twenty-eight loose objects careening around the interior with them as the car made several more spectacular barrel rolls. Twenty-seven of the objects were the nearly identical Ricola cough drops that had come loose from their bag, which had been tucked into a storage pocket on the driver's-side door and were not capable of doing any significant damage. They flew about the cabin recklessly, one connecting with Jørgen's chin, another hitting Vagns sharply on the ear, but any effect was swamped by greater pains, buffets, and concerns. (Had they been in any state to do so, they might have wanted to thank Jørgen, who did not allow snacking in his automobile, that they weren't battered with empty peanut jars, or half-full bottles of warm soda.) The twenty-eighth missile, the hardcover copy of Jack Ryback's *Death Rat,* had more inherent potential to wound, and it made good on that potential when it slammed into the ceiling and caught Bromstad a glancing blow off the side of his head, prior to hitting the seat again on the car's second somersault, bouncing up (perspective-wise, though in reality, down, toward earth's crust) before catching him on the forehead.

Several minutes later, when Bromstad awoke, he discovered how over the years he'd become so very dependent upon waking in a more or less horizontal position on a reasonably conventional sleeping surface—mattress, cot, even one of those accursed futons—to keep him from flying into a blind panic. When he realized that all of these expected conditions were absent, and that he was in a great deal of pain, he flew into a blind panic. This disgusted his Danish accomplishes, two of whom had already climbed out the broken windows of the Volvo. The third, Ülo, who was at least partially responsible for his consciousness, as it was he who had slapped Bromstad awake, now slapped him again when he beheld Bromstad's un-Danishly display.

"Get a grip on yourself, man!" he said, bits of broken glass dislodging from his hair with the effort of the slaps.

"Ahhhhhhhhhhhhhhhhhhhh!" shrieked Bromstad, who had remembered to wear his seat belt.

"Stop it, you blathering fool," shouted Jørgen, who was trying to make a phone call. He stood just five feet away from the spot next to the red oak where Bromstad was screaming, Ülo was slapping, and the car was still running, and paged through the menu of his Nokia digital phone in an attempt to find Stig Stou-Thorup's home number.

Ülo began pushing harshly on Bromstad's left side in a not-so-subtle (or medically prudent) effort to get him to make an attempt to climb out the only window accessible to him. He quickly realized that if this method were to bear any fruit, he would have to unbuckle Bromstad from his seat belt. He groped around the moist heat of Bromstad's midsection until he found the belt and followed it down to its source, pressing the buckle's release. It was a deep and unexpected flaw in Ülo's plan that he could not foresee a humid and panicked Bromstad falling fully onto him once he'd released him from his restraint, for that is precisely what happened.

It was at least twenty minutes before Vagns and Jørgen could extract both men from the Volvo by climbing atop its exposed driver's side and pulling them up through the window, Jørgen taking a moment after his rescue to slap Ülo, who had been screaming off and on for the full twenty minutes that he'd been forced to bear Bromstad's bulk.

Once all screaming had ceased and an inventory of wounds had been taken (total: one large bump on Bromstad's head, two slight hand marks on each of Bromstad's and Ülo's cheeks), the now carless party trooped back to the road under the leadership of Jørgen.

"We are lucky to have had the Volvo," Jørgen said somberly. "The Swedes aren't much as a people, but they understand the value of side-impact beams."

"*Ja,*" the remaining Danes agreed.

"Now what?" asked Bromstad in an accusatory tone suggesting that he'd forgotten that the crash was largely his fault.

Jørgen turned toward Bromstad, apparently intent on killing him with his eyes. "You, Mr. Bromstad," he said icily, "are going back to your home immediately, where you can do damage only to yourself. We are going on to Holey to reconnoiter and continue our surveillance of Mr. Ryback."

"What! How? The car's a wreck, isn't it?" Bromstad whined.

"You are correct. The Volvo is not operational. Per is bringing another unit to us, but you shall be returning home by found transportation."

"I don't get to go with you anymore?"

"You will have no more opportunities to kill us, no."

Several minutes later Bromstad was standing on the shoulder of the southbound lane on a bright, moonlit night, gazing toward the north with a sad, dazed look, like a man who has just lost his dog and is standing at his mailbox with the hope that his dog manages to drive itself back home. The Danes stood across the two lanes from him looking purposeful. The casual spectator, however, would have had no easy time discerning just what that purpose might be, as there was really nothing within a fifty-mile radius of the men that seemed to require having any purpose applied to it.

After a five-minute wait, headlights approached from the north, and Bromstad tentatively put out a thumb and pointed it roughly in the direction of St. Paul. The car, a white Saturn, whizzed by without slowing, although it did sound its horn, seemingly as a taunt to the hitchhiking author. Bromstad blinked heavily to remove road grit from his eyes. He then rubbed them like a tired toddler and yelled testily across the road, "Are you sure I can't go with you?"

"No," Jørgen said firmly.

"Why?" whined Bromstad. "It wasn't my fault you crashed."

"Ah, but it was," said Jørgen.

"Ülo did it."

"That is not true," Ülo yelled. Then he turned to Jørgen and repeated it in a quieter but firmer manner. "That is not true."

"I know, Ülo. Mr. Bromstad," Jørgen began, "like so many

Americans, is unable to admit when he—and he alone—is the cause of a single-vehicle crash."

"What?" said Bromstad, who really hadn't heard Jørgen's accusation.

"Just keep watching the road, you great oaf," Jørgen said irritably.

"Did you call me an elf?" an incredulous Bromstad asked.

"No. Can you not—" Jørgen began, but before he could explain to Bromstad that he'd referred to him not as a kind of pixie but as a fool, headlights in the distance cut him short. A dun-colored 1979 Chevrolet Impala roared past, then screeched to a halt several hundred yards down the road before backing up at high speed and stopping in front of Bromstad. The window rolled down, and he peered tentatively in, as though he were expecting it to be piloted by a bear. Instead he saw that it was driven by a young man of eighteen or so with patchy, unlaundered facial hair. Next to him sat a woman with no facial hair that he could immediately make out, although she did have bounteous hair on her head, mostly blond until it got within an inch of her scalp, where it turned dark brown.

"Climb in," said the man.

Bromstad stood up, looked over the road to the small knot of Danish men, and heaved a questioning shrug. "Should I get in?" he shouted.

"Yes," they replied in unison.

Bromstad attempted to open the door, but it wouldn't budge.

"Sorry, man. Door's busted. Gotta climb through the window."

CHAPTER 13

The staff of the Bugling Moose had never received an order for meringue larger than an amount that would fit atop a slice of already prepared lemon meringue pie. In fact, meringue had never been ordered separately from a pie, and certainly never in as great a quantity as fifty gallons. Their pies, when they had them, came from Wouton Bakery in nearby Eagle's Nest, so they had never even attempted to make meringue, chiffon, or any other whipped-egg-white-based confection. Patty Perpich, the owner of the Bugling Moose, tried to explain this fact to Gary.

"We don't do meringue," she said. "We could make you an omelette."

"No. I don't think that'll work. King Leo was very specific about the meringue," Gary explained, scanning a sheet of paper he held in his hands.

"What does he need fifty gallons of it for?"

"Says it's good for his skin or something," Gary said sheepishly.

"Wow. Even so, you'd think he'd gain an awful lot of weight from it," said Patty.

"Oh, no. He doesn't eat it. I guess he bathes in it or something."

"Well, I don't know what to tell you. We might get some pies in on Monday. If there are any lemon meringues in the batch, I could scrape the tops off and have those sent to him. But I don't want to overpromise, 'cause we don't get meringue pies very often. And of course I'd have to charge for the whole pie."

"Well, let's just forget it. I'll have to explain it to King Leo," he said, then sighed.

The Funkabus had disgorged its passengers the night before, and the crew of eight had rented out four units, the band decorating all of them to King Leo's taste immediately, accomplished by the use of liberal applications of draped silks and paper lampshade covers. In King Leo's unit, velvet upholstered pillows were also heavily utilized until the cabin's backwoods feel was almost completely obfuscated and replaced by a look not dissimilar to the set of Rudolph Valentino's tent in *The Sheik*.

Because of limited available space, Jack shared a cabin with Billy Moonbeam and Wigs Jackson (which turned out to be to his distinct advantage, because in his haste to pack he'd forgotten his dop kit, and Wigs had brought along toiletries in ridiculous abundance and lent all of them to Jack with extreme, almost excessive, largesse). King Leo took Cabin 7, known as the Snowshoe Lodge. (The titular snowshoes were now covered in pink and yellow silks.)

The morning after they arrived, Jack awoke, and though it appeared that they couldn't have been forced to care, made an excuse to Wigs and Billy ("I'm going to see if I can spot a loon"). He was sneaking his way over to Ponty's cabin when a voice from above made his spine stiffen and his arms shoot out at his sides.

"Jack, Jack, Jack, Jack," said the voice.

Jack scanned the sky around him and saw King Leo perched on the low branch of a medium-size white pine, his back resting against a branch above it. Jack made a conscious effort to quiet his aroused nervous system before speaking.

"King Leo," Jack observed.

"It's nice up here," he said.

"I'll bet," said Jack. "Um . . . whatcha doin' up there?"

"I couldn't do my meringue bath this morning, so I came up here for a little peace and reflection. Communing with whatever I could find."

Jack's concentration was so absorbed with slowing his breathing that he let King Leo's sentence slip by him without even attempting to comprehend it.

"Uh-huh."

"We belong here, Jack. Are you feeling it?"

"Sort of."

"Just a moment ago, as I sat here in this tree listening to the birds, watching the hamsters scamper across the damp forest floor, I felt a profound sense of peace. And apprehension, too."

Jack put his hands in his pockets and looked down while trying to find the handle on what King Leo had just said. Though he recognized immediately some deep problems with it—among them, how one could simultaneously feel a sense of profound peace and apprehension (and because they were standing among sparse trees, he might also have quibbled about the term "damp forest floor")—he asked for clarification on one particular point.

"Hamsters?"

"Yes. They have been very active this morning. Putting on quite a show for me," King Leo said with a bucolic smile.

"There are hamsters running around in the woods?"

"Oh, yes. If you wait with me, you'll probably see one come out of that little stand of brush over there," said King Leo, pointing.

Though Jack felt he'd be wise to let it pass, he pressed on out of morbid curiosity.

"What do they look like?"

"You've never seen a hamster? Ooohhh, Jack, Jack, Jack, this place is going to be good for you," King Leo said with tender condescension. "Hamsters look like smaller squirrels, only with playful little stripes on their backs and little white spots," he said, as though he were passing on a treasured family secret.

Jack blinked at him. "King Leo? Those are squirrels. Ground squirrels. I don't think we have hamsters here in Minnesota."

"Jack, you been in the city way, way, way too long." He dismounted the tree limb nimbly. "Walk with me, Jack. Let us talk of many things." Jack looked about nervously as King Leo threw an arm over his shoulder. They walked with apparent aimlessness for several yards. Finally King Leo spoke. "Jack," he said. Jack had not yet become inured to King Leo's habit of prefacing innocuous statements by saying his name in a preposterously weighty manner.

"Yes, I'm here," Jack replied solemnly.

"Did you sleep well?" King Leo asked.

"Okay. Billy Moonbeam snores."

"Should I fire him? I will if you want me to."

"No. No. It's fine, really."

"Jack?"

Jack decided not to respond this time in order to find out if answering King Leo was a requirement for hearing what was coming next. He waited some fifteen seconds. Finally King Leo spoke.

"Take me to the spot where it happened, Jack. Take me to the mine."

"What?" he said, his voice breaking slightly. "Now?"

"I think we should see it together, you and I."

Jack wondered why King Leo persisted in thinking there existed a "you and I" made up of he and him. He thought quickly, intending to add another person to the formula.

"You know, there's a guy I want you to meet. He's a local, and the real expert on the mine."

Before King Leo could object, Jack walked deliberately for several hundred feet, approached Cabin 2, and knocked loudly on the door. While they waited, King Leo leveled a reasonable question: "He lives here at the Bugling Moose?"

In his haste Jack hadn't thought of this, or much of anything, really. He realized how threadbare was the fabric of their lie that it could be so easily shredded by King Leo. But he did not intend to give in.

"His place is being bug-bombed."

King Leo's curiosity seemed sated for the moment, though Jack knew that his response naturally led to more questions about how he could have such up-to-date intelligence concerning the pest-extermination practices of the residents of Holey. Before that line of questioning could be pursued, however, Ponty appeared, to Jack's eye looking a touch riled, like a raccoon roused from a hollow log.

"Ja—"

"Hello, *Earl*," Jack said pointedly.

Ponty looked over Jack's shoulder and, seeing King Leo, felt for his top lip.

"Hello," said Ponty as Earl. Though his Earl voice was indistinguishable in tone from his regular voice, it was obvious he was trying to add something Earl-ish by the way his body moved differently from the effort of it.

"Earl, I'd like you to meet King Leo. King Leo this is Earl.

Earl . . . Topperson." Jack used his eyes to apologize to Ponty for the poor choice of a last name. "Earl is staying here while his house is being bug-bombed."

"Hello, hello, hello, Earl Topperson. You can call me King Leo, or you can call me the Sovereign Ruler of Groove, Milord Nasty Pants, the Magistrate of Penetrate, the Pharaoh of Funk, Maharaja of the Mojo, Caesar the Pleaser, Benevolent Despot of the Lower Places, the Commander in Chief in the Over-stuffed Briefs, or the Exchequer of Milk Chocolate Soul."

Ponty was staring wide-eyed at King Leo when he finished. Jack rushed to fill the horrified silence that ensued.

"Or, as he said, you can call him King Leo, Earl," Jack said nervously.

"Muh . . . muh . . . Milord Nasty Pants?" Ponty asked weakly. Clearly, of all the pseudonyms, he was most trauma-tized by this one.

"Yes, yes, yes. Or Sheik Shake and Bake, or the Mogul of Rock 'n' Roll-gul, or the Crowned Head of the Squeakin' Bed. Wooo!" King Leo added enthusiastically.

"Or King Leo," Jack added.

"Milord Nasty—" Ponty began, but he was cut off by Jack.

"He wants to see the mine, Earl. And I know that as a *local expert on it*, you'd want to be the one to take us there."

Ponty shook his head like a boxer shaking off a well-done uppercut.

"I was just going to take a nap. I've been doing quite a bit of turkey hunting this week. And, you know, if you want to catch a turkey off guard, you gotta get up pretty early."

Jack gripped Ponty deliberately by the front of his new flan-nel shirt. "Earl. Earl. Friend Earl. So happy you've been having fun turkey hunting, but"——and here he nearly picked up Ponty——*"he wants to see the mine."*

If King Leo was bothered or embarrassed at all by Jack's sudden forcefulness with this kindly-looking resident of Holey, he didn't show it. While Jack was lightly roughing up Ponty, King Leo was lifting his tangerine-colored sleeveless turtleneck, absentmindedly touching the taut muscles of his abdomen and humming a tune, as though scenes such as these were something he had become accustomed to seeing.

Ponty responded to Jack's persuasion. "Ouch. Okay. Okay. Watch the shirt. Let me just get ready, and we'll go see the mine."

"Good," said Jack, and he honored Ponty's request concerning his shirt.

"All right, then."

"Yes, all right."

"I'll just be a second," said Ponty, brushing at his chest as though Jack had grasped him with soiled hands.

"Take your time."

"King Leo, you'll excuse me?" Ponty asked regally.

"Oh, yes, yes, yes, yes, yes."

"Hang on, then," Ponty said to Jack.

"I'll be right here."

"I'd ask you in, but——"

"Would you please just get going?" Jack demanded.

Ponty slunk quickly back inside, and Jack heard faint noises of Ponty-style bustling——in Jack's opinion a staggeringly inefficient state for him to be in, what with its needless redundancy of action and frequent incidences of glass breakage. Jack, remembering himself, checked in with King Leo, who seemed quite undisturbed by recent events, as he was currently dispensing some sort of cream or unguent from a small white tube into a mound on the fingertips of his left hand. He deftly replaced the cap, put the tube back into a tiny over-the-shoulder bag (Jack presumed it was not to be taken as a purse, despite having all the traditional earmarks of one), and, after rubbing it between his hands, smoothed the emollient into his close-cropped hair. To Jack's questioning look he replied, "Flaxseed sculpting gel. You need some?" he offered.

Jack refused graciously, withholding his own strong opinions concerning the rubbing of flaxseed derivatives into one's scalp.

"It'll keep that flaking down," King Leo said.

His dudgeon still near the surface, Jack considered and rejected the idea of grabbing the front of King Leo's sweater and giving him a few shakes. A second scheme involving flinging him to the ground by his purse was also set aside for the moment as Jack's better man prevailed. Both schemes, however, were reconsidered briefly when King Leo then produced what Jack at first assumed to be a lip balm of some sort, but King Leo corrected him by identifying as "peach glaze lip essence." Again Jack conquered his baser instincts.

When Ponty reappeared a moment later, Jack couldn't help but notice that his top lip—moments ago free of any facial hair—was now thoroughly covered by a thick layer of mustache. He leaned toward Ponty in disbelief, blinking as though perhaps the newly acquired cookie duster was just a spot on Jack's contact lens. King Leo stopped the process of recapping his peach glaze lip essence to stare at "Earl" for a second. Ponty, a man sensitized over the years to the disbelieving stares of others, looked from one staring man to the other.

"What?" he asked.

King Leo said nothing but simply cocked his head to the side in a questioning manner before shaking it off. "Nothing, nothing, nothing at all, Mr. Earl. Lead on to that magic place."

"Well, I don't how much magic is there. It's all boarded up. Pretty junky-looking. And the mine itself is actually on a guy's property, so we'll have to check with him first."

"Oh, it'll work out. I know it. Big things are gonna happen there, Mr. Earl. Big things."

"What kinds of things, do you think?" Ponty asked as they walked.

"Gonna be a revival."

"Yeah, Jack mentioned that. A revival of what, exactly?"

"Oh, my, my, my, Mr. Earl. I'll tell you what. What it will be is a revival of the one Funka-Lovely-Creative-Spirit-Being that all people used to share. The same one that was at work when your Mr. Lynch was rescued from the beast in that mine. We've lost that in our time, and we need to get it back. But we're gonna do it. Me and Jack—with your help. We're gonna get it back."

"Well, okay. We can take my Tempo."

King Leo insisted on taking the backseat, despite objections from Jack. This turned out badly for King Leo. For when Ponty shifted his weight in his seat and pushed back, the improperly repaired seat collapsed yet again and reclined, Ponty ending up in King Leo's lap.

"Ooh, ouch, Mr. Earl," said King Leo, looking down at Ponty.

"Son of a . . . sorry. So sorry. They were supposed to have fixed this thing!"

"Ponty, get out of the man's lap," Jack said.

"I'm trying, okay? King Leo, could I ask you to just reach behind the seat and give me a push?"

"It would be my pleasure," said King Leo, and he did.

Ponty played around gingerly with the seat adjustments until he was satisfied that he would not be flying backward anymore. Just to be safe, King Leo moved to the spot behind Jack.

Once they'd started driving and the remaining awkwardness of the seat incident had dissipated, no one spoke for a moment, so Ponty attempted to get something going.

"So . . . King Leo. You do much fishing?" he asked, looking in the rearview mirror.

Jack, who had spent more time with King Leo, knew that Ponty had just opened himself up to a conversation-killing response, like "I am fisher of love" or "I fish the body electric" or some such thing, so he was surprised when King Leo responded simply.

"No," he said. "No, I'm afraid not."

"Well," said Ponty, "we could get after the walleye while you're up here. How long you planning to stay?"

"Until we are all saved by the universal spirit being."

Ponty was rocked somewhat by this reply, but he pressed on. "Well," he said, "if that's not gonna take long, you can always get a temporary license. They're a lot cheaper."

"Perhaps I'll do that," King Leo said, and there followed a long pause before he spoke again. "Mr. Earl, I could not help but notice that you have an unopened hot-dog steamer in the backseat of your car. Can you tell me about that?"

"Oh, yeah. It's kind of funny. I got it as a gift, and I have to say, I have almost no occasion to steam a hot dog of any kind, but I just never got around to returning it."

"May I have it?" King Leo asked respectfully.

"You want my hot-dog steamer?"

"I'll pay you."

"No. You can just have it."

"Thank you."

"You like hot dogs, huh?" Ponty asked pleasantly.

"Not particularly, no."

After another moment of silence, Ponty spoke. "King Leo, can I ask why you want my hot-dog steamer?"

"I'd rather not say," he replied. "Can I still have it?"

"I guess so," said Ponty tentatively.

They drove through town till they came to County Highway P, traveled on that for just under a mile, pulled off into a dirt driveway, traveled down it a quarter mile, and stopped the car in front of a large chain-saw sculpture of Linus Pauling.

"Mr. Earl, I have to ask you—what is that?" asked King Leo after they'd gotten out to get a closer look at Pauling's likeness, carved from the stump of a large oak. Before Ponty could answer, Jack guessed, with a fair amount of what turned out to be unwarranted confidence, that it was a sculpture of Robert Loggia. Ponty corrected him, explaining that the owner of the land they (and the mine) were on, Gerry Iverson, was a fan of Pauling. King Leo and Jack nodded knowingly, tipping Ponty off to the fact that neither one had the vaguest notion of who Linus Paulins was. Ponty was just giving them a brief biography when from around the backside of a large grass mound a savagely barking black dog took the vanguard position ahead of a far less fierce-looking man in a flannel shirt and white painter's pants.

"Firesign, man, knock it off," said the man to the dog. The dog obeyed but then ran excitedly toward them, choosing King

Leo to jump up on, smudging thick mud all over the front of his sweater. "Firesign!" the man cried sharply, and Firesign the dog shrank away and lay down on the ground, his tail wagging in apparent eagerness to leap on King Leo again.

"Hey, I'm really sorry, man," the man said. He was a thin-legged fellow of about fifty, with a small potbelly, a shiny bald pate, and long, dark hair pulled back into a ponytail and secured by a small band of beaded leather. His voice was a rough tenor, and he spoke with a vague accent or affectation, though his face was open and gave the impression of guilelessness. His eyes were surrounded by wrinkles and crow's-feet, and they were slightly rimmed with red. He touched the dog with the toe of his heavy sandal. "Firesign isn't used to guests, man."

King Leo was obviously in some sort of sartorial state of shock and could not speak. The man looked at Ponty. "Hey, Ponty," he said, and then he squinted and leaned in to get a better look at Ponty's mustache.

"It's Earl, actually . . . um, Gerry," said Ponty, not at all smoothly.

"Earl? You told me your name was Ponty."

Indeed, there was every reason in the world for Gerry to hold the belief that the newly mustachioed person now identifying himself as Earl was really named Ponty. For when Sandi had taken Ponty there several days before, he'd been nothing but Ponty.

"No. No, my name's Earl."

The man looked understandably confused. "But I called you Ponty the other day, didn't I, and you didn't correct me?"

"Well, they sound a lot alike. Sorry about the mix-up," said Ponty.

"Well . . . okay, man. Earl it is."

Ponty introduced Gerry to the other men, and Gerry took the opportunity to again apologize to King Leo for his dog's having soiled his "sweater set," as Gerry called the sleeveless turtleneck. King Leo had recovered enough to accept the apology gracefully, telling Gerry that it was okay, as he had dozens more sleeveless turtlenecks (which was quite true), but he did not offer his standard list of alternate names, for which Jack and Ponty were grateful. The introductions complete, Ponty asked if they could speak with Gerry for a moment, and he invited them into his house.

"Gerry has an earth home," Ponty informed the others.

"Yeah, me and Bilbo," Gerry laughed.

"Now, Gerry, is Bilbo your wife?" King Leo asked good-naturedly.

Gerry checked to see if he was kidding and, discovering he wasn't, said, "No. No, Bilbo's a hobbit, from the Tolkien books." They walked around the other side of the large earth mound toward the entrance, Firesign the dog tagging along behind. They had to walk past a large array of flat panels mounted about four feet off the ground. "My solar collectors," Gerry explained, though no one had asked. And he continued, "I got off the grid back in '84. Just couldn't take it. Saw an episode of something called *Night Court*, and that was it for me. I was done. Now, here, see, the aluminium"—he used the British pronunciation—"plates heat up in the sun and warm the water in the coiled pipes, and I pump that into reservoirs under the foundation." Not reading his audience very well, he kept the solar-collector information coming as they entered his earth home. "Works well until it gets really cold, and then I'm forced to use our dead ancestors as heat. But I suppose that's better than burning our friends the trees," he said, sounding a little sad. "I use photovoltaic panels for my lighting, but they're way pricey, man, so I can't use 'em for heat."

They stepped into his rustic kitchen, and he offered each of them a chair (and though all the chairs he offered were unique in style and color, the two similarities they shared were their chipping paint and an immediate need to be shimmed and glued in order to be considered structurally sound), and they pulled them up around his fiberboard kitchen table, a remarkably stained piece of wood set atop two sawhorses. "Can I get you some stinging-nettle tea?" he asked them.

"I—I don't think so," Jack said. "Or is it good?"

"Oh, it's great. I throw a little comfrey leaf in there, too," he said, hoping to close the deal.

"It won't sting when I drink it, will it?" Ponty asked.

"No, it shouldn't."

They all reluctantly accepted, so he drew water into a battered old aluminum teapot, lit a small can of denatured alcohol, and set the pot on a grid above it. "It'll take a while," he said. "But every good thing does." He took a large plastic pail from a spot next to the sink, overturned it, and sat down near his guests. "What can I help you guys with?" he asked.

"Well, King Leo here—Are you familiar with him, by the way?" Ponty asked.

"Just what I know of him from when we met a minute ago to now," Gerry said honestly.

"Well, he's a . . . a singer-songwriter from the Twin Cities, and he'd like to take a look at the mine. Is that right, King Leo?"

"Gerry, I want to see the mine in preparation for a funkadelic

cosmic event such as history has never known," King Leo clarified.

"What'll that involve?" Gerry asked.

"The coming together of many into one. An up-and-down,
whacked-out, joyous, dizzy funk being laid down in praise of
the Source, the . . . the, Spirit-Being, the Funky One, the Rat of
Dee-vine Power."

Gerry whistled. "How many people we talking about?"

"Gerry, if I'm right, and I am right often, the Source, the
Funky One does not require a certain number of people in
attendance to show his Dee-vine will and pour out the funk on
those involved in the revival." "I see . . . So . . . ?"

"I couldn't imagine more than forty to sixty-five partici-
pants."

"Would that be okay?" Ponty asked.

Gerry passed a hand over his balding head. "Well," he said,
"as long as you leave it in the condition you found it in, I don't
have a problem with that."

"That is excellent," said King Leo. "Gonna be a revival.
Thank you, Gerry Iverson."

Gerry waved off King Leo's praise. "Bah," he said.

"No, really, thanks," added Ponty.

"Ahh," Gerry croaked, with another demure movement of
his arm. He paused while looking King Leo over. "So you're a
musician, huh?" he said. "You know, I used to do a little finger-
picking and whatnot myself. Hang on a second." He left the
table with surprising alacrity, disappeared around a half wall
behind which the sounds of enthusiastic rooting around could
be heard, and returned a moment later with a battered Ovation
six-string and a banjo. Jack looked at Ponty with concern, but

Ponty was looking at King Leo, who in turn was watching Gerry with a mildly amused expression.

"While we're waiting for the water to heat up, what say we jam?" Gerry said, thrusting the guitar at King Leo. "We can start with a few Weavers tunes and see if we get anything clicking."

It was during the fourth stanza of the Irish Rovers' setting of "The Unicorn," King Leo strumming along with Gerry, that Jack felt a hollow sense of revenge for King Leo's poetry assault. Then Gerry swung immediately into "The Gandy Dancer's Ball," and Jack's feeling of revenge was swamped by one of intense personal misery.

CHAPTER 14

It was 8:45 A.M., and Bart Herzog, the governor of Minnesota, was rappelling out the third-floor window of the governor's mansion to greet his guest.

"Bromstad, you son of a tinker's son, how the Hec Ramsey are you?" he asked, unclipping from his carabiners to shake Bromstad's hand.

Bromstad had expected a more conventional approach, something along the lines of Herzog's opening his door in response to Bromstad's knocking upon it. He answered Herzog with a question of his own. "Governor, are your stairs out?"

Herzog began the process of laughing, extracted an El Rey del Mundo Churchill maduro from the breast pocket of his

military-issue M-65 field jacket, paused his laughing to bite the
end off, resumed laughing, pulled a pack of Ohio Blue Tip
matches from the thigh pocket of his BDU tiger-stripe trousers,
took one out and struck it on the side of his lifted boot, interrupted his laughing again to light his cigar, and, after some
strenuous puffing, threw the match over his shoulder, took a
long drag, and resumed his laughing on the exhale.

"No, no. That little toadstool press secretary of mine," he
said, pointing a thumb back toward his mansion, " 'advised' me
not to talk to you, and I didn't want to have to fight with him, so
I just came out the window. Didn't even wake the wife."

"Why do you think he advised you thusly?" Bromstad
asked, accidentally producing a rather archaic sentence while
trying to be nonchalant.

"He says you're as dead as a stuffed mule deer. 'Wouldn't be
good for my approval ratings to be seen with you,' he says,"
Herzog stated matter-of-factly before taking a puff of his
Churchill. "Hey! I'm sorry—you want one of these?" he
asked, gesturing with the already very wet end of his stogie.

Bromstad just shook his head sadly.

"What?" Herzog asked upon noticing Bromstad's hurt look.
"Oh, hey. Don't worry about it. He doesn't know what he's
talking about. You're not as dead as a stuffed mule deer. Sure,
you been shot by this Ryback fellow. But there ain't no reason
in the world you can't drag yourself through the woods, find
some heavy brush, and lay down to lick your wounds." A passing car honked its horn. "Hey," said Herzog, "they've spotted
us. Let's break up this little powwow and reconvene in my
study."

Once inside—they entered through the front door—Bromstad peered at Herzog through a thick fog of cigar smoke and attempted small talk. "How's the governor game going?" he asked.

"Beats pickin' cotton," Herzog said, "Though not by much. I suppose you heard about my recent trouble?"

"No. I've been busy."

"Are you kiddin'? Busy doin' what—spelunking? It's all over the media."

"I've been . . . out of town."

"Well, a protester got personal on me the other day, so I had to bust a move on him. Dropped him like a hot buttered anvil right there on the capitol steps. Unfortunately, a picture of me standing over him taunting Ali style made the front page of the paper." He took a long pull off a can of vanilla-flavored Sports Shake. "Big uproar. Lots of negative press. I suppose they would have liked it better if I'd held him in my arms and rocked him to sleep singing 'All the Pretty Little Ponies.' No. I did the right thing. I stand by it."

"Well, good for you," Bromstad encouraged, though he was really just waiting for Herzog to be done speaking.

"And what's happening with you? The latest Dogwood book just went in the toilet after the second week, huh?"

Bromstad pulled up the arms of his sweater. "No. No. It's still posting strong sales, and we expect to tie up some more foreign-rights deals within—"

"You can't fool an old soldier. This Ryback fellow's taking a big boardinghouse bite out of your sales. There's only so many book-buying dollars per household, and right now that rat-adventure book is eating your lunch. It happened to me when *Stamp Your Ass MINE!* came out. Bunt Casey's was released right after it, and sales took a little hit. They recovered, though." Herzog's personal memoir had turned out to be a giant success, and it was at the Dwee Awards, where Bromstad and Herzog had met and formed their friendship after discovering a common love of drinking too much table wine, throwing wadded-up bits of dinner rolls at other attendees, and heckling the presenters.

"Well, I'll admit it. I'm disappointed by recent events. I don't like or trust this guy. I want him taken out as a viable threat to our way of life."

"What can the governor's office do to help you?" Herzog asked while exhaling the largest cigar cloud yet.

"Well, here's the thing. I've got Stig and the boys from Den Institut Dansk working surveillance for me."

"Be careful. They're Danish. I hope you know what you're doing."

"Well, in fact, we ran into difficulty when an unfortunate incident caused the Volvo to roll, many times. We barely got out alive."

"Swede cars aren't worth the paper they're printed on. They would roll just as soon as look at you. Buy American." Bromstad was puzzling over this nonsensical automotive jingoism when Herzog continued, "How's their intelligence? What have you got so far?"

"Well, so far only this. He used to work at Medieval Burger. And he's got large feet."

"That's not a lot to go on."

"No, it's pretty thin—but we'll get more. He's up in Holey with King Leo right now, and—"

"King Leo! Jumping Jerry Rice in a flatboat, man! What's that panty-wearing freak of nature up to?"

"That's what I'm—"

"Eroding our hard-earned Minnesota dignity, no doubt," Herzog said, slamming fist down onto his table, overturning his empty sport-shake can.

"No doubt. That's—"

"What do you need? Troops?"

Bromstad did a double take. "Can I have some?"

"No. I got carried away there. Sorry. Now's not a good time anyway. The heat on me is too intense. Diverting the National Guard for personal use is not going to endear me to anyone." The governor looked around the room as though he smelled something. "What about a steak?" he asked suddenly.

Bromstad looked as puzzled as a man to whom the offer of steak has been unexpectedly made. "I . . . I don't see how that will help."

"You want one? I'm gonna have a steak."

"No thanks. It's a bit early for steak."

"Okay, I guess I'll wait, too," said Herzog, his voice betraying his disappointment over having to forgo the breakfast meat. "King Leo," he said, shaking his head. "His last album was nothing but a filthy rant over a bass line and fuzz guitars. It was an aggressive criminal act. My wife loves the guy, though. Figure that out."

"There's no sense to be made of it. But if this Ryback person has aligned with him, they can't possibly be up to anything good. That's where I need your help."

"I'm listening," said Herzog, though it was clear to Bromstad that he was still busy being disgusted over King Leo while relighting his cigar and therefore not listening at all. Bromstad coughed loudly, and Herzog disengaged from his own thoughts. "Okay. What do we do?" he asked.

"Well, I'll tell you. Number one, I don't believe that this Holey Rat story is true in the first place."

"What? That's a pretty serious accusation. What proof have you got?"

"It's the story of a man being attacked by a six-foot rat, Governor."

"Yeah, that's what I've heard. Sounds like an amazing story."

"Governor! A six-foot rat! When's the last time you heard of a rat that grew to be six feet long?"

"I haven't. But just to play devil's advocate, I know that sturgeon can get to be a thousand pounds or more if left to their own devices. Maybe rats are the same way."

"What does . . . ?"

"And I certainly wouldn't want to tangle with a rabid capybara in a dark alley, would you?"

"I don't know. But—"

"I saw him interviewed. He said he researched it pretty thoroughly. And his publisher, you don't think they checked this out? Look, you know I'm behind you.

You're good for Minnesota, just like I am, and Minnesota in turn is good to us. This guy with the big feet, I've got no more love for him than you do, but it seems like you're the only one who has a problem with his story being true."

"What if I could prove it wasn't?" said Bromstad, narrowing his eyes and angling his head down significantly, unfortunately undermining the effect of the look by hiding it from Herzog under the brim of his hat.

Herzog lowered himself to see under it. "Then I'd be behind you one thousand and ten percent."

"And you'd see to it that he was brought to justice?"

"Swiftly and surely."

"Lying to his trusting fellow Minnesotans like that, it's inhuman."

"It's in-Minnesotan, too, to coin a phrase. I don't like that kind of thing."

"What could you do to a fellow like that?" asked Bromstad, pretending to mull.

"Well . . ."

"Yes?"

"Say, you're not suggesting . . . ?"

"I could be."

"The Minnesota Cultural Sedition Act?"

"I am."

"The Minnesota Cultural Sedition Act," Herzog repeated ominously. "Do I have the power to invoke it?"

"You're the governor."

"I am, aren't I?" said Herzog. "Yes, if he's guilty, we could invoke the Minnesota Cultural Sedition act. It might be fun. Liven this state up a little. Steak?"

CHAPTER 15

About the four strangers in the Taconite Saloon, one thing was known for certain: They had recently shopped at Pamida, the discount store in Fishville, eighteen miles away. This was evident to the others present by the fact that all four were wearing identical brands of flannel shirts that had very obviously just been removed from their packaging (there was even a piece of cellophane tape featuring a redundant XL pattern adhered to one back). One was a red check, another yellow, and the two remaining were blue, and identical, and none looked very comfortable in their sizing-stiffened, almost crunchy states. The men's just-off-the-shelf blue jeans looked even more oppressive, and those who beheld them felt a firm conviction that some very uncomfortable pinching simply had to be going on beneath.

The strangers were eerily similar, though not identical, as though they'd been created in a factory whose quality control had slipped and begun allowing previously tight machine tolerances to loosen somewhat. They had about them a serious purpose, but for some reason appeared not to want that to be evident to the people of Holey and so put on a feigned nonchalance that was as stiff as their clothing.

"Ha, ha, ha, ha," laughed one in a stilted, nearly chilling manner as they walked in. "That's very funny, Vagns." The man it was directed at, Vagns, it seemed, did not appear to have said anything. They took four stools at the bar, and Ralph approached with as much courtesy as he could muster for such an odd quartet.

"What can I get you?" he asked, starting with Ülo.

"Oh, dear, dear, dear," said Ülo, looking above the bar, ostensibly for a drink menu that did not exist. "Oh, it is early, so I'll just have a Klar Høker snaps—Aalborg, if you have it, please," he added. He was immediately elbowed strongly by the man in the yellow shirt who sat next to him. "Or, actually, just a beer."

"I've got Grain Belt, Grain Belt Premium, Bud Light, and Leinenkugel's."

"Leinenkugel's? Is that Austrian?"

"Nnnnooo. Chippewa Falls, I think."

"I'll try one of those."

The other three echoed his order, and Ralph filled them all.

Conversation was light at the Taconite and decidedly lighter among the four strangers. Ralph leaned against the back of the bar, employing his remarkable ability to simultaneously stare at and think of nothing in particular. The four peered vacantly around the bar, their heads shaking, pleasant smiles on their faces. The man in the yellow shirt spoke.

"Ha, ha, ha, ha," he said.

This earned him a look from Ralph. "You all right?" he asked.

"Oh, yes," said the man. "I was just thinking of something Ülo had said earlier."

Ralph nodded, a gesture acknowledging that he had heard the response while at the same time confessing that he found it spectacularly uninteresting. He resumed his previous activities.

"So this is Holey?" the man said.

" 'S that?" asked Ralph.

"Holey? This is it?"

"Yes, it is," Ralph confirmed.

"Wasn't—wasn't there a mine or something here? Something like that?"

"Yes, there was."

"*Ja. Ja*, I thought so. My name is Jørgen," he said, extending his hand.

"Ralph," said Ralph, accepting the handshake in a Ralph-like manner; that is, betraying nothing that would indicate how he felt about meeting Jørgen for the first time.

"These are my friends Vagns, Per, and Ülo." Ralph greeted them all, and there was some difficulty getting him near a proper pronunciation of Ülo.

"Where you guys from?" Ralph asked.

"Minneapolis," Jørgen answered.

"I live in St. Paul, actually," Per added, looking over the tops of his glasses.

"Well, welcome to Holey," Ralph said, and he meant it, though perhaps with somewhat muted passion.

The men from Minneapolis (and St. Paul) resumed their looking around as Ralph got back to the business of staring.

"How's the fish—" Jørgen was just starting to say, but Ralph put up a finger indicating that he would be right back, as he was being summoned at the end of the bar by another patron who put in an order for a Jack and Coke and something called a Slow, Comfortable Screw. Ralph poured the drinks and returned.

"What were you saying?" he asked Jørgen.

"Oh. I was just inquiring how the fishing had been around here in Holey."

"Season ain't open yet. Unless you want to go after rock bass," Ralph said, in a tone suggesting that to go after rock bass would be something akin to dancing down Main Street in a powdered wig and bustier.

"No," Jørgen objected, "I don't want to go after rock bass. No thank you!" He laughed at this, and, inexplicably, so did his companions.

Jørgen and his friends had loitered at the bar for nearly an hour when Ralph suddenly produced small tubs of pasteurized processed cheese spread and set four of them at regular intervals on the bar, following them up with individual sleeves of saltines.

"For me?" Jørgen asked.

"For everyone," said Ralph.

Jørgen had never seen or tasted cheese in paste form before (he'd been brought up on Havartis, Esroms, flavorful Kumiosts, and Danish Blues), so he was somewhat mystified as to how he was to handle Ralph's gift. He picked up a tub of cheese, looking for directions.

"All-natural cheese spread. Port wine flavored," he said out loud to no one in particular. He opened it and plunged a cracker in with gusto, snapping it in half and polluting the pristine surface of the cheese spread with the broken piece and bits of shattered saltine detritus. "Son of a . . ." he said, displaying irritation for the first time since entering the Taconite Saloon. (Inside, he was filled with loathing over having to touch pasteurized processed cheese food, as he was convinced of the fact that Americans' consumption of such an abomination was clear evidence of their moral failings.)

As he passed by, Ralph noticed Jørgen's difficulties with the spread and, letting loose with a subtle but perceptible sigh, fetched four cheese knives from under the bar and set them near each of the tubs, placing the one near Jørgen with an especially heavy hand.

"This is a very thick cheese," Jørgen offered as his excuse.

"Yeah," Ralph concurred.

Jørgen and his associates responded to an unspoken command to consume and pretend to enjoy some of the offered spreads, probably reasoning that it was a way to endear themselves to the locals. Halfway through masticating his second cheese-encrusted cracker, Jørgen resumed his small talk with Ralph, who was again leaning against the bar.

"Mmm, this is very tangy and good."

Ralph nodded.

"Say, that mine, isn't that the one that that guy wrote a book about—or something like that?" Jørgen asked, brushing cracker crumbs from his new shirt.

"Yeah, that's the one."

"It involves a large killer rodent, if my memory serves me."

"Yeah, it sure does."

"Yes . . . yes," said Jørgen, hoping that doing so would lead Ralph to give up more information. It did not work. "Yes," he continued somewhat desperately, "yes." After a moment he added, "Yes. Seems like an interesting fellow, that guy. Saw something on him on a television program not terribly long ago." Ralph was unmoved by this piece of news, so Jørgen attempted a more direct approach. "Do you ever see him up this way?"

"Now and again," said Ralph. That was the end of his information on the subject, and Jørgen, who wanted to remain inconspicuous, decided not to press further. They finished their drinks, thanked Ralph, and left, huddling on the sidewalk out in front to discuss their next move.

"That was a big, giant, fat dead end," asserted Ülo. "And the cheese was ungodly."

"True, yes. It tasted of freshly expelled vomit. And I admit our subject was not as forthcoming as I would have liked. But it should not be that difficult to find out where he's staying, if only we keep our eyes and our ears open. Our next move should be—"

"Jørgen! Jørgen, traveler is at your six!" warned Per.

"What?" Jørgen said irritably. He turned to look where Per was pointing, and indeed Jack Ryback was striding toward them in the company of two other men. One was the mustachioed fellow from the park meeting, the other was King Leo, looking fresh and fetching in a peasant blouse of a delicate

ocean hue. They were closing in on the knot of Danish men
fairly quickly.

"Okay, move! Move!" said Jørgen urgently, underscoring his
command by pushing his comrades roughly, first Per, then
Vagns. "Come on. Come on."

"Ow," said Vagns, who did not like being pushed, especially
when the pusher had a hangnail and his push had missed its
mark, the jagged nail raking open a small cut on his top lip,
which is precisely what had happened.

"You must move now," Jørgen ordered. They walked
briskly down the sidewalk, away from the approaching author
and his strange entourage, ducking into an open shop, the
Jurkovich Family Pharmacy. The bell tinkled as the foursome
tumbled into the store, invading the quiet, Muzak tinged air.

"Ow. You cut me," said Vagns incredulously.

"Quiet, you little baby," said Jørgen. He looked around to
notice that the only person in the store, a placid-looking man of
forty wearing a blue smock, was staring at them with a pleasant
but subtly accusing look.

"Help you find something?" he said, and all were aware that
he really meant "Don't bring your trouble in here."

"We are just looking," Jørgen said, and he began nosing
around the nearest rack, which happened to be an area displaying barrettes, colorful brushes, various hair ornaments, and
ponytail scrunchies. He was pretending to examine a purple
Goodie-brand nylon hairbrush—as the others looked on—
when the bell tinkled again and the very three men they were
attempting to elude walked into the store, their progress
stopped short by the presence of the four Danes blocking their
way in the cramped entrance.

"Whoa," said Ponty.

"Hey, man," said King Leo as Jørgen, with terror in his eyes, looked up at him.

"Full house, huh?" Jack said energetically to them all.

"Ah. So sorry," said Jørgen. "Just needed to . . ." he said weakly, and grabbed a yellow flower-print scrunchie off the display rack. Per, Vagns, and Ülo just stared nervously. In order to clear a path for the threesome, Jørgen and company walked toward the register, their leader setting the scrunchie on the counter, ostensibly with the intent of purchasing it. Jørgen had assumed that this would allow Jack Ryback and his friends to spread out into the store, but they only followed the four up to the counter. Noticing this, Jørgen said nervously, "Ah. Would you . . . ?" and gestured weakly toward the cash register.

"No, you go ahead there," said Jack.

"Yes, please, we are in no particular hurry," said King Leo.

"Thank you, most gracious of you," said Jørgen, pushing the scrunchie several inches farther toward the clerk, who didn't notice because he was watching Vagns dab at the bleeding cut on his top lip.

"Um . . . you need something for that?" said the clerk.

"I suppose I should bandage it," said Vagns, pulling his hand away to reveal a red smear.

"Yeah, mouth wounds really bleed," said the clerk, who walked to the end of his counter, lifted a hinged section, and hustled off, leaving the seven men standing in a loose and uncomfortable knot at the front of his store.

"Sorry," said Jørgen, shrugging.

"*Ja,* sorry," said Vagns, from under his hand.

"No, no, no, no, don't give it second thought," said King Leo. "Happened to me more times than I care to remember."

Ponty looked at King Leo curiously for a second when he'd finished saying that.

"How'd you do it?" Jack asked Vagns.

"I don't remember," Vagns replied vaguely.

"How . . . how long has it been bleeding?" asked Ponty.

"Not long," said Vagns. "Oh, I remember. I must have cut it when I was having some cheese and crackers at the pub down the street." Jørgen was thinking that, on the whole, Vagns had done a less than acceptable job of coming up with a better explanation than "He pushed me," but he would not be able to say so until some later time.

"You . . . you cut yourself with cheese and crackers?" Ponty asked.

"Perhaps a jagged cracker edge. It's all a blur to me now," Vagns replied.

The clerk returned with bandages, a small generic yellow tube of triple-antibiotic ointment, and two cotton balls.

"Will that do you?" he asked.

"That looks dandy," said Jørgen, though the clerk was talking to Vagns.

"Okay . . . bandages," said the clerk, ringing a price into the register. "The ointment . . . and a scrunchie. The cotton balls are on the house."

"Thank you ever so much," said Vagns, reaching for them.

"That'll be two eighty-five," said the clerk. Jørgen paid as Vagns swabbed at his lip with one of the complimentary cotton balls. "Need a bag?"

"No thank you," said Vagns. "I will probably dress it here."

"Let's dress it in the car," suggested Jørgen strongly.

"Fine," Vagns acquiesced, leaving it unclear to the clerk whether or not they needed a bag.

"So . . . should I bag it up?"

"Yes," said Vagns.

"It won't be necessary," said Jørgen, snatching the items off the counter and hustling his crew out of the store.

"Strange fellows," King Leo said before turning his attention to the clerk. "Say, my man, I need a high-quality stain lifter to hand-wash soil out of mohair, some Chakra Pure-Fume Body Mist by Aveda, and I need these three prescriptions for amoxicillin filled, please."

CHAPTER 16

Much like Mr. Spock playing a difficult tridimensional chess match against an intellectually lively opponent, Ponty was feeling assaulted on many levels, and consequently he was having a hard time keeping track of the many stresses he was supposed to be under at any given time. He could have reverted to a general sense of impending doom, but Ponty was into the details.

At present he was worried because he had not been on a date in more than thirty-five years, and that last one had ended with tensely and grudgingly accepted apologies from Ponty. They were necessitated by an incident, mid-date, when a lackluster investigation into just who had jostled their dining table, causing bisque to slosh freely into his companion's lap, had centered, unfairly, on Ponty and not on the large and clumsy-thighed passerby who had actually done the jostling and caused the offending bisque to leap from its bowl. The whole incident was especially upsetting because Ponty had laid out considerable sums—which were scarce at the time—for the dinner and was unable to enjoy his pricey lobster thermidor with the unpleasantness hanging in the air.

Because it had been more than a third of a century since he'd asked a woman out, he'd made some mistakes with Sandi. Asking her casually if she'd "like to go bowling sometime" would have been a more effective lead-in if there were a bowling alley within a hundred miles of Holey, but there was not. This caused Sandi to interpret his question as a bad joke and to look at him with slight hostility. This in turn caused Ponty to sweat and fidget before recovering enough to ask her if she'd like to have dinner. She correctly interpreted this advance, graciously agreed, and Ponty had then retreated to begin recuperating from the stress of it all.

It was now time for their date, and Ponty felt like a foot soldier ordered to take a heavily fortified pillbox. It was a quiet and cool evening, a quarter moon visible in the still-bright sky as he piloted the Tempo to an avenue just off of Main Street, pulled into her driveway, and approached the house, compulsively attempting to smooth his hair down on the way to the door, to little effect. His hair had always had its own plan, an indecipherable internal logic as to how it wanted to situate itself on his head that no amount of tonics, combs, or smoothings could alter. Looking down at his left hand, he noticed that his knuckles were white, meaning that he had the flowers he'd purchased in an unnecessary death grip, so he relaxed it. He entered through a screen porch that had apparently settled more aggressively than the house, causing it to tilt alarmingly. He felt like he was climbing uphill to get to her front door. Ponty's fist paused a few inches from the door and then knocked cautiously. After half a minute with no discernible result, he debated whether to knock again, deciding that it would be better to wait so as not to appear too forward. He stood perfectly still, listening intently, for a full two minutes before knocking again, taking care to make it sharper in volume but still friendly in its effect. This second series of knocks fell short of its aim as well. He tried a third time, wincing from his discomfort with having to make such a potentially offensive racket. Four minutes passed, and still the door remained thoroughly unanswered.

After some torturous introspection, he decided to test the door and, finding it unlocked, pushed it open no more than a demure two inches. "Hello?" he yelled. "Sandi?" He steeled his resolve and took, to his mind, the extreme liberty of opening the door enough to push his head through. He tried to keep his tone light. "Hell-ooo?" he said, with mirth in his voice. "It's Ponty," he announced, but nothing changed. Pushing his shoulders through, he tried again. "I'm here!" For the first time in his life he used two words he had never used in combination: "Yoo-hoo," he said, and followed that up with "Woo-hoo." He glanced about Sandi's living room and felt the shock a man often feels when seeing so many knickknacks, tchotchkes, craft items, homey plaques, and decoupage all in one concentrated area. Everywhere he looked, notions and bric-a-brac assaulted his eyes. There were baubles, bibelots, and novelty items on every imaginable surface, many of them cat-based, though not exclusively. Before he could check himself, he had entered the room, a dazed look on his face such as the one Carter must have had when entering Tutankhamen's tomb.

Ponty saw Longaberger baskets and Snow Baby collections elbow to elbow with Hummel figurines and porcelain cats in various adorable poses. There were needlepoint wall hangings, doilies, and plants, potpourri in baskets and bowls, candles of various hues and shapes, all fragrant. He was having a difficult time comprehending all the trumpery. It made his eyes hurt.

Setting the flowers on the couch, he moved farther in, drawn there by an item on a half wall between the living room and dining room. It was perched next to a crocheted beanbag calico cat and a plaque reading IF YOU DON'T FEEL CLOSE TO GOD, GUESS WHO MOVED? It appeared to be a loaf of bread tied in red ribbons like a present, and when he picked it up, he concluded that it was indeed a loaf of bread that had been mummified in some manner unknown to him. He was turning it over in his hands, musing on what might drive a human being to preserve and decorate a loaf of bread, when he heard a sharp cry.

"Ponty!" said Sandi.

"Yes!" said Ponty, for there was no use denying it.

She was standing in a doorway toward the back of the house wearing overalls, a flannel shirt, and leather and canvas work gloves.

"What are you doing?" she asked.

"Oh, sorry, just examining the bread," he answered weakly. He held the calcified loaf out to her without realizing what he was doing. She approached him and gave the loaf an irritated, dismissive look. He withdrew it nervously, set it back down, and smoothed his hair.

"What are you doing in my house?" she asked.

"Yes. Well. I knocked. Quite a lot, really, and you didn't answer. So I thought you might be in the shower."

"So you came in?"

"No. Not to see you in the shower. I just—I'm sorry."

"And you have a mustache."

"Yes. I have to from now on. I'm Earl Topperson, remember?" She nodded in understanding, while leaving open the possibility that she still thought him insane. "Sandi, I'm sorry."

"It's all right," she said, though it clearly wasn't *all* right. She seemed to have more questions and perhaps a bit of resentment.

For the first time Ponty noticed her appearance, which suggested that yard work had just been, or was about to be, done.

"Ready?" he asked. "Or am I early? I mean, you look fine to me. I don't mean—"

"Ready? Ready for what?"

"Our d—" he said, and stopped himself. "Our thing. Our, you know, the dinner thing."

She relaxed. "Ponty. Honey"—she was using it sarcastically—"we said Saturday, remember?"

"Oh, yes. And if I'm not mistaken, today is in fact Saturday." He was beginning to perspire.

Sandi laughed a large laugh. Ponty looked at his watch for the date, even though it had no date feature, something he should have known instinctively as he'd worn it nearly every day for eighteen years.

"Ponty, today's Friday!" she laughed.

"No. No. I—" He looked at his watch again. "Is it?"

"Oh, it is, yes."

"No."

"Yes. It is." She was giggling.

"You're putting me on?"

"I wouldn't do that."

Ponty was still skeptical, so Sandi led him into her kitchen (it was decorated in a slightly more muted manner than the living and dining rooms, though it was still pretty adorable) and showed him a calendar, coaching him through the days of the week. Finally he could no longer deny the truth.

"I've come on the wrong day!" he said, looking as though he'd been recently hit with a carnival hammer.

"It's all right. It's a relief to know why you were in my house. I was thinking of macing you."

Ponty was focusing on his own misery and didn't hear her. "How could I do that?" he wondered, in awe at his own ineptitude.

"Happens to the best of us," she said. "You want to stay for some coffee?"

"No. No thanks. I'd better go," he said, his voice sounding dazed and hollow.

"Oh, come on. Stay. You can help me stack wood."

"I'd—I'd probably cause the pile to cave in and take our lives. The wrong day!" he said with amazement.

"Come on," she said, and, taking his hand, lead him past the tidy little kitchen and out through the mudroom into her expansive backyard, which was several acres of mowed grass abutting the deep pinewood beyond. To their left stood her one-car garage, a fairly decrepit old thing that listed dangerously, even more than her porch. On the right was an open woodshed, nothing much more than some green-treated poles sunk into the ground, steadied with some tongue and groove siding, and topped off with corrugated tin. Parked near it was an ancient gray Ford 8N tractor dragging a plywood trailer filled with a load of split elm.

"Make yourself useful," she said, dragging a log from the

trailer and tossing it to him. He caught it and those that followed and gamely began stacking them into the shed, even though it was not easy on his tender hands.

"I'm glad you messed up, Ponty. Stacking wood always makes me feel a little lonely," she said.

This embarrassed him, so he responded with a trite saw. "Well, many hands make light work," he said.

"I guess—hut, hut," she said to warn him of an incoming log.

"Oof, I got it."

"So I hear you been turkey hunting with Ralph?" she asked, offering Ponty a chance to brag.

"Oh, yeah. We got one nice tom, though we still haven't filled the other tag," he said, like a wizened old hunter who'd seen it all.

"Did you dress it, or did Ralph?"

"Oooh. Ralph did. I don't think I could handle that. Yuck. No, he's got it in his chest freezer now."

"Well, maybe we can all enjoy that turkey together sometime."

"Yeah, that'd be nice."

Sandi paused her labor and leaned against the trailer. "Oh, boy. This is gonna be a cool night, but it sure is nice now," she said, looking up at the sky. The sun was fading, the swallows were diving about the tops of the garage, and over the trees came the lonely call of the loon.

"That's all the way from the lake," said Sandi, smiling wistfully.

"It's nice," said Ponty, rubbing his hands together to warm them. "You never hear that in the city. Course, you probably

get pretty lonely for bus fumes from time to time," he joked
tentatively.

Sandi laughed. "Oh, there are plenty of fumes around these
parts, if you look hard enough." She grabbed a log, and they
resumed their work. Sandi began laughing to herself again and
did not notice that Ponty had interrupted the rhythm of their
work to do some fussy straightening of the logs he'd stacked.
Sandi turned to throw a log and, noticing he wasn't ready, awkwardly stopped her momentum, losing her grip on the log and
dropping it squarely on her toe.

"Ow, ow, ow!" she said, falling to the ground.

"Oh, oh! I'm sorry," said Ponty, realizing he was at least
partly responsible. He bent to minister to her but hadn't any
idea what propriety allowed him to do, so he simply hovered
over her nervously.

"Ow, ow, ow!" she went on, though she seemed to be laughing through the obvious pain. "That was so clumsy of me."

"It's me. There are always accidents and injuries when I'm
around," he said miserably.

"No, that's me! Ow, ow, take off my shoe, will you?" she
said, gripping her left leg, and it was now obvious that she was
at least half laughing.

Ponty was taken aback by her request. He had never in his
life unshod a woman and had no idea how to go about it. He fid-
dled lightly with the shoelace, accomplishing little.

"Come on, just pull off the shoe, will you?" She laughed.

"Yes, yes. Of course," he said, giving her light blue Etonic
tennis shoe a chaste and gentle pull.

"Come on. Get it off, will you?"

He then took the liberty that she had offered and gave her

shoe a good pull. It came off, and he set it aside, though there was still a short, terry-cloth sock to deal with, and Ponty hoped that the task wouldn't fall to him.

"Take off the sock. Is it broken?" she said.

"Hang on," he said, and his shaking hands orbited her foot unsurely.

"Ponty, it's not a tracheotomy. Would you just check to see if it's broken?"

"Yes, yes. I'm on it," he said, and with a quick, bold yank, he removed her sock. He was somewhat shocked to discover that her toenails were painted an unsubtle red.

"Ow, easy!" She laughed again, still clutching her leg. "Well?"

"How would I know if it was broken?" he asked.

"I think it would be written on there—*just look at it, will you?*"

"Which one is it?"

"It's the second one, I think," she said, and wiggled her toes. "Ow, yes."

"Second from which end?" asked Ponty.

This made Sandi giggle. "From the big toe in, of course."

"Right." Ponty gingerly touched her toe with his forefinger. "Does that hurt?"

"Did you do anything?"

"Yes. Here," he said, very gently pinching the end of it between thumb and forefinger and simultaneously blushing.

"Oh, I feel that."

"Sorry. Sorry," he said, withdrawing his hand.

"No, no. It's already feeling better. I don't think it's broken," she said, and sat up with effort. "Just caught it right on the end. It hurt."

"Yes, I see that," he said.

"Shut up, you," she said, and began pulling on her sock. "Let's go have some coffee. Hand me my shoe."

She limped into the house on a blushing Ponty's shoulder, and they talked in Sandi's kitchen for several hours over her terribly prepared, cheap coffee.

RALPH'S '81 MALIBU was smoking impressively as it pulled up to Cabin 4 at the Bugling Moose. He'd been meaning to get new rings and perhaps replace the head gasket on the Malibu's somewhat quirky 305, five-liter engine, but then he didn't. He had grown used to the smoke and the noise, but he didn't like to go on long trips because either one or the other, or a combination of the two, gave him a dull but substantial headache and, strangely, made him very hungry. He killed the engine, but it pinged and groaned under its own power for a good while, shaking the frame of the car, making it roll like a sailboat on its tremendously mushy, worn-out suspension, until finally it died and the rolling settled to a level safe enough for him to disembark.

He approached the cabin and was about to knock when the door opened and Jack appeared, an owly look on his face. Ralph also noticed that his hair was slightly moist-looking and stacked higher on his head than was normal. It contributed further to an overall owl-like appearance.

"Hey," said Ralph. "How'd you know I was here?"

"Your car announced you."

"Your hair looks funny," Ralph said without malice.

"I accidentally used a very powerful humectant."

"You kind of look like an owl."

Jack stared at him. "Are we ready to go?" he asked.

"Sure."

Ralph opened the rear door for Jack, made a gesture for him to enter that Jack guessed was supposed to be eloquent. They drove the few hundred yards to King Leo's cabin, and Ralph killed the engine, but its ensuing groans and explosions were so intense that the men stayed in the car to avoid injury until, after one final backfire, it quieted.

Before they had even made it to the door, it was flung open by an ebullient King Leo.

"You have got to be Ralph!" King Leo pronounced.

"Yup," Ralph agreed.

King Leo fairly ran past Jack, bounded at Ralph, and grasped his hand. "Pleased to meet you, Mr. Ralph. I'm King Leo, but you can call me the Secretary of the Pleasury, the Master of the Mattress, the Bedouin of the Boudoir, the Smooth Brown Czar of the Rocking Car, or President Erect of the Republic of Love! Woooo!"

"Yup. Heard a lot about you. Your car is ready."

"Yes! This is excellent! Jack, Jack, Jack, Jack, Jack. How are you, my friend?"

"Good. How are you, King Leo?"

"I am dead solid fine. May I say, your hair is disturbing me in some way I can't put my finger on."

"I borrowed some of Wigs's hair junk. Things went wrong. Mistakes were made."

King Leo sniffed at Jack's head. "Is that rapeseed and honey volume-building humectant?"

"Yes, so I found out."

"Jack, Jack, Jack. That's just not the right product for your thick hair. It's much too heavy. I wish you'd come to me."

"I didn't mean to use it. I grabbed the wrong stuff."

"Well, ask me next time before you rub anything into your hair. Promise me? I'll give you my personal cell number."

"I'll do that."

"You promise?"

"Yes."

King Leo took a long look at Ralph's car. "Mr. Ralph, my friend, is that an '81 Malibu?"

"Yup."

"With the 267 engine?"

"The 305."

"Mm. Kind of rare, isn't it, Mr. Ralph?"

"I guess most of them had the V-6s, but this is just the stock 305. But I'm thinking of putting in a 350,'cause this thing's almost shot."

"They had a lot of transmission problems, didn't they?"

"I guess. When I bought it from Dan, he said he'd put in a T-400 tranny, but—"

"King Leo, how do you know this?" Jack interrupted.

"Well, now, King Leo is a vast and complicated temple of knowledge, and if he reveals his secrets, his powers are diminished," King Leo said quite seriously.

"Did you work at a garage?" asked Jack.

"Is it possible that before time began, King Leo had a two-summer stint at Bosco's Specialty Automotive Repair? I cannot say," he said cryptically. "I simply cannot say."

"Can we get going?" said Jack.

"Yes, yes, yes, yes, I suppose we should. I'm very excited."

"Is the rest of the band coming?" Jack asked.

"They're very tired. They asked me to convey their regrets and to let everyone know that they'll be napping."

Ralph again opened the rear door and made his clumsily grand gesture inviting them into the interior of his Malibu.

"I'll sit in front," Jack offered.

"No. Please. You are my guest," said Ralph, redoing the gawky gesture, and Jack then discovered how low his threshold of tolerance for that move really was. He felt strongly that if Ralph never did it again, it would be too soon for his taste.

"Thank you" was all he said, and he climbed in next to King Leo.

"Ralph, this is a fine car," said King Leo once Ralph had settled his thick body in behind the wheel.

"Thank you, King Leo."

"Ralph, it smells like gas back here. Gas and sausage. Mostly I'm worried about the gas smell. Think everything is all right?" Jack asked.

"Ummm, yeah. Yeah, I'm sure it's fine."

"I don't want to step on these magazines. Can I move 'em?" Jack asked.

"Which ones are they?" said Ralph, seeming puzzled.

Jack pulled several off the floor. "Um, *Field and Stream, Popular Mechanics,* and *Sports Afield* from August of '97."

"Oh, that's okay. You can step on 'em."

Jack set them back on the floor and settled into the seat, only to have the process interrupted by a hard object that was jabbing him in the small of the back. He reached behind him and yanked out an eight-inch piece of angled high-impact plastic.

"Do you need this?" he asked, holding the piece up for Ralph's inspection in the rearview mirror.

"Hm. That's the handle for this cooler I had one time, I think," he said, somehow imagining that this would be of interest to Jack. "Um, I'll take it," he said reaching back. He put it next to him in the front seat and then cranked over the Malibu's aging engine. It did not cooperate immediately but rather made a sound similar to that of Watson's original steam engine, before he had made refinements. Ralph tried again, and this time it sounded much like a printing press being fed into a wood chipper.

"Ralph," said King Leo, "as a favor to me, press the accelerator halfway down and try again."

"Okay, King Leo," Ralph agreed, and he did as King Leo said. The engine turned over, made a sound like a front-end loader being demolished by a larger front-end loader, then caught and started. "That's the ticket," Ralph said happily over the noise of the engine.

They drove toward town, King Leo alternately chatting with Ralph (at high volume) about cars or lecturing Jack about hair products. As they turned onto Main Street, the small crowd that had gathered in downtown Sjogren Park cheered, but none of the trio could hear it over the din of the Impala's 305. Ralph again attempted to kill the engine, but it had other ideas. Sandi approached the car, prepared to officially greet Holey's famous guest, but it was still smoking and moving pretty wildly on its springs, and she didn't dare get too close and risk smoke inhalation and a head injury. Finally it settled down, and Ralph lumbered out and opened the door for King Leo (Jack waited for a moment, then got out on his own). The town cheered. The high school band, which consisted of a sousaphone player, a flautist, and a drummer, played "Tijuana Taxi" (it was the only pop song they knew). King Leo emerged from the Impala.

"My, my, my, my, my," he said, waving at the people. "Hello, Holey. Are you ready for a revival?" he shouted.

"Yeah," said some of the crowd.

"Sure," said a few others.

Sandi led him up to the small riser that was to act as their dais, motioned for him to sit in the place of honor, and approached the microphone.

"Welcome—" she began, and the sound system squealed out a hellacious feedback noise. The boy wearing the sousaphone shrugged it off, trotted over to the PA's amp, and made some adjustments while Sandi smiled pleasantly at him.

"Thank you, Erik. Welcome, all of you, and thank you for helping me to welcome King Leo. We're all big fans of your music and your dancing, and I know we all saw *NastyFantastic* and your wonderful performance in that more than once."

The population of Holey cheered loudly and then broke into spontaneous clapping to show their love of *NastyFantastic*. King Leo beamed. "Oh, stop it, now. Stop it. Come on, now," he demurred. But the clapping would not stop, so King Leo rose, went to the edge of the dais, and took a bow. When the applause subsided, he sat back down and Sandi continued.

"As mayor of Holey, I would like to present you, King Leo, with the key to our city."

As the applause broke out afresh, she pulled from behind the podium a three-foot-long plywood key, spray-painted gold. King Leo stood to accept it, but before he could actually grasp the key, Sandi pulled it back a bit and spoke to him sotto voce.

"You know what? Ralph just made it this morning, and the paint's still a little tacky. Might get on your hands. Why don't you let me hang on to it till tomorrow?"

"Oh, yes, yes, yes, yes, yes, of course."

"Sorry."

"Not at all, Your Honor."

"You're kind."

"My pleasure."

She faced the crowd again. "And now perhaps Mr. Leo would like to say a few words?"

"Yes, yes, yes, yes, yes, yes, thank you, Mayor Sandi. I'm very, very, very honored. You have a northern paradise here, and I thank you for making me feel welcome. This place you live is special. I feel the spirit of Edward Lynch and . . . and that other guy as I walk the streets of Holey, and I know that you all have a funk in your soul. Thank you," he concluded, gesturing to the key that Sandi was holding.

There was more applause, some spontaneous hooting, and one loud "Woooo."

Sandi then presented him with various small gift certificates and coupons: a free shampoo and haircut from Shear Amazement salon, a thirty-five-dollar gift certificate from Bill's Red Owl grocery store in nearby Darby, and 20 percent off his next prescription from the Jurkovich Family Pharmacy. King Leo thanked the town of Holey profusely, probably saying the actual words "thank you" more than 180 times during the presentations.

"Thank you, thank you, thank you all, thank you," he concluded, and was about to leave the dais when Sandi called him back.

"We have one more special gift for you. Earl, would you kindly bring that out?"

Ponty appeared from the side of the dais carrying something large, brown, and substantial and stood near King Leo, who offered him a goofy smile. Ponty in turn offered him a grudging nod.

"We would like to present you with a very special piece of Holey history. Please accept this giant rat pelt on behalf of all the people of our town."

The good people of Holey responded with as much raucous applause as can be mustered up by a crowd of fewer than forty. King Leo was absolutely thrilled with the preserved ratskin.

"I—I can't believe it. Is this . . . ?" he stammered.

"Yes. That's the one and only rat that attacked and stalked Ed Lynch in that mine so many years ago."

"This is it? This is the one he killed by the saloon?"

"Yes. There has been, and hopefully will be, only one giant rat in Holey—knock wood!"

"And you're giving it to me?"

"We know you will treat it with the respect it deserves."

"Oh, I will, I will, I will. This is—I'm speechless."

The crowd again let loose with unrestrained enthusiasm for the funk star and his new animal hide.

"This is clearly a sign from His Funkiness," King Leo said rapturously, looking up to the sky.

The crowd agreed and showed it by applauding wildly. The only people in Holey who were unenthusiastic were the four strangers in the stiff Pamida flannel shirts standing toward the back wearing odd and similar looks.

t was getting on toward evening on a warm and perpetually cloudy day as Ralph and Ponty crept like commandos through the woods fringing the Bugling Moose. Ralph, in the lead, stopped up short, and Ponty, who was trailing behind while checking their perimeters, smashed into Ralph's prodigious back area with some force, causing Ponty to fall backward.

"What was that?" Ralph hissed.

"Ow! That was me, you goon. Why did you stop?" Ponty asked as he struggled to his feet.

"I felt something," Ralph whispered.

"That was me crashing into you because you stopped. Wait, what did you feel before I crashed into you?"

"Maybe it was just you crashing into me."

"Then why did you stop in the first place?"

"Oh, right. I thought I saw something."

"What was it? Was it the police?" Ponty asked, his pulse rate rising even further.

"I don't think so. It was moving in those trees over there."

"Let's get going," Ponty said, and the pair took off in the direction of Jack's cabin.

Ralph stopped up short again, but Ponty avoided collision by steering himself around to the right of his large partner's back.

"What now?" said Ponty.

"There," Ralph answered, pointing into the thick brush behind the cabin area. Ponty couldn't see anything other than brush.

"Is it a turkey?" he asked.

"Not likely. Not around here."

"Come on," said Ponty, leading the way to Jack's cabin.

JACK WAS SITTING in a padded rocking chair reading an article entitled "Monster Crappies: Hit 'Em Hard with Spinners" from *In-Fisherman* magazine when he heard a light, almost effete, tapping on his back window. He looked up but, seeing nothing, went back to reading about slip bobbers. Presently the tapping resumed. This time he looked up to see Ralph's and Ponty's faces peering through the panes, Ponty's looking annoyed, Ralph's looking characteristically Ralph-ish. Jack leaned forward to see better as Ponty was mouthing words to him. He walked to the window and opened it.

" 'Open up' *what?*" Jack asked.

"I said, 'Open up, you idiot.' "

"Ponty! There's no need for that."

"I'm sorry. I'm sorry. I'm very nervous. We saw something out here. May we come in?"

"You have face paint on," Jack observed.

"Yes. We came through the back way. Didn't want to be seen."

"Sometimes I use it for turkey hunting," Ralph added.

"You look like Special Forces," Jack said.

"So can we come in?" Ponty pressed.

"Sure, sure," Jack said.

"Your bunkmates are gone?" Ponty asked, spying one of Wigs's lamé jackets hanging on the coat hook.

"Oh, yeah, they're at band practice. They'll be gone for another few hours," Jack said.

"They still call it 'band practice'? Even at this level?" asked Ponty.

"What else you gonna call it?" Jack said while backing up to give them room. Ponty scrambled through, and Jack helped him up.

Ralph looked at the window frame doubtfully. "I don't know. . . ." he said. "What if I make it halfway and stick?"

"Would you just come through?" Ponty said with irritation.

"No. I'm serious. It's happened before."

"What are you, Winnie the Pooh?" said Ponty. "Just climb through!"

"Why don't you come in through the front door?" Jack suggested. "No one's around."

Ralph looked questioningly at Ponty.

"Fine. Fine. Just come around—quickly and quietly."

Once they'd gathered Ralph inside, they lowered the lights and took chairs around the kitchen table.

"I think it's going rather well," Jack said.

"What?" said Ponty. "An entire town just presented a bearskin to King Leo and told him it was cut off a rat in 1865. How long do you think it's going to be before he finds out the truth?"

"Ponty, he thinks squirrels are hamsters. I think that buys us some time."

"So he doesn't suspect he's being had?"

"No, he's happy as a clam. He's glad he came to Holey. Now, listen, here's what's going to happen. He'll do his whacked-out, whatever-it-is revival, then he'll leave, and after a spell, a month or two or more, things will get back to normal."

"Well, perhaps there's something to that," said Ponty. "But all these tourists, the press—don't you think someone's going to start poking around and asking questions?"

"Let 'em ask. They're not gonna hear anything from our people. I mean, who's gonna give us up under pressure from the Eyewitness News Team's entertainment reporter?"

"I won't crack," said Ralph.

"See? Ralph won't crack. These Holeyites are made of sterner stuff than that. As long as the money flows, they're on our side."

"What about King Leo's bandmates? Are they so willing to believe along with him?"

"Have you spoken to Wigs for any period of time? Ever held a conversation with Billy Moonbeam?"

"No."

"What about Tarzan Moe? Ever played cribbage with him and Kaptain Kinetik?"

"No, of course not."

Jack paused for effect. "I wouldn't worry about the band, Ponty."

"You're so confident, but you forget one thing: I'm involved. Things don't go well for me."

"*Things,* bah" said Jack dismissively. "What things?"

"Life. Living day to day. Being a human. All of it goes very poorly for me. Schemes fare particularly badly."

"Ah, but you forget one thing."

"Yes?"

"You're in *this* thing with me. Things go *well* for me. I've got the magic touch."

"When I met you, you were an out-of-work actor peddling fast food at Medieval Burger."

"And look how quickly things have turned around."

"Have they?" Ponty asked, but Jack kept going.

"And Ralph is on our side. Ralph, you've been pretty lucky, haven't you?"

"Life's been good to me. What can I say?" Ralph said.

"See?" said Jack, as though the matter were settled.

"Okay. Have it your way. But what's the plan now?"

"Stay the course. Like Johann in *The Hour of the White Monkey*."

"I'm not familiar with that."

"I was in it years ago. It's a play by Gerhardt Schienke."

"A play about white monkeys?"

"No," Jack replied, as though it were a strange question. "No monkeys in it."

"But there was a guy who stayed the course?"

"Johann, yes."

"Did you get to work with real monkeys?" Ralph asked.

"Nnnoo. No monkeys in it."

"Well, then, why in tarnation is it called *The Hour of the White Monkey*?" Ponty asked, his patience cracking.

"I don't know. Perhaps it's not the fittest title. Still, I think my point is clear. If we just keep proceeding with the plan with confidence, everything will go just fine. Now, you'd better get going in case band practice breaks up early."

Once the area had been thoroughly scoped out, Ralph and Ponty exited through the front door, despite Ponty's reservations. They chose an alternate route for the return trip, going deeper into the woods. Halfway back to Ponty's cabin, Ralph's Ralph Senses began tingling.

"Sh," he said. "Hear that?"

"No."

"How can you not hear that?"

Ponty bristled at the implied insult. "What am I supposed to do? I can't hear—"

"Sssshhhh."

Ralph communicated to Ponty using hand signals they'd practiced while tracking their elusive and wily turkey quarry. He'd been instructed to circle around to his right, while Ralph went left to flank whatever was up ahead. Ponty, never confident in his ability to move his own body efficiently through space, had, however, recently made great strides in his ability to slink. And now he slunk around as Ralph had instructed until they were fifty yards from the spot where they'd started, ten feet away from each other looking back. Ralph signaled for Ponty to look closely at a tree ahead of them, and there, seated on a low branch, was a manlike object. When it moved, it was clear to Ponty that it was indeed a man. The pair tried as best they could to close in on him noiselessly and, as they did so, realized that it was hardly necessary to be noiseless. The man, who was wearing a new, fairly stiff camouflage jacket (of a type sold regularly at Pamida discount stores), was also wearing ear buds and listening to a small cassette player. From twelve feet away they could clearly hear the sounds of classical music, something European, probably Germanic, emanating from his ears. He was lightly humming along with it, a few times in the minute they observed him stopping to raise a pair of unnaturally large binoculars and scan in the direction of Jack's cabin.

Ralph lifted his eyebrows and held up a finger, indicating that he had devised a plan to deal with the situation. He walked up behind the man, grasped him by the back of the jacket, and pulled him backward off the tree, the man collapsing on the ground with a thud. Ralph took a seat on his chest and yanked out his ear buds.

"Ahhhhh!" the man shrieked, a wild look in his eyes. His face was painted in a camouflage design.

"What the heck you doin', bub?" Ralph asked him.

"I was, was . . . um, watching the ducks."

"Ducks? There ain't no ducks around here."

"*Ja.* I was having no luck at all."

"You were spying, is what you were doin'."

"I knew it," Ponty said. "I knew it. I told you."

"Spy—ha!" said the man. "But that is ridiculous. What would I be . . . *spy?*"

"You always look at the ducks wearing camouflage paint?"

"Yes, yes. I do, in fact. I took up the habit not two years ago, and it has completely changed the way I—"

"Shut up. Say. You look familiar. Where do I know you from?"

"Are you active in the duck-watching community? Perhaps—"

"I tell ya, shut up. What's so interesting about that cabin there?"

"Ask him who sent him," Ponty said, trying to be steely.

"Who sent—" Ralph began, and then he stopped to look at Ponty. "Why don't you just ask him?"

"Right," Ponty said, nodding. "Who . . . um, who sent you?"

"I don't understand."

"Who, you know, who do you work for?"

"I work as a buyer for a construction firm."

Ponty looked at Ralph apologetically. He had nothing more to ask.

"You done?" Ralph asked.

"Yes."

"All right, listen," Ralph began, but he was unable to finish his thought, as right at that moment he was hit from behind by something large and stealthy, knocking him off his perch atop the buyer for a construction firm. Ponty had no time to react, as he was simultaneously hit from the side by something of equal size and stealth.

Once on the ground, the stealthy object, identifiable now as a man, knelt on the small of Ponty's back and began to pull his arms behind him. At that moment all Ponty's training as a high school wrestler came flooding back to him. He realized that there were three things he needed to do: prevent his arms from being pinned behind him, get to his knees, and, if possible, grasp his attacker's right arm underneath his own and roll. It was his favorite reversal move, and he'd used it many times in practice. He tried it now, but, the conditions' being so dissimilar to those at Coulberry High School wrestling practice, the results were somewhat disappointing. Within seconds after attempting the move, Ponty was pinned, his arms trapped behind him, helpless. He could hear the sounds of Ralph struggling with his attackers and, presumably, the man they'd captured.

Ponty then attempted a move that was not sanctioned by either the Amateur Athletics Union or the NFHS official wrestling rules: He kicked wildly, like a toddler having a tantrum, at his assailant's back, perhaps one in three of the kicks actually landing.

"Stop it!" demanded the man on his back.

"Get off me!" Ponty yelled.

"Stop kicking me, you wildebeest!"

"GET! OFF!"

"Don't be such a baby."

"Shut your mouth, fool," a different, and oddly familiar, voice to the side of Ponty demanded sharply.

Ponty kicked again, a few of them landing with a beefy thud. He decided it was time to try his move once more, and when he did, to his complete surprise, it worked. He was now on top of the man who had attacked him, but the man obviously knew his way around a wrestling mat, for he immediately rolled to his stomach and got quickly to hands and knees. Ponty's instincts took over. He gripped a wrist and broke him to the ground, applied an aggressive half nelson and got him over on his back. Locking his opponent's head, Ponty stiffened his body and went up on his toes to maximize his weight on the man's chest. Once he'd subdued him, he applied another unsanctioned and wholly illegal move: He reached underneath the man, helped himself to a handful of his underwear band, and yanked with all his might.

"Here's a little wedgie for you," snarled Ponty. "You like that, huh?" He twisted the man's jockeys on the word "huh" for emphasis. The man whimpered but did not directly respond as to whether he liked it or not. Ponty applied more pressure and asked again. "How's that? That feel good, huh?"

He had no time to conclude his investigation into the matter, however because at that moment Ralph yelled, "Look out, Ponty!" and Ponty was hit from behind with something hard, something with a solid edge, and he slumped off the top of his captive, nearly passing out. Ponty was barely aware of some more sounds of struggling and then footfalls in retreat—a pair of them he thought, though he could not be sure—uneven, as though the man making them had just had his own undergarments pulled forcefully into the cleft of his buttocks.

Ponty saw Ralph's face materialize in front of his own, a bit blurry, but, Ponty noticed through his delirium, it was almost preferable that way.

"You all right, Ponty?"

"I've got to hurry to make my date," Ponty said, and then he passed out.

CHAPTER 18

n the newly cleared area near the entrance to the Holey Mine, tourists and townsfolk alike sat on blankets having picnics under the scorching sun, or wandered in small groups browsing the trinket and concession stands, or stopping by the official King Leo booth, which was selling T-shirts, his entire oeuvre of CDs—including rare bootlegs—a few choice pieces from his clothing line, and his pheromone-rich fragrance for men or women, called DewMe. Over all the proceedings an excited, carnival-like atmosphere prevailed. Everywhere, that is, but at Gerry Iverson's makeshift concession stand, where Walter Kuhnet, manager of the local grain cooperative, took strong issue with the percentage of Iverson's retail markup.

"Iverson, you fruitcake," Sturgeon began, "I ain't gonna pay three-fifty for a bottle of water."

"Clear spring water," Gerry corrected. "And, hey, I've got labor costs *and* I just put in a new drive point."

"And what in the holy Hector is comfrey?"

"Comfrey is pure deliciousness, Walter. And when you drink it like tea, it encourages the secretion of pepsin."

"Keep it clean, you hippy freak!" Walter shouted.

"Walter, take it easy, okay? I'll tell you what, why don't you have a tempeh hoagie on me."

Walter was somewhat calmed by Gerry's expansive hoagie offer. "I'll need water to choke down this longhair food," he said testily.

"Okay, okay. Have a spring water, too."

"Okay," said Walter, sounding mollified. "Thanks, Gerry."

A tall, salt-and-pepper-handsome-type man was next in line at Gerry's booth. Despite the unseasonable heat, the man looked quite natty and comfortable in a yellow pima-cotton polo shirt and sensible slacks, which appeared to have a touch of elastic for an easy feel.

"Hey, fella," the man said with advanced smarm. "How's the biz?"

"Can't complain. You?" asked Gerry pleasantly.

Daniel Turnbow was taken aback, as it was clear that Gerry Iverson did not recognize him or his famous hair.

"Good. Good. Daniel Turnbow . . . ?" he said, trying to get some recognition.

Gerry shook his head. "Don't know the fella. He from around here, or is he from up Tokesburg way?"

"No, no. *I'm* Daniel Turnbow. KMSR News?"

"Oh, okay. You work out of Duluth?"

Gerry could not possibly have insulted Daniel Turnbow more had he called him a big, water-added ham with bad hair and a lisp.

"N-ho, no, no, no, no. Out of the Twin Cities. Been there for years. Don't get down that way much?"

"Been off the grid since '84," Gerry said proudly.

Daniel Turnbow didn't know what this meant but assumed it was some sort of scary north woods hillbilly speak, so he did not pursue it. "So listen, pal. What's King Leo cooking up here anyway?"

"Revival, I'm told."

"Revival of what?"

"Well, I'm not altogether clear on that. The Funkalicious Spirit Mother or something like— Hang on." He leaned out the front of the booth and yelled at Ralph, who was putting a trash liner into a large garbage can. "Hey, Ralph. What's King Leo reviving again?"

"The Funka-Lovely-Creative-Spirit-Being, I believe, Gerry."

"Yeah, the Funka-Lovely-Creative-Spirit-Being," Gerry repeated to Turnbow.

"Yeah, I got that. What is it, this Funka-Lovely-Creative-Spirit-Being anyway, buddy?"

"Well, it's got something to do with the rat. You know about the rat?"

"Yeah, yeah. The rat. Read the book, sporto. Know all about the rat. But is the rat the Funka-Lovely-Creative-Spirit-Being?"

"I'm not sure. I always thought it was just a rat. Big rat, though. Seen the skin?"

"Skin?"

"The ratskin . . . pelt, hide—whatever they call it when it comes off a giant rat. The town gave it to King Leo in a big ceremony just the other day."

"Hey, move it along there, will ya? The revival's about to start." said a voice from behind Turnbow.

"Oh, yeah. I got customers stacking up. Can I get you something?"

"No, no. Perhaps I can interview you later, mi amigo?"

"Once I close the booth, sure."

"Super." Turnbow spun around and flashed a look at the impatient man behind him, a shorter, older fellow with a mustache. The man's head was bandaged substantially in the rear, and the dressing was held in place by one loop of gauze tape encircling his head like a sweatband. "It's all yours, there, Bobby Riggs," Turnbow said, and he took a step before stopping himself to give the man another look. "Have we met?"

Ponty started upon recognizing the man as Daniel Turnbow, who, if he was any kind of newsman at all, would know Ponty either from their brief encounter at Fetters's office or from his mug shot. Ponty half turned his face away as he answered, "Hm. No."

"Did I meet you at the Western Cable Show in Anaheim?"

"No. But I get that a lot," said Ponty, pretending to wave at someone in the distance.

"I don't know . . . ?" Turnbow said doubtfully, cocking an eyebrow.

"Not me," said Ponty with an apologetic shrug.

"Hm, have it your way," Turnbow said, and left with some irritation, seemingly over the fact that Ponty refused to be a person he'd met at the Western Cable Show in Anaheim.

Ponty stepped up to Gerry's concession. "Gerry, can I have a water?"

"Whoa. What happened, Ponty?" Gerry asked, grimacing at Ponty's bandages.

"Hey, careful. I'm Earl today."

"Oh, right. The mustache is the key, isn't it? Well, what happened, Earl?"

"I slipped in the tub."

"Man! What were you doing in there?"

"I was—"

"Hey! No. Nevermind. None of my business."

"No, look—"

"Stop! Not another word. Don't want to know. That's three-fifty for the water."

"What?"

"I just put in a new drive point."

"But I just gave you all that money for the— And what the heck is a drive point? Oh, fine. Here." He thrust a five at Gerry.

"I don't have change yet."

"Well, neither do I."

"I'll catch you next time, Earl," he said. "Okay, who's next!?"

Ponty hurried to get a spot near the stage (on the way dumping his water into a trash can, unable to get used to the strong notes of sulfur and a flavor suggesting several parts per million of dissolved fish). On the instruction of King Leo, the stage itself was situated in a semicircle around the boarded-up opening of the mine, in the event that if the Funka-Lovely-Creative-Spirit-Being made another appearance, he'd be in a position to "meld with it, in a cosmic embrace." Unfortunately, had it been constructed in such a manner as to accommodate this cosmic embrace, the stage would have violated the building code. A railing with a latched gate was built, so that King Leo could be safe but still have access to the Spirit-Being.

After a series of mike checks, in which Billy Moonbeam

nearly drove Ponty mad with the odd and incessant rhythm of it ("Check TEST, check, check, check, HEY, hey, HEY, hey, HEY, CHECK! SIBILANCE! SIBILANCE! Sibilance, CHECK!" over and over and over), King Leo's band came rushing out and laid down a thick bed of funk. A PA announcer then introduced King Leo, in what turned out to be a six-minute introduction that unfortunately led listeners to believe that it was over some fifteen times before it actually was. This was particularly hard on Ponty, what with his fresh head injury and a low threshold of tolerance for King Leo in the first place. Finally the Sovereign Ruler of Groove himself bounded onto the stage with a high-pitched scream.

Pontius Feeb did not often have flashbacks, and his ordered mind rarely indulged in free association, but now, as King Leo appeared before him wearing rainbow-colored silk pants that flared outward at the ankle a ridiculous amount—fringed with a great deal of frilly lace—a yellow peasant top, and a shockingly red kerchief tied around his head Aunt Jemima style, Ponty found himself remembering an incident that had occurred in 1978, at a small county fair in St. Charles, Illinois. Ponty, who was going to fetch his wallet from the car, was mooned by two clowns in a station wagon filled with clowns. He desperately hoped that the memory of seeing King Leo dressed as a kind of Mardi Gras hooker would not end up to be as indelible as the clown mooning.

"Yooooooouuuuuuu look like candy, baby/ Oooooooooh, I want to unwrap you, baby," King Leo sang, then grabbed a guitar off its stand and began a long, savage solo that made Ponty's head wound throb. When it was finished, he shucked off the guitar and threw it across the stage, and most of the frugal people of Holey were distracted by the action, wondering how much an item like that costs and what the repair bills might be.

It came as a surprise to Ponty that King Leo would lie down and begin grinding his pelvis into the stage so soon into his revival. Ponty had never been to a revival, but he believed unquestionably that the presider did not normally do this to any portion of the stage or equipment at any time during the event. In that respect King Leo was certainly a maverick in the area of revivals. His theatrical grindings continued until they were just beginning to tax the patience of the crowd. Then they ended, the band kicked it down, and King Leo wailed out the rest of the highly suggestive lyrics of his opening song, comparing a woman to a wrapped confection.

As unusual an opening as it was, it seemed to please the crowd. They cheered him on for some time, and he acknowledged the applause gratefully, while simultaneously toweling off.

"I love you, Holey!" he bellowed out, as though he were playing a show at Budokan Arena. The crowd of fifty or so let him know in return that they were, all things considered, somewhat fond of him as well. Ponty could manage only a lackluster "Yay."

"Before we continue with our revival, my friends, I've asked my guide, my guru, my leader in the ways of this mystic mine of yours, my friend Jack Ryback, to read an invocation. Jack!" he yelled and gestured offstage. Jack tramped up looking sheepish and stood in front of King Leo's microphone.

"Thank you, King Leo," he began tremulously, then pulled a folded sheet of paper from the back pocket of his jeans. He unfolded it and read slowly and somewhat flatly. "'We gather together as one before the thunderbolt path of pulsating rightness, in the divine hope that—'" He was interrupted by King Leo, whose whispers could be heard over the microphone.

"'Dee-vine.'"

"What's that?" Jack stage-whispered back.

"'Dee-vine,' not 'divine.' It's a different energy."

"Is it?"

"Oh, yes, Jack."

"All right, then."

"Gotta get the right energy."

"Understood." Jack got back to his paper: "'... in the dee-vine hope that forces, space, time, and matter align in a manner that allows for the transmutation of our beings to a level concomitant to the Funka-Lovely-Creative-Spirit-Being. That the Rodent of Divine'—dee-vine, sorry—'Power, um ...'" He stopped, seeming even more uncomfortable. "'... the Rodent of Dee-vine Power, um, suckles our beings with—'"

There was an involuntary moan of disgust from the crowd. Ponty let out a fairly loud "*What* the ... ?" and even Wigs Jackson said quietly into his headset mike, "Oh, man."

Jack shrugged almost imperceptibly at the crowd then turned to King Leo with a questioning look, but King Leo was wearing an expression of bliss and didn't seem to notice that anything was wrong.

"That's right, Jack. You're doing a great job."

Jack coughed softly and looked back down at his paper. "'... the rodent of dee-vine power suckles our beings with—'"

A nearly identical moan of disgust was heard, with Wigs again voicing disapproval, this time by saying, "Ohhhhh, come oooonnnn."

Jack kept going this time. "'... with,'" he repeated, "'the

alchemical miracle of body energy.' " When he had finished, he continued to look at the paper for a moment before turning it over in his hands to check the other side. Satisfied that he'd read everything that was required of him, he waved, said, "Okay then," and left the stage.

"Jack, Jack, Jack, Jack! Jack Ryback. His book, *Death Rat*, changed my life. And now we're going to change your life by funking it up, down, over the other side, and backward."

As clumsy as King Leo's transition was, the funk that followed was undeniable. Ponty guessed that it would last a while, so he strolled around, looking for a friendly face. After a moment of wandering, he came upon Ralph, who was eating an unidentifiable, but large item from Gerry's concession.

Ponty inclined himself toward Ralph's ear. "Hey, Ralph."

"Hey," said Ralph, red lentils falling haphazardly out of his snack. There was a pause as Ralph chewed and looked up at the stage. "I've never been to one of these. What happens now?"

"I don't know."

"It's loud."

"Yeah."

Another pause as Ralph chewed and watched King Leo gyrate suggestively.

"I'm not a huge fan of funk," Ralph averred.

"No?"

"Not a fan at all, in fact."

"I guess I'm not either," agreed Ponty.

King Leo was now mock-spanking Tarzan Moe with the headstock of his guitar.

"Do I have to stay for the whole thing?" Ralph asked a bit pathetically.

"I think we'd better stay. Got to mollify King Leo, you know."

Jack appeared next to them. "Wow, huh?" he said. "You don't hear something like that every day."

"You did a nice job," Ralph offered.

"I was little nervous. I'm not used to reading psychotic ramblings in front of a crowd." He noticed the amorphous red lump of food in Ralph's hand. "Ralph, are you eating your own hand? What is that?"

"Um, it's a red lentil, Swiss chard, and . . . um, fermented soybean wrap. It's good."

"I don't believe you," Jack said.

The music kept coming, and, aside from an occasional lightly obscene gesture or word, King Leo did nothing further to horrify the crowd. Just as Ralph was getting especially fidgety, the mood on the stage changed. The music shifted, becoming slower, meditative, more mystical. Kaptain Kinetik even used his tinkling, feathery bar chimes, which to that point had been silent.

"I'm scared," Ponty said.

King Leo was collapsed forward, his head on his knees. Two stagehands appeared carrying the bearskin and draped it over his back as he straightened slowly up. The skin had been smartly modified since its presentation to include straps that allowed it to be attached around King Leo's arms, and the stagehands now strapped it on and left. One of them returned immediately with a large, excellently crafted rodent head. (It was the head of *The Nutcracker*'s Mouse King that had been purchased at frightening expense from the Guthrie Theater's costume shop and delivered, also at tremendous expense, by courier just that day.)

"This is kind of weird," Ralph said.

Sir Shock-a-Lot appeared dressed in a tattered brown jacket and cowboy hat and carrying a rifle.

"Who's that supposed to be?" asked Ralph.

"Edward Lynch, I suppose," said Ponty.

"The guy that supposedly hunted down the rat?"

"Right."

"Looks like Jed Clampett."

The pair began an obscenely comic pantomime as Sir Shock-a-Lot's Lynch character stalked King Leo's Death Rat character around the apron of the stage for a minute or so. Sir Shock-a-Lot finally took aim at King Leo, and at that moment they both pantomimed falling, Sir Shock-a-Lot dropping his gun. King Leo leaped at Sir Shock-a-Lot, and they struggled in a highly stylized and not altogether dignified manner for a minute or two before they both sprang up. Sir Shock-a-Lot then spun off the stage as the music reached a crescendo and King Leo approached his microphone.

"It's time!" he shouted, and it was a good deal muffled by the heavy foam mouse head. The band struck a chord.

"It's tiiiime," he sang with effort, causing the head to jiggle.

"Time for what?" asked Ralph.

"Got to come to us now!" shouted King Leo, and then he began leaping up down. He continued to leap up and down in the same manner for some time, all the while shouting encouraging phrases to the Spirit-Being, the band making frenzied music as he did.

At reputable theme parks throughout the world, there is a fairly standardized safety procedure in place for those employed as mascots. Because of the tremendous heat buildup in the heavily insulated suits, there are always two people portraying the same character. One will work the park for but a brief ten to fifteen minutes before withdrawing into an air-conditioned environment, and the other will appear and work his ten-to-fifteen-minute shift, and so on. Some mascot suits even employ small, sophisticated cooling fans in attempt to deal with the overheating problem, but they tend to be of limited use.

King Leo was not aware of the stringent safety practices typically employed when one is wearing a heavy latex foam head, as he'd never been required to wear one. He had just jumped in the air and was about to shout the phrase "Got to come to us now, oh, holy rat," when, in midair, overcome by heat exhaustion brought on by the warmth of the bearskin and mouse head, he passed out and, when he returned to earth, crumpled down on the stage in a gray-brown heap. The crowd gasped. Two stagehands rushed out and yanked off King Leo's mouse head. They fanned him with a handkerchief and took his pulse. Sir Shock-a-Lot ran up, crouched over King Leo, and attempted to give him some water. After a minute they revived him, and the crowd cheered. The got him to his feet and were carrying him off when he stopped them and motioned for them to help him over to the microphone.

"My work is not yet done," he said weakly to the crowd before gathering his strength to shout, "We'll see you here tomorrow!"

t was 11:00 P.M., and there was one light on in Den Institut Dansk. Gus Bromstad sat in a chair in front of Stig Stou-Thorup's desk looking around expectantly at the many Danish faces in the room. There was about their Danish faces a far less imposing cast since last they'd met in Stig's office.

"Well? What news?" said Bromstad.

"It turns out, Mr. Bromstad, that you are correct. There *is* something fishy about this Jack Ryback character."

There was a pause, Bromstad still gazing at Stig expectantly.

"That's it?" he asked, looking around the room and seeing only downcast faces.

Stig, too, glanced down at some papers in a file on his desk. "Hmm . . . let's see . . . so far . . . yes."

"But—if you'll recall—I told you that."

"And through good, solid surveillance, we were able to confirm it."

"But that's good, solid squat, is what that is. I need proof. I've got to bring something to Bart Herzog."

"Egad! What dealings do you have with that buffoon?"

"He's going to help me put this pinchbeck behind bars."

"Yes, but is it worth it, do you think? Herzog is an ape in human clothes."

"Perhaps. But I need him."

Stig shuddered. "I hope you know what you're doing." He closed the file. "Well. I don't think there's anything else to—Oh, yes! I almost forgot to mention, there were some unforeseen problems with our operation in Holey. They were managed in a most expert fashion, but I'd be lying if I said they weren't unfortunate."

"Do tell," said Bromstad.

"Well, Jørgen, you were team leader on that particular stakeout. Why don't you fill Bromstad in on the details?"

Jørgen shifted in his seat. "Yes," he began. "Yes. Yes. Well, at six forty-five P.M. on the third day of May, we were posted in the woods observing our target from a safe distance when one of our company was set upon by two men. We were able rescue him, but the possibility exists that we were identified. Not ideal, of course, but there you are."

"Who did they set upon, exactly?" Bromstad asked in an agitated fashion.

"*Whom,*" Stig corrected.

Bromstad stared at him from under his hat.

"Not important," said Stig.

"It was I," Vagns admitted.

"What were you doing? How come you let that happen? I thought you were supposed to be so professional?"

"It's no good throwing stones. These men were experts. There was nothing I could do."

"He's right," said Jørgen. "These men clearly knew what they were doing."

"Who were they?" asked Bromstad.

"One works as a bartender in the town of Holey proper. His name is Ralph Wrobleski. Stig?" Stig handed Jørgen the file from his desk, and Jørgen extracted a photograph that he in turn handed to Bromstad.

"Wow! He's big," Bromstad noted.

"Yes. His size is indeed formidable."

"What's with his head?"

"All of us noted a certain asymmetry to it. But this fact most assuredly does not detract from his cunning."

"And who's the other guy?"

"We do not have a positive ID on him yet. He goes by the name of Earl Topperson."

"Topperson? What kind of name is Topperson?"

"Anglo, I suppose? Afrikaans? I don't know," admitted Stig. "This Topperson, too, claims to be a Holey resident, though we find no record of him at the courthouse." He handed several pictures to Bromstad.

"Not very photogenic, is he?" said Bromstad.

Jørgen ignored him. "We are running his plates, but there's some sort of a problem. We think his car may be stolen."

Bromstad winced at another photo. "That *hair*," he said.

"It is the unkempt hair of a criminal, yes. You will probably note that there is a certain cruelness to his eyes as well."

"Not a flattering mustache, is it?"

"The only other solid information we have on him is that he was a wrestler, probably at the college level. Ülo, why don't you fill him in on that?"

"Yes. While I was attempting to subdue him during our fracas in the woods, he administered several moves on me that I recognized as conventional wrestling moves. He applied some other less conventional moves as well. He's a very dangerous man."

"What other moves?" Bromstad asked, closing the file.

"Well, he kicked my back. And . . . it's . . . once he had overpowered me, he . . ." Ülo was becoming emotional.

"Go ahead. You have nothing to be ashamed of," encouraged Stig.

"He used my underpants as a weapon against me."

"What? What does that even mean?"

Ülo was having a hard time continuing.

"Please, go on, Ülo. Tell what he did with your underpants. It is a detail that could prove to be of some import."

"He . . . he," Ülo began haltingly.

"What? Did he take them off and strangle you with them? How can a man hurt you with underwear? Tell me?" Bromstad demanded.

"Well, grabbing the . . . the band, he pulled them with great force upward. As you might guess, they became wedged between my . . . my buttocks. My genitalia were also injured in the attack."

To the surprise of all the Danish men in the room, Bromstad did not laugh or mock, but rather a strange look came over his face.

"A wedgie, huh?" he said quietly, readjusting his hat thoughtfully.

"There is a name for this barbaric practice?" asked Stig.

"Yes. It's called a wedgie or, rarely, a snuggie. Horrible thing, a wedgie."

"Yes. Horrible," agreed Ülo.

"Pain, yes. But it's the shame that stays with you," said Bromstad authoritatively.

"It has not left me," said Ülo, shaking his head.

"There is a feeling of disbelief. And helplessness."

"Precisely!"

"In that way it's not unlike a double jock lock. Ever had one?"

"This is the first attack of its kind against my . . ."

"Right. Well, a double jock lock consists of bending both

legs back and holding them in place by looping the straps of one's own jock over the feet. Any struggling only results in . . . more . . . pain. . . ." Bromstad trailed off.

"I am glad I was not wearing a jock, or he most certainly would have used this lock against me."

With shocking suddenness Bromstad dug into the file again and began frantically leafing through the photos. As he examined them, a noticeable dudgeon seemed to build within him, until he was not only handling the pictures roughly but also doing something rather unexpected. He had begun to punch the photographs rather methodically, automatically disqualifying any notions that he might be doing it by mistake.

"Oh, yes, yes, yes, my friend. I've got"—and here he punched a photo—"you. You think you're so"—and again he delivered a punch—"tough, huh? You are going"—and yet another punch "*down!* Down."

The Danes, who until that moment had never seen another human being punching photographs, did not know what to do.

"Those—those are our only copies. Please. What are you doing? Gus?" said Stig. "We have the negatives, yes. But we'd like to keep those for our files."

Bromstad ignored him and continued punching them. Then, apparently dissatisfied with the lack of resistance from an item with relatively little mass, he began whacking the photos with the flat of his left hand. Punching them in this manner, he was able to get a decent-sounding smack out of them. When he'd punched five or six of the photos a couple times each, he then held one of them several inches from his face and, gritting his teeth asked of the photo, "You want to play, huh? Think you can hurt Gus Bromstad? Think you can steal *my* fame? My people? Huh, you freak!"

"Gus? Perhaps if you explain—" Stig said gingerly.

"Oh, ho, ho, ho. You're clever, my odd-looking little friend. You're very smart, aren't you? You're just as bold as a badger, aren't you?" The photo said nothing. Bromstad began punching it again, and, after a few of those, he ground his fist into it while emitting a kind of growling noise. After a bit of that, he began to form words again. "Got yourself a big stud to front for you, did you, you . . . troll? Climbed out from under your bridge and tried to take what's *mine*, didn't you?"

Bromstad had still not settled his score with the photo. He stood up, growled at it some more, threw it in the air, attempting to punch it on the way down, and, missing it, dove after it. He ended up on the floor near Stig's desk, rolling around with the photo, making animal noises.

Stig decided it was time to take action.

"Vagns, get some aquavit!"

Vagns dashed out of Stig's office and returned a moment later with a bottle and shot glass. He poured a dose of the liqueur, bent down, and tentatively held it near the growling Bromstad.

"Mr. Bromstad, please. You will hemorrhage. Please calm yourself. Take some of this."

Bromstad made a quick, spasmodic move and knocked the aquavit from Vagns's hand. The Danes started in shock, and Stig thrust himself out his chair.

"Bromstad, please!" he shouted.

This had the effect of causing Bromstad to stop his rolling, and Vagns was able to retrieve the shot glass and administer some liqueur. Bromstad sat back down in his chair, his face and ears red, smacking his lips and breathing heavily.

"Thank you. I . . . I . . . Lost it . . . there."

Stig, too, sat back down, the crisis of having a hysterical, foaming author rolling on his floor abated for the time being.

"Vagns, more glasses, please," he commanded.

Vagns dashed out for more glasses, and soon everyone was sipping aquavit. In a moment Bromstad was calmed enough to speak.

"That stuff works wonders," he said.

"It is literally the water of life," said Stig with pride in his nation's grog. "Now, do please tell us why you punched and growled at the photographs of Mr. Topperson?"

"Topperson, ha! Earl Topperson is an alias, and a remarkably stupid one at that, don't you think?" he asked, becoming slightly riled again.

"Well, now that you mention it, I have never met anyone with the surname of Topperson."

"That's because until he took it on, the whole of human civilization was wise enough, took enough time and care to make sure that no one ended up with the name Topperson!" Bromstad's face was reddening.

"Do be careful, Bromstad. Take another sip."

Bromstad obeyed. "I should have known. Should have suspected. That ridiculous rat book is dripping with dull history, isn't it? That's his unassailable prose, I'd bet my hat," said Bromstad, slapping his meaty thigh. "A history author! *Old von Steuben Had a Farm*," Bromstad said with thick disgust.

"Perhaps that is enough liquor for the time being," Ülo suggested.

"Yes. You are not making sense, Mr. Bromstad," Stig added.

"Oh, I'm making sense, for the first time since that rat book came out, my Danish amigos. More water of life," he

demanded, thrusting his glass at Vagns. When Vagns had filled
it and Bromstad in turn emptied it, he said in a low tone, "This
man, the man who got the best of you, the man who assaulted
your underpants"—he was looking at Ülo—"this man who has
evaded us at every turn, I know who it is. And believe me when
I say he is the mastermind pulling the strings of this Jack
Ryback's *Death Rat* scam. I assume it is not just I who has a
stake in seeing that he is found out, and justice done," he concluded, pointing his head significantly at Stig.

"No, I would enjoy seeing that as well. Indeed, more than
that. I think it essential that we make him pay."

"I'm going to make a trip up to Holey. Someone there knows
the truth. Stig, you're clean. I'd like you to come with me."

"Well, as you might guess, there are matters to attend to here
at Den Institut. I—"

"And given the cunning of our foe, or foes, I feel it's important to bring along one thing that was missing on the last mission," said Bromstad.

"Yes?"

"I think we should bring firearms."

"Gus!"

"He won't come easy. He'll be a desperate man. And we
know how dangerous and committed he is."

"Yes, I see that, of course. But as I said, I have the Kiwanis
Friendship Lunch coming up. I should not be taking time off
for gunplay."

"I ask you to remember our deal—and to be Danish about it."

Stig's expression became serious and firm. "Yes. Yes, of
course. I will accompany you to Holey."

"And you'll bring your firearm?"

"I'll bring a firearm, yes."

"And one for me?"

Stig paused, appearing to think. He opened his top desk drawer and pushed some items around. Then he opened a side drawer and rooted in that as well. Finally he straightened up.

"Yes. One for you as well," he said.

CHAPTER 20

Dean, you're wrong! You're always wrong, and it's we honest Minnesotans who suffer!" bellowed Bart Herzog, Minnesota's duly elected governor. He was splayed out on the couch in the entertainment room of the governor's mansion, alone, wearing combat boots, Zubaz, and a sleeveless Gold's Gym cutoff T-shirt, watching the nightly news. He was becoming agitated over what he perceived as a lack of competence in the weather-forecasting abilities of Channel 4's Debbie Dean. "That's what you said last year, and I didn't get my jet ski in the water till June, liar! Filthy *Liar!*"

Barb Herzog. Minnesota's first lady, pushed her head into the room.

"You all right, honey?" she asked.

He let out a groan that sounded like a bus decelerating. "It's this Dean character. She really frosts my strawberries, is all."

"Well, try not to let her get to you," Barb counseled, adding, "Would you like some cereal or something?"

"Huh? No. No, I'm fine."

She paused in the doorway. "I got you your Count Chocula. You're sure?"

"I'm right as rain," he said, putting his combat boots up on the Rhodesian-teak coffee table.

His wife bade him good night and withdrew, leaving him alone with Debbie Dean and her web of lies. When Debbie had finished spreading her poison, she tossed it back to anchor Alisha Poole, of whom Herzog was fond, mainly because he imagined she looked like the dark-haired woman from ABBA, only with blond hair.

"Thank you, Debbie. Looks like it's going to be a pleasant Thursday," Alisha said pleasantly.

"It should be," agreed Debbie.

"Liar!" shouted the governor.

Alisha thanked Debbie again and then announced their final feature of the evening, something called the Holey Watch.

"What in the grits and gravy is this?" shouted the governor, and then he watched in horror as Daniel Turnbow lubriciously reported from the site of the mine. He became especially agitated when King Leo appeared onscreen in a jumpsuit filled with cutouts.

"Filthy freak!" he cried. "You defile our state. Real estate prices are declining because of you!" He reached for his *Sports Illustrated* football phone and quickly dialed.

In just one and half rings, his press secretary answered. "Adam, what are you doing?" the governor demanded.

"Um, I was just putting away some socks. Why?"

"Never mind. Turn on the TV."

"Okay. Hang on," and the governor heard the sounds of his

press secretary moving away from his sock drawer to get near a television, then the sound of it switching on. "Okay."

"Tell me what you see," the governor demanded.

"I see an African lungfish. Of course, I'm trusting the graphic on this one."

"What the Buddy Guy are you watching? I mean turn on the news. Channel Four, man."

"Okay. Yes."

"What do you see?"

"I see King Leo singing upside down and backward through his own legs."

"Exactly. And where is he doing this?"

"Oh, it's this Holey thing. He's started some strange rat-based religion up there."

"Why wasn't I kept abreast of this situation?"

"I thought you weren't a fan of his stuff. I guess I misjudged."

"I'm not, you toadstool! I want to put a stop to his brand of anti-Minnesotan filth. Hang on. Check out this three-dollar bill," he said as Jack appeared onscreen answering Daniel's questions and looking fit and rugged. "Oh, that's right, milk it like a junkyard nanny goat, you phony."

"Me, Governor?"

"No, dolt. This four-flusher, this Jack Ryback."

"Why do you say that? I like him."

"You like everything that isn't tied down. You have no barometer, that's your problem. You're barometerless. We need a good war to temper people like you and give you barometers. Okay, who's this piece of work?" asked the governor.

"That, I believe, is the mayor of Holey."

"Really? I thought I knew all the mayors in Minnesota. Didn't I throw a luncheon for them all once? Planet Holly-wood, right?"

"No, sir. Those were producers. You were courting Holly-wood at the time, trying to entice them to Minnesota, turn it into a destination for film production, Governor."

"Did it work?"

"No, sir."

"Well, remind me to try again sometime. Whoa, whoa, whoa. Look at the screen. Who's this Peter Yarrow mutant?" asked the governor, referring to Gerry Iverson.

"Who's Peter Yarrow?" asked his press secretary.

"Peter, Paul and Mary? He was Peter."

"Oh, right. Well, then, perhaps it's Peter Yarrow," Adam suggested.

"No, not his type of thing. Now, listen, Adam, this whole boondoggle up in Holey has got to stop. It's not good for our state."

"What do you mean? We're getting a lot of attention on a national level," Adam objected.

"Gigantic rats, big-headed lugs in logger's shirts, abandoned gold mines, filthy funk stars, ponytailed hippy rejects, rat-based worship—is this all adding up to 'Minnesota' by your reckoning?"

"Except for the rat stuff, I'd say it's not far off."

"Well, the world can't know that! It's your job to see that they don't! Now, how do we go about it?"

"I don't know that there's anything we can do. It's very hip right now. King Leo's got a bunch his cronies up there. The press is crawling all over it. You rain on that parade right now and your approval rating's bound to take a hit."

"Feh! To the dogs with my approval rating!" the governor announced bravely. "How many points, would you think?"

"Let me do some quick calculations. Mm-hmm. Mm-hmm. And . . . okay. All right. I'd say at least fifteen points."

"Fifteen points! That's Wilson Cott territory!" he said, referring to his predecessor, a hardworking but bland career politician whose rating always suffered because of an unfortunate comb-over.

"A couple points lower than his term average, actually."

The governor wailed. "That can't be good for the upcoming book."

"No. I'd certainly call Williamson-Funk before making any kind of move."

Herzog's voice rose, sonorous and bold. "You think I call my publisher before I make a move in my position as governor of this state, a title entrusted to me by the good people of Minnesota? That's *your* job. Call them and see if it's worth the risk of me busting up this little cadre of freaks in Holey."

"Got it."

"Remind them how well it worked out when I beat up that protester."

"Right."

The governor snapped the elastic band of his Zubaz. "And, Adam? Tell them I'm out of cigars."

TERRACE BERRY COURT Lane was completely unfamiliar to Gus Bromstad, and that was too bad. Making a left from Terrace Berry Court Lane onto Linden Grove Boulevard Circle is difficult; the turn was easy to miss. But making that left from Terrace Berry Court Lane onto Linden Grove Boulevard Circle and then taking a hard right onto King John's

Plaisance Way was the only way to get to 1287000 Friar Tuck's Path, and 1287000 Friar Tuck's Path was the address to Stig Stou-Thorup's duplex at the Sherwood Forest Dell housing park in Brooklyn Center. Gus, lamentably, missed the turn onto Linden Grove Boulevard Circle and ended up in the City Park East Northern Technology Center, where he got lost. He had to ask for directions in the DigiTelCo Building, at the offices of Brite Ideahs Marketing, LLC, just as they were opening their doors for the day. His presence there caused something of a fuss, and he was forced to sign the receptionist's teddy bear before he could get any useful information out of her.

Thus, when Gus eventually showed up at Stig's place, he was late, tense, and highly intolerant of people who live in duplexes in the Sherwood Forest Dell housing park.

"Have you no self-respect, man?" he asked Stig. "Your lawn looks like it was just unrolled yesterday. Your trees are no taller than your trash cans."

"I like it here. It's quiet, and there's a Mamma Pepperoni's Pizzeria Italiana right up the street."

"There's a Mamma Pepperoni's Pizzeria Italiana right up every street in Minnesota. They're like snowflakes in this state. You're Danish. I thought you people liked old, crumbling things?"

"We are a practical people as well, and if by living here I can get a gingerbread latte within ten minutes of waking, then so be it."

"Mother of pearl, man! You like those dissolved baked goods? You're more of a freak than I ever would have been bold enough to imagine."

"Mr. Bromstad, if you're angry that my Volvo is in the shop, I assure you, I can contribute toward petrol for the drive."

"Let's just get going."

With Stig's guidance they were able to get on 169 headed north without wandering into any office-park snares, and they made the nearly five-hour trip up to Holey having spoken a total of eleven words between them.

"You were lucky to get a room," said Patty Perpich when they arrived at the Bugling Moose. "Everything within miles of here is filling up because of King Leo's revival. But for Gus Bromstad we just had to do it." She smiled sweetly.

"You got my keys?" Bromstad said.

"Thank you. Thank you so much," Stig added.

They had found their cabin, unloaded their belongings, and staked claim on their separate rooms when Stig appeared in Bromstad's door naked save for the towel he was holding. Since this was really covering only a portion of four fingers on his right hand, he was in practice naked.

Bromstad shrieked, calmed himself, and then summed the situation up accurately.

"You are as naked as a newborn."

"Yes."

"Will this be happening frequently during our stay together? If so, I'll need to make some plans to blind myself."

"I am going to sauna."

"There's a sauna?"

"Yes. It's fifty yards on toward the lake."

"And you're going there naked?"

"Yes."

"I see you have a towel. Might you not want to use that to cover things?"

"No."

"I strongly advise it."

"The Danish way is to sauna naked."

"And to actually *go* to the sauna naked as well?"

"When one has one's aquavit stowed in one's towel, yes. Are you ashamed of the male body, Mr. Bromstad?"

"Yes. Deeply. It is a travesty of engineering."

"So be it. I came to ask if you wanted to join me." Stig said.

"Well, you've got the aquavit, so I suppose I'm in."

Soon there were two naked, sweaty men in a small cedar-lined room flogging their own backs with birch branches.

"Not so much force, Mr. Bromstad. Just gently flagellate yourself," Stig advised.

"Don't get fresh."

"And you really should take your hat off."

"I take my hat off for three things, and that's it: haircuts, showers, and bed. Well, most nights anyway. Now, loose your grip on that hooch."

Stig poured out two shots, and they quickly disappeared.

"Ah," enthused Bromstad. "You know, we should have brought along a bag of pretzels or something. You getting peckish there, Stig?"

"*Ja,*" Stig said automatically. He then leveled a question that has been bandied about in saunas since man first stripped and got into one. "Do you think, ultimately, one is punished for one's sins?"

"What? You mean failing to bring pretzels? I shouldn't think we'd be in big trouble when the cosmic bill's all tallied up."

"I mean it. Kierkegaard would have us believe that there is no logic that would lead us to a belief in God, and despite that, *he* believed strongly in Him. Is there—"

"Kierkegaard: Danish?"

"Oh, yes."

"Copenhagen, right?"

"Oh, yes. Excluding a few travels, his entire life was spent there."

"That explains the apparent dichotomy right there. I was on a book tour in Denmark for a week, so I think I can help. You see, anyone living in Copenhagen who has ever tried getting a taxi is bound to conclude that there is no God. And yet, when one is living in the pallid despair of a taxiless city, one needs something to believe in besides bad coffee and boiled fish. Hence Kierkegaard's invented 'loving' God."

"Bromstad, you are—"

"Well, down the hatch."

Stig shook his head sadly. "Sooner or later we will all have to answer, Mr. Bromstad. As for me, I am going to jump in the lake." He stood up to leave.

"What? Where are you going?" asked Bromstad.

"It is tradition after one has experienced the heat of the sauna, what the Finns call the *löyly,* to run into a cold body of water or roll in the snow. There being no snow to roll in, I'm going to jump in the lake."

"I'm coming with you."

The naked men splashed about in cold Lake Vermilion and soon returned for more *löyly.*

Once they'd thrown some water on the stones and got down to the business of sweating a whole lot, Stig asked Bromstad, "So who is this man, this person whose photo you punched? Why is he so significant?"

Bromstad gently flagellated himself several more times without responding. Then he stopped his hand and stared at the wall in front of him. "His name is Feeb," he said.

"Feeb?" asked Stig. "Feeb what?"

"Feeb. Pontius Feeb. He's a history writer. You know the type."

"I confess I don't," said Stig.

"Bookish. Smart-mouthed. Face like a conch. Often they smell of rancid salad oil. They're jealous, corpulent little freaks with no social skills, and yet they . . . *they've* got the gall to get on their on high horses and preach down from Mount Wisdom at the rest of the world as though some high council had given him permission to write *All the Rules to Everything in the World*, as opposed to dusty little volumes on German immigrants—"

"Bromstad. Mr. Bromstad, calm yourself. We want no more rolling."

"Yeah, yeah. I know. What happened was this: Many years ago we were both attending the Dwee Awards, he for some little piece of tripe, me for a book I'm very proud of, called *Letters from Jenny*. He got jealous that I won, so he wrestled me to ground, right there in front of everyone, and he gave me a tremendous snuggie. Horrible, horrible thing. I was humiliated. On what should have been a night of my most treasured memory, I ended up pulling myself off the floor and limping away to the bathroom for some serious extraction procedures. And to think, he was so jealous he let it stew all these years, and now he's cooked up this plot to try to do me in. Who knows how long he could have been planning this thing?" Bromstad concluded, still having not looked at Stig.

"Hm. I see."

Now he looked. "What do you mean, 'hm'? And what is 'I see'?"

"I beg your pardon. I meant, of course, 'I understand' or 'I have no difficulty comprehending what you have just communicated to me.' "

"That doesn't explain the 'hm.' "

"Purely contemplative."

"What's there to contemplate? The guy's a jealous, wormy, illiberal dolt in bad pants. So you can lay off the contemplative 'hm's, all right?"

"Okay?" agreed Stig.

"What do you mean 'okay'?—as though it were a question?"

"Did I say 'okay'? I meant to say 'okay.' English is not my first language, of course."

"Well keep working on it."

Stig threw more water on the rocks, trying to increase the *löyly*.

Bromstad suddenly exclaimed, "Okay, look—I threw a roll, and it hit his friend, so he came over like some high-handed egghead to set me straight—"

"A roll?"

"A roll, a bun, a bap, as the Brits say. This one happened to be a spongy little dinner roll. Slightly yellowish color to it. No flavor. Simply a medium for butter."

"Ah, yes. I believe I have seen them at weddings."

"I wadded it up for better trajectory and threw it. I meant to hit him—never had much of an arm. He looked so funny sitting there in his bad little suit. That *suit!*"

"Unfashionable?"

"A crime against humanity. Brownish, it was. Some sort of

pale shirt lurked beneath it. The pants were high, of course—
that's to be expected of a history writer. The shoes, wrong.
Anyway, the roll hit this woman, this friend of his, in the eye.
Not ideal needless to say, but kind of funny. That's when he
strode over like Galahad in polyester."

"And demanded an apology?" Stig suggested.

"Yes, demanded. As though those things can just be summoned out of the air. Even if there was cause for one, which
I'm not prepared to admit."

"And you said . . . ?"

"I demurred, naturally."

"By saying . . . ?"

"It's been so long. . . ." Bromstad pretended to think. "It
may have been 'Ram it, clown' or perhaps 'Stuff it, oaf.' As I
said, it's been so long."

"And that's when the attack against your . . . um, yes?"

"Yes."

"Well, sounds like an unpleasant man. Drink?"

Bromstad accepted. Stig leaned back, crossing his legs, an
unexpected blessing for Bromstad.

"So what kind of a writer is he, do you know?" Stig asked.

"Histo— Have you been listening?" Bromstad snipped.

"My question was referring to the quality of his writing."

"The quality? Lacking, I would guess. The guy's only sold
about twenty-three books. Most of those got returned."

The men became quiet. The stove clicked gently.

"All right, I read *Old von Steuben Had a Farm*," Bromstad
said.

"One of his?"

"Yes. It, too, was up for the Dwee Award."

"Not good, I trust?"

"No. No, it was good," said Bromstad, looking down.

"Really?"

"Yes. I read it before the Dwee Awards, trying to get a sense of the competition. I also had to read *Reach Not the High Shelf* by someone named Lonnie Dich and, what was it . . . ? Oh! *Complainer's Moon* by Ingrid Stufflebeam. I didn't feel either was serious competition. *Complainer's Moon* I remember as being particularly insufferable."

"But *Old von Steuben* was competition?"

"Yes. Yes, it was good. And you want to hear something that stays within the walls of this sauna?"

"Of course," said Stig, holding up a hand.

"*Dogwood Downs* never would have been written were it not for *Old von Steuben*."

"No!"

"It's true. His manner of not only reporting the history but also bringing these Minnesota towns and their people to life, it inspired me. *Old von Steuben* set me on my course as Minnesota's greatest writer."

"Astounding. You don't think he knows that?" Stig asked.

"No. I don't. . . . You don't think he does, do you?"

"I don't know."

Bromstad thought about it. "Well, soon he'll be in jail, so what difference does it make?"

"And what is the plan for tomorrow?"

"I go and visit the mayor of Holey and get the truth about this town from her."

"What if he's got her in his pocket, as you Americans inexplicably say?" asked Stig, using his right hand to squeegee sweat from his left arm.

"She's a woman from a small town. I'm Gus Bromstad. She doesn't stand a chance," said Gus coolly, and he leaned his head back, drops of sweat falling from his beard. "If my charms don't work, I offer her ten percent of my next Dogwood book. And, as you know, my next book isn't going to *be* a Dogwood book," Bromstad laughed, then took some of the water of life.

CHAPTER 21

I t was now the fifteenth time that Ralph had heard "LoveDeathTomorrowJelly," and he was becoming less enthusiastic about it with each fresh hearing.

"There! There! What does that part mean? What is that?" he asked irritably of Jack as they did their part in what was becoming a fairly massive revival.

"Is that a rhetorical question, or do I have to answer?" said Jack.

"I'd like an answer. I really would," said Ralph, becoming quite agitated. " 'Crystal frogs, the amniotic fog, and daylight breaks upon your paper skin,' " Ralph quoted with some mockery in his voice. "What is that?!"

"Amniotic fog? Yikes. All the time I thought it was Amenhotep fog."

"Amenhotep? What's that?"

"Egyptian king, I think."

"No. No, it's amniotic. I looked it up on the Internet."

"Ralph. Why?"

"It was bugging me. I've heard the thing four hundred times now, and I think I deserve to know what amniotic fog means."

"Well, amniotic, that's . . . What is that?"

"In mammals it's a membrane that contains the fluid in which the embryo is immersed."

Jack looked at Ralph questioningly.

"I looked that up, too," Ralph explained.

"Well, then, clearly, amniotic fog is . . . Heck, I don't know."

"That's my point. No one knows, and yet this idiot is a trillionaire, while I bust my hump at a bar every day."

"You've got the book money."

"Yeah, and I'm busting my hump for that, too. Every second spent here listening to this moron is like a full shift at the happy hour bar in hell!" Jack had never seen this much passion from Ralph, who usually preferred to communicate in short grunts.

"Well, he's got a lot of energy," Jack said, gesturing toward the stage, where King Leo was currently running at full speed, his high-heeled cowboy boots a blur.

"So do most three-year-olds, but they don't get trillions for it. And what's he trying to prove with this new religion crap of his? You want religion? Go to church. They've got one just sitting there. They'll be happy to explain it to you anytime."

"I think he just—"

"I'll tell you what it is. It's because people weren't looking at him enough, and he needs that. He doesn't exist unless people are looking him. What else could explain that jumpsuit he's wearing?"

"That thing does raise some questions."

"And how long is this thing going to go on? What's he looking for?"

"Well, I can only tell you what you already know. He's waiting for an appearance of the Funka-Lovely-Creative—"

"Creative-Spirit-Being, I know. If I hear him say that stupid name one more time, I swear I'm gonna run up onstage and bust him in the teeth. Then I'm gonna snap the high heels off his stupid little cowboy boots. What's he supposed to be anyway, a cross-dressing Dale Evans?"

"Ralph, you seem tense."

"I want this to be over. I can't drive around my own town, for *these* idiots," said Ralph, singling out a man to his right to point a thumb at.

King Leo and his band finished "LoveDeathTomorrow-Jelly" on a high note, and the crowd of five hundred loved it (excepting Ralph, of course).

"Thank you! I love you Holey!" shouted King Leo to his flock.

"Get off the stage, you freak!" Ralph shouted back. Tourists all around him turned to look.

"Ralph, take it easy," counseled Jack.

"Freak," Ralph repeated, more quietly this time.

"I'd like to take a moment and acknowledge some of the familiar faces in the crowd. Some of those fine, fine, fine, people who've made the pilgrimage. Shā, is here. Come on up, Shā and say hello."

"What in tarnation is a Shā?" Ralph asked irritably.

"She did that song 'Love is a Brick,' " Jack informed him.

Shā tottered up onstage in tight jeans, her thong underwear readily visible above the waistline, wearing a sequined, midriff-exposing halter top and high heels that put to shame King Leo's attempt at height. The crowd was electrified by her appearance.

"Thank you! You're beautiful. I love what you're doing here. It's so spiritual," she purred into the microphone.

"Shā just came out with a killer new CD that will funk you up. It's on the Spangle label. Little sister, you wanna do a song with the crew and me?" King Leo asked.

"Oh, King, I don't know," she said coyly.

"You got to, got to, got to, little sister," King Leo pleaded. He gestured toward the crowd, and they dutifully erupted in cajoling applause.

"Would you guys be able to do 'Love Is a Brick'?" she asked, looking around sweetly at the band. They all nodded coolly in turn.

"Yeah, man. Not a problem," said Wigs.

"Yeah, then we got to do it!" King Leo exploded. "One, two, three, four—"

"I seen him!" shouted Ralph, who had suddenly materialized onstage next to King Leo.

Shocked, Jack looked to his left and noticed a decided lack of Ralph. He must have slipped off during Shā's introduction. The crowd, too, was shocked, and there began a torrent of questioning murmurs.

"Whoa, whoa, whoa, hold on there, Ralph," said King Leo, taking his microphone out of its stand and putting an arm around Ralph. "Everyone, I'd like to introduce you to my friend here, from Holey. This is Mr. Ralph. And you saw who?"

"The Rat of Dee-vine Power. The Funka-Lovely-Creative-Spirit-Being . . . of Power," Ralph added unsurely. "Well, you see, I been to every one of your revivals just a-waiting on the Funka-Lovely-Creative-Spirit-Being, just feeling the funk and all that?"

"Bless you, Mr. Ralph," said King Leo, giving him half a hug.

"Uh-huh," said Ralph, trying to get the hug over as quickly as possible. "Well, anyway, it finally happened. He came to me."

The crowd was hushed with the electric excitement of the revival's first sighting. Shā stood there looking uncomfortable.

"Oh, Mr. Ralph, Mr. Ralph, Mr. Ralph, tell us all about it, brother," said King Leo excitedly. He had forgotten about Shā.

"I was standing over there," said Ralph, pointing to a spot where he had not been standing. "And that's when I seen it."

"Mr. Ralph, that is excellent news. And now you must tell us, was it a human form that it took?"

"No. It was . . . well, it was kind of ratty, if you know what I mean?"

"Oh, yes, yes, yes, yes, I know what you mean indeed, Mr. Ralph. What else can you tell us about it? Did he walk up to you, or did he float up?"

"Um, he walked, and then it seemed like, if he got a little tired, he'd float. Just a little bit off the ground. Some of his tail was still dragging."

"Was he glowing?"

"Glowing. Oh, yes. He was a glowing gray color."

"A glowing gray," King Leo repeated rapturously. "And what did he look like?"

"Well, as I said, he was rattish, but not totally like a rat."

"No?"

"No. It had on a jacket," Ralph vamped.

"What kind of jacket?" King Leo asked.

"One of those jackets like what kings wear. With the stuff on it?" he said, looking to King Leo for help.

"The crinoline? The gilding."

"Is that the gold stuff?" Ralph asked.

"Yes."

"Yeah, that's it, then. He wore a gilded jacket that was real long in the back. Nice-looking. Fit him real nice. And he was carrying one of those things."

"A crown," guessed King Leo.

"No, no. One of those poles with the knobs on the end."

"A trident? A staff? Oh, a scepter."

"Yeah, one of those, and it was gold, too."

"Was his face beautiful?"

"Well, remember, he *is* a rat. But, yeah, it was beautiful because it was so wise-looking. His whiskers were long and white. Real noble-looking . . . um, what you call it? Muzzle. Real noble-looking muzzle."

"Mmmm," said King Leo, closing his eyes.

"And he walked on his hind legs."

"Yes, yes!"

"That's about it, I guess," said Ralph peering out at the crowd of eager faces.

"Did he say anything? Did he have a message for us?"

"Oh, yes. I almost forgot. He said, 'I have a message for you.' "

"Yes, yes?"

" 'Tell them I appreciate them coming,' he said. 'It's real, real nice of everyone to have traveled so far. And I thank them.' And he said, 'Go forth now, and spread my message.' "

"Yes! Yes! Yes! Was there anything else? This is important, Mr. Ralph. Did he say what his message was?"

"Yes, I almost forgot that part. He said, 'Funk on, my people.' "

"Yes, what we've done here has mattered, my brothers!" King Leo shouted to the crowd. "Praise the Holy Holey Rat! And lets it hear it for our faithful brother Ralph!"

The crowd applauded wildly for their prophet Ralph, who simply nodded impatiently back at them.

"Well," said Ralph, "thanks everyone. I'm gonna do what the rat told me. I'm gonna get going, gonna funk on as best as I can. I suggest you do the same. Drive safely, everybody."

"Whoa, whoa, whoa, brother. Didn't he say, 'Funk on, my people?'"

"He sure did."

"Then I think we ought to do just that. If we stay and funk long and hard into the night, perhaps we will all be blessed with an appearance by the Funka-Lovely-Creative-Spirit-Being, the Rat of Dee-vine Power!"

The crowd agreed. Ralph tried to silence them.

"Well, now hang on there, brother. Remember he said, 'Go *forth* and spread my message.' Go *forth*. He was real specific about that. I forgot to tell you, but he said, 'Don't forget that part, Ralph.'"

"And so you shall, brother Ralph. *You* shall go forth. It is clear to me that that was *your* message. You are to go forth and spread the message. We are to stay here and wait for our own messages."

"Well . . . I'm not so sure you're doing the right thing, but you think I should get going, right?"

"Oh, yes. Go forth at once," King Leo encouraged. "Tell them what you saw here today."

"My staying here would serve no one?" Ralph double-checked.

"No, brother. Take your '81 Malibu and spread the word."

"All right! Woo. I'll see you all later!" Ralph shouted and ran offstage. Wild applause followed after him.

"The visions are the start, people. Individual visions will precede the collective vision that we await. We are close, people. I can feel it!" King Leo exclaimed. "Have there been any more individual visions? Don't be shy, we are all friends here."

"I saw him!" said Shā from a spot just behind King Leo.

"Praise the Rat," said King Leo.

CHAPTER 22

Sandi Knutson was furiously rearranging her cat figurines. She hadn't spoken to Ponty since he'd stood her up for their date more than a week ago. It made her angry, even though she knew he had a good excuse. (He was unconscious.) Still, a date was a date, she thought. He could have called and made other arrangements.

She was moving Alistair Q. Kitty, the yellow tabby, off the shelf by the recliner and into the growing window next to the plants when she was startled to see a famous author's head suddenly appear before her.

"Ah! Gus Bromstad?" she said to the head that was currently hovering outside in her yard.

Now the head was joined by a hand, waving at her. It really was Gus Bromstad, standing on her lawn, looking mightily overdressed for such a warm day in his Greek fisherman's cap and his Irish sweater.

She pointed him around to the side door and met him there.

"As I live and breathe. Gus Bromstad. What are you doing at my home?" she asked him.

"Are you Mayor Sandi Knutson?"

"Yes, I am she."

"May I be so forward as to ask if I might have a few moments of your time? I know you're busy, what with the bar and the mayoral duties and King Leo's popular new religion."

"Oh, please. Do come in," she said cordially, if a bit stiffly.

She led him into the living room and showed him a seat among the bric-a-brac. He smiled warmly at it all.

"Is that Purressa White Boots?" said Bromstad, pointing to a black-and-white ceramic cat on an overcrowded end table.

"Why, yes that is. How did you know that?" she asked.

"Oh, I've signed so many of them. They're very popular with mid—" and he was able to stop himself, redirecting the word "miss—miss—misses. With the misses. And the men, of course. Ladies and men. I've noticed that everyone seems to enjoy the whole Pretty Kitty line."

He finished stammering his cover, and she fetched them both some weak coffee that Bromstad was able to fortify with sugar and generic white creamer powder and pretend to enjoy. She told him how much she loved his books, and he pretended not to be impressed with himself. When that was over, he got down to business.

"The reason I'm here is the same reason so many are. I'm fascinated with the history of this town, what happened with those two men, and, of course, that giant rat. So big."

"Yes."

"Big, big rat."

"Very, yes."

"Massive. Very, very, very, unusual."

"Yes."

"His ears must have been the size of milk cartons."

"That big, do you think?"

"I'm thinking half-gallon size."

"Oh, right. I suppose they could have been. I would have thought about the size of a . . . well, like the size of my coffee cup," she said, holding it up for him to see how big a coffee cup is.

"Well, no matter. We could speculate on rat ear sizes all day and not get to the bottom of it. What I was wondering is, as the mayor, Ms. Knutson, I'm sure—"

"*Mrs.* Knutson, actually."

"Oh. But they said you, you—"

"My husband is dead."

He seemed relieved. "Oh, well, too bad. Anyway, I'm sure you have all the documentation of the Holey rat event. The newspaper clippings. Court records of any transactions the men might have made, that type of thing? I mean, I could go to the courthouse and get them, but I took a guess that you might be safe-holding them here in Holey."

"I . . . uh, I don't believe we have them here in Holey," she said, doing a very unconvincing "thinking" face.

"Really? Well, lash me to a pig and roll me in the mud. I thought sure they would be. So when that Ryback fellow was doing his research, where was he getting his information, do you happen to know?"

"I suppose he must have gotten it from the courthouse in New Sligo."

"Really? But you've seen the materials, haven't you?" Brom-stad asked.

"Oh. Seen the materials? The clippings and things that he used?"

"Yes."

"That's what you're talking about? Like that kind of thing?"

"Yes, yes. The research material."

"Oh, yes. I've seen it."

"No kidding. What kind of stuff was it? What did it look like?"

"Oh, well, it was old," she volunteered.

"I'll bet."

"It was about this big," she said, holding up her hands.

"Newspaper stories? Pictures? What kind of stuff was it?"

"I don't remember. I just remember being very convinced that the story was true."

"Really?"

"Yes. Quite. Very convinced."

"But you don't remember what the material consisted of?"

"No, I'm sorry. I wish I could be more specific."

"So someone showed you a scrapbook full of giant-rat mem-orabilia and reportage, and you swiftly forgot it?" he said, his voice gaining an edge of incredulity. "But you retain the thor-ough belief in the story you don't remember? Is that correct?"

"Well, I guess," said Sandi nervously.

He held up his hands to represent the material. "Remember the *result* of the stuff; don't remember the *stuff*, is that it?"

"I suppose so."

"Okay. Okay. Let's pretend I'm a guy. I walk up to you and say, 'Hey, lady, want to see some stuff I have that proves there was a guy a long time ago who killed an impossibly large animal?' I ask. And you say, 'Sure.' So I show you the material, and you're looking at it and saying, 'My goodness, that story sure was true. I can see it right here in these newspaper clippings and eyewitness reports.' Then I take them away from you and ask you, 'So, you're convinced, then, eh, lady?' and you say, 'Oh, yes. Very convinced.' And I say, 'What was it that really got you?' and you say, 'Oh, I don't remember. *You know why?*" Bromstad's voice rose. "'Cause I just forgot what kind of things you just showed me. Did you show me an antique sock? A picture of your Aunt Frieda? I don't remember, you see. I know it was old. And I know it was about this big. But I'll be darned if I can recall whether it was an old piece of scrimshaw or Danny Kaye's hat. Gosh, I sure do believe unquestionably in all the stories about that large animal, though.' Is that it? Is that pretty much what went down? That's what you're asking me to believe?"

She gave him a hard look and after a pause said, "Yes. You described it to a tee just now."

"Well." Bromstad considered this for a long while. "Yes. That is something. When you think you've heard everything. Yes. I wonder if you could to me a small favor?"

"What?" she said coldly.

"Could you possibly *cut the crap, lady?* Do I look like I just fell off the turnip truck to you?"

"A little."

"Where is he, lady? Where's Pontius Feeb? Is he in here? Is he hiding? Hello? Rat-book author? Treacherous rat-book author? The jig is up, my friend!" he yelled in the direction of the back of the house. It occurred to Bromstad that perhaps he wasn't adhering as closely to his plan to charm her as he might have liked.

"Could you please leave now, Mr. Bromstad?"

"Not until I give you all the facts, Little Miss Ratty Pants," said Bromstad, veering unexpectedly off into the puerile. "This Feeb character is in a lot of trouble. Think huge, gigantic piles of trouble—and then double them. That's how much trouble he's in. My friend the governor is fully prepared to try him on the charge of cultural sedition, and if you're in this thing as thick as I think you are, you'll be having steamed burritos at the Shakopee woman's prison every Tuesday for the next thirty years."

"I have no idea what you're talking about," she said.

Bromstad, knowing that it would be a tough sell, tried to switch to charm anyway.

"Sandi," he said with sudden softness. "Sandi, my dear, dear, lady. This Pontius Feeb is a dangerous, hair-trigger, criminal possessing a total disregard for the law and an unnatural obsession with other people's underwear. You don't want to get mixed up with a man like that, no matter how much money he's paying you. And unattractive? Goodness! He looks like an artist's rendering of a crazy uncle."

"I don't know about that," said Sandi.

"Sandi, Sandi, Sandi. You don't want to spin out your retirement years in a room with striped sunlight. I know how it is with these men from the big cities. They come into a town like this, drag their spotty little abdomens around, and begin spinning webs of bitter, bitter deceit. They imagine that the 'innocents' in this wee burg aren't smart enough to see what they're up to, but if there's anything that my writing about small towns has taught me, it's that you are smarter than that. You can see a Ponty Feeb for what he is. A poisonous, silver-tongued mountebank. Now, if you—"

"What the heck's a mountebank?"

"I beg your pardon. Perhaps I should have said a . . . a Janus-faced bamboozler." He was losing her, and he knew it. "A swindler. A cheater."

"Now, look, Bromstad, I told you, I don't know anything about it. I thank you for stopping by but I want you out of my house," Sandi said firmly.

"How much? How much is he paying you?"

"Leave."

"I'll double it. I'll triple it. Just give up the goods on this Feeb. I'll quadruple it."

"I have nothing more to say to you."

"I'll quintuple it."

"Out."

"I'll septuple it!"

A ceramic cat parted the air next to his ear and crashed into the wall behind him.

Bromstad's eyes widened. "Your Pretty Kitties! Are you insane?"

"Get out."

An unidentified knickknack hit him sharply in the shoulder.

"Ow! You're crazy! He's going to drag you down with him! You're in a deep quagmire, lady. This Feeb is no good!" He saw a Snow Baby tumbling through the air toward him and, pausing to decide whether to dodge left or right, he was caught flat-footed. It smacked him on the bridge of his nose. "Ow!" He retreated toward the exit. "I'm going to see that two-bit hoaxer take a fall, with or without you! Ouch!" he added, for a Lilliput Lane cottage had just caught him in the small of the back. "Have it your way, harridan! But if you think they allow bric-a-brac in prison cells, you've got another think coming!"

He turned to see Sandi reaching for another impromptu missile, so he said quickly, "You've got one day to give him up! Then I go to the governor, and I'm going to advise him to put you in a cell so deep they'll have to pump daylight to you! And forget about Pontius Feeb. He'll die in prison!" He saw her propel what appeared to be an Emmett Kelly Jr. clown statuette, so he quickly exited, and it shattered in the spot where he'd been.

CHAPTER 23

Sandi waited till darkness covered Holey and then slipped out her back door. No stranger to the art of camouflage, having had so many hunters pass through her bar, she'd chosen black slacks, a navy blue sweatshirt with a lighter-colored teddy bear on the front that she had taped over with black cloth tape, a black stocking cap, and black face paint. She avoided the wide pool of illumination thrown off by the "scaredy" light on the pole in her yard and slunk through the woods the quarter mile to her neighbors', Lindy and Bette's. They were just pulling up in their Saturn SL1 when Sandi arrived.

"Sandi? Got a minstrel show tonight?" Lindy asked.

"Shhh. Come on inside."

"Oh, thank you. I *will* go into my house," he said.

"Oh, Dad. Quiet now. It must be important," Bette scolded. Though married with four grown children, they still called each other Ma and Dad in the event that if a child would stop in unexpectedly, they wouldn't be caught accidentally displaying affection for one another. "We just got back from the revival. Looks like it's going to go all night. You, come on inside now, honey," she said, taking Sandi's arm.

"I think I'm being watched. Can I borrow your car?" she said once they were in the Lindburgs' kitchen.

"You runnin' bathtub gin to the next county again?" said Lindy.

"Dad. Stop it. It sounds serious."

"Oh, it's nothing," said Sandi. Bette looked pointedly at the perimeter of Sandi's painted face, then at her taped sweatshirt. "Well, it's something, but it's not that bad," Sandi added.

"Of course, dear. You take it," said Bette, handing her the keys, as Bette was always the one who drove.

"Careful, though. It's got impact-*resistant* panels. That don't mean you can roll it or crash into other cars," said Lindy, who had just made himself a brandy and water.

Checking to make sure she wasn't being followed, Sandi drove at once to the Bugling Moose.

PONTY WAS SO used to oddities that when he heard the sound of fingernails dragging eerily over the pane of his cabin window, he assumed it was some undead creature of the night who'd had trouble shape-shifting into a bat and been unable to fly through the chimney. Or, he reasoned, it might be a timid bear, shyly trying to lure him to the window for an easy meal. Or, more remotely, it could be Eartha Kitt kindly scraping bugs off his window for reasons only Eartha Kitt could fathom. Whatever the case, Ponty didn't really care. He wasn't interested in whatever the window's eerie scratcher was trying to sell.

When the scratching sounds changed and became a tapping at the window, ruining his concentration so that Ponty had to stop writing, he became annoyed, but still not enough to get up and get to the bottom of it. When the tapping changed fully into knocking, accompanied by a voice saying, "Ponty? Ponty, it's Sandi. Please open up," Ponty finally was forced to consider alternative theories about its source. He opened the sash.

"Ponty, didn't you hear me?" Sandi asked.

"Um, I was otherwise engaged."

"I saw you sitting right there. Well, never mind. May I come in?"

"Oh, certainly," said Ponty, grasping her arm and helping her through. The procedure of actually getting her through the window hit a snag when Ponty failed to support her and she fell on the floor. "Sorry," he said numbly. "I do have to ask, though I think I know the answer, why do you feel it necessary to crawl through my window as opposed to walking in the front door?"

"Because I didn't want to be seen," she said, pulling closed the drapes.

"Yes! I was right! That's what I thought." He noticed the tape on the front of her sweatshirt. "What is that covering? Something dirty?"

"No, it's just for camouflage. Are you all right, Ponty? You seem a bit poleaxed."

"Oh, yes. I was just doing some writing," he said. "Um, getting back to my question, whom didn't you want to see you just now?"

"Gus Bromstad," she said, as the pair moved over to the living area, Ponty choosing the threadbare armchair and Sandi the threadbare couch.

"I suppose I can see that. He's not a pleasant man. But, really, is there much danger of that?" he asked.

"He's here in Holey."

"I mean, he lives in St. Paul and really doesn't know you—I beg your pardon?"

"Here in Holey. He came to see me."

"Are you even a fan of his work?" Ponty asked listlessly.

"No. And after his visit I'm even less of one. He's a horrible man. And his head is so big."

"I could have told you that. You didn't have to have him to your house to find that out."

"How do you . . . ? Never mind. I'll tell you all about it in a minute. Let's back up. Why didn't you call me after your . . . your accident? Ralph told me you fell in the tub, which I completely understand—most injuries are tub-related, I know. But after that it was like you seemed to just fall off the face of the earth."

"Well, Sandi, I didn't fall in the tub. It was thugs. They hit me with—I don't know—hard things."

"Oh, that's horrible. Did they hit you while you were in the shower, or did they drag you out of there?" she said, craning to look at his injury.

"No, no. I wasn't in the shower. I told a lie because I was too cowardly to let everyone—well, you, really—know how dicey this whole thing had become."

"You think the men who hit you had something to do with the book? You don't think they just wanted to hit you? You know, for money or whatever?"

"No. No, I'm positive it was because of this . . . business. And I guess I pulled away because I was ashamed of myself. I didn't want you to have to spend time with such a miserable, cowardly, wormy . . . coward like me."

"Ponty!"

"It's true. That's another reason I've been out of sight. I've been writing my confession."

"Confession?"

"Yes. What I've done is wrong. I know right from wrong, and yet I talked myself into ignoring it—for what? For this? Everything, from the start, I'm the one, the one who did everything: wrote the book—a cynical act to begin with— talked Jack into pretending he wrote it. Being too cowardly to confess my mistake when things went wrong. Talking you and these good people of Holey into lying for us. Despicable. You want to know another thing about it? I couldn't even tell the truth to the people who were going to lie for us. It wasn't our publishers who made the mistake with the book. Jack didn't write any of it. He didn't 'punch up' the text. He said that because I was doing a bad job of convincing you all to lie. From the very start it was me who made up everything, because I was too cowardly to face my old age like a man and, I don't know, too insecure to admit that I really haven't made much of my sixty years here on earth."

"Ponty," said Sandi quietly.

"Well, I'm going to fix things as best as I can. There's a couple of small lies in my confession, but I feel good about them. I've absolved Jack. I've confessed that I fed him the idea for the story, that I showed him forged documentation, but otherwise he did write it. I've said that my motivation was revenge for having seen him act in *Strindberg's Wallet*. I think that should do the trick. And that he paid me for the material and the research—there's nothing unusual about that. As for the town of Holey, it works the same way. I showed you the proof. Everything else, of course, is all true. The players are all real— Lynch, Fuller. None of you had any reason to doubt me. When I turn this in, you're all free and clear," he said, holding up his notebook. Though his eyes were cast down, Sandi could see that they were about to spill over with tears.

She was making a motion to touch his face when Ponty's door was flung open and two naked men with guns burst in.

"Well, isn't this cozy?" said Bromstad.

The other man just stood there dangling.

Gus bromstad, whether he knew it or not, lived in a continual state of mild irritability. This was his baseline, and he never fell below it; circumstances caused it to rise by varying degrees, but catch Bromstad at his best and you still had a man who was moderately prickly.

After his visit with Sandi, upon returning to the Bugling Moose, Gus Bromstad had added to his baseline considerably, and the irritability needle was spiked into the red.

"Morons, all!" he'd announced to Stig as he flopped onto their couch.

"Who are all morons?" asked Stig, looking up from his book, *Man One, Mountain Zero.*

"Everyone! Everyone I've ever met since first I drew breath upon this earth." Stig looked at him questioningly. "The jury's still out on you. But this Knutson woman, bah. She didn't give me anything, and she threw a cat at me! No one's ever thrown a cat at me!"

"Was the cat seriously hurt?" Stig asked.

"A ceramic cat, you jackass! And a clown statue."

"You have a cut on the bridge of your nose."

"That would be the Snow Baby," said Gus, touching his injury lightly. "Idiot! She'd rather take a fall. Well, that's fine with me. Someone in this Podunk little bulge in the road is going to talk, and when that happens, then they're all going to the big house," Bromstad raged, poking his forefinger into the air for extra emphasis.

"You allow events to influence you too much, Mr. Bromstad. Evenness is the key. We Danish have long understood that. In fact, there is an oft-cited Danish proverb, *Ingen ko p°a isen,* which means "No cow on the ice." He shook his head meaningfully.

" 'No cow on the ice'?"

"*Ja. Ingen ko p°a isen,* " Stig repeated.

The men looked at each other. "Perhaps you hadn't noticed that I was waiting for you to explain that," said Bromstad.

"It means that there is no problem. If one of our cows was out on the ice, that would be something to worry about. As it is, our cows are safe on land. No problems. Do not become agitated until your cows are out on the ice."

"That's what you Danish people worry about, is it? Cows out on the ice? That's the ultimate tragedy for you?"

"Within the internal logic of that one saying, yes. I don't think you can generalize all Danes through the lens of that one proverb, however. If that were the case, I would judge all Americans by any number of sayings. Take, for instance, 'Well, I'll be a monkey's uncle' or, more comparably, 'Why buy the cow when you are able to enjoy the milk for free?' I certainly *could* judge Americans by those, but I have taken care not to, and—"

"All right, all right. Lay off. I think we should go into to town, check out that bar. Maybe poke one of the locals and see if he howls."

"I'll get my shoes."

In the car Bromstad mulled over Stig's adage. "Let me tell you something: I got plenty of cows on the ice, you square-headed simpleton Dane! They think it's their pasture right now. The ice is cracking, and there are hooves poking through into the water."

"Oh, I don't think it's all that—Um, please, watch the road, Gus Bromstad. You nearly hit a rabbit."

"Good," said Bromstad. They angle-parked in front of the Taconite Saloon, and as they climbed out of Bromstad's Acura, Stig advised, "Mr. Bromstad, you are agitated. Why don't you let me cast about to see what I can find out. In your state you might rile them."

"Oh, I shall rile, my friend. Let the riling begin," said Bromstad, a hard look in his eyes.

"Have it your way."

They pushed open the door and entered a fairly lively saloon. The pinball machine, pool table, and video games all were occupied, and the sound of Molly Hatchet from the jukebox only added to the mood of rowdy festivity. Stig and Gus helped themselves to the last remaining vacant stools at the bar. Stig, recognizing the barkeep as Ralph Wrobleski, tilted his head and mouthed the words, "It's him," to Bromstad.

"What's your problem?" said Bromstad, looking down at the front of his sweater and then wiping his mouth. "What? What?"

"Nnnn," said Stig out of the side of his mouth as Ralph approached and leaned his mass toward them.

"Hey," he said suspiciously.

"Hello, stout fellow," said Stig, who was still learning the language. "May I have some vodka on the rocks, and my friend will have . . . ?"

"Same."

Ralph withdrew with a backward glance toward the pair, and Stig leaned in to Bromstad. "That's the one from the photo, the one with the head," he said, making a gesture with his hand that was supposed to represent an asymmetrical skull.

Gus, however, was not at his best and could not pick up Stig's gist. "The one with the head? Have you gone mad, you fish-creaming freak?"

Ralph returned before Stig could clarify. Stig broke off and asked Ralph in honeyed tones, "So why, may I be so bold as to ask, is it this busy?"

"Revival," said Ralph impatiently.

"Oh, the King Leo–sponsored event at the mine, is it?"

"Yeah. He's going 'round the clock now. People take their breaks here, I guess."

"I see, thank you. I wonder if I might—"

"So listen, buddy, just what the heck is this flimflam about the rat anyway? I happen to know it's not true, and I've got the goods—" Bromstad began, but he was interrupted when Ralph pulled him halfway over the bar by the front of his sweater, taking dozens of Bromstad's chest hairs out in the process.

"IT'S TRUE, YOU GOT IT, PAL?" bellowed Ralph as he shook Bromstad like a can of paint. "I will not be answering any more questions about that. That rat was real, okay? As real as you or me."

Bromstad, who had first sounded off with a high-pitched shriek at the shock of being manhandled by this publican, now made gruff vocalizations each time the air was forced out of his chest.

"Yeah, 'ugh, ugh, ugh' better be the only thing you say, pal," Ralph encouraged. "I am not going back there, you hear me? I refuse to listen to any more hoo-ha about amniotic fogs and tomorrow jellies, you got that?" he asked of Bromstad, and then, without really giving him a fair chance to answer, dropped him on the floor. "I'm doing my mission work. I'm spreading the word. This is my going forth," he hollered in a rather unorthodox method of proselytizing. "All right, who's thirsty?" Ralph said to his stunned clientele.

"He just roughed up Gus Bromstad," said a tourist with pool cue as Stig scraped his partner off the floor.

"WHAT DID YOU say to tick that guy off?" Bromstad asked from a reclining position on his couch at the Bugling Moose, sipping an aquavit that Stig held to his lips.

"Perhaps I just have that effect on people."

"Well, tone it down a bit, will you?" he asked, sipping some more. "That guy's not going to give us much, I'm going to guess. So what next?"

"Perhaps I am going to sound like a broken record, but the day is coming to a close, and I think we should sauna."

"Sauna?"

"Yes. Things always seem better after a sauna. They are almost magical that way."

"I have to ask, what part of speech is sauna? You seem to use it as a noun and a verb?"

"I am taking liberties with Danish speech as I speak it in English. *Sauna* is the place, the hot room, *saunoa* is the action of enjoying it. I use them interchangeably in English. Many Danes do this in America. Please forgive the liberty."

"Forgiven."

"So. Sauna?"

"Yes. But it must involve the water of life."

"And so it will," promised Stig.

Soon they were ensconced in their favorite location at the Bugling Moose, the humid, superheated cedar room that stood alone among the cabins.

"So the nudity? It's so horrible. Why?" asked Bromstad once the *löyly* was thick in the air.

"It is a custom. Finnish, to be certain, but we have adopted it, as have the Swedes. What can I say, except that it is like your custom of eating turkey at Thanksgiving or of going to brunch on Mother's Day?"

Bromstad considered this. "Well. I suppose once you've seen so many naked men, nothing can ever, ever match it in terms of shock and horror and pure mental trauma. So as far as inuring one to tragedy, perhaps it serves a purpose," he allowed. "I'm going to shake hands with a millionaire," Bromstad declared, and stood to leave.

"I'm sorry?"

"I'll return shortly," he clarified, slipping on his sandals.

"Oh. Oh, of course," said Stig, getting the gist.

Bromstad wandered out into the brisk moonlight and immediately regretted his decision not to wrap himself with a towel, given the night's average low temperature of fifty-nine degrees.

"Whew," he said, recognizing the distinct danger of shrinkage. He looked up at the moon and, noticing how it undulated, discovered that he was tipsy. He stood for some time in the wood, allowing his eyes to adjust to the darkness, and when they did, he saw to his surprise that a female rear end was protruding from the side of Cabin 5. He crept up to investigate. Staying a discreet distance away, concealed for the most part by a thick tamarack, he could make out the words of the voices inside.

"Um, getting back to my question, whom didn't you want to see you just now?" said a male voice.

"Gus Bromstad," came the answer, and in an instant Bromstad knew all. He listened for just a moment more and then ran to his cabin at the top speed that his sandals and nudity would allow, fetched their two pistols from Stig's leather travel bag, and ran back to the sauna.

"It's go time!" he announced to Stig, who was leaned against a wall, dozing. Bromstad pitched him his towel. "Put this on for a change."

"Huh?"

"And take this. We gotta go!" he said, throwing a Beretta into his lap.

Stig, awoken effectively by the cold metal, secured his towel, slipped on his sandals, and followed Bromstad without question.

CHAPTER 24

"Gus Bromstad!" exclaimed Ponty.

"Pontius Feeb," said Bromstad.

"And you are . . . ?" Ponty asked, looking at Stig.

"I'd rather not say."

"I understand. Well, pleased to meet you anyway," said Ponty.

"Likewise," said Stig politely.

"I'm sorry, Ponty. I started to tell you," said Sandi.

"That Gus Bromstad would appear in just a towel? Sandi, I like and respect you a great deal, but you should have tried harder. This is a nightmare."

"Oh, this is too perfect," said Bromstad, narrowing his eyes at Ponty.

"It is?" asked Ponty incredulously.

"Let's drive, sweethearts," commanded a new and purposeful Bromstad, gesturing with his pistol.

The gunmen checked the immediate area before leading them out through darkness to their parked cars.

"What are you going to do with us?" Ponty asked. "Also I need to ask—and this is very important—does your being nearly naked figure into the plan at all?"

"Oh, please, no. It would kill me if you thought that," said Stig. "We were simply taking a sauna when the call to action came. I am sorry."

"Shut up," Bromstad commanded. "We're going to take a little drive."

"Can we please not take the Saturn?" Sandi asked. "It's not mine. It's my neighbor Lindy's, and he will go nuts."

"Oh, no. We're taking this little beauty," Bromstad said, tapping the side of the Tempo with his Berretta.

"Careful, please. I'm trying to preserve what little resale value it has," Ponty pled.

"You drive, Pontius Feeb," said Bromstad, his voice fuzzy with drink.

The foursome loaded into the Tempo, Bromstad selecting the seat behind Pontius so he could more effectively threaten him with his firearm.

"All settled in up there, Mr. Wedgie?" asked Bromstad, who was warming to his role as a naked ruffian.

Ponty was formulating a plan. "Oh, sure, just let me give you some legroom back there." Hoping to knock the gun from Bromstad's hand and crush his lap, Ponty pulled the seat lever and thrust his legs backward with all the force available to him. Nothing happened. The Tempo's seat froze without moving an inch.

"How you doing on that legroom there?" Bromstad asked.

Ponty sighed. "Seat's broken. Sorry. You'll have to make do."

"Drive on," said Bromstad. "The mine."

Ponty drove, grinding the gears several times out of nervousness. He could smell Bromstad's alcohol breath and hear the Berretta brushing against the side of his head restraint. Once on the road, he snuck a look over at Sandi.

"Sorry," he said softly.

Sandi shrugged and offered him a weak smile.

"You okay on heat back there?" Ponty asked.

"I could use a little, I must confess," said Stig.

"It'll just take a bit for the engine to warm."

They drove for several minutes in silence through the dark night. A dim glow in the sky glowed brighter as they

approached Gerry Iverson's property. There were more cars in
the makeshift lot than Ponty had yet seen.

"Oh, my, look at all the cars! Looks like King Leo's got himself a nice little revival business going here," said Stig as Ponty
maneuvered through the somewhat illogical parking scheme.

"We'll see if we can't throw a little cold reality on that," said
Bromstad. "Okay, park it, Feeb."

"This is pretty far away. Do you want me to try to find something closer?"

"Yeah, yeah. Just don't do anything funny."

"I think this guy's leaving," Ponty said, and he followed a
young man wearing big madras shorts. "Oh, no. He's just getting a jacket from the car."

"Oh, there's a spot," said Stig.

"Think I can squeeze in there?" asked Ponty.

"It will be tight," Stig agreed.

"Well, let's try and see if you can get out on your side."

"Look!" yelled Bromstad. "Just stop the car here! It doesn't
matter!"

"Okay, okay. Just don't kill me," Ponty requested, stopping
the car in the middle of a traffic lane. As they unloaded, Ponty
looked at the Tempo's placement and shook his head. "Someone's going to key it."

"Get moving," said Bromstad, and he poked Ponty.

Gus and Stig walked their prisoners as near as they could to
the stage area, but further progress was prohibited by the crush
of people, all watching raptly as Jack gave a reading from his
book, *Death Rat*. King Leo looked on.

" 'All throughout that dark, cold night,' " Jack read, his voice
pleasant and sonorous, " 'Lynch huddled in the wetness, shivering and afraid, not knowing if at any moment the hot muzzle of

the rat would be upon him. Doom spread over him like a cloak.' "

"Lousy spread over your prose like a cloak," Bromstad said to Ponty, and then he fired his pistol into the air. "All right, make a hole, people!" he shouted to the crowd.

There were some screams and exclamations, and the crowd parted dutifully.

"No one make a move, or the mayor and the history author get it!" Bromstad instructed.

"I told you we were being followed, Jack!" Ponty yelled up to the stage.

"Shut up," said Bromstad.

They moved through the crowd, and as they did, there were many exclamations of "That's Gus Bromstad" or "Hey, it's the Dogwood guy!" They came to the foot of and then mounted the stage, a move that particularly upset the crowd when performed by the two men wearing only towels.

"Oooohhhh," the people with the best views groaned as Stig and Bromstad swung their legs up onto the stage.

King Leo tried to manage the situation. "Now, men, whatever your beef is, you know it cannot be settled with violence, but only through the intercession of the dee-vine and cosmic nature force that—"

"*Shut up!*" said Bromstad, leveling the Berretta at King Leo's exposed belly button. Bromstad stepped up to the microphone. "I have a strong feeling that church will be breaking up for the night right after you all hear this reading from St. Ponty. Ponty? Why don't you go ahead and tell them what you were telling the mayor here? And I want the real story, not your little fiction of a confession, got it?"

Ponty nodded, stepped slowly up to the microphone, scanned the crowd for a moment, and said, "Ahem." He was going to continue when he noticed just how many television camera crews were taping the event. He turned back. "Gus, I—"

"Go ahead and tell 'em, lover boy." Even in such a stressful moment, Ponty had time to wonder why Bromstad had called him "lover boy."

Ponty turned back. "Ahem," he repeated. "I, um . . . should probably introduce myself. My name is Pontius Feeb. Some of you may know me as Earl. Earl Topperson, but that's just a clever pseudonym. As you can see, I don't have my mustache, and Earl did have one." There was some murmuring from the assembled crowd.

"Shut your mouths!" ordered Bromstad. He leveled his pistol toward the crowd. "You in back—stay where you are. Go on, Feeb," he urged Ponty.

"Yes, thank you, Gus. I'm actually Pontius Feeb, and I am the history author, that, um . . . Mr. Bromstad was threatening to shoot just a moment ago." He saw recognition on the faces of some people near the stage, so he continued, "Right. So thank you for not making a move. Anyway, last summer, I wrote a pretty silly little book that I hoped would be a nice summer read, you know, something to throw into the beach bag or take on a plane. Nothing too serious or deep. Anyway, I couldn't sell it, so I asked Jack Ryback there—hi, Jack—to pretend he wrote it. As you can see, Jack is better-looking than I am by a long chalk. Not a judgment, you understand, just an observation. So Jack did sell it, but by mistake he sold it as a piece of nonfiction and . . . well, here we are. You see, that book was *Death Rat,*" Ponty said miserably.

The crowd emitted a collective gasp. Jack pushed past Ponty and said sloppily into the microphone, "No, no! Don't worry, everyone. Just a little joke. It's all part of the show here. Well, show? Heck—*revival*. It's all meant to increase your faith in the funka-, you know, lovely—" Jack turned to notice a weapon near his ear. "Ah! Mr. Bromstad. You have something to add?"

"The truth, *Ry*back," he said, pressing the gun into Jack's ear.

"Oh, Mr. Bromstad, please don't shoot me there. Okay, okay. Ponty was right, everyone. Sorry."

Ponty took over again. "That's right. There is no Holey Rat. Never was. Rats don't get to be six feet, you see. Capybaras, as I wrote in the book, get big, sure, but they are a different kind of animal, and their growing seasons are much longer than here in Minnesota so . . . Well, anyway, the town of Holey backed me up on the story because . . . well, I paid them. Who can blame them, right?" he quickly added. "I'm sorry. I didn't mean for it to get this out of control. Or rather I guess I did mean for it to get like this, because I could have stopped it and I didn't. It's all my fault. I betrayed the reading public." He turned to King Leo, who was staring at him wide-eyed. "I'm sorry, King Leo. No rat. No dee-vine help from anything. Lynch was just a citizen of Holey, nothing special. Never did battle with any rodent, that I know of. I am sorry. And, Jack, I'm sorry I got you into this thing."

"Oh, please. It's been fun," Jack said, and then he looked at Bromstad's gun. "Tonight could still turn sour on us, but . . ."

"Yeah, yeah. That's right, that's right," Bromstad encouraged, seeing the shocked and saddened faces of the faithful. He brushed Ponty aside and stepped up to the microphone. "So you can stop lining the pockets of these frauds,'cause your little Minnesota fantasy is over! Six-foot-long rat. You idiots. You deserve your disappointment! Now," he said, pointing his pistol out at the crowd, "break it up, everyone. Nothing to see here. Let's go. Get in your cars and let's head home."

The crowd, many of whom did not want to get shot, started to break up.

"*No!* Stop! All of you!" shouted King Leo. "He's wrong. Wrong, wrong, wrong, wrong. There is something to see here," he continued, taking the microphone from Bromstad, who was too shocked to stop him. "History is about more than just what happened. Isn't that right, Ponty?"

"Well, 'what happened' is certainly part of it, but you're right, it's—" Ponty began.

"That's right, see? Well, that goes for faith as well. What did you come out here to see? A six-foot rat? No. You came to get yourself funked, is what you came here for. And the source of that funk *is* the Rat of Dee-vine Power, whether he was invented by Earl or Ponty or Jack or whoever. He *is* real! Brother Ralph, he saw him. And since that time dozens of people have seen him. Now, that's what I call faith." King Leo started to ramp it up. "Faith in the rat. Can you feel it? Can you feel it, people? Are you ready for a revival? Wooooooo!"

The people let King Leo and the rest of them know that, yes, they were ready for a revival.

"That's right! You have to believe! Now, I don't know what motivates Mr. Bromstad and his naked friend here to try to bust up our faith like they have, but I would guess it's because they don't have anything of value in their lives. Nothing to believe in. But I'd like to thank Jack and Ponty for giving us all something to believe in. The Rat of Dee-vine Power. Thank you, Jack," said King Leo, and he dispensed a hug.

"Oh, you know. I've been only too happy to help."

"And, Mr. Earl—Ponty. My thanks to you for your fine work," said King Leo.

"I, um . . . I'm not much of a hugger. Okay, okay. Thanks," he said, and Ponty finally received one of King Leo's much-talked-about hugs.

"As for you, Mr. Bromstad, let go of that bitterness. Can you feel the power melting it right out of your heart?" King Leo asked, and though the expression on Bromstad's face was somewhat enigmatic, it was clear that there had been no dissipation of bitterness quite yet. "Take my rat cloak, Mr. Bromstad. Here, give me that ridiculous gun," he said, taking it from Bromstad. "Give me that ridiculous towel, too," he said, snatching it away from a seemingly passive Bromstad. There were only a few snickers from the crowd. "Now, take this cloak, cover your nakedness, and find a place in your hard, hard heart for the Rat of Dee-vine Power." He covered the immobile Bromstad with his rat cloak and fastened it around his arms. "There, there," he added as the crowd applauded, moved by emotion and by the apparent addition of another proselyte.

King Leo stepped back, looked at his new church member, and joined the crowd as they applauded. Bromstad appeared to be looking back at King Leo, so King Leo threw wide his arms for a hug. But Bromstad was not looking at King Leo. He was looking past him into the eyes of Pontius Feeb, who in turn was looking back at him. Ponty was looking back at him because for the first time in his life he saw murder in the eyes of another human being, and he found it oddly fascinating.

A feral cry of rage tore forth out of Bromstad's body, and he ran at King Leo, went under his outstretched arms, and slammed himself into Ponty, who stumbled backward but did not lose his footing. His wrestling instincts took over again as he widened his stance, grasped Bromstad around his chest, and executed a nice takedown throw. Unfortunately, instead of a mat upon which to land, they had only the stage's railing, which promptly broke, sending the two hurtling down toward the boarded-up entrance to the mine. The boards themselves had not been properly maintained, and years of weather had worn them to the point that they would easily break if landed on by two grown men.

When Bromstad and Ponty plunged into the boards, the boards gave way, and the pair plummeted down into the Holey Mine.

CHAPTER 26

Most mines of the era were constructed with something called an adit, a horizontal opening through which to enter the mine without falling tens of feet and hurting oneself. The Holey Mine had been constructed hurriedly in the race to find the richest lode, so sacrifices were made. It was given only a vertical shaft, out from which levels, or horizontal tunnels, were cut, and it was entered by standing in a kibble, or Cornish bucket, and being lowered by winch. Months after his fall Ponty would curse the Holey Mine's lack of a good, quality, horizontal adit, but at this point he did not know it lacked one. He fell into the mine painfully, without even giving the shoddy mine construction a thought.

"Oof!" was the sound he made when he landed, for Bromstad had fallen on top of him. Once he'd pushed Bromstad off, he felt a strong desire to lie there on his back, moaning for at least a minute or two, but there was no time. Bromstad almost immediately began choking him.

"You rotten usurper! You ruined my life!" Bromstad said as he squeezed Ponty's neck. That it was Bromstad choking him Ponty established by deductive reasoning only, for he could see nothing but utter blackness. He arched his body, pushed Bromstad off his chest, stood up, and ran, smashing his head into the low ceiling of the level running off the main shaft. Feeling in front of him, he discovered just how low the level was and, crouching, made his way down it, his pace understandably slow.

"Where are you? Usurper! Lying, thieving usurper! Did I make it clear that I wanted to kill you? Where are you, usurper?" Bromstad yelled.

Ponty chose not to tell him. Because he heard Bromstad's rat cloak rustling, a growling noise issuing from his mouth, and also an indiscreet drinking burp, he knew that the author was in pursuit. He widened the distance from Bromstad, which was not difficult given Ponty's sobriety and his motivation not to be choked to death. He had no idea how far down into the level he had traveled when he finally stopped and, hearing nothing, sat on the cold, damp ground.

Though he was shivering, fatigued, and hurt in places he could not immediately identify, and despite the fact that he was being pursued through a deserted mine by a drunken rival author intent on his death, and setting aside the detail that he might just have implicated his friend—a woman he quite liked—and an entire town in what could turn out to be criminal charges and countless lawsuits, Ponty felt pretty good for the first time in a long time.

I F THE CROWD of people that had gathered at the Holey Mine for King Leo's revival were shocked by the sudden and oft-changing rush of events, they were not calmed by the appearance overhead of a Bell 206L-4 helicopter training its powerful spotlight on the stage. Nor did the voice that issued from its loudspeaker soothe their jangled nerves:

"All right, you monstrous perversions of nature, break it up down there, or I'll have no choice but to open fire on your freaky love-in!"

Screams and panic were the result as the crowd did indeed disperse. After all that had transpired, they were inclined to believe only those who threatened them with violence.

Once he saw an appropriate amount of fear and running, Governor Herzog rappelled from out of the hovering chopper and dropped down onto the stage. He then signaled for the chopper to land, making those next to him wonder why he didn't just land with the chopper.

"All right," he asked of a group made up of King Leo, Jack, Sandi, King Leo's band, and a naked Stig-Stou Thorup, "just what in the double-jointed Jack Dempsey is going on here?" Then, noticing Stig and his lack of approiate attire, he added, "A pasty Dane in a towel! Can you think of any reason at all that I shouldn't pop you on the button and drop you like a plumb bob?"

"It's Gus Bromstad. He and Ponty Feeb have fallen down into the mine," said Stig, either misinterpreting or ignoring his governor's question.

"All right, well stand back, give 'em some air. Everyone spread out," said the governor, even though they were ten feet up on the stage looking down at the mine entrance and couldn't possibly be crowding either Bromstad or Ponty. The governor leaped off the stage, taking reasonable care not to land in the mine, and surveyed things.

"Hm. I'd say they fell through here, is that right?"

"Yes, sir," said Stig.

A television camera pressed in on the governor.

"All right, all right, all right, people," he shouted to unseen people around him. "Here are the problems as I see them, and the events that are going to transpire in an attempt to right these problems: Number one, we've got Gus Bromstad trapped down in that mine. Number two, we've got . . . some other guy down there with him, doing who-knows-what to our beloved author."

"Governor," said Jack, "it's another author, a Mr. Pontius Feeb. Bromstad attacked him, and they fell into the mine. Bromstad was trying to murder him."

Herzog considered this new information. "All right, all right, all right, people. Here's what's going to transpire: I'm going to rappel down into that mine and try to stop our beloved Minnesota author from killing this . . . this—"

"Pontius Feeb, sir," the naked Stig offered.

"*Pon*shius Feeb, yes, thank you, Mr. Stou-Thorup," said the now-irritated governor.

"Um, I would be remiss in not pointing out that Mr. Bromstad is naked save for King Leo's rat cloak, so a speedy rescue is
essential," added Stig.

"Noted," said the governor. He yelled for some materials
from the chopper, and after his pilot brought them over, he
attached a fair amount of hardware to his beefy body and prepared for his descent. "All right," he said, giving the thumbs-up
to the television camera and flicking on his headlamp, "let's go
rescue some authors."

Probably because he was playing somewhat to the camera
and not paying full military-style attention to the task at hand,
the governor failed to attach some critical carabiner clips to his
rope, so that when he let go of solid ground, he, too, plunged
tens of feet straight down and hurt himself at the bottom.

Pontius had not been huddling in his corner for long when he
heard a crash and then, inexplicably, the very gruff and recognizable voice of his governor.

"Uh-oh, son of a butter bean! I busted my darn fool leg!" his
state's leader complained. "Bromstad? What in the name of
Jim Kelly are you doin' down here? Bromstad? Help me!"

Ponty got on his hands and knees and, feeling ahead of him
in the blackness, tried to find his way toward Herzog's voice,
which continued steadily, complaining and chastising. After
crawling for ten minutes or so, he came to a spot in the level
where it seemed to continue straight ahead but also fed off to
the right. He tried to concentrate as much as his strained and
fading faculties would allow, but he simply could not remember
which path he'd taken as he ran from the foaming Bromstad,
nor could he determine with any certainty from which direction
the yelling was originating.

"Hey, up there!" Herzog shrieked. "Tell that moron Adam to send out the National Guard. You hear that? Tell him I can do that—I have the authority!"

"Hey!" Ponty yelled. "Mr. Governor, sir?"

"Who's that? Is that Feeb?"

"Yes, sir, sir."

"Feeb, you've got us in a mell of a hess, you know that, man?"

"I'm very sorry, sir," said Ponty, who was near to tears. "But right now I'm very lost, and it's very dark, and I don't know how to get to where you are."

"That's what happens when you join up with a freak like King Leo," Herzog admonished.

"Yes. Yes, I know that now, Governor. It was a huge mistake."

"That ain't no bean dip, for sure, Feeb. Now, listen, we'll get you out of here. Follow my voice, man."

"I'm trying, but it's very hard. Do you think you could just keep talking, and I'll try again to make my way to you?"

"Yeah, yeah. Heck, I'll go you one better. I'll just keep singing. You'll find me. And if you stumble across Bromstad, drag his carcass along, too, will you?"

"Yes, sir."

"Okay. Here goes, Feeb. Let's see. This is one from Billy Ray Cyrus's album *It Won't Be the Last*. It's called 'Ain't Your Dog No More.'"

Ponty crawled wearily and blindly through the tunnel while the governor shouted out a few by Billy Ray Cyrus, half of a song by Styx that he couldn't remember all of, 'Beth,' by Kiss, and two songs from *Paint Your Wagon*. But there was a maze of levels spreading out from the one down which he had initially traveled, and Herzog's voice was so diffuse that it was of little help. While Herzog was belting out 'Hand Me Down That Can o' Beans,' Ponty blacked out and collapsed facedown on the cold stone floor of the Holey Mine.

CHAPTER 26

Ponty regained consciousness three days later in the logy funk of the recently medicated. The room seemed unnaturally bright, the lights above him ringed with hazy coronas. He could not have been blamed if he had misidentified his room as heaven, and indeed he might have if Jack's large and very mortal body hadn't appeared suddenly above him.

"Hey, Ponty!" Jack said cheerfully.

"Jack?" Ponty croaked. "Am I in jail?"

"Jail? No, no. Food's the same, though. No, you're in the Fishville hospital. Took them a while to get you out of the mine, Ponty. You had us worried."

"What happened? I remember Herzog singing from *Paint Your Wagon*, and then everything went black."

"Well, that's probably for the best," said Jack. "Let me ring for the nurse."

"Wait," said Ponty, shifting himself up in his bed.

"Careful," said Jack, helping Ponty with his pillow.

"What happened after that?"

"Well, the rescue was not the smoothest ever. Herzog's a big man. He got wedged sideways in the main shaft as they were pulling him up. As you know, because of the rock there, it was impractical to get in behind him, so basically they had to give him a good yank and he came free. Sad, though. He came up blubbering like a baby right in front of the TV cameras. Didn't do his image much good, in my opinion," Jack poured a cup of water for Ponty, stabbed a straw into it, and held it up for him. "Here."

"What about Bromstad?"

"Well, the trouble with him is, he didn't want to come up, apparently. Finally, though, they dragged his naked body out for the world to see. Ewww." Jack shivered. "He got checked out medically and then went right to jail, along with Stig. I imagine they're sprung on bail now. But you— they had a tough time finding you. It was the next afternoon before they got you out. You were pretty dehydrated, and your core temperature was not where it needed to be."

"See? I mess everything up. Can't even keep a decent body temperature going."

"Enough now. I'm calling the nurse," Jack said, thumbing the call button. "Then I want to give Sandi a call. She's been here all she could, but she had to go tend bar today."

"No! No," said Ponty. "Keep her away from me, will you, Jack?"

"What? Why?"

"Just do whatever it takes. I can't see her, okay?"

Jack shook his head. "All right, Ponty. Anything you say."

Though pressure from the media was intense, Jack ably handled it, taking a lot of the scrutiny off the recovering Ponty. Consequently, Ponty's convalescence at the Fishville Community Hospital did not last more than a week. His brother flew in

from Tucson and helped him get back to his home in Minneapolis.

"Come on, bro," Thad pleaded. "What's here for you? Fly
back with me to Tucson."

But Ponty would not go, and Thad, shaking his head, left
him in the charge of his roommates.

Two weeks later Sags, Phil, Beater, and Scotty found a new
place, nearer to the university, and Ponty was not invited to join
them.

"You probably want to be with your own kind anyway,"
Sags had helpfully suggested.

Ponty had already packed his scant belongings and moved into
a dingy walk-up with a shared bathroom when the subpoenas,
forwarded from his old address, started showing up. He rang
Jack.

"Yeah, it's raining lawsuits, isn't it?" said Jack with wonder
in his voice. "Fetters is suing us, there's a class-action suit from
the readers, and P. Dingman is hopping mad. They're bringing
the big guns. I never saw it, but apparently it was right in the
contract that the book was supposed to be true. Looks like the
ride is over, Ponty. It's too bad,'cause *Death Rat* is still selling
like hotcakes—morbid curiosity, I guess—but I don't think
we'll be seeing much of that moola."

"Jack, I'm really sorry I dragged you into this."

"Hey, enough of that. It was a good time. Ponty, I got to go.
I'll see you in court."

As the year wore on, Ponty would spend a fair amount of
time in court. He appeared at the arraignment of Bromstad,
Stig, and the others from Den Institut, but neither he nor
Sandi, who only sent a deposition, wanted to press any charges

against them. Bromstad was ordered to undergo therapy. While Stig's henchmen got off scot-free, he was not quite so lucky: He got three months, but after pressure from the Danish consulate, he was shown leniency and allowed to serve it out in Copenhagen. Bromstad, who was responding well to therapy, was publicly contrite. At a press conference, tears in his eyes, he apologized and told his readers that his recovery process had made him realize how important it was to keep a promise. Because of that, his next book would not be a Dogwood after all.

"What's it going to be about?" a reporter asked.

"Beauty, truth, nobility . . ." he said with a faraway look, and then he trailed off, mumbling something that had the reporters looking at one another for help.

" 'Herring,' did he say?" the asked each other.

Bromstad went to work immediately on his thorny and impenetrable Danish historical epic *Gesta Danorum*, which would sell only eight thousand copies. Of those, more than 83 percent would be returned for a full refund. It sold far less even than Bart Herzog's disappointing account of the Holey incident, *Ain't Nowhere I Won't Go*.

Ponty took a job at a mall store, avoided Jack's phone calls, and after a time faded back into a thin but anonymous existence. There were days when he would not think about *Death Rat* at all. Pontius Feeb was Pontius Feeb again.

Ponty sprinted down Washington Avenue and arrived at the Wick 'R Baskit with just three minutes to spare. Though he'd been there nearly a year, he had no desire to get on the bad side of his store manager, Jessica, who at nineteen was as hardened by life as any veteran unpromoted slaughterhouse worker. Ponty hung up his jacket and began assembling soap-based gift baskets, and, hearing him, Jessica came in from the front of the store.

"Big day," she said. "Big, big day. I hope you're pumped and ready to assemble truckloads of gift baskets."

Ponty, who had spent a full sixty-one years on earth never having felt any emotions at all about any gift baskets, ever, pretended that he was. "Are you kidding?" he said. "This is going to be an eighty-seven-gift-basket day or I'll eat a eucalyptus wreath whole."

Jessica frowned at him.

"I mean it," he said, and for a moment he actually believed that he had nothing to lose by eating a eucalyptus wreath whole.

Thirty-four soap-based gift baskets into his day, Jessica came in from the front of the store, her attitude more clipped than usual, something Ponty hadn't imagined was possible.

"There's . . . ah, someone here to see you," she announced with irritation. "She said she wants to 'talk,' to you, but I don't want her here in the back. I suggest you go to the bench by the Sox It to Me."

Ponty entered the front of the store for the first time in months and was even more overwhelmed by soap, candle, and potpourri stench than he was while leaning his face over baskets of the stuff all day. He blinked and rubbed his eyes.

"Ponty," said Sandi.

"Sandi," said Ponty. They hugged awkwardly, and Ponty blushed.

"Sorry," he said, "my boss says we have to go sit by the Sox It to Me."

They crossed the mall in silence, and Ponty wordlessly offered her a seat at a bench opposite the sock store.

"Oh, Ponty," said Sandi once they'd sat down.

"Sandi," said Ponty.

"The Wick 'R Baskit?"

"I get an employee discount on tea candles," he said, then coughed lightly into his hand.

"You keep disappearing on me," she said, looking him up and down. "I like your little beard and mustache thing. Real?"

"Yes. Disguise, you know, so kids don't chase me down the street like the elephant man."

"I've called you so many times."

"The phone is at the end of the hall, and Mr. Panniermeyer usually gets it first. He doesn't even give me my messages because he thinks I'm evil."

"Are you really that broke that you have to live there?"

"Lot's of lawsuits. My Wick 'R Baskit check is garnisheed pretty heavily every week. Maybe that's why Jessica doesn't like me," he mused, looking back in the direction of the store.

"When they pulled you out of there, after Herzog and Bromstad had come out looking so bad, I thought you were dead for sure."

"No. No. Cold. But not dead," he said, looking down.

"Do you see Jack much?"

"Oh, yeah. Now and again. Going to see him this weekend, in fact. He's doing a showcase at the Theater of the Broken Mind. After this I think he's going out to L.A. for good."

Sandi laughed. "I don't hear much from his good buddy King Leo."

"No, that ended pretty quickly. King Leo became Darren Johnson again. Jack says he's in L.A., producing."

"Oh, I'd like to see Jack again," Sandi said fondly. "Are you writing?" she asked.

"Me? No. Well, just code numbers on the side of the gift baskets."

"Things are still pretty happening up in Holey, Ponty. Lots of young people up there. They think the whole thing is very cool. Gerry, he's making money hand over fist. You should come up sometime. Ralph misses you. Dying to go hunting with you. And, of course, needs to pass on his walleye secrets to someone, and you know he doesn't get along with Chet."

"Ah, well, say hi to him, will you? And now I'll take my leave, for if I don't get back soon, Jessica will have *me* hunted and killed."

Sandi put a hand on his, and he did not withdraw it. "Come on up to Holey and help us work the Taconite. We've got a deal with the Bugling Moose— we're putting in a bar there at the main building. We need a good man."

"Ha," he snorted. "I'll let you know if I can think of anyone."

"Think about it, Ponty. You'll have plenty of time to write. Think about it, and then come up," she said. Ponty promised to think about it, said good-bye, and went back to his powerfully malodorous job at the Wick 'R Baskit.

He was able to assemble more than ninety gift baskets on his shift, so when he got back to his rented room on Walker Street, he was even more tired than usual. Just as he reached the second floor, the phone at the end of the hall rang, and Ponty was in a position to answer it before Mr. Panniermeyer could even get his gray, cranky body out the door.

"I've got it, Mr. Panniermeyer," Ponty announced to the man's skull as it poked out of its room.

"Unggrh," said Mr. Panniermeyer.

"Hello?" Ponty said into the greasy phone.

"Hey, you big Feeb! I finally got you."

"Hey, little Feeb. How are you, brother?"

"I'm good. How about you? The dust settling?"

"It's still feels somewhat dusty, I must confess."

"So? You coming out here? That was a heck of a winter you had."

"They're all bad."

"So come out. We've got the pool. Nice little place picked out for you? Come on, big bro."

Some choice, thought Ponty. *Freeloading off my little brother or winding down my life making stinky gift baskets for a bitter teen. I can do more with myself than that,* he thought. *Maybe not a whole lot more, but something.*

He thought of turkey hunting and how much he'd loved it and how there just had to be a book in there. With the proper research and some fieldwork with Ralph, he was sure he could get something out of it. He could not deny that he'd been playing with a title—*Bald, Fat, Wattled, and Proud: The History of the Wild Turkey in America*. It sounded like a winner.

"No. No, Thaddeus. Why don't you come and visit me? I

think I'm going to live up in Holey. I'm going to hunt a little. Do a bit of fishing. Run a little bar up there. You bring the family. Come up there."

"Hey, that sounds like heaven! I'll see what I've got this summer."

"Yeah. Do that, brother. Meet me up in Holey."

"I'll see what I can do. And hey, you watch your step up there, okay?"